The Victorian Detectives
An Appointment with Destiny

J.B.Bass

First published in Great Britain as a softback original in 2022

Copyright © J.B.Bass

www.jbbass.co.uk

The moral right of this author has been asserted.

All characters and events in this publication, other than those clearly in the public domain, are fictitious and any resemblance to real persons, living or dead, is purely coincidental.

All rights reserved.

No part of this publication may be reproduced, stored in a retrieval system, or transmitted, in any form or by any means, without the prior permission in writing of the publisher, nor be otherwise circulated in any form of binding or cover other than that in which it is published and without a similar condition including this condition being imposed on the subsequent purchaser.

Typeset in Warnock Pro

Editing, design, typesetting and publishing by UK Book Publishing
www.ukbookpublishing.com

ISBN: 978-1-914195-97-6

*Dedicated to **PJ***
A brother, a fallen ghost.

Contents

PRELUDE: LONDON, 1898.		1
1.	'THE ISLE OF LEWIS.' 'AUTUMN, 2020.'	3
2.	'A BRIEF DIVERSION.'	8
3.	'A MOST IMPORTANT WARD.' 'LONDON, 1898.'	18
4.	'WINSTON.'	25
5.	'SEVERIN.'	38
6.	'OUTWATER.'	57
7.	'LEVIATHAN.'	68
8.	'OUT OF THE FRYING PAN, INTO HELL!'	76
9.	'CAPTURED.'	84
10.	'LIBERTY.'	95
11.	'A LIBERTY, OF SORTS…'	112
12.	'A SAPPER'S FIRE.'	123
13.	'AN UNEXPECTED TURN OF EVENTS.' ('FROM THE JAWS OF VICTORY.')	128
14.	'THE LEGENDS ARE ALIVE!'	136

15.	'A HARSH REALITY.'	139
16.	'THE 13TH MEISTER.'	160
17.	'AN APPOINTMENT WITH DESTINY.'	165
18.	'FAMILY.'	170
19.	'THE ANATOMY OF FEAR.'	179
20.	'RETURN OF THE GHOSTS.'	192
21.	'INTO THE VIPER'S NEST.'	198
22.	'NETTIE.'	211
23.	'THE BARON OF BANKSIDE.'	220
24.	'A FORTRESS OF STEEL AND GLASS.'	232
25.	'THE FALL OF OLYMPUS.'	251
26.	'A MOST RHADAMANTHINE PAIR.'	257
27.	'A STRANGE SENSATION OF DEJA-VU.' 'PRETORIA, 1899.'	269
28.	'COMPLETELY HUMAN.'	280
29.	'A CURIOUS TALE RECOUNTED.'	290
30.	'A PHOENIX RISES.' 'JUNE 18TH, 1940.'	297
31.	'THE UNLIKELIEST FAREWELL.' 'JANUARY 4TH, 1965.'	300
32.	'SONATA FOR A PAIR OF TIRED, ORDINARY MEN.' 'WHITECHAPEL: NOVEMBER, 1898.'	309
33.	'THE LAND BEYOND THE FOREST.' 'WINTER, 1898.'	319
	'ACKNOWLEDGEMENTS.'	322
	'ABOUT THE AUTHOR.'	323

Prelude

London, 1898

Tiberius Blackmore was experiencing something of a troublesome day.

On several occasions, during both recent and long past altercations too numerous to recall, he had found himself outflanked and pinned down, as he was at this precise moment, by a potentially lethal barrage of enemy crossfire, with any hope of a miraculous victory or salvation by a timely intervention of welcome reinforcements appearing less likely with each second that elapsed.

Whilst searing projectiles of deadly lead bit into the great stone northern arch of Tower Bridge, where he had sought to secure what meagre cover was available to shield himself and his bold companions from the potentially deadly shards of masonry shrapnel that arced dangerously about their ears, Blackmore turned towards his colleague and great friend Detective Inspector Marcus Jackson and shouted to be heard over the cacophony of gunfire and impacting ordnance around them...

"I fear that venturing out onto the bridge might prove to have been a grave tactical error, Marcus, one that might yet cost us dear. The 'Black Guard' now have us at a major disadvantage on both of our flanks."

"Our revolvers, high calibre though they might be, are no match for their heavy gauge rifles, shotguns and C96 Mauser semi-automatic pistols," retorted Jackson as he proceeded to re-load the spent chamber of his smoking-barreled, over-burdened revolver...

"I fear that my ammunition reserve is almost exhausted," he added with an air of resigned acceptance.

Prompted to review his own personal cache of ammunition immediately, Blackmore was quick to reply...

"Mine as well, Marcus. I hope that the safeguarding of our young companion here is worth the potential loss of several good men's lives here today," he alluded, as he glanced across towards the dapper young man who was the beneficiary of a human barrier made up of himself, Marcus Jackson and a small group of 'Covert Special Forces' operatives, who appeared to exude an air of untroubled calmness despite the scene of chaos and confusion that continued to erupt all around him...

'Almost, one might assume, as if this young gentleman had prior experience of being involved in an altercation such as this...' Blackmore allowed himself to ponder for a brief moment prior to another insistent volley of ordnance impacting into the brittle stone blocks above his head...

"Would that James were here with us at this moment," imparted Jackson hopefully, a sense of rising desperation not unnoticed by Blackmore in the tone of the young Detective Sergeant's voice.

Remaining silent within his own thoughts, Blackmore mused to himself as a stray spent round penetrated the upper left sleeve of his old overcoat, grazed his outer shoulder lightly and fortuitously passed clean through the thick tweed cloth and out the other side.

'James, my oldest friend. If ever there was a moment in time more suited to your arrival, then please, by the good grace of God, let that moment be now.'

Tiberius Blackmore was experiencing something of a very bad day indeed.

Chapter 1

'The Isle of Lewis'

'Autumn, 2022'

The opportunity to lose oneself, frequently and completely, within the ranging, spectacular vastness of the northern-most Hebridean landscapes, that graced with such exquisitely picturesque beauty the northwestern highlands of Scotland, had always greatly appealed to James Bass.

Where the rolling green glens of Glencoe give rise to the towering mountains of the northern ranges, reaching ever higher to touch the seemingly endless blue highland sky, the crystal blue lochs of Stornoway and the most northern tip of Lewis was the place of almost absolute solitude, save for a few random crofts indigenous to this alluring highland wilderness, chosen by Bass and his wife, Constance, as the sanctuary where he could finally seek the inner peace for which he yearned.

A place, too, where the lycanthrope spirit that constantly wrestled for the exclusive ownership of his soul could be freed at will to roam, unburdened by any inhibitions and completely unchallenged by the all too easily offended eyes and often oppressively cruel and misinformed prejudices of humankind.

Connie Bass was becoming accustomed to many hours being spent alone, patiently waiting for the wolf to return from its most recent nocturnal roaming; hoping that her husband had finally managed to find some peace from somewhere, anywhere, from deep inside himself, praying silently to herself for an end to his inner torment, perhaps also in her own heart, though in all probability in her mind a forlorn hope, anticipating with ever increasing optimism the miracle that she was well aware might never come.

Standing alone once more, as a light sprinkling of snow began to fall at the beginning of another brisk early winter's morning, Connie patiently surveyed the breathtakingly beautiful vista of the barren Lewis landscape that surrounded the modest crofter's cottage that she had shared with her husband, James, on a good many similar occasions before.

How beautiful the purple heather looked to her, stretched out carpet-like over the endless wilderness until it reached the angular borders of the peat trenches that scarred the landscape and provided them with the earthy scented fuel for their constantly burning fire.

It was not unusual for her to first hear the wolf as it howled its feral protestations directly towards the smiling, taunting face of the moon, as if it were the single cause of anguish for the great white beast.

Often, upon hearing the wolf's forlorn cry, a sound that would chill the blood of any unsuspecting innocent party, but a sound to which Connie had nonetheless become totally accustomed, she would wonder to herself in moments of private contemplation...

'Is your call on this night one of happiness, my husband? Is it a cry of sadness, of anguish, a protestation of anger or perhaps frustration, or even one of pain?

'I truly hope that one day, during your travails beyond the boundaries of our earthly reality within the fourth dimension, you will be able to discover true inner peace. Then on that day my sweet, kind man, my heart shall truly rejoice.'

The customary sense of inner turmoil he always experienced was, on this occasion, remarkably absent. Alternatively, a feeling of almost tranquil calmness enveloped the great white wolf akin to the comforting, all-encompassing, warming embrace of a king-sized eiderdown quilt.

Quite possibly, for the very first time, James Bass was able to appreciate being totally at one with his majestic, yet still unpredictably dangerous, alter-ego and, under the circumstances of this new-found, unhindered freedom, able to find both contentment and a comforting inner peace.

Bass was also becoming more aware of the remarkably advanced capabilities he now shared with the wolf. His ground speed over any kind of terrain, coupled with his great physical strength and his enhanced agility had improved beyond any level he had believed humanly possible;

'Accounting for the fact that I am no longer exclusively human, anything at all would seem likely to be a very real possibility whilst inhabiting this form...'

he mused to himself...

He was now able to determine the distinctive pheromone present within the rogue DNA of potential suspects, as he too seemed to have developed a sixth-sense that enabled him to identify either the threat of imminent menacing confrontation or the possibility of any potentially hazardous situation.

On this morning, however, as the all-enveloping cloak of unpolluted night receded to be replaced by the broken, orange-tinged cloud of a new autumn sunrise, the wolf remained conspicuously silent.

Even as he stealthily approached the smallholding where Connie faithfully kept her lone vigil, the only sound made by this great beast was the laboured breath emanating from his exhausted lungs.

Confident in the knowledge that the wolf retained enough of her husband's spirit to guarantee her safety from harm, Connie welcomed the arrival of the werewolf with the loving greeting she had rendered time and again to her returning husband...

"Welcome home, James, my love," she imparted tenderly as the wolf began its agonizing metamorphosis from monster to man...

"Good morning, my sweet Connie, and what a particularly good morning it promises to be," came the rather surprisingly chipper greeting from James Bass to his relieved wife...

"You appear to exude unconditional happiness on this most pleasant of mornings, James; might one be so bold as to suggest even the sense of a mood of undiluted elation perhaps?"

"Indeed, you might, Connie, indeed you might," replied Bass jovially...

"I cannot begin to explain the exhilaration and the feeling of complete oneness which this remarkably re-invigorating environment we have both come to adore brings me. Here in this place, with you beside me, my love, I truly believe that I can really learn to live once more, as opposed to merely existing throughout the cycle of the wolf moon."

Bass embraced his wife as she wrapped them both in the large sheepskin rug that had hung about her shoulders, and they turned to greet the brand-new sunrise together.

"Ahh," sighed Bass as he gazed out contentedly over the seemingly endless expanse of open country stretching before him. Inhaling deeply and fully inflating his lungs, the air tasted pure and clean, untainted by the pollution of any century, be it past or present. An unfiltered, natural sweetness that could only be experienced in this most unspoiled of environments.

'Could a simple man such as I dare to believe that here, in this wondrous place, is to be found everything that he could ever desire.'

CHAPTER 1

His thoughts lost momentarily inside the perfect marriage of an almost hypnotic, tranquil calm and the breathtaking panorama surrounding him, Bass was rudely re-introduced to his earthly plane of consciousness by the intrusive trilling of a cell phone...

Connie had returned the few steps back to their cottage in order to answer the insistent beckoning of 21st century technology...

"Pontius calls, James. We must away back to our London of 1898 with some urgency where our presence is required at the Tower."

Chapter 2

'A Brief Diversion'

"One could scarcely have believed that one day it would be possible to traverse such great distances so swiftly by road, and in such comfort to boot," imparted Bass as he throttled their black Toyota SUV as much as he dared between the required speed warnings that seemed ever more present on the southbound carriageway of the M1 motorway between their current location of Sheffield and London.

Connie afforded herself a wry smile and waited a few seconds before she answered her husband's observation, recognising full well that their still almost naïve wonderment with the many advantages that 21st century technology offered to all people, and not just the privileged few, was still very much in its infancy…

"Indeed, James… A journey that would once encompass three days of constant, harsh travail by hard-sprung mail coach bumping uncomfortably along less than adequate roads, that is now achievable in but a scant few hours; quite a remarkable thought even though we are both now experienced cognoscenti with regards to understanding the principle and practice of modern high-speed travel in all its many and varied forms."

Connie returned to her idle gazing out of the rain-flecked passenger's side window.

CHAPTER 2

The largely uninteresting, somewhat dilapidated landscape of South Yorkshire's once proud iron and steel industry flashed inconsequentially by, as too did the repetitive uniformity of several red brick and breeze block new-build middle class commuter villages, and the multitude of designer shopping outlets each boasting exactly the same corporate retailer brand names, an identical plot situated at the exit of every single motorway junction hawking '2 for 1 meal deal special', 'All you can eat carvery' family pubs that appeared to be structures indigenous to every one of these purpose-built, self-contained estates; all of these traits synonymous with the complacency associated with twenty first century consumerism darting by in an inseparable blur, conspired to lull a weary Connie into drifting towards a peaceful slumber.

Waking with a start as their vehicle came to a stop, Connie was momentarily disorientated by her unfamiliar surroundings...

"Where... where are we, James?" was the obvious first question posed to her husband...

"Chesterfield. The small market town in North-East Derbyshire where I was born," came the immediate retort from Bass.

"Since one inherited the ability to meander through time, I formulated a notion that when an opportune moment presented itself, I would visit the place of my birth, in a not-too-distant future, and assess how time might have altered the essence of the place, if indeed at all."

Leaving their vehicle parked on a byway that Bass recalled immediately as being Spencer Street, they proceeded towards the main road that lay a few metres in front of them.

Turning to their right, they continued a further few metres towards a new build of properties, the bland frontages of which concealed behind them a large building of austere appearance which Bass recognised instantly.

Even though he was sporting his favoured long tweed overcoat over an ancient, weather-worn denim jacket and a black beany hat pulled down tightly over his ears in an attempt to keep out the biting early winter cold, an icy chill ran through his entire body as they approached the glowering façade of what was once known as The Chesterfield Union Workhouse.

Bass allowed himself a few moments of private contemplation whilst standing before the front entrance to the impressively preserved building...

"This is the place where I was born, Connie: The Chesterfield Union Workhouse. My mother passed away within these cold stone walls whilst in labour with me. It was to present for the first 12 years of my life a living hell on earth where I suffered unimaginable grief and tribulations.

"Finally, I mustered the necessary courage and absconded to Whitechapel, where I was to experience more untold hardship aplenty before a fortuitous and life-affirming association with a certain Alan Tiberius Blackmore began but a few short weeks after my arrival on those harsh London streets."

Bass fell silent as he allowed himself a moment longer to reminisce on hard times long consigned to a distant past. It was a period in his own history that had quite obviously left an indelible mark on his deepest inner psyche and assisted greatly in contributing early noticeably obvious character traits, such as a remarkably advanced, street-aware cunning, a brazen youthful guile and a tendency shown towards a ruthless, uncompromising yet somehow instinctively measured brutality in order to achieve his aims, thus nurturing a fearless inclination for survival at any cost...

'To live on this day affords us the opportunity to continue the fight on another...'

...he remembered imparting to Blackmore on more than one occasion, which now seemed like several lifetimes ago...

CHAPTER 2

"I needed this closure, Connie," mused Bass, his voice tinged with an almost melancholic timbre as he spoke...

"Just to stand before this place once more, where once my soul was so unhappy and troubled, to witness this once formidable, dour façade, now preserved as a modern domestic domicile, fills my heart with joy and cleanses my soul...

"I do believe the many once tormented spirits who undoubtedly wander its labyrinthine corridors to this day might have finally found their own lasting peace."

Turning to leave the concourse in front of the old workhouse, Bass looked over his shoulder once more and uttered wistfully...

"Goodbye, Mother. Rest assured, we will finally meet some day, far beyond this mortal plane of life, and on that day, of all days, my heart will be glad."

All the while, as they made their way the short distance back towards their parked car, the sight of a certain street name, or a piece of familiar architecture would be recognised and stir a distant memory...

"So many of these buildings were not here, Connie, and yet, I still feel as though a small part of me in some way will always belong here," imparted Bass to his patient wife...

"That row of cottages at the top of Abercrombie Street look almost exactly as they did when I was a child."

Bass stopped for a moment and perused the many and varied items of interest that made up the well-dressed display of a corner shop window. Noticing that among the veritable cornucopia of random items expertly arranged so as to court maximum interest from the casual browser, were several examples of quality pottery and other various pieces of object d'art that he immediately recognised as being of 19th century origin.

Glancing up at the signage above the door and window lintels he read out to himself 'The Newbold Fair Trade Emporium' before first excusing himself to his wife, and then entering to explore this curious 'earthly portal in time' further...

"Please indulge the whim of a curious old soldier; for just a few moments more, Connie, I promise you."

Upon entering, almost immediately they were greeted by a very handsome, slim and genteel young man who wasted little time in engaging Connie in the warm and welcoming conversation usually reserved for family, or perhaps the closest of friends.

Bass gave the confident young gentleman what he considered to be his politest expression of silent recognition, a single nod of the head, and promptly disappeared into an adjoining back room full to its rafters with books, pictures, pottery, glassware, general bric-a-brac and all manner of potentially interesting treasure trove, in order to continue with his spontaneous browsing spree...

"James, come out here and meet Justin," called Connie to her husband, who, whilst perusing a shelf almost too high to be easily accessed by anyone under six feet tall, had discovered a selection of interesting old books...

Suffering from threadbare spines and water foxing on some of their ageing pages, one book in particular nevertheless made an instant impression on the old detective as he thumbed its yellowing leaves.

Bass emerged from his cavern of hidden gems to re-join his wife and her beaming young companion...

"Aye' 'oop, duck, I'm Justin French and I'm very pleased to make the acquaintance of a local lad."

Accepting the strong and hearty handshake offered by Justin, and upon offering his own cordial introduction, Bass found himself so remarkably relaxed as to engage in a normal and pleasant conversation with this polite, refreshingly articulate young man...

"James Bartholomew Bass. The pleasure is indubitably mine, sir. So, Justin French; you're from around these parts, one would deduce as much from the colloquialisms apparent within your Derbyshire accent alone."

"That's very perceptive of you, James. One might even observe the keen acumen of a professional journalist, or possibly even the silently brooding analytical mind of a detective perhaps?" enquired Justin, displaying a layman's aptitude of his own for detective work...

Slightly taken aback by the perceptiveness shown by his young interrogator, Bass found himself uncharacteristically stammering his initial response as Connie, a wide grin forming across her face, proceeded to garner her own amusement from her husband's momentary loss of his customarily stoic composure...

"I... erm... I... well... I suppose my reading and writing is adequate at best, a handicap that pretty much negated any aspirations one might have harboured with regards to a career in journalism, but I have been known to have solved the odd case or two for the London Metropolitan Police Force, ahem..., a hundred and twenty or so years ago, give or take a year or two either way of course"

Eyeing the old detective with his friendly, smiling visage remaining perfectly intact, whilst private thoughts of ...

'Ahh... poor old sod; I'll bet he's well capable of spinning a fantastic yarn or two though' ... running through his head, Justin continued...

"Oh, lovely. Well, if it kept you busy and out of trouble, 'duck'..."

"My work has a tendency to keep me very busy still and, more often than not, rarely out of trouble, Justin French of Newbold, Chesterfield!" interjected Bass somewhat tersely as he eyed his startled inquisitor intently from behind the dark lenses of his spectacles...

Sensing a rising tension developing in her husband's demeanour, Connie was swift to steer the rapidly disintegrating conversation into less troublesome territory...

"I notice that you have selected several books from Justin's rather handsome collection, James. Pray tell what points of interest their subject matter might offer to the casual reader."

First continuing to survey Justin's still smiling features intensely for a good few seconds longer, Bass then turned his attention to the four well-thumbed books in his hands which he proceeded to caress with a rare, gentle delicacy, as though he had unearthed a hoard of priceless artefacts...

"Four first edition copies of novels written by Herbert at the turn of the 19th century. Do you recall, Connie, when the notion came upon him to write of the Earth being invaded by extra-terrestrial beings, and of his bold foresight when presenting the idea that the possibility of fourth dimensional time travel might be scientifically possible? How perceptive he was with his what he considered to be fictional depictions of what would eventually come to pass as an acceptable reality."

"Oh, those musty old things came from a house clearance on Cromwell Road a few weeks ago. Just give me a fiver for all four and our charity will benefit nicely from your generosity. 'Ta' very much, luv," Justin chirped cheerily into the inscrutable blackness of Bass' darkened spectacle lenses.

Merely nodding once to signify his approval of Justin's generous offer, then turning his head slightly towards Connie as if to silently implore her to produce some cash in order to purchase the books, Bass remained silent...

"What did you say you'd found, 'duck', four old books by Herbert... oh, H. G. Wells," observed Justin as he read out the author's name on the cover of one of the books.

"It's just that I could've sworn you spoke earlier as though you actually knew him very well," enquired Justin of Bass as Connie reached into her purse and produced a five-pound note...

"Herbert George Wells. A very perceptive individual, a possessor of great intellect and advanced foresight who was able to challenge the accepted boundaries of human thought and yes, I would say a very good and trusted friend indeed," deadpanned Bass with absolute sincerity towards the now incredulous visage of his young inquisitor.

After a few seconds, Justin retorted...

"Right, ok then... so that'd make you quite old, James, if you count H. G. Wells as being among your personal friends," he imparted, an air of light sarcasm now seemingly tempering his words as he spoke...

"I notice from hearing a familiar phrasing of words as you speak that you're from around these parts yourself, James?" he enquired, in the hope that his attempted light sarcasm would be immediately excused by this seemingly harmless storyteller, whose shielded eyes, however, continued to conceal the true soul of this mysterious visitor to his store.

Retrieving his books from the shop counter, Bass answered as directly and sincerely as he had done during their whole conversation, leaving the dumbfounded young vendor visibly shaking his head in disbelief...

"Yes, how perceptive of you, indeed I was, young fellow. I was born a mere short footfall away in the old Chesterfield Union Workhouse here on what is now named Newbold Road...

"Accepting today's date as a marker for the approximate time of my birth, the exact date of which I am not altogether certain, you understand, oh, perhaps a hundred and sixty-two years ago, give or take a day or so either way...

"Many thanks for being the custodian, if only for a short while, for these most precious of memories. You have on this day made a very old man extremely happy. Now I bid you a fond good day, sir," came the final, courteous parting words from Bass as he turned to leave the shop, followed closely by a smiling Connie, obviously greatly amused by her husband's attempt at imparting a generous slice of his legendary dry wit upon his hapless young victim...

"You, sir, are incorrigible! How unashamedly wicked of you to tease that charming young man so, James Bartholomew Bass," exclaimed Connie lightheartedly to her grinning husband as they stood on the pavement outside the shop...

"The opportunity, when presented to one so readily by one so innocently ignorant to the truth, was too fortuitous to forego, my love," imparted an almost jovial Bass to his wife...

"The books, James. What significant subject matter, other than their author of course, drew your attention to those four rather dilapidated little tomes?" Connie enquired about the four outwardly uninteresting books still being so carefully caressed in the black leather gloved hands of Bass.

Drawing a copious intake of breath, Bass waited a few seconds before he began to speak...

"As you so correctly observed, Connie, outwardly and to all intents and purposes four 'dilapidated little tomes', each one insignificant, unremarkable and innocuous even to any but the most observant eyes. However, to the eyes that see beyond the rather worn superficial exterior condition of each book, the first thing of significant note is the fact that each volume is a first edition copy; 'The Island of Doctor Moreau' written in 1896, 'The Invisible Man written in 1897, 'The War of the Worlds' written in 1898 and last but not least, and without doubt the most precious jewel belonging to this whole treasure trove 'The Time Machine' written in 1895."

"Yes indeed, my husband, a fortuitous discovery, but what more might one expect beyond them being regarded in high esteem by anyone but the most avid collector of late 19th century first edition fictional literature? A significant financial value; perhaps if the condition were better..."

"The true value here lies in the personalized inscription written inside the front cover of 'The Time Machine', Connie," interjected

CHAPTER 2

Bass...

"It reads thusly:

'To my great friend and mentor Pontius... My trusted colleague and my brother 'Grand Meister'... My love and respect to yourself, Beatrice and Leopold always...

'Free at last to explore beyond the boundaries of human understanding. I thank you from the bottom of my heart...

Your humble servant...

'Herbert George Wells...'

"Do you not see, Connie? H. G. Wells is one of the Council of 13 'Grand Meisters' of the 'Time Enforcement Agency'."

Connie gave a wry smile in recognition of her understanding and waited a few seconds before her attempted answer was unceremoniously curtailed by the trilling of her cell phone. Giving just one sentence in acknowledgement of the short-texted request made by Pontius Aston:

"Connie. Return to London 1898 with some urgency if you please. Tiberius is in mortal danger and requires immediate defensive support from James. With all possible haste, Pontius."

Connie addressed her husband with some urgency...

"Tiberius is in grave danger. Even as we speak, both he and Marcus fight to preserve their lives, those of several 'Covert Special Forces' operatives under their command and that of a very important mystery ward whose life it seems must be protected at all costs, in an altercation with members of 'The Black Guard' on Tower Bridge back in our London of 1898."

Bass merely moved his head simply from side to side, once in each direction, and imparted with an air of familiar acceptance clearly present as he sighed...

"Ah, but of course. When is Tiberius not in grave danger?"

Chapter 3

'A Most Important Ward.'

'London, 1898.'

"Tiberius, you are wounded; there, blood on your sleeve..."

Blackmore glanced down at his left upper arm for a brief second or two before shrugging dismissively and returning his full attention as to how best to quell the deadly firefight that threatened to wipe out his entire squad of brave companions...

"I have neither the inclination nor the time to bleed at present, Marcus. My immediate priority is focused solely on preserving the lives of my command and preserving the well-being of our very important charge...

"I fear, however, that our rapidly diminishing cache of ammunition, coupled with our lack of adequately defendable territory, will, on this day, be the joint key factors responsible for our inevitable capitulation in the wake of such insurmountable odds, my young friend.

"The tenacious manner in which these 'Black Guard' fellows are going about their extremely well-ordered task suggests to an old, experienced soldier, that affording any survivors their basic breathing privileges upon conclusion of their mission, is not a mandatory requirement on their part. If you offer affiliation to a God or religion

CHAPTER 3

of any denomination, Marcus, I suggest that you speak up now and make your peace accordingly."

Just as Blackmore's final few words were drowned out by the incessant barrage of deadly lead projectiles, which relentlessly continued to bombard their now virtually indefensible position, Jackson noticed positive murmurs emanating from some of their beleaguered companions' mouths...

"SEE THERE, TIBERIUS, TO THE REAR OF THE ADVANCING NORTHERN TROOP; AND THERE, BEHIND THE SOUTHERN RANKS OF 'BLACK GUARD.' IT WOULD SEEM THAT OUR THOUGHTS OF IMMINENT DEMISE WERE SOMEWHAT PREMATURE...SALVATION IS AT HAND."

Offering a devastatingly effective rear-guard counter attack behind both of the advancing northern and southern groups of 'Black Guard', were units of the Duke of Wellington's Red Jackets brigade led by the welcome sight of 'League of Ghosts' colleagues Pontius Aston, Don 'The Undertaker' Blackmore, Leopold Aston, Phineas Jefferson and Detective Chief Superintendent Frank Abilene.

Confounded by the surprise incursion from behind each of their advancing ranks, The Black Guards' tactical discipline, exemplary up to this moment, fell into complete disarray as they attempted to compensate for this unexpected counter assault by hastily altering the initially conceived two-pronged assault upon their prime objective target to a less manageable three-point strategy, thus turning their seemingly unassailable tactical advantage of a few short seconds ago into a desperate fight for their own survival.

From his own position beneath the great northern arch of Tower Bridge, Blackmore was now aware that his group's capacity to retaliate effectively had improved greatly due to the timely intervention of James Bass, who had silently materialised by his side and proceeded to unleash his own form of instant retribution upon the now rapidly depleting personnel of 'Black Guard' who remained alive.

Utilising first his 'yellow boy' Winchester repeating rifle until its chamber was spent of ammunition, then drawing his pair of Smith and Wesson Schofield revolvers, Bass proceeded with devastatingly precise accuracy to administer what had become his signature kill shot, comprising two chest taps and one forehead tap to each specific target, a distinct trademark that was achieving something of a legendary status all of its own amongst the ranks of both his own colleagues and the criminal fraternity alike...

"I would recognise that haphazard style of gunplay anywhere!" exclaimed a somewhat relieved Blackmore to his newly arrived comrade...

"Good afternoon, Tiberius, and Marcus. I offer most humble apologies with regards to my late arrival. I'd been informed that you might be in need of a little assistance," quipped Bass dryly, displaying an almost casual demeanour in between dispatching continuous volleys of unerringly accurate, deadly lead towards the now hapless and helpless remnants of their all but vanquished assailants...

"Tiberius, might one suggest advancing from our enclave and exploiting the tactical advantage that we now hold over our enemy in order to secure captives for the purpose of interrogation? Perhaps we might yet glean valuable information as to the motivating factor that guides the murderous intent of these hapless minions here today."

"Agreed," spat Blackmore as slivers of sharp sandstone and grit forced him to shield his face for a second before addressing his men...

"YOU, YOU, YOU AND YOU; WITH MYSELF AND COLONEL BASS; YOU TWO, COVER AND PROTECT OUR WARD WITH YOUR LIVES... MARK ME WELL, GENTLEMEN... WITH YOUR LIVES!"

Up until this moment, the young gentleman, to whose safety was being paid so much attention, had remained silent and remarkably calm considering the chaos that was ensuing all around him. Just as Bass, Blackmore, Jackson and their men busied themselves re-loading spent weapons' chambers and preparing themselves to advance from their position, the young man rose to his feet and began to speak, exhibiting great clarity of voice and exuding the composure of an experienced military tactician for one of such tender years...

"Gentlemen, if one might be so bold as to offer a suggestion as to how our little band might progress?"

As he continued to lay down a suppressing covering fire making way for his group's imminent advance, without turning his attention away from the immediate task at hand, Blackmore remarked...

"If you please, sir, our mandate is clear. Protect the young gentleman at all costs. We shall only be able to carry out our orders if you agree to..."

"Hand me a weapon, Colonel Blackmore!" exclaimed the young man, somewhat brusquely.

"I am well versed in the use of small arms and close order combat techniques as I shall gladly demonstrate... IF ONE MIGHT BE GRANTED THE USE OF A WEAPON!"

Overhearing the young gentleman's request, Bass reached into the right-hand pocket of his long overcoat and produced his old Webley service revolver which he duly tossed towards the young man in the same sweeping movement.

As though eager to demonstrate the combat prowess about which he had just a few seconds earlier so vociferously boasted, the young gentleman levelled his revolver at a trio of advancing 'Black Guards' and put a single round directly into the centre of each of their foreheads.

'Very impressive,' thought Bass and Blackmore simultaneously as they glanced at each other and nodded once before commencing with their advance.

Sensing that their assailants' ammunition reserves must be all but depleted, as were their own, Bass and Blackmore opted to engage their enemy in hand-to-hand combat.

As combinations of perfectly executed punches and kicks rained down on their now demoralized and defeated attackers, it became clear to the detectives that the young gentleman that they had been tasked to protect at the expense of their lives was more than capable of protecting himself as he proceeded to offer a rather impressive demonstration of his own extremely disciplined and very effective pugilistic skills.

Whilst surveying the aftermath of their spontaneous counter-offensive, Bass barked out the command to all the 'Black Guards' left alive who were capable of hearing his voice…

"All of you. Yield now and clemency will be considered. Choose to continue with your offensive, however, and the consequences for you all will assuredly be swift and final."

Selecting the 'Black Guard' lying closest to him, Bass raised the severely beaten excuse for a man to his feet by the lapels of his long black greatcoat and began his impromptu interrogation…

"Listen to me well, 'Black Guard'. I am not accustomed to asking questions for a second time. Who sent you here today on this 'forlorn hope'?"

Silence…

"COME ON, MAN… NO ADVANTAGE FOR YOURSELF CAN BE GAINED FROM MAINTAINING YOUR CONTINUED SILENCE. TO WHOM DO YOU OFFER FEALTY? WHAT IS THE TITLE OF THE OVERLORD WHOSE IDENTITY YOU CONCEAL TO THE DEATH? SPEAK!"

Using his great physical strength, Bass lifted his helpless interviewee clean off the ground and proceeded to shake him from side to side like a limp rag doll. As he did so, his patience reaching its tolerance, Bass became acutely aware of a strikingly familiar odour that seemed to be emanating from somewhere about the person of his frustratingly unresponsive interviewee…

'Almonds' he thought to himself in the precise moment that his 'Black Guard' captive uttered a final short sentence of defiance before falling dead to the ground…

"To forfeit one's life at this moment comes as a welcome reprieve from the ten thousand torments that the 'Master' would bestow on the one as payment for failure."

"CYANIDE! THEY HAVE CYANIDE CAPSULES CONCEALED INSIDE THEIR TEETH!" Bass exclaimed in vain, as all around both himself and his colleagues what remained of the 'Black Guard' assassination squad fell lifeless at their feet.

**

Upon greeting their colleagues, Bass and Blackmore stood alongside them observing a few seconds of silent contemplation over the corpses of their enemy, almost as though paying tribute to a band of fallen brothers upon the field of battle…

"Whomsoever orchestrated their very ably-conceived tactical offensive on this day must be regarded as a formidable opponent indeed. One simply cannot ignore the plain fact that these 'Black Guard' were once highly skilled and very capable soldiers and it is for those former brothers in arms, and not the misguided agents of darkness and chaos they became latterly, that I mourn. What an unnecessary waste of human life this was," lamented Blackmore solemnly as he bowed his head in a show of genuine, heartfelt sorrow…

"Remember this, Tiberius, that regardless to whatever nation's armed forces their allegiances were once honourably pledged, these men were coerced, wilfully or not, into making the choice that led them to their sorry end," alluded Bass sagely, his wise counter-observation duly noted with respect as his old companion responded with a customary single nod...

"Where is your ward, Tiberius; does he remain unharmed?" enquired a rather anxious Pontius Aston of Blackmore...

"He is over there, safe and sound, conversing with Marcus. A remarkable young man who bears the heart of a lion and displays very obvious leadership and command capabilities. Fights and kills well, too. This boy is a soldier, is he not, Pontius?" enquired Blackmore as the young man and Jackson joined Aston, Blackmore, Bass, Abilene and Jefferson where they stood...

"That he is, Tiberius, a very fine soldier indeed, whose great potential must be allowed to develop and flourish precisely on schedule for the sake of all humanity and in order to help preserve the future freedom of the entire world," imparted Aston gravely.

Needing no prompting whatsoever to speak, the young man proceeded to surprise everyone further with his obvious prowess as a knowledgeable, gifted orator...

"Gentlemen, please accept my gratitude for your rather impressive and most enthusiastic efforts with regards to preserving my well-being. I have no doubt that a complete briefing as to the reasons for this lively skirmish will be forthcoming, but for the present, please allow one to formally introduce oneself:

"My name is Churchill, former Cornet Second Lieutenant of the 4th Queen's Own Hussars; Winston Leonard Spencer Churchill, at your service, and I am deeply indebted to you all."

Chapter 4

'Winston.'

Following a round of brief but nonetheless formal introductions, Churchill was hurriedly escorted the relatively short distance from their compromised Tower Bridge location to the more secure confines of the Tower of London where, upon locating the concealed entrance behind Traitors' Gate that led into the labyrinthine maze of tunnels known as Trajan's Vaults, the eventual safe haven of 'The League of Ghosts' headquarters, located deep beneath the 'Bloody Tower' keep, was a welcome sanctuary where stock of their immediate situation could be properly taken, and a robust, tactically achievable strategy formulated...

"I assure you, gentlemen, that I am unharmed, though I must confess to still being at something of a loss as to why my continued wellbeing should be of such paramount importance and should merit your brave and selfless interventions on my behalf, for which I remain deeply indebted to you all," imparted Churchill whilst exuding a noticeable air of self-confidence.

Allowing a few seconds before he answered, Aston began what he was all too aware would prove to be a lengthy dialogue between the two of them...

"Mr Churchill, sir, please be aware that whenever our services are called upon by the highest authority, then rest assured the matter brought to our attention is one of potentially world-altering importance."

"Whenever 'your services are called upon by the highest authority', Captain Aston?" enquired Churchill, presenting the immediate impression to all those assembled that any questions offered on his part would be well considered and used intelligently to glean the information deemed necessary in order to satisfy the keen and enquiring mind of this, as yet, insignificant and untested young former second lieutenant…

"But am I not merely at present a somewhat quite ordinary man of tender years? Ambitious and hungry to achieve high purpose without doubt, but as yet relatively untried and one who boasts an unremarkable, anonymous presence on the home front, let alone on the world stage?…

"What facets of an average at best scholar's unimpressive curriculum vitae would pique the interest of mysterious strangers bearing hostile intent upon one's life?"

The initial attempt by Aston to offer his riposte was curtailed as a result of the exuberance openly displayed by the brash young Cornet…

"Mr Churchill sir, if I might…"

"Winston, Captain Aston, if it pleases you. After sharing the field of combat together and undergoing the necessary ritual of formal introductions, Winston will suffice…

"Whilst recently serving with the Queen's Own 4th Hussars my rank of Cornet Second-Lieutenant was never bettered and indeed, I find myself outranked on a military level by most of the gentlemen, and no doubt the ladies here assembled…

"Considering therefore my immediate aspirations erring towards a career in journalism, I fail to understand why the continuance of one's existence should be of such great importance to the regular clientele of an east end public house, let alone to the realm."

CHAPTER 4

"If one might be allowed to continue for a moment, Winston, I'm sure all of your enquiries will be addressed," was Aston's immediate response.

"My colleagues and I represent a brace of covert organisations that operate with the full blessing and sanction of both the British and World governments, but whose actions remain unhindered and unburdened by any of the stifling bureaucratic shackles or official protocols that might unduly hamper swift and decisive progress on their part."

Immediately sensing a keenness within Churchill to unleash a torrent of probing questions, Aston raised his right hand sharply in order to silence the young man's eagerness to speak and pressed on with his own dialogue, beckoning towards the group seated around the grand oak table...

"'The League of Ghosts' comprises the seventeen exceptionally gifted individuals seated here, each one in possession of the exacting criteria and, erm, shall we say for want of a more technically detailed explanation, singularly unusual attributes deemed necessary to be considered for eligibility of membership into this most elite and unique of organisations...

"Their anonymity, which remains jealously guarded, affords them the luxury of operating as would any ghost; silent spectres able to exploit their hard-won privileges of rank in order to infiltrate the highest echelons of government office and the protected palaces of aristocracy; skulking shadows experienced in manipulating the more questionable darker arts of law enforcement, testing their resolve selflessly and without question at the most basic levels of existence in order to melt seamlessly into the less salubrious areas of humanity in order to achieve their ultimate goal of protecting and preserving both homeland and world security."

Once again, Churchill took it upon himself to intercede...

"Forgive me, Pontius, but I feel compelled to enquire: what possible significance a life thus far so ordinary has, or possibly will have, with regards to securing the future freedom of humanity from an as yet undisclosed, potentially cataclysmic human catastrophe?"

Aston offered a knowing, wry grin in recognition of Churchill's remarkable ability to pose the most pertinent question at precisely the correct moment...

"Of course, my dear Winston. Finally, you pose the question of prime importance, the answer for which, fantastic though it may at first appear, is the sole reason why your life must be preserved regardless of any sacrifice that must be made in order to achieve that end."

Churchill used the ensuing pause allowed by Aston to gather his thoughts before answering simply...

"The intrigue is almost too much for a man to conceive, Pontius. Pray continue, if it pleases you, sir."

Aston duly obliged Churchill's request, beginning with a question of his own...

"Please, enlighten us if you will, Winston. Did you not once allude casually unto a school friend in a moment of private conversation that one day it would be by your hand that Britain would be saved from a foreign invasion?"

"What if I were now to inform you that the then somewhat naïve, yet robust and bold prediction of a sixteen-year-old schoolboy would indeed come to pass in less time from this very day than it would take five decades to elapse."

Churchill eyed Aston incredulously and answered almost immediately, an expression of disbelief appearing upon his youthful features as he exclaimed...

"Then I would be compelled to enquire if one would be able to substantiate exactly how in God's name a pithy, somewhat naively arrogant boast of future bravura and unbridled ambition during a conversation held in supposed secrecy between two adolescent school friends could possibly be made common knowledge in this house today!"

"How indeed, my inquisitive young friend, how indeed?" countered Aston.

"Earlier, if you care to remember, I alluded to the existence of a second covert organisation that would be of vital importance with regards to the successful outcome of our intended mission of protection...

"Consider for a moment the simple and elementary rules of physics concerning the three dimensions of physical movement already proven possible on this plane of consciousness...

"One is quite obviously physically able to move backwards and forwards, from side to side and, albeit over a limited distance from standing still, upwards and downwards; these are the three dimensions of physical movement, as explained in non-scientific layman's terms."

Raising his right hand sharply in order to halt the impending torrent of enquiry from Churchill, Aston continued...

"Please indulge me for a moment longer, Winston. I assure you of this, the true facts will out very soon and your full understanding of all things relevant to this conundrum of sorts will be complete and to your satisfaction...

"Imagine then, if you will, the reality of a fourth dimension. An alternative physical plane that exists outside the parameters of most human consciousness and thought that, if it were able to be in some way accessed, would allow persons to travel either backwards or forwards in order to visit any fixed point in time...

"I put it to you that an accessible conduit exists between the established three dimensions of the physical plane inhabited by all of us, and the fourth dimension of time."

Unable to contain himself for a moment longer, Churchill seized upon his opportunity to re-enter Aston's briefing...

"One might suppose then, that, if one were to accept the rationale for such bold revelations were based upon valid, trustworthy intelligence, then access into such a conduit would essentially require a specially commissioned task force in order to police it, so as to negate any risk of criminal agencies both accessing and utilising it themselves in order to further their own unscrupulous ambitions, and therefore subsequently risk altering the true course of time as it should naturally unfold."

Aston sat back in his chair and smiled knowingly in Churchill's direction, his respect for the young man growing markedly with every new exchange of dialogue that passed between them...

"Your insight is flawless, as too is your uncannily accurate perception of the facts quite correct, Winston. The second covert task force, to which you so intuitively refer, the very same organisation to which oneself alluded earlier, is named 'The Time Enforcement Agency' to which myself, my wife Beatrice, my son Leopold, Colonel Bass and Colonel Blackmore are commissioned to serve as agents...

"Our remit is very simple in principle. We are charged to supervise the timelines for any presence of the criminal element who possess the knowledge to traverse the corridor between ours and the fourth dimension. In short, as you so perceptively reasoned earlier, my friend, we attempt to cancel out the random elements of chance that could potentially jeopardise the future security of our world and even threaten to destabilise the very fabric of our existence as it was so intended."

Churchill reclined in his own chair and carefully pondered Aston's words for several seconds...

"Were it not for what I consider to be a rational, disciplined mind witnessing first-hand the events unfolding as they have done so on this day, one would feel compelled to dismiss such fantastic revelations as ones made directly by your esteemed self, Captain Aston, as being little more than the fanciful ravings of an over-stimulated, overtly-creative imagination...

"However, having witnessed with my own eyes the courageous and selfless actions on your part towards preserving one's personal well-being, regardless of the potentially fatal consequences to both your own life, and to the security of your valiant companions, I find myself compelled to conclude that today, regardless of what history will be made and by whom, and given that the adventures of this somewhat as yet quite ordinary young man will undoubtedly continue, the personal ambitions of that same young man will be realised no matter the risk or hardship involved during that long and arduous travail, and that the solid foundations upon which lifelong friendships are constructed, have on this day been set."

Nodding his head in sage agreement, the retort offered by Aston was instantaneous...

"Very well then, Winston. Taking into account that you accept as the sincerest truth the content of my briefing, it follows that I must insist that you will therefore please divulge your immediate intentions to this assembly, with regards to any plans you may already have in place, to further your ambitions, however trivial you might at present consider them to appear."

"Sir, with the greatest respect intended, my plans are conceived for good reason always, as is their meticulous formulation finalised implicitly prior to their commencement," snapped Churchill, his belligerent reply denoting the indignant manner of a person whose hitherto sacred personal boundaries had been invaded once too often...

"My immediate intention is to take up my commission as a war correspondent reporting for both the Daily Mail and Morning Post newspapers directly from the front line of the second Boer War in Ladysmith, South Africa...

"Following a brief sojourn in Calcutta during March, then possibly traversing on to Cairo until late April, I shall return to England in order to place my immediate affairs in order at home, from where I intend to embark next autumn for Ladysmith where I shall commence my new employment immediately."

"Rest assured, Winston, you are and shall always remain the single key protagonist during the course of these proceedings," Aston interceded, the sincerity of his demeanour instantly recognised and appreciated by Churchill.

"Your personal security will be trusted to the auspices of both Colonel Bass and Colonel Blackmore," he continued as he gestured towards the two ageing enforcers seated opposite them who simply nodded once their affirmation towards both Aston and Churchill...

"They will move as would the most anonymous of ghosts. Discreetly, silently, inhabiting the darkest shadows that surround you until such time as their presence is required, and in this knowledge you may be confident, my young friend, their presence to assist during vital moments that will shape your destiny will undoubtedly be required...

"Our intelligence network provides flawless, accurate information; each of our agents retain the capability to traverse time itself in order to ascertain exactly the precise moment at which our pair of designated enforcers here are required to act...

"Now, I believe that concludes my briefing. Upon divulgence of your immediate travel arrangements in minute detail, you are free to leave, but I ask of you, Winston, with all humility and with the greatest of respect intended, to be wary at all times of that anomaly, however trivial it might appear, which may seek to entice even the most prepared and disciplined mind from its intended course, and remember this well: we will be watching your life as it unfolds with a great deal of interest."

As he rose from his chair and prepared to be escorted through the intricate labyrinth of tunnels leading from the secret enclave and upwards towards Tower Hill, Churchill's parting words denoted to all present an air of unmitigated self-confidence, possibly even suggesting traits of the reckless arrogance demonstrated by some of the great and proven aristocratic leaders of generations long past...

"Once more, gentlemen, and ladies of course, I thank you for your timely interventions on my part. As you are all now aware, my personal ambitions were formulated at a tender age and will, it would appear, with your assistance in the fullness of time, be realised...

"I must, however, confess to finding quite absurd the notion that my well-being should merit the constant vigilant attentions of our good Colonels Bass and Blackmore, even though, with the greatest humility and respect intended, I am certain that their lofty military ranks are well-earned and their capabilities to carry out such a mission are more than adequate."

Turning towards Bass and Blackmore and addressing them directly Churchill continued...

"All I feel compelled to add in conclusion as something of a footnote to this quite extraordinary exchange, is that I look forward to our next encounter with great anticipation as I am sure that your combined presences will provide for quite an interesting raft of rather fine adventures, and with that, gentlemen, and ladies, I must with no shortage of haste be away to my next appointment, for which I am now excruciatingly and inexcusably late! Good day, good day... now come, gentlemen, let us away from this cold stone mausoleum out into the open air of old London town..."

Even before his final words were completed, Churchill turned away with some purpose from his perplexed audience and was escorted from the library by half a dozen dark attired and burly Covert Special Forces operatives.

Waiting for a few brief moments until he was certain that Churchill was beyond earshot, Aston proceeded to address Bass and Blackmore directly...

"Quite the assured character it would appear, young Mr Churchill."

Blackmore returned Aston's comment with an expressionless gaze, mirroring exactly the one offered by Bass. The two detectives then answered simultaneously, as if bound by some telepathic bond to do so, with a single word...

"Quite."

"James, Tiberius, your mandate is clear: the prime directive of your mission parameters will be to visit key points in the personal timeline of Winston Churchill that have been identified by the 'Grand Meisters' of the Time Enforcement Agency as being those deemed most vulnerable to incursion by a potentially random rogue element...

"Your mission is one of a direct and quite simple nature in principle, gentlemen: to cover and protect your mark. At all human cost, above all else, Winston Churchill must survive in order to fulfil his youthful promise to become the leader of our government and to deliver Europe from the inevitable rise of a fascist tyrant. Gentlemen, this is without doubt an opportunity for you to make your own appointment with destiny."

Altering his perspective slightly, Aston continued by posing a question to the two detectives...

"Might one enquire, gentlemen, in that now being made aware of the imperative requirement for the success of your mission, and that you will be seconded in close proximity to your charge during key personal moments that will occur throughout his lifetime, what were your first impressions of the man himself?"

Bass and Blackmore eyed each other across the great round table; Bass being the first of the two to speak...

"Erm... Tiberius. Would you care to... erm...?"

"Oh, no, James, please do continue. I'm sure that my allusions regarding the subject in question will mirror your own... in the main," was Blackmore's condescending, yet mildly humorous response to his grinning colleague...

"Very well, then. Mr Churchill exudes confidence, of that fact there is no doubt. He is courageous and tactically aware, denoting an educated and well-drilled military acumen. His speeches rendered unto this house showed us exceptional oratory skills and his understanding of both military techniques and the complexities that abound within the political arena suggest that his future success in commanding and leading nations on the world stage is to be built on strong foundations here, in this time...

"However, for every one of these positive attributes, the man's character is, even to the layman's perception, quite obviously flawed."

"As is the character of every person, even if only in some minute detail, James," countered Aston.

"Just so, Pontius. Our human flaws might be perceived as being necessary components set within the well-ordered machinery of a stable persona; components that require constant attention with each malfunction or weakness, however minute, immediately addressed and repaired in order for that machinery to function perfectly, as it should.

"One might even suggest that these character flaws are a necessary trait to be regarded as something of an educational experience of sorts. Trifling, even somewhat annoying encumbrances experienced on the way towards attaining one's own level of emotional enlightenment and professional achievement...

"As a matter of the utmost importance, therefore, I would recommend that a professional, in-depth evaluation of our young Mr Churchill's mental capacity be carried out by both of our resident psychologists, Connie and Florence."

"Valid points duly noted, James. Does anyone else have more points of relevance to add?"

The final words of Aston's speech were curtailed somewhat abruptly by Blackmore's perceptive intervention...

"Might one be correct in the assumption that Churchill has in fact been 'green lit' by our nemesis of old, 'The Architect'?"

Aston's answer was direct and succinct in its content...

"It would be a safe assumption that this is indeed the case, Tiberius. We are informed by a reliable source that 'The Architect' himself is responsible for the conscription of former soldiers to swell the ranks of his 'Black Guard'. Disenchanted, lost souls discarded as would be the day's rancid refuse to the streets after giving years of unquestioned service to what they now perceive as an ungrateful, uncaring government and shunned by the very public that they were once sworn to protect...

"A highly trained, lethal force lying dormant, awaiting radicalisation by a manipulative genius in aid of a twisted cause: to believe in and subsequently carry out with impunity pledged to all who would serve the will of their now completely-trusted commander in chief and absolute overlord: 'The Architect'.

"We have it on reliable authority that 'The Architect' is responsible for the conscription and the subsequent deployment of 'The Black Guard' under the command of one Septimus Mortecai Severin, late of Her Majesty's Covert Special Forces unit."

"SEVERIN!" exclaimed Bass.

"Septimus Severin. Without doubt one of the finest, most courageous soldiers with whom Tiberius and I had the good fortune to serve."

"And aside from both myself and James, without question the absolute best of the enforcers ever to emerge from within the ranks of the military," interjected Blackmore solemnly...

"Now, as we are all well aware, enforcers are employed specifically to exploit their rather singular set of special skills with regards to the enforcement of designated mandates, or..."

Bass continued the thread...

"Forgive me, Tiberius; or for their ability to terminate a mark with extreme prejudice, without suggesting the slightest hint of hesitation or displaying any sign of either regret or remorse for their actions."

Just as he completed his sentence, a sudden bitter coldness sent a chill to the very core of his soul as Bass processed the obvious truth of this latest revelation...

"Good lord, Septimus Severin has been contracted by 'The Architect' to assassinate Winston Churchill!"

Chapter 5

'Severin.'

"SEVERIN! Known affectionately, and with good reason among the many ranks of recruits within Her Majesty's Covert Special Forces unit who were fortunate enough to benefit from the wealth of knowledge that he bestowed upon them, as 'The Teacher'," the admiration and high esteem held for this man by both himself and Blackmore wholly apparent in the voice of Bass as he spoke...

"Septimus Mortecai Severin. One of our most highly revered and trusted colleagues. The most decorated and highly respected soldier ever to rise from the ranks, one of our closest allies and a man one was proud to regard as a friend. How in the name of all that is holy can this be, Pontius?"

Aston pondered the question posed by his old comrade for a moment prior to answering...

"Loyalty, given in the service of any cause, is literally dependent upon the strength of will possessed by the individual. Interpretation of the ideas formulated and presented by any ruling body rely solely upon the fragile parameters that bind those ideas together and in utilising the authority deemed necessary that exists within the highest echelons of governmental jurisdiction wisely in order to enforce those ideas as acceptable law...

"In all honesty, who is to determine which of those ideas provides the correct cause to support? The reasoned, balanced idea of a so-called righteous truth convincingly presented by the government to whom your unmitigated support has been duly pledged or..."

"Or the persuasive influence of a very convincing counter-argument, cunningly conceived by a psychologically superior, extremely manipulative entity; one quite capable of turning the strongest of constitutions towards the darkness with the power and fortitude of persuasive word alone," retorted Bass gravely...

"So, it would appear that Septimus has somehow allowed himself to be coerced into supporting the systematic implementation of an extreme new world order to be presided over by the ultimate master of deception and deceit, 'The Architect'," interjected Blackmore, openly displaying concern in his voice as he spoke.

"Indeed it would, Tiberius," answered Aston.

"Possibly the single human factor present within this equation with whom one would least relish the prospect of a final, fatal confrontation...

"Nevertheless, Septimus Severin remains the catalyst whose participation in these proceedings must be ended as a matter of extreme urgency," an authoritative sternness remaining present in his voice as he spoke...

"If for reasons appertaining to the strong personal feelings you both harbour towards the man becoming a compromising factor that may hinder your ability to complete the designated mission successfully, I am willing, under these most extenuating and delicate circumstances, to..."

"YOU WILL DO NOTHING, PONTIUS!" exclaimed a most perplexed Bass...

"The mission parameters are set in motion. Both mine and Tiberius' course is precise and our consciences are clear, as our focus remains resolute to enforce our mandate with extreme prejudice, should the need arise...

"Our resolve will not be compromised by remnants of personal feelings once held for a brother now swayed towards an alternative path, but know this, we shall endeavour to uncover the truth of Septimus' change of allegiance by using every resource available to us...

"If he is indeed to be permanently 'retired', his termination will be implemented when, and only when, this remains the absolute final option left to us in order to cease his intended course."

"And lest we forget, the protagonist and perpetrator of all things that are set into motion here, the brilliant and yet inherently evil mind of 'The Architect' once more rises up and engages to challenge the fundamental ideas upon which our civilisation is founded...

"Should opportunity present itself, the sanction parameters must extend in order to cover his own immediate and unquestioned termination," added Blackmore in no uncertain terms.

"Absolutely, Tiberius. Without question," agreed Aston immediately.

"Severin is merely the directed 'asset' of these proceedings. The real and unequivocal threat posed to the continued natural and unhindered evolution of our race should never be forgotten...

"Should adequate and clear opportunity present itself during the course of forthcoming events, you are hereby sanctioned to retire 'The Architect' with extreme prejudice, with no quarter considered, nor any plea for clemency granted...

"Now, gentlemen, even as we speak, Mr Churchill sets fair on the first part of his intended course to Ladysmith, South Africa from the Eastern Dock at Whitechapel aboard the converted man-o-war HMS 'Rocinante', now the flagship of the great East India company...

"Your tickets are procured, as are your berths on board the 'Rocinante' and your identities as independent agents sent to broker trade deals with the South African government on behalf of the East India Trading Company have been formally logged and your commissions made active...

"Embarkation commences in three hours in order to take full advantage of the early evening tide, so I would advise you both to use that time wisely and make restitution with your respective families. Your presence on the maiden part of the voyage is imperative as it would almost certainly be expected that an opportunistic attempt will be made on Churchill's life, even at this early juncture...

"Remember, gentlemen, endeavour to exercise discretion at all times with regards to your presence aboard ship, but absolutely no quarter must be granted to any assailant who may show their hand...

"Now, away to your task and know that all of our hopes and prayers accompany you as you strive towards facilitating the successful completion of this most extraordinary of commissions."

***

Towards the latter part of the nineteenth century, the combined area of the east and west London docklands had become one of the busiest ports in the world and had gained the enviable reputation as being the single most important harbour through which a great portion of the world's lucrative trade passed.

The densely populated, multi-racial population throughout the port of London suggested to both Bass and Blackmore that the perfect opportunity for an attempt to be made on the life of Churchill was not merely a distinct possibility, but more than likely a written-in-stone certainty.

The pair of newly commissioned faux trade envoys attempted to remain inconspicuous by furtively concealing themselves behind several large pallets of cargo amidst the throInging tide of humanity busying itself on the quayside, so as to facilitate a favourable view of the gangplank belonging to their ship 'Rocinante' remaining clearly in view.

Blackmore took a long pull on his old clay pipe and proceeded to air his concerns as to the immediate security problems which they faced...

"An attempt on our man's life could potentially occur at any moment, from any number of locations on this blasted dock, James. Tactically, at this precise moment, we face our first logistical problem."

"The first of many, one would surmise," answered Bass in full agreement with the concerns aired by Blackmore as he casually flicked the stub of his still glowing stogie into the rapidly rising evening tide of the Thames...

"See there, Tiberius; our man Churchill approaches, displaying, it would appear, no shortage of the confidence that we previously ascertained he possesses...

"His lack of any discernible effort to promote even the merest hint of discreet anonymity on his part reflects either a demeanour of youthful recklessness, or one of blind stupidity," observed Bass as their obviously bold but naïve young charge strolled confidently towards his awaiting passage, seemingly oblivious to even the slightest notion that an attempt might be made upon his life at any moment.

"Observe too, James, the seemingly random deployment of 'Black Guard'. No doubt with the intention of confounding the untrained eye, they move freely among the embarking passengers and crew. As we correctly surmised, we are not alone...

"Stand you prepared to act swiftly, my brother, for I fear that our immediate attentions regarding this matter, primarily both our cunning detective guile and our ability to soldier with stealth and decisiveness, will surely be required presently."

Taking great care to maintain a discreet anonymity, Bass and Blackmore proceeded to board the 'Rocinante' a few minutes after Churchill, making certain that he was safely berthed in his cabin before conducting a thorough and painstaking deck-by-deck reconnoitre of their sizeable ship.

CHAPTER 5

***

The 'Rocinante' set sail on the high evening tide towards the mouth of the Thames and out into the cold and brutally unforgiving embrace of the North Sea before reversing course in a southerly direction through the narrow English Channel and then onwards, navigating through the Bay of Biscay towards the coastal markers of Spain and Portugal.

Bass and Blackmore prowled the curiously deserted lower decks and took stock of a tactical situation that they were both well aware had, in all probability, already been compromised...

"Our course, as yet, maintains close proximity to the coastline," observed Blackmore...

"We tease the edge of French sovereign waters around the Bay of Biscay and steer ever more southwards, skirting the Portuguese coastline towards southern Spain and onwards through the Straits of Gibraltar along the well-travelled African trade route. Our Mr Churchill has elected to follow the lengthier journeyman's passage towards his intended destination of Cape Town."

"And do you notice, Tiberius, though the passenger and crew manifests respectively offered no discernible evidence of either suspicious title or military rank, I fear that our presence aboard ship, and the grounds appertaining towards our true intentions, are already common knowledge to our enemies," noted Bass, displaying possibly the merest hint of consternation prior to Blackmore alerting his colleague to an altogether more disconcerting threat...

"More immediately so than you might imagine, James; one-hundred and eighty degrees about face: A trio of hostiles bearing down on your position with undoubted malicious intent in mind!"

Bass reciprocated by issuing a warning of his own to a now fully-prepared Blackmore...

"And to your rear, Tiberius. Three more 'Black Guard'. Assume each one bearing intentions fully prejudicial and with the express intent to cause fatal harm!"

Without the need for prompting or direction as to what course of action to pursue next, Bass and Blackmore commenced upon violent, non-compromising engagement with their assailants, displaying an impressive selection of the lethal skills accrued by the pair of ageing warhorses initially whilst leading harsh lives on the dour, unforgiving streets of Whitechapel, honed to accurate, deadly perfection as a result of the iron handed discipline later to be so forcefully administered by their battle-hardened and often brutal military taskmasters.

Armed with a selection of weapons designed to facilitate as silent an altercation as possible, the assault began, with their assailant's intent from the outset of allowing the two detectives no quarter a primary tactic.

Nor was any offered in return, as firstly Bass reciprocated by mercilessly smashing the right knee of his first attacker by utilising a perfectly aimed kick from his heavy-booted right foot.

At once, deftly manipulating the body of the disoriented 'Black Guard' and using his semi-incapacitated bulk as a human shield in order to hamper the advance of his knife-wielding second and third assailants, Bass proceeded to release his captive with some force directly into the path of one of them...

This tactic was sufficient enough to occupy a pair of his opponents momentarily so as to afford himself the opportunity of engaging, unhampered, the third 'Black Guard' in direct single combat.

Whilst drawing a blade from concealment beneath his heavy overcoat, Bass was able to avoid the pair of gleaming meat cleavers being wielded threateningly by his opponent as he deftly crouched down below their dangerously arcing swathes. As he did so, Bass was able to administer several swift stabs to an invitingly exposed torso.

His mark falling to the ground, momentarily incapacitated, Bass turned his attention once more towards his remaining pair of 'Black Guard', one of whom he decided to retire immediately with an expertly directed punt of his blade finding its resting place deep within the centre of an unprotected chest.

Satisfied in the success of his fatal assault, Bass squared up to his final cleaver-wielding aggressor and proceeded to advance fearlessly into the oncoming swathes of potentially deadly arcing steel.

Disarming his startled opponent with a deft 'slapping' of each blade from unwary, much weaker and less skilled hands than his own, Bass brought his forehead to bear squarely across the brittle and openly inviting bridge of the 'Black Guard's' nose, thus stunning his aggressor and exposing the weakened body to the precisely landed salvo of terminal pressure blows administered by a pair of extremely capable and mercilessly lethal hands.

The second trio of 'Black Guard' who had been allotted the task of extinguishing Blackmore's life light, discovered the course of their own fortunes took a turn even less favourable than those of their luckless, vanquished colleagues.

Dispatching the first of his assailants with relative ease, employing his own trusty blade to good advantage, Blackmore swiftly reinforced his already knarled warrior's fists with a pair of brass 'dusters' and proceeded to decimate the two remaining 'Black Guard' whilst openly displaying the skills, grace and lightning speed of a champion prize fighter.

Blow after relentless blow reigned down virtually unchallenged until another pair of mercilessly bested souls lay motionless at the lethal old soldiers' feet. The moment his final, brass-enhanced blow was landed, Blackmore immediately sought to address Bass; an extreme concern was obviously evident in his voice as he spoke…

"This detachment of a half-dozen 'Black Guard' was deployed as something of a hindrance, James, sent to draw us out into the open. A cleverly conceived strategy designed to test both our strength and resolve during battle, and to divert attention away from our prime directive...

"In the seconds we tarry here, Severin presents this cunningly conceived confounding tactic as his opening gambit and proceeds, in this very moment, to capitalise upon our absence in order to make an attempt on Churchill's life."

All at once, Bass became acutely aware of the slightest movement occurring not more than twenty yards immediately in front of the position where he and Blackmore conversed.

In one swift movement, Bass recovered his blade from the chest of a stricken 'Black Guard' and sent it spinning and arcing on a precisely judged trajectory into a vertical wooden post, embedding itself at the eye height of their not so stealthy interloper, whilst simultaneously calling out a stark warning, first towards his unwary companion, and then in the direction of their skulking voyeur in the shadows...

"TIBERIUS, WE ARE ONCE MORE COMPROMISED!"

In one second of habitual action, both Bass and Blackmore simultaneously each drew revolvers and levelled them, hammers cocked and readied for discharge, towards their now obviously terrified interloper...

"STAND YOU FAST; STEP FORWARD WITH ALL DUE CAUTION AND BE RECOGNISED," came the forcefully delivered command from Blackmore.

"D... don't shoot! Fer 'faks' sake d... don't shoot me. I 'ain't with them 'fakkers'. I've no designs on your wellbeing nor no interest in your business affairs, sirs, such course as they might take: As if I could 'ope to match 'wot' I just seen anyhow but fer 'faks' sake, please God don't shoot me!"

CHAPTER 5

"ON YOUR KNEES, HANDS BEHIND YOUR HEAD!" ordered Bass tersely, the petrified young man complying immediately...

"NAME, REASON FOR YOUR PRESENCE HERE SKULKING IN SHADOWED CONCEALMENT? SPEAK!" continued Bass as he segued seamlessly into his very well-practised field interrogation mode...

"J... Jennings P... Pike, sir" stammered Pike awkwardly.

"F... first mate. I'm nowt' but the 'fakkin' first mate an' this is my 'evenin' watch, mores the 'fakkin' pity. The cargo decks this time of night is usually quiet as the grave... usually!"

"First mate Jennings Pike; pay very close attention to what I have to say. I require you to divulge the exact whereabouts aboard this ship of a Mr Winston Churchill. His unencumbered existence upon this Earth very much depends entirely upon myself and my colleague ensuring that his continued ability to draw breath goes unhindered, from this night onwards and for the duration of at least the next forty-seven years or so," Bass requested, his taciturn manner lightening for a moment as a result of his unintentional aside of humorous wit.

Accounting for the impressive display of hand-to-hand combat that he had just witnessed moments earlier, and the efficient, military-like precision with which both of these gentlemen went about their business, each of whom had exuded both the confidence and menace that suggested their credentials identifying them as travelling merchants were bogus, Pike's answer was given based purely on the instinct that this pair of extraordinary strangers' presence here was somehow fated in order to contribute substantially towards the facilitation of a greater, possibly even humanity-preserving good...

"Starboard side, deck two, berth number four," Pike blurted out, self-preservation being his key motivation for divulging such classified information as was documented within the pages of the usually closely guarded secrets of the crew and passenger manifest, with little prompting from Bass...

"Then without wasting another precious second, lead on, Jennings Pike," snapped Bass as he hauled the young first mate to his feet and beckoned for him to lead both himself and Blackmore to Churchill's berth...

"And pray to God that the often darkly humorous nature of time does not conspire against us and become our enemy on this night."

Pike proceeded willingly to lead Bass and Blackmore towards a solid bulkhead which separated the cargo bay from a combined galley and crew dining area before alighting a steep set of steps into the dimly lit upper deck corridor...

"This 'b... be' deck four, sirs," stammered Pike, his initial fear dissipating somewhat in the wake of his realised new-found usefulness towards this most intriguing cause...

"The berth that you seek lies at the far end of this corridor, exactly where that dark suited gent makes furtive attempt to enter the cabin door."

Just as Pike had observed, a dark figure, clad in a heavy, military-type greatcoat and sporting a black bowler hat, not dissimilar to the one favoured by Blackmore, was indeed attempting to access the door of cabin number four: Churchill's cabin.

Recognising the plain, somewhat austere style of attire sported by the mysterious dark figure immediately as that more than likely belonging to someone whose probable proclivity towards regularly instigated and expertly controlled violence they should be very wary of, someone both Bass and himself knew very well from a dim and distant other lifetime of many years ago, Blackmore bade Pike to seek safer refuge behind both himself and Bass before announcing their presence in no uncertain terms...

"SEVERIN! SEPTIMUS MORTECAI SEVERIN! RAISE YOUR HANDS AND STAND YOU DOWN... YOUR BLACK INTENTIONS

CHAPTER 5

HERE ARE COMPROMISED!"

Turning almost nonchalantly towards the direction from which the very familiar, confidently commanding voice from his distant past came, a voice that had somewhat rudely interrupted his intended course, Severin, for it was indeed he whose tall, powerfully imposing frame stood before them, began to speak in a tone that was eerily parallel to both Bass' and Blackmore's usual personification of calmness when confronted by extreme pressure...

"Of course, Tiberius Blackmore, and James Bass. Esteemed company indeed, and, aside from that other preening, pompous, soon to be obsolete brace of ancient, old school soldiery Pontius Aston and Phineas Jefferson, the only effective pair of enforcers even remotely capable of offering adequate challenge towards thwarting my immediate intentions...

"Yes indeed, the 'Grand Meisters' chose their agents wisely, but mark these words well, my bold comrades of old; just as I nurtured and honed from rough, raw stone my pair of lethal masterpieces here before me standing, be under no illusion whatsoever that I am more than capable of breaking you both into a thousand fragments in an instant."

Bass and Blackmore looked on in silent incredulity as Severin continued his diatribe, their pistols already habitually unholstered and aimed towards their mutual target...

"So, here we stand. Weapons primed of course as your conditioning denotes, aimed towards each other threatening malicious intent and yet therein already has each of us committed the one potentially fatal error that an enforcer of prime, tested quality such as we three should never make. Neither one of us instantly discharged our weapons. Why is that do you suppose, James? Tiberius?

"Accounting for everything you were once taught: To retire instantly with extreme prejudice; To fulfil the parameters of your sanction without question; neither showing, nor feeling any sliver of emotion or regret. WHY?"

Surprising the dumbstruck pair by choosing to holster his own weapon, Severin slapped his chest forcefully with both hands, as if to indicate himself an open, willing target and persevered with his now somewhat emotional rhetoric...

"HERE IS YOUR MARK, MY FINE, BRAVE WARRIORS. FOR HERE, IN THIS MOMENT, MIGHT BE YOUR ONE OPPORTUNITY TO ACT; TAKE THE SHOT! TAKE... THE... SHOT!"

Bass and Blackmore remained stock-still, both their pistols primed and ready to fire. However, in that single, eternal, crystalline moment both men realised that had they displayed the slightest sign of hesitation before any enemy other than this one, then the pair of them would almost certainly, by this time, be lying fatally wounded; yet still neither man discharged his weapon.

Instead, perhaps harbouring the intention to at least offer some small professional courtesy to a once loyal and trusted colleague, Blackmore enquired...

"Why, Septimus? What overbearingly persuasive rhetoric exists that could motivate the infallibly patriotic, once-unbreakably resolute iron will of the absolute best of us to become the abominable worst?

"What despicably malignant force is able to exert an influence so strong as to turn the ultimate champion of truth and justice from the path of light towards the shadows of darkness?"

Now offering a wry, knowing grin as he answered, Severin retorted...

"Ah, Tiberius, as ever, the benevolent, compassionate diplomat. I fear that were I reliant solely upon the mercy of James alone then, alas, my life light would have been well and truly extinguished moments ago...

"I mean no disrespect, James, but yours was always the mentality best suited to the dispassionate sensibilities required by the assassin. The relentless stone-cold killer of killers, the instant harbinger of doom towards all supposedly unrighteous causes. A proud and conscientious artist such as myself could only fantasise in his wildest dreams of creating such a perfect weapon. Thank God, then, for the intercedence of your human conscience: Tiberius Blackmore."

"Explain to me then, James, if I could beg your indulgence for a brief moment longer; why do I still draw breath? Taking into account that the seemingly endless hours of intensive conditioning, coupled with the unforgivingly brutal and systematic deconstruction of your mental faculties were components in part of a meticulously conceived process, a process designed to facilitate the ultimate human strike weapons, devoid of all compassion and feeling...

"...nothing more than an obedient pair of assets designed to be systematically deployed against the most malignant forces imaginable bearing criminal intent. To believe always that even when there remains the slightest modicum of doubt, kill! So, I ask of you once more, James: why do I still live?"

Bass took no time to consider the musings made by Severin; the blunt, economically worded message sent forth on the back of his reply left his ex-colleague under no illusion as to the undoubted course upon which his train of thought travelled...

"Respect, Septimus. The only tangible reason as to why you yet draw breath is out of the respect that both Tiberius and I held for a once trusted and greatly admired colleague. A respect that guarantees him a single opportunity, perhaps for redemption, or perhaps merely to explain the motivation for his proposed actions...

"And so, Septimus, I reiterate the question previously posed by my so-called 'human conscience', the only question necessary before I surely consign your treacherous carcass to Hell. WHY?"

Without pause, Severin answered...

"Hell, James. A desolate place. A last bastion of damnation and torment, the like of which could scarcely be imagined, surely awaits those of us deserving of its tantalising welcome...

"A place whose portals we have teased to enter on many occasions. The sprawling 'Underverse' where we will join our fallen compatriots already serving their sentences of eternal suffering in return for the many lives they, and we, have brought to a premature end; the horrors that we have so willingly endorsed in the name of our government and Crown, both of whom we served so faithfully and without question...

"The Master offers light and a new hope for the future of our race as a new age of order and benevolence rises from the ashes of the existing decrepit, worn out and malignantly corrupt establishment..."

"Your so-named Master, 'The Architect', proposes nothing more than a contrived dictatorship," rebuked Blackmore disdainfully...

"A harshly disciplined autocracy offered in return for surrendering unchallenged fealty in support of an undemocratic, dictatorial overrule. Hardly the benevolent, utopian democracy one who might be easily persuaded, or perhaps more to the point of fact, coerced into believing in the validity of such a fantasy would expect as the ultimate reward for pledging one's allegiance to such a cause, eh, Septimus," Blackmore continued, a knowing eyebrow raised towards his old drill Sergeant Major...

"A jaded concept exploited to great lengths and varying degrees of success by many skilled orators, soldiers and opportunistic politicians alike, throughout the course of history...

"Alexander the Great, The Persian Dynasties, The Egyptian Pharaohs, The Roman Emperors, Genghis Khan, Napoleon Bonaparte; all were quite brilliant and yet morally flawed minds intent on forcing their concepts of total rule upon a malleable and subservient populace...

"I concur with you, Septimus, that the world order we have now: the bloated, all-powerful trade organisations, supported by culpable, unscrupulously corrupt governments grown fat on the wages of sin, who choose to turn a blind eye to all transgression, however corrupt, so long as the overflowing coffers of the wealthiest and most powerful remain full, must be addressed and held accountable for their sins with all possible urgency...

"However, 'The Architect' has sold you a lie, Septimus. A falsehood based on a single promise to deliver a utopian myth that was neither his right to make, nor one that he should ever attempt to deliver outside the parameters of officially sanctioned channels...

"He manipulates the trust placed in him by all those weaker minded, easily coercible souls who believe his convincing rhetoric, and wields with reckless abandon the manipulative influence he possesses in order to achieve his own ambition, that of achieving his one prime directive of securing nothing short of total world domination...

"Quite obviously, in this particular instance, 'The Architect' seeks to exploit the inevitable rise of fascism that will spread like a festering plague across eastern Europe during the next forty-seven years...

"His goal is quite simple in that he wishes to alter the equilibrium of time as it should unfold by systematically erasing from existence the key protagonists responsible for writing history's true pages, thus paving the way for an alternative era of dictatorial rule and chaos throughout the World...

"You, Septimus, whether subliminally coerced or otherwise, remain nothing more than a 'facilitator', a mere 'cleaner' dispatched at the behest of a madman to remove any obstacle that is deemed to offer a distraction towards his scheme."

Severin took a few moments to consider Blackmore's perceptive, very well-conceived oratory, all the while remaining wary of the possibility that perhaps, on just this one occasion, the uncharacteristically courteous diplomacy displayed towards an old colleague by the human conscience of James Bass, might be at any moment discarded and the enforcers' creed restored.

Bearing this in mind, whilst retaining a wary eye on the still raised and cocked pistol brandished by Bass and with cold beads of perspiration working their way from under the brim of his hat and down through each of his 'mutton-chop' temples, Severin offered his answer to Blackmore...

"As always, your impeccable choice of words is to be commended, Tiberius. For their eloquence, and, if I am correct in making this assumption as to at least part of their meaning, of course, is that within lies hope that a decision made lately by a once-trusted old friend might still yet be turned...

"Taking into account, therefore, allusions made previously concerning the present establishment of bloated and corrupt overlords, yes, Tiberius, I would see them fall, even if an act of subversion against both our corpulent government and the archaic monarchy it supports were facilitated by the black hand of 'The Architect'. Henceforth, I shall not be turned; my resolve will remain steadfast and I shall play my part with no deviance nor lack of conviction upon the stage of a new world order."

"Then you leave me no further options to consider, Septimus," interjected Bass with blunt disdain clearly evident in his voice as he spoke...

"Opportunity for redemption was offered as a courtesy to a once valued and respected comrade; termination is the mandatory sentence meted out as punishment for a proven traitor towards the Crown and the Regimental Colours, and a traitor you are to both of these noble institutions without question, sir."

At the precise moment Bass orated his final phrase, both he and Blackmore readied themselves to administer the fatal sentence. As they did so, Severin removed an unremarkably ordinary looking silver watch from inside his left-hand waistcoat pocket and opened the lid that covered its deceptively ornate Roman numerated face...

CHAPTER 5

Meeting the direct eye contact with his perspective executioners and smiling broadly as he spoke, Severin's speech faded away into another dimension, accompanying his not inconsiderably proportioned, somewhat imposing frame...

"So, it is with some regret that I bid you adieu for now, my old friends. Opportunities for both parties to attain a satisfactory conclusion to their mission parameters will, I assure you both, manifest themselves in the future; of that fact you can be certain."

"THE SLIPPERY OLD BASTARD POSSESSES A PORTKEY!" exclaimed Bass at the precise moment both he and Blackmore proceeded to unleash three full chambers of lethally accurate, searing lead projectiles into the now vacant bulkhead where Severin had stood a mere few seconds before.

Amidst the cloying white fog and acrid stench generated by the ignited gunpowder that hung in the stale, rancid air permeating throughout the forward berthing quarters of the ship, the door belonging to cabin number four opened inwards, through which stepped a somewhat sleep-dishevelled, obviously just rudely awoken Churchill...

"What in God's name could justifiably explain such a hellish cacophony of... Bass, Blackmore! Might one assume then that our association has, in these last few seconds, been officially sanctioned?" enquired Churchill of his bold, if somewhat frustrated protectors, who each habitually proceeded to reload the spent chambers of their weapons...

"A relationship that is now most assuredly well and truly consummated," quipped Blackmore dryly as he clicked one of the four fully loaded nine-round chambers, that he always carried about his person, into the frame of his old LeMat revolver...

"For your continued safety, Winston, please enter your berth and we three shall take stock of a fresh tactical conundrum which offers some immediate cause for our concern."

"And what to do about what one would assume to be the random presence of our young first mate, Master Pike?" enquired Churchill, upon noticing the obviously terrified form of Jennings Pike cowering against a bulkhead a short distance down the corridor.

Turning sharply, his pistol instinctively raised, the hammer cocked and ready for immediate discharge, Bass deadpanned menacingly towards Pike, his words spoken at a volume easily heard by their somewhat perturbed young interloper...

"What to do about Master Pike indeed."

Chapter 6

'Outwater.'

Holstering his weapon, purposefully displaying a conscious effort to ease the tension, uncertainty and fear that he sensed must be raging within the obviously petrified Pike, Bass spoke first, adopting a lighter, more tactful tone...

"Steady yourself, young man, we mean you no harm. The focus for our anger is now, for the present at least, passed."

"THE FOCUS OF YOUR 'FAKKIN' ANGER, SIR, JUST PROCEEDED TO PASS RIGHT THROUGH FOUR INCHES OF CLINKER-BUILT, NAVY REINFORCED, PITCHED-SOLID, OAK PANNELLED BULK 'EAD! 'OW IS THAT EVEN 'FAKKIN' POSSIBLE? AN' MORE'S TO THE POINT, WHERE 'AS THE FOCUS OF YOUR 'FAKKIN' ANGER TODDLED OFF TO? THE BOTTOM 'O' THE 'FAKKIN' POND TO 'AVE TEA AN' CRUMPETS WIV' OLD NEPTUNE 'IMSELF. I MEAN, STRIKE A 'FAKKIN' LIGHT, GUV... S... SIR... DO ME A 'FAKKIN' FAVOUR... YOU'RE 'AVVIN' A 'FAKKIN' LAUGH, MATE... 'AIN'T 'CHA?"

"Do you see me laughing, Jennings Pike!" snapped Bass, openly displaying mild consternation in response to Pike's somewhat surprisingly spirited outburst, whilst inwardly admiring the admirable attempt made by the young first mate to exhibit the very familiar characteristic of east London levity...

"Now join us within the relatively secure confines of Mr Churchill's cabin where we shall discuss our next course of action."

As Bass and Blackmore entered Churchill's cabin, Bass turned back towards Pike, who remained ensconced in what he perceived to be his enclave of relative safety, hoping that some deep-rooted inner compassion, hitherto not sensed from within Bass, would surface which would allow him to decide for himself not to be involved, and to continue about his mundane duties as though everything he had witnessed during the last few minutes was perhaps merely the result of an over active imagination, fuelled to overwhelming flights of fancy by an extra crafty nip of the rum ration, first mate's privilege, of course...

"My last remark was not made merely as an idle request, boy," afforded Bass ominously as he motioned backwards with a simple nod of his head towards the cargo hold where the corpses of the six 'Black Guard' still lay...

"Make your next life choice very wisely, Jennings Pike."

Instantly aware that the persona of Bass the enforcer had well and truly returned, and that he was now indelibly bound twice to this waking nightmare, firstly in bearing witness to the multiple dispatching of six souls to the afterlife, then to becoming an unwitting eyewitness to some inexplicable fairground magic caper, Pike decided that if he chose to cooperate, at least for the time being, he might learn a great deal more about the reason that had motivated such extreme proceedings and, most importantly of all, he may just live a little longer...

"Colonel Bass, Colonel Blackmore, what a not unexpected delight to see you both again so soon. Please enter and let us re-acquaint ourselves whilst imbibing a tumbler of rather fine Italian brandy," blustered a somewhat invigorated Churchill. Noticing the furtive frame of Jennings Pike following tentatively in the wake of the two detectives, Churchill continued...

CHAPTER 6

"Ah, Mr Pike. Might one strongly suggest that one takes Colonel Bass at his word. Please, in order to preserve your own well-being, for I do now surmise that your fate has become irrevocably entwined with our own, meaning in short that you now, in all probability, face the very same dangers and tribulations as do we bold three. I implore you, at all costs, heed my words...

"The balance of your life is now tainted by association with us alone. For the duration of this caper, however long may it continue, you are now a marked man, Mr Pike," stated Churchill ominously.

Prior to entering the cabin, Blackmore scanned the corridor: first forward and then astern as far as he could see, satisfying himself that for the present their privacy was assured.

He then proceeded to close and bolt the heavy cabin door behind him. Somewhat surprisingly, Pike was the first to speak, albeit tentatively, directing his words at Blackmore...

"Th... those six dead souls back there in the cargo 'old. They set about you an' 'im 'wiv' malicious intentions, but I swear on my mother's life, I 'ain't never seen anythin' like wot you two 'dun...

"'Alf a dozen well capable an' granite 'ard rough 'ouses', soldier types if I was guessin', sent willingly to meet whatever end awaited 'em, courtesy of you two devils stood 'ere among us. I 'ain't so much scared of wot's outside that door, I 'is' more 'shit-scared' of wot's 'fakkin' in 'ere, standin' right in front 'o' me!"

Bass surveyed Pike coldly, betraying no sign of emotion as he removed the dark-lensed spectacles that he always wore, to reveal his pitch-black eyes...

"Believe all that you see with your own eyes, Pike. All that you have encountered thus far, and what you will no doubt experience from this moment forth, will continue to contradict all forums of logical reason in which you believed, and the ordinary and accepted processes of rational thought to which you adhered...

"Now steady yourself and listen with an open mind for you will hear things that will conspire to confound and confuse your wits towards the boundaries of unhealthy distraction. Be seated over there and contribute only when invited to do so."

Pike perched uneasily on a three-legged stool by the washstand situated in the far corner of the small cabin. The final instruction... 'Contribute only when invited to do so'...offered by the seemingly perpetually taciturn Bass still ringing bell-like in his ears, Pike shuffled nervously on his seat and in what amounted to an act of naïve spontaneity chose to contradict the explicit instruction he had momentarily received, by enquiring of the ageing enforcer...

"A qu... question please, sir, if I may?"

As anticipated, Bass fixed the young first mate with a withering glare that made the beads of perspiration that were already seeping from every pore in his young body, seem as though they were instantly turning to droplets of ice. The retort Bass gave was simple and, accounting for the warning he had issued to Pike just a few moments earlier, quite tolerant...

"Ask your question."

"Those m... men you killed. 'Oo' were they to you? Wot could they possibly 'ave dun' to deserve such a violent end by your two's 'ands?"

Somewhat uncharacteristically, Bass chose to ponder for a good few seconds before delivering his measured answer...

"The complexities of our lives, and the manner in which they unfold, whether experiencing the ecstatic highs offered to us usually upon receiving good fortune and perhaps whilst reaping the rewards earned through hard, honest toil, or alternatively the catastrophic lows enveloping a soul fallen victim to misfortune or harsh treatment as administered by a random third party, rely solely upon the simple choices that we are all compelled to make at some juncture during each of our unique, extraordinary journeys through life...

"Rest assured, Mr Pike, those men made their own choices and their spilled blood is not worth a single tear. The choices they made on this night sealed their fate."

Blackmore interceded immediately, as if to purposefully divert proceedings towards more relevant business matters...

"Apologies for the abrupt nature of our re-introduction, Winston. A matter of pressing circumstance required our immediate attention, but please be at ease. A potential threat to your well-being has been neutralised; alas, I fear, only for the present."

"An attempt made to end one's life, so soon? I believe that our association will be one coloured throughout with the brightest hues of adventure and 'derring-do'," blustered a buoyant Churchill, much to the annoyance of Bass, who snapped back venomously...

"OUR MISSION PARAMETERS WERE NOT DEFINED SO AS TO PRESENT YOU WITH ENTERTAINING ASIDES, CHURCHILL!

"To preserve your life, as you are very well aware, is the task that has been allocated to us as our prime directive; it is a mandate that we both shall honour to the death, if such be destiny's course for us."

Churchill pondered the vehemently delivered words of Bass for a considerable time before delivering a character defining response...

"You... do not much care for Churchill the person, Colonel Bass. One understands completely your chagrin with regards to one's outwardly conceited, steadfastly opinionated and often unashamedly forthright and rude character, for which traits I nonetheless make no apology, neither to your esteemed self, nor to anyone else...

"Please then, I ask of you to search beyond this veneer of privileged arrogance for both the heart and soul belonging to Churchill the man...

"I am compelled onwards by an irresistible inner force towards my pre-ordained appointment with destiny, an appointment that I fully intend to honour in my own fashion. I shall willingly, and with unflinching resolution, face my enemies and ultimately triumph against all the trials and tribulations that may be sent to test the strength of my character, but of this one thing you can most definitely be assured, Colonel, I shall prevail. TOGETHER, WE SHALL PREVAIL!"

The response Bass afforded Churchill's speech, a single, silent nod of his head, could not have been any more understated. This provoked an expression of incredulous consternation upon the face of Churchill, who was accustomed to, at the very least, having his opinions being challenged in some part by a robust verbal response...

"Please, Winston. Our recent 'altercations' with 'The Black Guard' should have presented conclusive proof beyond all doubt as to the intent of our shared nemesis," interjected Blackmore, perceiving that a more diplomatically inclined approach was required...

"It remains entirely your prerogative always to believe what you will, to go forth and embrace the myriad opportunities that your life will surely present, but rest assured, my headstrong, opinionated friend, that this pair of spectres will haunt moments throughout your life from this time forth until the forces that conspire to make their prime concern the termination of your existence deem their mission parameters fulfilled. Do I make myself perfectly clear?"

Now it was Churchill's opportunity to answer with a single, silent nod of his head in the wake of such a profound statement.

Turning to face Pike, who had listened intently to every uttered syllable, Blackmore proceeded to address him directly...

"As for you, Pike, your role from the outset with regards to these proceedings was never one of random chance. The introduction of Jennings Pike into this public arena was always a certainty, to be played out in some form during this extraordinary drama as it unfolds, though any attempt to explain at this precise time the complexities that necessitate your involvement would consume vital precious minutes that we simply cannot at present afford to squander...

CHAPTER 6

"However, I feel compelled to enquire of you with all humility intended: In light of the many strange occurrences that you have witnessed on this night thus far, will you now consent to aid our noble cause?"

Rising to his feet, and now exuding an altogether calmer, more self-assured demeanour, Pike answered immediately whilst noticing in his peripheral vision that Bass had drawn a dangerous looking blade from concealment beneath his heavy overcoat, and proceeded to move it from hand to hand displaying a mesmerisingly dexterous display of juggling prowess the likes of which Pike had never before witnessed...

"Yeah, 'course I will, guv'. When I lays a bet, I 'ave an instinctive notion to back the winnin' 'nag' an' from 'wot' I just seen, you'se two 'ain't likely to be commin' 'ome no close second."

"Very well then," continued Blackmore with some degree of urgency returning to his voice as he addressed the whole group, whilst Bass, much to Pike's great relief, desisted at once from his intentionally intimidating, yet nonetheless impressively deft, blade wielding display and re-sheathed his weapon as swiftly as it had been brandished...

"Full perimeter sweep, standard clean-up protocols to be initiated, no traces. Winston, join us, if you please. Four pairs of hands and eyes will assist immeasurably in shortening the duration of our rather weighty and cumbersome task, and help to maintain the level of discretion we shall require."

And so the unlikeliest of alliances made its way along the deserted, dimly-lit ship's passageways towards the cargo bay where they wasted little time in dispatching the six 'Black Guard' cadavers into the cold, dark ocean where any physical evidence that they had ever existed would at once become Neptune's closely-guarded secret forever.

Noticing an expression that encompassed both trepidation and fear etched upon the features of Jennings Pike, Bass attempted to steady the young man's resolve by offering a reminder of a significant moment during their previous conversation...

"Remember, Pike, for better or worse, their life choices were made a good long while ago."

Upon completion of their grim task, Bass continued to address Pike directly...

"Return to your duties for the present, Pike. Secure quarters, ensuring all is well throughout the ship and no suspicion has been aroused, and when the earliest opportunity manifests itself return with haste to Churchill's cabin where further debate as to how we are to proceed will ensue. Announce your arrival with three knocks upon the door, followed by a brief pause, then a further two knocks."

***

Ensconced once more within the relatively safe haven of Churchill's cabin, the three companions began a thorough de-brief of the evening's curious occurrences...

"Gentlemen, first allow me to thank you for your timely interventions on my behalf. I..."

Churchill found his sentence abruptly curtailed by Blackmore's somewhat brusque interruption...

"Forgive my rude interjection, Winston. The purpose behind the maiden assault of our formidable foe was not so much designed as an assassination attempt, though of course a successful strike by our enemy tonight would've proved prematurely advantageous to their cause, but more so designed as a stern test of the security protocols set in place in order to dissuade such an attempt...

"Now Severin is aware of against whom precisely his cunning strategy is pitted by committing to a forlorn hope those six hapless 'Black Guard' recently dispatched overboard...

CHAPTER 6

"His resolve will become inordinately keener by being made aware of both mine and James' involvement in proceedings."

A robust three knocks upon the cabin door, followed by a brief pause, then a further two knocks silenced Blackmore in mid-sentence. As a matter of deeply ingrained habit, Bass drew his side-holstered Schofield revolver, but nonetheless proceeded to open the cabin door immediately upon recognising the pre-arranged signal that he had imparted to their young accomplice a brief moment ago.

Jennings Pike entered the cabin, preceding the arrival in his wake of two other men, one of whom was greeted heartily by both Bass and Blackmore...

"Marcus, thank the Gods!" exclaimed Blackmore, obviously somewhat relieved by the arrival of their fellow League of Ghosts compatriot, Marcus Jackson...

"Marcus, it pleases me that you are the agent designated the task of field commander in charge of this mission in our absence. Your presence alone improves the odds of a satisfactory conclusion in our favour tenfold. How fare you, my very dear friend?" enquired Blackmore as he proceeded to greet his colleague with a strong clasped handshake...

"I am in rude health, Tiberius, and made all the better for clapping eyes upon you two reprobates," responded Jackson jovially as he returned his friend's genuinely enthusiastic greeting with interest.

Bass reciprocated the clasped handshake with Jackson and offered the hint of a grin and a single nod of his head in recognition of his friend's arrival. He then fixed a stare so icily cold upon the stranger accompanying Jackson that were it to be visited upon any unprepared mortal heart would set it racing to an anxiety-teased bursting point.

Whilst still glaring directly into the stranger's Mediterranean blue eyes, Bass enquired of Jackson when he had satisfied himself that the distinctively handsome, olive skinned, mid-European complexion belonging to this intriguing newcomer were not familiar to him...

"And who, pray tell, Marcus, is your shadow?"

"Allow me please to introduce myself to the room, Colonel Bass, Colonel Blackmore, Mr Pike. My name is Sabinas Lucius Sura, Centurion and field commander of the Seventh, Eighth and Ninth cohorts of the Imperial Legion of Rome for virtually the duration of the reign of Trajan from 100-117 AD," answered Sura, bearing the confident tone of a man fully justifying his alleged high-ranking credentials...

"Might one ask then, Commander Sura, what advantages such a high-ranking Roman officer might offer to our cause?" enquired Bass, surmising that little profit would be gained by frittering away precious minutes in an attempt to validate Sura's impressive roster of credentials further.

Bass also accounted for the fact that so many and varied had been his and Blackmore's experiences appertaining to their dealings with supernatural anomalies and all manner of strange phenomena these past few missions, how could the details just this moment imparted by Sura amount to anything but legitimate facts.

It came as no surprise, then, to each of the detectives that Sura answered Bass, his Italian-Latin flavoured accent adding a certain mid-European continental romanticism to his near-impeccable delivery of the English language, with the disciplined decorum and confident manner his purported officer's station befitted...

"Of course, Colonel Bass. If I may refer your attention to a moment I alluded to earlier: Whilst serving as an active Commander Centurion, responsible for the command of three cohorts of the Imperial Roman Legion, my duties placed me among the higher echelons of both the Imperial High Command and the villas of high-born aristocracy, including close associations with the Senate of Rome and even the Royal household itself...

"I was a close confidante of the emperor Trajan himself and became an associate and friend of one of his most trusted allies and closest courtiers; he was a fellow centurion in command of the first, second and third cohorts, related to the bloodline of future emperor and namesake Septimus Gaius Severus, the man known to both of you very well, I believe, as Septimus Malachai Severin."

Chapter 7

'Leviathan.'

Bass and Blackmore were both stunned into momentary silence in the wake of Sura's startling testimony, each man initially harbouring inner feelings of nonplussed disbelief...

The simple realisation dawned on them both, however, that all of the remarkable situations they had experienced together during the extraordinary course upon which their lives had steered them thus far, made the fantastic revelations presented recently by Sura appear all the more plausible...

"A Centurion once in command of three cohorts of the Imperial Roman Legion, you say?" alluded Bass matter of factly, as though intelligence of this magnitude were mandatory every-day vignettes of information nestling within the acceptable parameters of normal conversation...

"Well, who are we to argue against the validity of your remarkable testimony, Commander Sura?"

"Please, Colonel Bass, though formally introduced but a few minutes ago and surely as we are to be working together towards the same goal, could we not dispense with resorting to the somewhat cumbersome, increasingly archaic and often stereotypically trite formality of rank when addressing each other directly? My name is Sura."

CHAPTER 7

Bass reciprocated by merely glowering towards Sura from behind the mysterious opacity of his dark-lensed spectacles as though offering his own silent affirmation that as far as he was concerned, trust and familiarity were prized accolades that needed to be earned over a period of time.

Sensing an ambience of tension already developing between his taciturn brother at arms and their latest companion, Blackmore felt obliged to speak first, possibly sensing that logical explanation of the mindset required for entering into the sacred covenant of an accepted and trusted brotherhood was necessary and that cordial, perhaps even convivial, language should be employed, even if only as a means of momentarily deflecting attention from the obvious aura of latent menace so apparently emanating from Bass...

"One might surmise that your presence here denotes a certain commitment on your part to serve our mandate, Sura. Both myself and James choose to support wholeheartedly a cause more deserving of our undivided attention than any that we have previously encountered; in short, we strive to preserve the soon to be hard won freedoms of the democratically solvent, relatively stable humanity of the near future from an omnipotent enemy who possesses great powers of manipulative cunning and guile."

Gesturing towards the intently listening Churchill with his battered, wooden wolf's head cane, Blackmore continued...

"We are assured, by a trusted higher authority, that for the sake of the future, both our own, and the future belonging to our descendants, this man must survive!"

Pointing his battered wolf-headed cane towards Bass, Blackmore proceeded to raise the intensity of his speech as, all at once, a stark and deeply concerning realisation of a possible concealed truth came to his mind...

"Our mandate is simple and clear. Both James and I protect the life of the one, to preserve the lives of the many.

"This thing I ask you now, Sura, and I would expect the integral honesty befitting a high-ranking officer of the Legion of Rome to be present as you answer: What inner flame burns deep within your soul? What monumentally compelling force drives a man to traverse the centuries? The persuasive tongues of the 'Grand Meisters' undoubtedly played some part in your decision, perhaps key historical knowledge personally held by you appertaining to one of our adversaries is a reason for your involvement, namely Septimus Gaius Severus almost certainly, but I suggest further that a darker agenda yet remains sequestered deep within your soul, does it not, my Roman friend?

"A centuries-old wound that still festers, open and exposed, waiting all of these many long years past for the gilt-edged opportunity to arise when that wound could be healed once and for all."

A wide smile informed Blackmore immediately that the undisclosed details regarding the Roman Commander's secondment to the mission had been expertly anticipated and were only a moment away from being confirmed.

Lowering his gaze momentarily whilst nodding his head in approval of the wily old detective's subtle interrogation technique, Sura answered, with his growing admiration for Blackmore apparent as he spoke…

"Bravo, Colonel Blackmore, a truly excellent strategy. Your legendary prowess as a great detective reveals itself in this moment to great effect and proves to be a well-earned attribute, my new-found friend."

Turning to address Bass directly and without pausing to take a breath, Sura continued…

"And you, Colonel Bass. Your guarded, ice-cold, outwardly stern persona suggests to one that any number of the rather interesting, and in some cases quite disturbing metaphors one has heard used to describe, err, how shall we say, the more extreme character traits that

CHAPTER 7

you have been known to exhibit, might well have their basis in fact. I sense that your friendship will prove to be a harder won prize, and all the more valued for it, I think."

This time, taking several breaths whilst momentarily pausing to compose himself, Sura discouraged signs of interruption from all of his companions by sharply raising his right index finger towards his lips in an attempt to crave their silence for a little while longer...

"I was convinced many centuries ago, whilst still in the employ of Rome, that time, with regards to both its past and future dimensions, was a physically accessible anomaly. My insatiable curiosity soon became something of an obsession as I scoured the vast known reaches of the Roman empire, and even beyond its long-established borders into exotic and often hostile foreign territories hitherto uncharted by any exploratory expedition or cartographer, to seek out the greatest intellects and scholars belonging to science and philosophy in an attempt to further broaden my research into the possibility that the barrier of time could be crossed at will by a mortal...

"After a while it became apparent that my often illegally intrusive inquisitiveness had not gone unnoticed by the all-seeing eyes of the 'Time Enforcement Agency' when I was contacted directly by one of the thirteen 'Grand Meisters' of the High Council, a Captain Pontius Maximillian Aston to whom both our parties are well acquainted, I believe, and was afforded the once in a lifetime opportunity of undergoing the rigorous induction protocols required in order to become an effective field operative, pledging lifelong service to the agency."

Bass continued to conspicuously eye Sura coldly, all the while toying provocatively with his unsheathed knife, waiting several uncomfortably tense seconds before finally breaking his silence...

"Should you not substitute the phrase 'personal interest' for the altogether and wholly more appropriate 'personal grudge' with regards to your previous statement?

"Take heed, Sura, and mark these words as a warning: From this moment forth we demand total transparency and unremitting commitment from you if yours be the will to remain a viable, effective asset to our cause; and be under no illusion that should your proposed resolve falter in the slightest, or your pledge to serve deviate in any direction but set fair on its honourable course, then your new-found friend over there, Colonel Blackmore, will see fit to end your impressively lengthy tenure here on Earth even more swiftly than I."

The unnerving tension, the expanding pressure of which now appeared to press outwards towards the four walls of the tiny cabin, was fortuitously interrupted by an insistent, continuous clanging of the ship's bell...

"ALARM!" exclaimed Pike as he leapt to his feet and instinctively made for the cabin door...

"GENERAL QUARTERS ALARM! ALL CREW TO STATIONS... Gentlemen, for your continued safety I must ask you all to remain..."

Before Pike was able to complete his mandatory delivery of safety protocols to those he perceived to be civilian passengers, and now that a general quarters alarm had been sounded, Bass, Blackmore, Jackson, Churchill and Sura forced their way past the hapless first mate and out into the now densely populated passageway outside the cabin...

"Please remain inside the cabin for your own safety," Pike remonstrated demonstratively to no-one.

Logically conceding that whatever authority he might have possessed as first mate in command of this situation had evaporated completely, Pike reluctantly decided to join his new-found group of companions.

As they proceeded to be swept along in the cascading human tide of both crew and passengers, who had all been stirred into a single, organic, undulating mass of hysteria by the immediate and urgent clang of the still insistently tolling alarm bell, one word seemed to permeate the deafening cacophony of almost unintelligible gibberish, a word that each of Churchill's bold protectors, and the man himself, recognised instantly...

...A single, simple and quite innocuous enough word, one would imagine, if it were overheard when idly uttered during normal, polite conversation, well beyond the context of their current situation. An intrusively threatening, terrifying word nonetheless that instantly chilled each one of them to the innermost core of their soul: 'LEVIATHAN!'

"If we are able to access the 'fo'c'sle' through this melee, we can get topside through the officers' mess an' see wot all this 'fakkin' fuss is about," suggested Pike to his companions, as they continued to be involuntarily swept forward on the relentless tide of highly-agitated, now almost deliriously euphoric humanity.

Upon reaching the 'fo'c'sle 'their access to the upper forward deck proved virtually unhindered when finally, upon emerging topside into a clear spring Atlantic evening, it became obvious, by the due easterly direction in which all eyes seemed to be trained, as to what fantastic anomaly was commanding everyone's attention off the starboard side of the 'Rocinante'...

'LEVIATHAN!'... 'GOD 'ELP US ALL, THE BEAST 'AS RISEN'... 'DOOMED, WE'RE ALL 'FAKKIN' DOOMED'... 'LEVIATHAN 'AS RISEN TO CLAIM ANOTHER SHIP OF SOULS'... 'THE GREAT MONSTER OF THE DEEP 'AS AWOKEN ONCE MORE'...

The consensus of both passengers and crew alike appeared to suggest the physical manifestation here, in this exact place, at this precise time, was the great mythical beast that had roamed the world's oceans for centuries, preying mercilessly upon the lives and vessels of the hapless mariners who were unfortunate enough to cross its path.

Thought of by most people capable of exhibiting rational reasoning and logical thought processes as being at best a mere figment of imagination from within the confused, rum-addled ramblings of a handful of ageing seafarers, their frail human constitutions sun baked, poorly nourished and without fresh water for much too long to the point of witnessing spectres from ancient tales of fable and folklore, it would appear that the legendary ghost of 'Leviathan' had indeed risen up once more from the ocean deep to claim its next group of defenceless seafaring souls.

Their eyes instinctively joined all others as they beheld what appeared to be the silver-scaled tail of a giant serpent-like beast dive majestically beneath the ocean surface, not more than forty feet off the starboard bow of the 'Rocinante.' Blackmore, averting his attention from the spectacle unfolding out to sea for a few seconds as he turned towards Bass, noticed the merest hint of trepidation in the eyes of his old comrade as his own eyes focused once more upon proceedings unfolding off the starboard baffles...

"How fare you, James, my old friend?"

Without averting his eyes for a second, Bass reciprocated immediately...

"Have no concern, Tiberius. Even though on this eve the 'wolf moon' will rise to its perigee during this lunation, my resolve and commitment to the success of our mission remains resolute, as does my suppression of the powerfully insistent lycanthrope spirit residing within me remain totally and unequivocally absolute."

Even though appreciating the heartfelt request as to his wellbeing made by Blackmore and as though with the intention of instantly diverting attention away from what he considered to be the petty trivialities concerning his ongoing inner conflict, Bass continued...

"See, Tiberius, how the rising, clear full moon glow illuminates the scene as it plays out, almost enchantingly, before us. I see enough tangible evidence to ascertain, without any doubt, this anomaly that has traversed the annals of time and human consciousness throughout the notions of conjecture, folkloric myth and hearsay is no mammalian, Piscean, nor any form of living, physical beast. The 'Leviathan' is undoubtedly a man-made, mechanical ship."

Chapter 8

'Out of the Frying Pan, Into Hell!'

Blackmore looked on as the great silver and gold scaled, intricately engineered, meticulously detailed articulated tail of the machine-beast arced majestically upwards for one final time prior to disappearing below the surface of the moon-illuminated ocean...

'Impressively deft control for a mechanical craft of such size'

Just as the last swell of rippling water closed around and over the giant tail fin, Blackmore could have sworn that, just for the briefest second, he caught sight of a great eye set directly into the belly of the craft;

'The legendary single eye of the Leviathan, perhaps'

"A controlled ship you say, James? A vessel that is able to travel at great velocity deep below the surface of the world's oceans."

"Consider this for a moment, my friend," answered Bass...

"A ship that also boasts the capability to traverse freely within the fourth dimension, thus substantiating the many alleged sightings documented throughout the centuries past of a monstrous, serpent-like beast striking terror into the hearts of mariners the world over as it roamed throughout Earth's many vast oceans...

"A ship whose title was taken from the petrified utterances of those mariners who had witnessed this phenomenon throughout time and unwittingly added to its burgeoning legend; the legend of the 'Leviathan'."

"Yes, Tiberius; 'Leviathan'. A fantastic, mechanical submersible vessel. Brilliantly conceived and designed to withstand what we assume to be the great pressure that exists at extreme ocean depths, a craft that is also capable of achieving great velocity as it scythes its way forth, effortlessly, below even the most violent and hazardous of open water conditions...

"Imagine then, the swathes of rampant, unanswerable chaos throughout the oceans of time such a ship could unfurl should its master prove to be our primary nemesis, as I very much suspect might well prove to be the case," alluded Bass as a slight expression of concern became apparent to the ever-observant Blackmore upon the usually stoically impassive features of his colleague...

"Hmmm..." he murmured...

"Might not the presence of such a vessel also offer explanation as to how Severin was able to walk through a solid oak bulkhead and disappear without a trace?

"Let us assume, then, that the ship was positioned at a precise bearing in the immediate vicinity of our own, perhaps waiting but a few seconds either into the future or indeed the past, enabling one who commands both the knowledge and the power to 'shift' between dimensions to make good their escape."

"Indubitably so, Tiberius. I will offer one more point worthy of consideration at this juncture, as something of an afterthought, if I may: A ship able to harness such power, one too, that potentially harbours great destructive prowess, would almost certainly, at any moment of its commander's choosing, be capable of decimating any vessel of this era sent to challenge it...

"The fact that our good ship 'Rocinante' yet remains above water suggests that the lives of a certain person aboard, or indeed persons, are of prime importance to the enemy, and whose continued existences would undoubtedly, at some time in the future, benefit the cause of our foe in no small fashion...

"I believe that whilst Churchill remains a passenger on board and ably chaperoned by capable agents loyal to our cause, his continued safe-keeping will prove a somewhat less complicated task to fulfil."

Blackmore glanced in the direction of Churchill whose attention remained rapt, as was the focus of all others aboard it would appear, on the final few ripples made by the 'Leviathan' as it disappeared completely from view into the depths of the Atlantic Ocean...

"Agreed. If one may tender a suggestion that might aid in hastening considerably our frustratingly steady progress in real time...

"I propose that we change ships. The Royal Mail cutter 'Dunator Castle' is scheduled to re-supply in Gibraltar at exactly the same time as the 'Rocinante' is due to berth, before setting a direct course through the Straits of Gibraltar on its standard course along the Northern and then Eastern African trade routes towards its eventual destination of Cape Town in the south."

Bass reciprocated his colleague's proposal with a most uncharacteristic outward expression of first frustration, then puzzlement...

"CHANGE SHIPS? Alight from the relatively secure confines of a proven man-o-war, made even safer by the presence of several capably endowed members of its human cargo one might add, to a smaller, infinitely more vulnerable craft. Explain the logic, Tiberius, if you will."

Blackmore countered immediately...

"Undoubtedly, James, the 'Dunator Castle' is a much smaller vessel, but has the distinct advantage of being several knots faster than the good old lady 'Rocinante,' even when taking into consideration its smaller sail ratio...

CHAPTER 8

"In addition to this, my friend, worth considering is the presence on board the 'Castle' of one General Sir Redvers Buller, Commander in Chief of the British Expeditionary Force in South Africa whom history dictates Winston Churchill will surely meet at some juncture during the remainder of this voyage."

Bass reflected for a moment before offering his considered answer to the flawless logic submitted by Blackmore, his reasoning being based solely upon the realisation that history must, at all costs, be allowed to run its true and unhindered course, with all protagonists remaining both totally focused upon the prime mission directive, and in full acceptance of any potential outcome that might occur...

"We should, therefore, endeavour to take great care that our change of vessel goes unnoticed, especially by agents co-opted to the service of 'The Architect'.

"Churchill, Marcus, Sura and young Pike need to be briefed as to our intentions, though this Sura still offers me cause to doubt his inclusion as a key asset going forward towards the successful conclusion of this mission."

***

Bass and Blackmore, together with Churchill, Marcus Jackson, Sura and Jennings Pike rendezvoused back in the relatively peaceful and secure sanctuary of Churchill's cabin where Bass wasted little time in briefing his companions thoroughly as to his and Blackmore's immediate intentions prior to pressing Sura further upon the validity of his credentials as a Time Enforcement Agent, and to clarify once and for all his true motivation with regards to his personal agenda...

"In order to maintain the correct equilibrium within the intended timeline, we change ships at the port of Gibraltar. It is imperative that the remainder of Churchill's journey to Cape Town take place aboard the 'Dunator Castle'."

"Why in God's name should we concede the relative security of a more than robust, solid old English man-o-war for the uncertain, substantially less armoured payload of a lightweight Royal Mail clipper?" questioned a perplexed and visibly agitated Churchill...

"Please, Winston, my very good friend..." interceded Sura, catching both Bass and Blackmore completely off guard with his outwardly public display of familiarity towards Churchill...

"...Know that if either Colonel Bass or Colonel Blackmore propose any deviation from our intended course, then it will be for a valid reason. Please, trust their judgement implicitly, as you have come to trust my own."

A single, silent nod of the head from Churchill in the direction of Sura confirmed at once to the pair of wily old soldiers that indeed Churchill and Sura were very well acquainted, initially provoking an incredulous retort from Blackmore...

"You know each other?"

Waiving attempts by both Churchill and Sura to instantly voice their opinions by rapidly raising his right hand as he met both men's eyes with a withering glare, Blackmore continued, the frustrated tone of his voice apparent for all to hear...

"For how long exactly have the pair of you been acquainted, and for precisely what period of time have you, Commander Sura, been tasked to this cause?"

Churchill beckoned with raised index finger to his lips for Sura to remain silent and then began to speak...

"Please, Lucius, if I might be allowed to respond in part to Colonel Blackmore's enquiry. On the very day that I graduated from Sandhurst Military Academy, in the month of December 1894 if memory serves, awarded the rank of coronet second lieutenant, and commissioned to the Queen's Own 4th Hussars, I was befriended and subsequently

CHAPTER 8

mentored by a refined, rather dashing and ever so slightly reckless, youthful Italian Captain...

"This was a man with whom I shared an instant rapport. Custodian of a spirit that positively effervesced with the powerful vitality for life that I myself yearned for, and possessing the already proven experience of many past glorious campaign exploits, of which I was particularly envious and vowed to emulate one fine day, after my own fashion.

"Capitano Sabinas Lucius Sura proceeded to physically, as well as subliminally, ensconce himself as a constant and trusted companion throughout the commitments of both my burgeoning social diary and my numerous military campaigns abroad, during which, over the last four years on numerous occasions through merit of his conspicuous presence, has employed his considerable cache of impressive soldiering skills in order to preserve my continued existence on this Earth."

"My initial and prime mandate was always one of unequivocal protection, your protection, Winston," interceded Sura...

"Yes indeed, my great Roman friend," continued Churchill...

"Ah, how we stood firm alongside our Spanish allies as we faced Cuban rebels, rode tall together along the skirmish line on the North-West frontier during the Indian campaign and charged full-bloodedly into the faces of the Mahdi forces with the 21st Lancers at Omdurman...

"My Mauser pistol spat forth its deadly payload time and again as our maiden charge bore us into what appeared to resemble the very mouth of hell itself...

"Repelled after that initial sortie, the bold lancers of the 21st, undeterred in the face of a stubborn Mahdi resistance, regrouped and galloped forth once more upon the gait of thunderous hooves, this time to victory...

"Ah, my friends, I tell you plainly and in all honesty that the spectacle created by such conflict will undoubtedly never be witnessed again, consigned to the dusty pages of history as the last great victory won by utilising such a mounted cavalry charge."

"So, here we are," deadpanned Bass, as though unimpressed by the revelations of 'derring-do' just recounted with such enthusiastic zeal by Churchill...

"Tiberius and I were present during the charge of Omdurman," he stated matter-of-factly, piquing the attentions of both Churchill and Sura immediately...

"Ours was the task to organise and command 'special operations' designed specifically to infiltrate Mahdi enclaves and confound their progress, both from within the supposed security of their own infrastructure and on the open field of battle."

Bass contemplated for a moment before recounting further his own recollections of the charge...

"Churchill? Yes, of course. A distant, dusty old memory returns to me with more clarity now: Talk throughout the regiment of a brash, glory-seeking Second-Lieutenant whose high-placed and extremely influential socialite connections persuaded Lord Kitchener himself to grant a commission with the 21st Lancers, for whom harsh action had already been assured on the field at Omdurman."

Blackmore continued the thread...

"...And equally was the word passed through the ranks of an Italian Captain named Sura, the constant chaperone always by Churchill's side, whose remarkable prowess when wielding a pair of Roman 'gladii' in battle became something of a regimental legend, some eye witnesses stating quite categorically that through deft movement of his twin blades he was even able to deflect oncoming volleys of bullets...

"A curious choice of weapons for one to favour upon a field of modern 19th century warfare to be sure, but now, taking into account the circumstances appertaining to your presence here, and the divulgence recently of your personal history, quite an understandable one."

CHAPTER 8

Sura interrupted Blackmore's speech, somewhat irritated by a situation that was seemingly manifesting into something of an interrogation and shot a disparagingly icy glare at the pair of wily old detectives as he answered...

"My 'gladii' and the manner in which I choose to use them is really of little consequence in context of the grander scheme of things, wouldn't you agree, Colonel Blackmore, Colonel Bass?"

Then addressing the whole group, Sura continued...

"Each of us here shares a common cause. Let us proceed from this moment as a unified whole; our past histories and recent posturing are to be regarded as nothing more than an introductory aside. Our actions henceforth will purport to prove the validity of each other's loyalty towards our cause and the level of commitment towards achieving our shared prime directive."

Listening intently to Sura's summation, Bass and Blackmore glanced briefly towards each other and offered a single nod of their heads, as if to confirm subliminally that they each agreed upon their immediate course of action, then turned towards Sura and offered him an identical sign of affirmation.

Blackmore then uttered a single syllable to finally conclude this most curious conclave...

"Onwards..."

Chapter 9

'Captured.'

Subsequent to a brief, unhindered rendezvous with the Royal Mail cutter 'Dunator Castle' at the North African port of Tangier, the most unlikely group of colleagues boarded their new vessel swiftly.

Designed primarily for speed, and sleeker of build, rather than hosting the robust battleship characteristics of the 'Rocinante', 'Dunator Castle' was able to cut a swift passage through the southern Mediterranean Sea towards the isthmus of Suez and one of the true wonders of modern-day engineering, the Suez Canal.

Once granted passage through the vast sea level waterway and on into the calm waters of the Red Sea, progress was swift and unhindered as the sprightly little cutter glided effortlessly through the 120-mile length of the canal from the northern terminus of Port Said to its southern equivalent of Port Tewfik located in the city of Suez.

Here, the 'Dunator Castle' once more docked briefly in order to fulfil part of its official commitments to the Royal Mail and to replenish depleted supplies before re-commencing its voyage eastward through the Gulf of Aden, then altering course due south around the northern tip of Somalia and along the seemingly perpetual eastern coastline of Africa and onwards towards first a potentially hazardous traverse through the often perilous waters of the Cape of Good Hope, then

CHAPTER 9

briefly charting a northern course towards their final destination at the port of Cape Town that was located in the south western corner of the country...

"This confounded east African coastline gives one the distinct impression that it will never relent!" grumbled Blackmore as he proceeded to load a generous brick of newly-crushed 'Hindu Shag' tobacco flakes into the bowl of his old clay pipe...

"A necessary irritant that is to be endured for the present, you impatient old goat," riposted Bass in what could best be described as an almost glib response to his colleague's obvious chagrin.

Gazing out over the port side of their ship, into the vast expanse of a calm evening Indian Ocean, Bass continued...

"'Leviathan' remains at close quarters. I feel its silent, secretive presence as it slips beneath our bow, as one would be aware of a constant, attentive shadow."

Blackmore remained in silent repose for a while before imparting...

"Forgive me, James, I find my mind occupied by thoughts of how we will proceed once we make landfall at Cape Town."

Without averting his keen eyes for a second from his port-side vigil, Bass afforded Blackmore an answer that was as simple in its construction as it was logical in its intent...

"We become one with the shadows until such time arises that our undivided attention becomes necessary, and rest assured, my brother, our keenest attention will undoubtedly be required henceforth if we are to be successful in the completion of our mission."

***

The second Boer War, that lasted three years from 1899 to 1902, was waged with some ferocity between the British Empire, the Afrikaans speaking Dutch settlers of the Orange Free State and the Transvaal

Republic over the ever increasingly intrusive influence the Empire exerted within the country of South Africa.

Initially bested by a strong, well-armed Boer force whose non-uniformed guerrilla tactics provided early victories over the under-prepared and somewhat over confident British Expeditionary Force, a combination of superior numbers and the implementation of harsh and uncompromising tactics saw the conflict's fortunes eventually turn favourably towards the British.

Upon arrival at their destination in the south western port of Cape Town, which remained relatively untroubled by the conflict that raged more towards the eastern and mid-townships that remained under the control of the Dutch Afrikaans speaking settlers, Bass, Blackmore, Churchill, Jackson and Sura bid a fond farewell to their new-found ally, Jennings Pike, and wasted little time in securing transport, courtesy of a Captain James Aylmer Haldane, with whom the group of companions had cultivated a useful friendship during their long voyage, onboard an armoured patrol train that had been dispatched towards the town of Chieveley, located 100 miles north-east of Durban, in order to confirm reports that Louis Botha himself was operating in the area...

"The conflict presently unfolds in favour of the Boers, or so I am reliably informed," blustered Churchill, the extraordinarily cheerful manner he vociferously displayed giving both Bass and Blackmore some concern as to what exuberant public outbursts might follow...

"It becomes ever more imperative that I secure an active commission with a front-line unit upon our return so I might have at these feisty Boers myself...

"Ah, Haldane, my fine fellow, how I do so envy your captaincy and the laurels that surely await you. There is glory to be won here that would transcend immeasurably the one-dimensional, inane scribblings of a mere scribe, I would imagine."

Haldane wasted little time before answering Churchill, lines of concern clearly etched across his dour features, his usually stoic composure tested to its limits by a sudden tidal wave of anxiety, enhanced primarily by the seemingly reckless bravura his friend was openly presenting...

"Have a care for what you desire, young Winston. These Boers are fierce, well-ordered, battle-hardened soldiers who boast a wealthy experience of cunning guerrilla tactics designed specifically in order to constantly test and confound our courageous forces' resolve...

"They now, too, possess an exceptional command structure that exhibits excellent knowledge of these tactics led by Generals Louis Botha, Jan Smuts, Christiaan de Wet and Koos de la Rey; indeed, Botha himself is reported to be present in the very state to which we travel, hence the urgency of this ill-advised patrol that is supported by a mere handful of Dublin Fusiliers and Durham Light Infantry."

All at once, controlled logic turned to blind fury as Haldane vented his anger in the direction of the absent commander who had issued orders for the patrol to deploy...

"DAMN COLONEL CHARLES LONG AND A THOUSAND CURSES BE REINED UPON THIS FOOL'S ERRAND FOR BEING CAST INTO A DESTABILISED MAELSTROM OF UNCERTAINTY AND MISFORTUNE FROM WHICH FEW OF US, IF INDEED ANY OF OUR EXPEDITION AT ALL, SHALL HAVE THE GOOD FORTUNE TO RETURN HOME SAFELY!

"As commanding officer of this mission, I suggest that upon completing a swift, incisive reconnoitre of Chieveley, we make all possible haste on the return journey to the relative safety of British held lines."

Appearing as though he were at last being compelled towards imminent glorious conflict by some insatiably irresistible force, Churchill responded as if the sage, passionately delivered words of the infinitely more experienced Haldane had been wasted on closed ears and a mind racing with the anticipation of imminent engagement with the enemy a certainty and momentarily non-receptive to the suggestion of a more sensible tactical strategy …

"Excellent, Haldane, my good man, excellent. Shall we not soon then be directly engaged in open conflict with the absolute best of our foe, presented in our midst to test the mettle of our resolve and courage in battle? A fine maiden tale of first-hand bravado with which to regale my attentive readership back home, would you not agree?"

Noting with some concern the brash, vociferous manner which Churchill adopted in order to share his exuberance, not just with the perplexed Haldane, but rather with the entire population of their carriage, Blackmore imparted his obvious misgivings to his colleagues in a more discreet manner…

"Churchill imparts his somewhat brash oration at some considerable volume, displaying little regard, or perhaps more likely a blind ignorance, to whatever agents bearing dark intent may lurk in concealment, awaiting their prime opportunity to strike…

"For all of his irksome arrogance and a tendency towards immature, rash decision and action, the man possesses some modicum of courage, but…"

Bass found his repost sharply curtailed by the screeching grind of metal on metal and the sharp cessation of their forward motion as their train carriage at first seemed to rise upwards, then lurch sideways and continue on an indirect, random trajectory before coming to an abrupt halt several uncomfortable moments later…

"OUR CARRIAGE IS DE-RAILED!" exclaimed Bass as he correctly surmised the truth appertaining to the unceremoniously rough cessation of their journey.

Barely pausing for breath, Bass continued to address his colleagues with some urgency…

CHAPTER 9

"Look directly to Churchill for it is at this precise moment that I fear the natural course of history is about to be challenged, with maximum prejudicial intent intended by our enemies."

Even before Bass was able to complete his sentence, several volleys of high calibre gunfire began to strafe their stricken carriage, providing a potentially lethal combination of splintering wood and searing lead projectiles around all those who survived the initial impact of the derailing...

'BOTHA'S GUERRILLA FORCES ARE ALREADY THIS MOMENT UPON US!'...claimed a desperate, random voice out of the ensuing chaos that proceeded to unfold all around them...

'HE SEEKS TO LIBERATE THE ENGINE AND OUR '7 POUNDER' FOR FURTHERANCE OF THE BOER CAUSE' ...issued forth a warning from another anonymous voice, this particular sliver of information connecting immediately with Churchill's patriotic sense of duty towards protecting a vital component of valuable British military ordnance...

'AT LAST'!...

...he supposed to himself upon being made cognisant to the fact that both his commanding officer, Captain Aylmer Haldane, and his closest subordinate officer had been temporarily incapacitated during the ensuing chaos...

'NOW IS MY OPPORTUNITY TO COMMAND!'

"Liberate our engine, and our heavy ordnance bound for front line action, the property of her majesty Queen Victoria herself; never into the charge of these Boers will valuable property belonging to the Empire fall; never, my brave boys, without offering our most resolute, stubborn resistance!"

His natural instinct for command rising immediately to the fore, Churchill, now in his element, commenced issuing clear and concise orders to any surviving military personnel amidst the ensuing cacophony of the skirmish that proceeded to envelop them all.

First laying eyes upon a group of perplexed, shaken and obviously leaderless Durham Light Infantrymen, appearing devoid of any notion as to how they should proceed, Churchill was swift in seizing his opportunity...

"You men; who is your commanding officer here?"

An extremely youthful looking private answered nervously...

"Er, 'dunno', sir; Captain 'Aldane is out 'fer' the count over there, an' Lieutenant Dodds... well sir, 'e's... 'e's... there, sir, and there, and over there an' all, sir... bits of 'im all over the 'fakkin' shop; beggin' your pardon, sir."

Not wasting a moment to the folly of indecisive thought or deed, Churchill acted immediately...

"Right then; you men, to my command. Prime your weapons, apply due diligence and summon all inner reserves of guile and courage as we go forth; firstly, in order to assess the validity of our tactical situation, and secondly, to potentially present a robust counter-offensive upon our ambushers."

His C96 Mauser pistol locked, loaded and firmly to hand, Churchill proceeded to lead his newly-acquired command towards the rear door of their precariously sideways listing compartment. Meanwhile, Blackmore took a brief moment to address his remaining companions, offering a strategy of his own...

"Whatever course of action Churchill decides to pursue here must be unhampered by any interference on our part, save for the sole purpose of preserving his life."

Turning his attention directly towards Bass, Blackmore continued...

"James, might one make the suggestion that we two join Churchill's 'scratch' command as willing soldiers and in so doing attend directly to his personal security?"

CHAPTER 9

Altering his focus towards Jackson and Sura as Bass nodded his approval, Blackmore continued…

"Marcus, Lucius, return at once directly to Cape Town and devise a sound strategy to secure our liberty from the imminent capture and subsequent incarceration that will surely befall us here."

Realising instantly the extreme importance that their phase of the mission now entailed, offering neither protestation, nor raising any question of negativity towards the order given by Blackmore, both Jackson and Sura nodded their affirmation and swiftly exited the compartment by means of an alternative rear exit mere seconds before an overwhelming force of Boer guerrilla fighters proceeded to mount an assault on their position…

"God speed and good fortune be your companions, my friends. We shall return bearing both sound strategy and healthy reinforcement soon when your freedom will be secured," were the parting words of encouragement offered by Sura to the remaining group as they prepared to focus on what was almost certainly to be their forlorn task at hand.

Bass eyed Sura for a second, then proceeded to offer a single, silent nod of affirmation before taking up his designated position as the rear guard of Churchill's courageous squad.

Re-united once more at Blackmore's side, Bass was the first to speak amidst the seemingly relentless barrage of deadly ordnance that continued to explode all around them…

"Marcus and Sura are away safely to Cape Town. For all our sakes, I pray that their return is swift. As for our current standing, should our somewhat over-exuberant commander choose to pursue a frontal assault upon the prevailing Boer force, well, the forlorn hope at Sevastopol that we two were a part of held better odds in its favour for a successful outcome than the meagre odds we shall encounter here…

"The Boers boast greater numbers, carry superior armament and advantageously hold the higher ground. These obvious tactical and logistical advantages alone would assure any such endowed opponent possessed of any organised military worth a swift and decisive victory, regardless of the stubborn fortitude shown by a resisting force."

Listening intently to the bleak tactical assessment offered by Bass, Blackmore offered a sombre response...

"I fear that Churchill's personal mandate is clear; regrettably, quite abundantly clear...

"See how he circles the engine, displaying little regard towards his own safety, no doubt with a view to raising the spirits of his men in order to achieve greater purpose...

"Every last morsel of our fortitude, guile and energy reserves must be channelled towards protecting the man, regardless of thoughts appertaining towards both our lack of tactical advantage and what should be considered the best military course of action to be undertaken here...

"A measured, tactical retreat protected by a stoic rear-guard in the face of such overwhelmingly insurmountable odds would be my command decision, but..."

Bass, his pistols instinctively now ready to hand and primed for immediate discharge, merely shrugged his shoulders in acknowledgement, and in acceptance of the stark realisation that both he and his trusted comrade of old were once more about to set forth selflessly into the potentially cataclysmic embrace of a tactical nightmare.

With both Bass and Blackmore taking up positions in close proximity to each of Churchill's flanks, attempting as best they could to protect their charge from the constant barrage of searing lead that proceeded to rain down upon their position, they were welcomed to a scene of ever unfolding chaos by what was incredulously perceived by the pair to be a gleeful greeting from their surrogate commanding officer...

CHAPTER 9

"James, Tiberius, my bold protectors. Welcome to the war! We must, at all costs, keep the engine and its valuable munitions payload from falling into Boer custody. The robust iron body of our momentarily incapacitated transport will suffice as a more than adequate shield behind which we shall bide time until their ammunition cache is exhausted. Then, one suggests that..."

"EVEN ACCOUNTING FOR ALL OF OUR UNDOUBTED RESERVES OF FORTITUDE AND COURAGE, WE CANNOT PREVAIL HERE, WINSTON!" spat Blackmore venomously as the relentless hailstorm of deadly lead pelted mercilessly down onto their ever-more precarious position, ricocheting randomly and with deadly consequence from the incapacitated iron carcass of the engine directly into the helpless group of brave British soldiers who were now relying on its stricken bulk as their sole cover and appearing outwardly bereft of any obvious tactic or act of fortitude that might enhance their seemingly-futile situation...

"YIELD NOW, WINSTON. HOLD UP YOUR HANDS SO THAT WE MAY YET BE ABLE TO FIGHT ANOTHER DAY, WHEN THE TACTICAL ADVANTAGE WILL, WITHOUT DOUBT, SHIFT ONCE MORE IN OUR FAVOUR," was the sage advice offered by Blackmore, a vastly experienced commander and respected veteran soldier of many a past campaign, to a relatively inexperienced young coronet second lieutenant, whose own insatiable quest for personal glory now threatened to jeopardise his prime responsibility as a commanding officer with regards to preserving the lives of the dependent group of frightened and disorientated soldiers in his charge.

Even as Churchill attempted to provide Blackmore with his reply, a tumultuous surge of Boer guerrilla fighters swarmed downwards from either side of the high cutting where the de-railed train lay helpless and besieged, and proceeded to overwhelm what remained of the inadequately-armed and ill-prepared British soldiers with some considerable ease.

Displaying both reluctance and a good deal of frustration on his part in the wake of what he conceded to be the total and abject failure of his inaugural command, Churchill bade the survivors of his bold command to lay down their weapons and surrender to their Boer vanquishers...

"Who amongst you commands here?" came a gruff, authoritative demand from a tall, imposing, bearded man whom Churchill, Bass and Blackmore instinctively perceived to be the Boer Commander.

Attempting at once to rise and claim the title for himself from the dishevelled, beaten group of soldiers, Churchill found himself forced down by a well-placed boot administered by Bass to the inside of his left knee.

Glaring disdainfully at Bass as he unceremoniously toppled back to earth, his inevitable outburst was instantly curtailed by the venomously hissed warning issued by his insistent colleague...

"Remain silent, you fool, lest the powers of evil that surely even now permeate the Boer high command, and possibly even its government, seek to end your, at present, worthless existence here; in this very moment...

"Desist from your posturing and prepare to be taken."

Chapter 10

'Liberty.'

"Prisoners of war we are then once more, my old friend," alluded Blackmore, a resigned acceptance of their immediate standing apparent in the tone of his speech as he raised his manacled hands and proceeded to rattle the heavy iron chains that bound the surviving companions together.

In reciprocation of his colleagues' actions, Bass, raising his own chained wrists as though attempting to break the heavy cast iron links asunder, was immediately aware that his words, though borne out of a deep frustration from within at relinquishing their liberty whilst offering little resistance, ought nevertheless to be delivered with discretion in mind...

"These chains would shatter as brittle glass were the wolf spirit that lies dormant inside me to be rudely awoken from slumber, as would the lives of these miserable Boer maggots be forfeit with equal ease of effort, if only I..."

"Steady yourself, brother!" exclaimed Blackmore, a calming hand laid upon the shoulder of his frustrated companion...

"Our captors must not yet be made cognisant of the telling advantage we possess, an advantage that we might yet still have need to engage should our situation worsen...

"I would also advise against Churchill learning of your formidable capabilities for the present, at least until such time as they are called upon to aid our cause."

Bass nodded once in acceptance of Blackmore's wise counsel and paused in contemplation for a moment prior to diverting his attention towards Churchill, who sat to Bass' left sporting an outwardly downcast demeanour, and breaking his silence with the sternest admonishment that he could muster in little more than the whisper he dared to use...

"Desist from further notion to proclaim yourself commander of our group. Advantage lies in our favour if the Boers remain ignorant of yours, and indeed our true military ranks lest we all suffer the same fatal consequences as do all apprehended, non-uniformed British officers."

"But one merely intended to offer bold and decisive leadership in the moment when necessity beckoned for one to do so. I..."

Churchill was silenced abruptly and proceeded to recoil as best he could from his close partner in chains by the most vitriolic of rebukes administered from the venomous tongue of Bass...

"YOUR BRAGGADOCIO, PONCING AND PREENING WILL LIKELY GO TOWARDS SEEING US ALL SWING LEST YOU CURB YOUR INSATIABLE, FOOLHARDY DESIRE TO ACCRUE CHEAP LAURELS AND GLORY FOR YOURSELF AT ANY COST!

"Forced discomfort and intense interrogation remains a certainty, administered more than likely by their most experienced, highest-level inquisitor, possibly even Louis de Souza himself, with his prime directive being discovery of true military rank and, in your case, social standing...

"Regardless of discomfort suffered, seek to convince the impending inquisition with all humility of your true purpose, that of civilian war correspondent sent by the British broadsheet 'Morning Post', sent to report on daily front-line activity. Offer both legal reference for proof of identity and a reliable contact, including an address in England who remains willing to corroborate your admission of true intent in this country."

Softening his vitriolic, sobering tirade a little, Bass adopted an almost advisory tone as he continued…

"There will be time aplenty for soldiering, should you desire the opportunity to engage in further skirmish during this very conflict, of that fact I have little doubt, but this is neither the time nor the place for any further thoughts of such matters for the present…

"Have patience and seek to trust the judgement of both Tiberius and myself, and anticipate the arrival of our colleagues, Jackson and Sura, who, even as we speak, hasten towards Cape Town and the procurement of ample reinforcements in order to aid us in securing our liberty."

Bass then offered, by way of conclusion, words so ominous in their intent that even in the stifling, airless heat of the midday South African sunshine Churchill's blood ran so cold as to suggest it was turning to ice…

"Tarry with both myself and Tiberius a good while, young fool, and we shall willingly transport you to places that lie beyond the boundaries of common decency where your darkest imagination thought never likely to exist…

"City streets stripped bare of both humanity and dignity where life is regarded as nothing more than a cheap, disposable commodity by the ever-increasing numbers of well-ordered crime syndicates, and where survival on a daily basis is the accepted way of life…

"…Or alternatively, if your preference be such, to the battlefields of carnage where thousands of conscripted men fight to appease the will of a handful of blustering, clueless commanders and politicians; fields of brutality, horrors beyond your imagination, misery and even murder from where hell itself would prove to offer a welcome respite; yet a place where, nevertheless, all of the glory and laurels that you so wantonly crave associated with such organised degradation and suffering grow freely and are present to pick for the taking as one would harvest ripened fruit from the tree, if one is able to lower one's own moral standards to such a base level as to earn such worthless, meaningless trinkets...

"The choice will be yours, should we survive our current predicament, of course."

The uneasy silence that befell the whole group, Churchill included, was the only immediate answer that Bass required...

***

From 1899 the State Model School in Pretoria served a dual function as both hospital for the care of Boer War casualties and as the main prison where captured British army officers were held.

Despite airing their insistent protestations that they each held no active military commissions, it was nevertheless behind the Stinkwater village sandstone and red brick walls of this recently-fortified edifice in Gauteng Province, Republic of South Africa, that Bass, Blackmore, Churchill and a re-united Captain Aylmer Haldane were incarcerated in early November 1899.

"Our situation conspires towards worsening with every passing minute," alluded Blackmore as a set of heavy iron gates clanged shut behind them and they were unceremoniously marched through a narrow, iron caged corridor towards a second set of high iron gates.

Once navigated beyond these, Bass, Blackmore, Churchill and Haldane were separated from what remained of the bold Durham Light Infantry and the Dublin Fusiliers, and led out into a small courtyard which was totally exposed to the searing heat of the midday sun.

Here they were forced to stand, without offer of water or respite in the punishing, hell-fire glare for what seemed like an eternity until a

CHAPTER 10

door was flung open on the northern side of the high-walled courtyard.

Several men attired in the familiar khaki Boer military uniform filed out, followed by a tall, finely attired gentleman bearing a full set of dark, immaculately groomed facial whiskers, whom both Bass and Blackmore recognised immediately...

"De Souza!" hissed Bass, just loud enough for the benefit of his companion's hearing before their reception committee moved into earshot.

Halting directly before the group, the accompanying half dozen Boer sentries brought their high calibre, British-made Enfield magazine rifles to bear as senior Minister for War Louis de Souza eyed each one of the rapidly de-hydrating companions intensely for some considerable time before he began to speak...

"Welcome, gentlemen, to the British officers' prison in Pretoria. As you must now surely be aware, due to your presence within this particular facility, it is futile to deny further or to employ subterfuge to the contrary, that each one of you holds active commissions as officers serving with the British Expeditionary Force here in South Africa!"

Concentrating his address firstly towards both Churchill and Haldane, de Souza initially proceeded cordially, offering a formal introduction of himself, before skilfully unleashing a barrage of awkward questions designed to unsettle the now somewhat exhausted, disoriented and dangerously de-hydrated pair...

"Gentlemen, please forgive my poor manners regarding the correct recognition and implementation of both etiquette and protocol towards fellow officers of rank; my name is Louis de Souza; I am the senior Minister for War for the South African government..."

"You, sir, are Winston Spencer Churchill, Cornet Second Lieutenant of the Queen's 4th Hussars Regiment, late of the 21st Lancers; already a decorated veteran at the tender age of 25 years old of the Spanish/Cuban conflict of 1895; seen active service during the Indian North-

West Frontier skirmishes of 1897, and lately in 1898 a willing and very capable participant in the cavalry charge upon Mahdi forces at the battle of Omdurman."

His manner suddenly rising towards a harsher, less cordial crescendo, de Souza continued...

"DO YOU STILL PERSIST IN DENYING THAT YOU HOLD AN ACTIVE COMMISSION AND WILFULLY COMMAND BRITISH TROOPS AGAINST BOER FORCES LOYAL TO THE REPUBLIC OF SOUTH AFRICA? YOU KNOW THIS TO BE FACT, SECOND-LIEUTENANT CHURCHILL; DESIST WITH ANY NOTION OF EMPLOYING SUBTERFUGE IN ORDER TO SUBSTANTIATE YOUR QUITE LUDICROUS CLAIMS TO THE CONTRARY...

"WE ARE FAMILIAR WITH YOUR PRIVILEGED ORIGINS AND WE ARE WELL AWARE OF BOTH THE POLITICAL AND FINANCIAL ADVANTAGES TO BE GAINED IN FAVOUR OF THE BOER CAUSE IN RETURN FOR YOUR PROMPT RELEASE AND UNMOLESTED PASSAGE BACK TO THE RELATIVE SAFETY OF THE BRITISH-HELD LINES IN CAPE TOWN."

De Souza paused briefly in order to collect his thoughts and to hydrate himself from the generously sized trough of water that had been cruelly placed just a few paces in front of the dishevelled, sun-scorched line of men...

"Ah... God's own sweet elixir of life. A simple resource from Mother Nature's abundant larder that we all shamelessly, and with little thought, take for granted every day; something of a necessity, especially when one is fool enough to loiter uncovered for any length of time under this intolerable, high-noon sun, do you not agree, gentlemen?" de Souza taunted, all the while knowingly provoking his captives mercilessly as he tantalisingly sipped the precious, restorative liquid...

"Oh yes, we know of you, Cornet Second-Lieutenant Churchill, as we too are aware of you, Captain James Aylmer Lowthorpe Haldane.

CHAPTER 10

Your history of past achievements reads almost as impressively as that of our esteemed Second Lieutenant here."

Switching his attention towards the impassively brooding visages of Bass and Blackmore, de Souza initially marvelled inwardly as to how little the pair appeared to have been affected by their prolonged exposure to the searing heat...

"You two gentlemen, however, remain for the present the unfathomable enigma of this piece. You both exhibit a remarkably stubborn tolerance to the effects of dehydration, prolonged heat exposure and forced parade as would a very select few military personnel who had been specially trained to do so."

Blackmore countered immediately, his calm demeanour and ordered speech belying the fact that adequate hydration and sleep had eluded him for a good many hours...

"Alas, sir, you mistakenly hold myself and my esteemed colleague at some considerable fault. Please, allow one to make formal introduction. My name is Archibald Stephan Le Matt. My rather surly looking rogue of a companion is called Daniel Jenson Schofield. We are agents operating in the interests of the precious stone mining company of Schofield and Le Matt, based in the town of Castleton that lies at the heart of the English county of Derbyshire...

"We merely, and quite independently of any military involvement, one might add, accompany the British Expeditionary Force as civilian prospectors bound for a meeting with agents belonging to the De Beers diamond mining syndicate, with a view to brokering a rather lucrative trade deal between our two companies; a very important engagement which I now fear we shall not be able to honour due to the unfortunate, and most probably for the present, inextricable circumstance within which we now find ourselves infuriatingly embroiled...

"We travel with the full sanction of the East India Trading Company, whose offices in London, I'm certain, would corroborate any formal enquiries lodged as to the validity of our credentials."

De Souza raised his right index finger and proceeded to wag it in Blackmore's direction, a knowing grin forming beneath his full-set of distinguished black whiskers...

"Very astute phrasing, Mr... Le Matt, you say? A calm disposition and a faultless appraisal given with reference to your business affairs in our country, and of course those of your silent, brooding colleague: a dark, feral, yet perversely alluring menace emanates from behind those perfectly black eyes of his. Intriguing, to be sure...

"What price, I wonder, to have in our midst an elite pair of British special forces operatives, set fair to be taken immediately from this place for trial as British spies? Need one remind you, gentlemen, that the outcome of such a trial, should you be found guilty of espionage against the Republic of South Africa and the Orange Free State during a time of war, would, of course, be swift and very final."

Throughout this speculative, yet nevertheless unnervingly perceptive and marginally accurate assumption of the truth, Bass glowered directly at de Souza, barely able to conceal the rising tide of murderous intent that he longed to unleash upon the South African Minister for War.

Turning his attention momentarily towards the six Boer soldiers, brandishing their Enfield rifles trained at point-blank range towards the vulnerable hearts of each member of the group, then back towards de Souza, Bass attempted to formulate some semblance of a strategy that might offer them a minute sliver of tactical advantage; ruminating meticulously his silent tactical appraisal of their currently dire situation several times over in his mind, he returned always to the thought of unleashing his own interpretation of hell on earth upon these unsuspecting, potentially hapless Boers...

'A single, crystalline opportunity to strike with lethal intent. Just one precious, unguarded second allows the wolf time enough to remove

CHAPTER 10

arrogant, unwary heads from shoulders, to rent still-beating and blood-warm hearts from beneath splintered ribs, to tear weak, tender human flesh from bone; Ah, to savour the sweet-scented essence of the kill once more'...

His increasingly intense concentration upon the single notion of issuing murderous intent upon their captors, all the while agitating the raging spirit within him to rise and commit such an atrocity, the total humanity of James Bass was instantly re-engaged by yet more perceptively observant asides delivered by the very shrewd cross examination expertly managed by de Souza...

"And you, Mr Schofield: You do possess a curiously familiar surname, sir. Your favoured choice of sidearm, perhaps?"

By way of intentionally issuing a mocking response, Bass merely took the two lapels of his dusty old black velvet jacket in-between the thumb and forefinger of each hand and proceeded to open it wide, revealing to de Souza that he carried no concealed weapon, and uttered simply...

"No sidearm hangs here where none is required."

Sensing what he perceived to be the merest hint of a grin forming on the stubbled, now almost unnervingly gloating features of Bass, the answer given by de Souza was both direct and delivered with remarkable candour. The timbre of his voice, however, betrayed more than a hint of restless unease, much to the delight of two ageing detectives...

"Yes... quite... well then, gentlemen. I think that your stay here with us will prove to be a lot more comfortable, and the cordial hospitality you are hereafter shown will reflect our gratitude quite substantially, should we be able to corroborate your statement to our satisfaction of course...

"If, on the other hand, cause is given for harsher measures to be implemented... well, let us just be clear that if that were to be the case then your tenure here will conclude abruptly and with an altogether less favourable outcome."

Unexpectedly softening his manner towards the severely parched group somewhat, de Souza finally offered them the life-saving refreshment which they craved...

"Come, gentlemen, and generously slake what now must be your overwhelmingly powerful thirsts, if you please, then you shall be escorted directly to quarters befitting of your station and rank."

Requiring no second bidding, Churchill and Haldane were first to drink copious amounts from the barrel and then proceed to refresh themselves as best they could by ladling the precious liquid over their gratefully accepting heads...

"Ah, a simple resource that I shall never take for granted again for as long as I live," was the immediate reaction from a grateful Churchill.

"As God surely bears witness to my wholehearted agreement with your somewhat perfunctory, yet nonetheless accurate statement, Winston, nor shall I," concurred Haldane as he took his much-appreciated turn at the barrel.

At precisely the moment both Bass and Blackmore shared measured sips of the precious, restorative elixir of life, the single heavy wood and iron-hinged door into the courtyard opened and all four prisoners were escorted briskly towards the relative comfort of a shaded corridor.

As they were about to step over the threshold, Bass noticed that in an adjacent corner of the courtyard was situated a perfect sphere of what appeared to be of a standard red brick and mortar construct.

He estimated its diameter to be approximately seven or eight feet from pole to pole, making the circumference of the sphere a tad over 24 feet, though he conceded to himself that his knowledge of physics and the calculation of both mass and surface area had always proved avenues of study he thought best left to those scholars boasting a keener aptitude for the subject.

CHAPTER 10

What occurred to him as quite odd was that the presence here of such a curious object as this quintessentially English type of garden ornament, appearing totally out of context to its current surroundings of the four stark courtyard walls and the scorching hot sand underfoot.

Aware of the fact that this incongruous brick orb would not have gone unnoticed by Blackmore, Bass chose to remain silent for the present and instead focus his concentration upon the altogether more pressing matter: to precisely where they were being escorted, and to whom.

Bookended by their escort of six Boer soldiers, three towards their point, three more towards their rear, the four captives were chaperoned along the passage for approximately thirty feet before being halted inside what appeared to be the high-ceilinged, cathedral-like central hub of the prison.

From this open plan area, perceived by both Bass and Blackmore as being the processing concourse where new arrivals were inducted into the prison population, seven more identical corridors branched off at equidistant intervals around the circumference of the circular walls of the central hub, to where Bass supposed...

'Seven routes leading to seven potential discomforts anew'

Here, they were momentarily halted as de Souza was approached by a uniformed guard. Following a brief exchange of words between the two, de Souza promptly excused himself and as he turned to take his leave, much to the guarded amusement of the four colleagues, displayed the brusque, confident gait of a man whose daily achievement quota had been surpassed beyond all expectation, by presenting a quite ludicrous and somewhat comically theatrical flourish incorporating an amateurish and quite unnecessarily thespian-like posture and emanated an air of almost camp over-exuberance...

"You must excuse me, gentlemen. Pressing matters arise elsewhere that demand my full attention, but rest assured, we shall speak again very soon of a great many things."

As de Souza climbed an ornately cast-iron spiral stairwell to a landing that Blackmore estimated to be not higher than twenty or twenty-five feet above them, the sight that met his eyes forced Blackmore to turn his back sharply, as though to conceal his appearance from recognition, and instantly bade Bass to emulate his action...

"AVERT GAZE AT ONCE FROM OUR PREENING HOST, JAMES! ON THE LANDING DIRECTLY ABOVE US."

"Several darkly-attired men, almost certainly a squad of 'Black Guard' and there, among their number and being cordially greeted by our preening host as though they were each one a trusted acquaintance of long standing, our familiar and formidable adversaries, Septimus Severin and 'The Architect' himself."

"Yes, brother, I was certain that I had caught a hint of their putrid stench the moment we left the courtyard but a few moments ago. I had hoped to reach the relative privacy of secluded incarceration prior to revealing their presence here, but alas, our current predicament curtails any such notion," hissed Bass as he too attempted as best he could to conceal his appearance from detection...

Well aware of the fact that he risked drawing unwanted attention upon both himself and Blackmore by persisting with his speech, Bass nonetheless continued with some urgency...

"Our adversaries seek to liberate Churchill directly from the custody of the Boers. A prime opportunity indeed for 'The Architect' to press his plan towards a successful conclusion here, on this very day!"

Blackmore considered the comment made by Bass for a brief moment before offering his answer...

"The extradition of Churchill by the Boers into the custody of a legally non-proven authority may prove to be a formality should 'The Architect' prove successful in bringing his powerful influence to bear...

"Indeed. Much depends on the strength of resolute defiance that de Souza is able to muster with a view towards resisting what is sure to be such an overwhelming display of willpower on the part of 'The Architect'," countered Bass...

"I pray that we are granted time enough to formulate a sound plan of escape prior to the inevitable failure of de Souza's resolve and until our presence here is surely discovered."

Whilst simultaneously daring to dart momentary glances towards the upper balcony in an attempt to glean even the merest hint of body language that would offer a clue as to what course their immediate fate might take, it was with some mild reassurance then that Bass and Blackmore were able to hear de Souza offer clear and concise instructions to the commander of his personal guard...

"Commander Pretorius; please see the prisoners directly to the main officers' quarters where they are to await further interrogation at my pleasure."

Just as they were being ushered from the processing hub towards one of the seven branching corridors, however, the collective feelings of relief shared by each member of the group were immediately dashed by a loud and commanding bellow from the landing above... 'HOLD THAT GROUP!'

Clearly made audible by the natural echo which resonated around the high-ceilinged room and dropped directly to where they stood, the four companions were able to discern every syllable of the conversation that commenced between de Souza, Severin and 'The Architect', who spoke first and with whose voice both Bass and Blackmore were instantly familiar...

"So, Mr de Souza, you have in your custody one Second-Lieutenant Winston Spencer Churchill, a personage who holds great interest to me, who, and I state this in no uncertain terms, must under no circumstances, be allowed to return behind the safety of British held lines. It is imperative that this officer be handed over to me, with immediate effect and without question."

As he began to reply, de Souza was interrupted by 'The Architect'...

"Well, Mr?"

"Bloemfontein. Commissioner Tremaine de Rufus Bloemfontein, acting upon the express instructions of President Paul Kruger himself."

"Well... I... that is to say...," stuttered de Souza, perplexed by the audacious demand made by 'The Architect'.

"Of course, you must understand, sir, that your credentials will require official verification. One simply cannot transfer custody of such a high-profile prisoner without receiving ratified authorisation to do so from the highest authority."

Irked profusely by the sliver of stubborn resistance offered by de Souza towards his initial attempt at employing his mind-numbing tricks, 'The Architect' was forthright in openly displaying his irritation...

"YES, YES, BY ALL MEANS SEEK YOUR OFFICIAL VERIFICATION; I WOULD ADVISE YOU TO DO SO WITH ALL POSSIBLE HASTE LEST YOU COURT THE DISPLEASURE OF PRESIDENT KRUGER HIMSELF!"

Visibly shaken and emotionally unsettled by the threatening undertone of the obvious warning so convincingly delivered by 'The Architect', de Souza began issuing hurried instructions to one of his waiting subordinates.

As he did so, Septimus Severin, after scrupulously surveying the group of chained prisoners below them for several minutes whilst 'The Architect' spoke, posed a very pertinent question...

"And what of the other two prisoners attached to this group, sir? Captain Haldane is known to us and we remain satisfied that his presence offers little or no feasible influence upon our officially sanctioned mandate. There is, however, a certain familiarity present regarding the gait of those others."

CHAPTER 10

With uncomfortable beads of ice-cold perspiration now making their way down the length of his spine towards the small of his back, and his starched rigid shirt collar beginning to resemble the steadily tightening grip of a thuggee garrotte around his neck, de Souza answered Severin as growing anxiety approached its peak with every tense, unnerving second that passed...

"Oh, they are of little importance. A pair of British mining consultants apprehended whilst being chaperoned by their British military escort to a rendezvous with prospective business colleagues at the headquarters of the De Beers mining company here in Pretoria...

"Should their submitted statement appertaining to such matters be corroborated, as I expect it to be presently, then I would be compelled to release them without charge so they may continue about their proposed business."

His interest suddenly piqued by this aside from de Souza, 'The Architect' initially imparted his words with his characteristically measured control before perceiving in an instant the truth of the matter and issuing specific and forcefully delivered instructions to Severin, to the 'Black Guard' and to the Boer prison guards simultaneously...

"Mining consultants, you say? Interesting... Very interesting indeed...

"HOLD THAT GROUP. ISOLATE THOSE OTHER TWO AND COVER THEM WITH DUE DILIGENCE, LEST ALL OF YOUR MISERABLE LIVES BE FORFEIT THIS VERY MOMENT!"

"WE ARE DISCOVERED, JAMES!" exclaimed an exasperated Blackmore as they were unceremoniously separated from Churchill and Haldane to await the imminent attendance of their once great friend and mentor, Septimus Severin and his 'Black Guard'.

"Ah, of course; the keen instinctive insights of the Master are rarely in error. James, Tiberius, please step away from your colleagues and resist any notion that you might be harbouring with a view towards securing your liberty, lest both yours, and their lives end here in this moment, even before official sanction is granted by higher government authority."

"Septimus, you traitorous lap-dog!" spat Bass venomously as he instinctively readied himself for what he now perceived to be inevitable, brutally uncompromising conflict...

"STAY YOUR ANGER, JAMES," implored Blackmore, instantly aware of the fact that offensive action taken immediately on the part of the two very capable detectives would be met at once by a decisive counter-action that would almost certainly result in a potentially catastrophic outcome concerning the continued well-being of Churchill.

Satisfied that security had once more been established, Severin looked back towards the gantry where he observed the smirking bearded features of 'The Architect' as he proceeded to give a single nod confirming that a pre-conceived order should be carried out with immediate effect...

"A thousand apologies, my once great friends, for it seems as though your tenure on this earth has finally run its course, as would the tenure of any non-uniformed British officers apprehended whilst overseeing covert operational espionage behind enemy lines...

"Goodbye then, James, Tiberius, and I pray that we may meet once more on another spiritual plain and under more amiable circumstances."

Addressing the commander of his attending 'Black Guard' unit, Severin barked out his final, fatal order...

"Take these two out for immediate termination, full military honours to be observed both during and post execution of sentence."

Mystified by the portion of the order granting full military courtesy to the condemned men, the 'Black Guard' commander proceeded to make the fatal error of questioning the order given by Severin...

CHAPTER 10

"Begging your pardon, sir; full honours to be observed, for this scum..."

The commander's enquiry was instantly curtailed as a single, accurately aimed bullet from the revolver drawn from a side holster underneath Severin's heavy black greatcoat popped into the centre of his forehead, killing him instantly...

Turning to his second in command, with pistol still to hand and poised as though threatening to deliver a second fatal round if necessary, Severin imparted dryly...

"Full military honours to be observed, pre- and post-execution of sentence; do I make myself perfectly clear, Captain?"

The young 'Black Guard' Captain, now made completely aware of his new responsibilities as commander of the group upon witnessing the harshest possible example of discipline, stuttered nervously...

"Y... Yes, sir... Qu... quite c... clear, sir... At once, sir."

Chapter 11

'A Liberty, of Sorts...'

Wasting little time offering further explanation or idle words of any description, Severin instructed six of his elite 'Black Guard' operatives to reinforce further the six Boer soldiers who had been ordered to stand as the primary execution squad.

Taking up flanking positions to the two detectives, their purposefully over-compensated escort proceeded briskly towards the end of one of the seven corridors that Bass at once recalled as being the one that led to the courtyard where, but a few moments ago, their interrogation had taken place.

Anticipating that their time was becoming an increasingly more precious commodity with the passing of every second, Bass divulged his fleeting thought process to Blackmore, who reasoned that the somewhat desperate course of action suggested by his remarkably calm colleague was, under the circumstances that they found themselves in, the only logical short-term option available to them both worth considering.

At the precise moment they were ushered through the now familiar heavy wooden door out onto the sand that covered the floor of the square compound, it became clear to all that night-time had fallen and the entire area of the courtyard was clearly illuminated by a very bright, full moon risen to its perigee; a wolf moon...

"Tiberius, prepare yourself to engage in uncompromising, full-blooded combat. I shall proceed with summoning the wolf spirit to aid our cause... please... distance yourself as best you are able... I..."

His final words curtailed somewhat abruptly by the all-too familiar sound of the sickening cracking of bone and sinew, first breaking, then re-aligning; the razor-sharp claws bursting from elongated fingers; the snarling, hungry fangs salivating and eager to tear unprepared flesh set within the wolf's gnashing jaws, Bass began his bizarre and quite horrific metamorphosis into the beast.

Initially displaying all of the unpredictable character traits with which Blackmore was all too familiar, the unfettered, feral monster that stood before him was now fully formed and prepared to wreak unbridled carnage upon their startled, would-be executioners; yet, in the wake of, without question, the most remarkable and unanticipated occurrence to which he had yet borne witness with regards to this extraordinary phenomenon, Blackmore immediately sensed that this transformation differed significantly from any other which he could recall.

The elongated fingers, from the ends of which razor-sharp talons protruded, remained a familiar feature, as did the characteristic snout of the wolf bearing its set of snarling, gnashing fangs.

Of noticeable and significant difference to Blackmore, however, was that, contrary to its previous coat of pure white, the wolf's fur now adopted a hue of dark ochre that was flecked with what might be bizarrely alluded to as resembling distinguished streaks of grey.

A further pair of features that became instantly noticeable were that the wolf also now retained not only the majority of its garments, but also the upright human stature of James Bass as it reached the obvious zenith of its metamorphosis and readied itself to attack.

Using the element of surprise generated amongst their stunned escort by the unexpected appearance of the wolfman, Blackmore utilised every precious moment of this welcomed distraction to his advantage by first overpowering, with relative ease, one of the dumbstruck Boer turnkeys, and relieving himself of the heavy iron manacles that had secured his wrists.

Arming himself with a handsome, heavy bone-handled hunting knife from the utility belt of his incapacitated guard, Blackmore set about both Boer and 'Black Guard' opponents alike in a cascading torrent of direct and uncompromisingly brutal retribution that was directed upon those present who had wished to visit fatal harm upon both himself and his great friend, Bass.

In what appeared to be very little time at all, four Boer soldiers had forfeited their lives as they attempted, in vain, to stay the savage tide of precisely targeted, mercilessly ferocious violence meted out by Blackmore.

Whilst concentrating on his grim task, Blackmore was able to notice momentarily that the altered appearance of his lycanthrope companion was not the only interesting aspect that had undergone a distinct alteration.

Though the wolfman's initial assault proved to be as uncompromisingly lethal as his own had been, it too showcased the unique, meticulously controlled and precise combat skills that could only belong to one man...

"James, my old brother at arms; you are here by my side in much more than the lycanthrope spirit, I think."

Through the blackened voids, where once rested a pair of human eyes, the wolfman glanced momentarily towards Blackmore in order to signify his recognition in the form of a grotesque snarl whilst continuing without pause to scythe across unguarded faces and chests, employing his claws with lethal, controlled precision, as would a master swordsman wield his weapon of choice in a similarly impressive and deadly manner.

CHAPTER 11

With each of their twelve erstwhile executioners lying dead in the courtyard within a matter of seconds, Blackmore instinctively turned towards his wolfen colleague, still for the present electing to err on the side of caution in maintaining a discreet distance between them, but now appreciating that the beast understood his every word and was capable of both following, and acting upon, a logical thought process of his own...

"James, we must away from this desperate place post-haste and take time to formulate fresh strategy with regards to the liberation of Churchill. To live now makes certain the opportunity to fight another day."

Without pausing for a second longer than he required in order to hear and understand the sage words of his greatest friend, Bass made instinctively for the heavy wooden door that appeared to offer them their only avenue of escape.

Whilst moving towards the solid, securely bolted door, with the initial intention of mustering his great lycanthrope strength to effortlessly tear it from its iron hinges, Bass noticed in his peripheral vision, a rusty old drainpipe that ran from the rooftop down the full length of the south wall of the courtyard and disappeared into an iron grating. Could this welcomed element of chance, he reasoned to himself, offer a more instantly accessible and safer avenue of escape for the desperate pair?

As Blackmore looked on, whilst simultaneously guarding the door in anticipation of the imminent arrival of Septimus Severin and a host of 'Black Guard' reinforcements, Bass proceeded to lift the heavy iron grating and toss it to one side with seemingly little effort, exposing an opening that was barely wide enough for a man to squeeze through and drop down into the filthy black sewer water below.

Turning towards Blackmore, the wolfman gesticulated coarsely towards the now open grating and snarled a wordless request for his friend to enter the sewer first, almost certainly regarding the well-being of his more vulnerable human companion of prime importance to his own.

As though instinctively understanding the thought process of Bass instantly, and not wishing to tarry a second longer than was necessary, Blackmore duly obliged his lycanthrope companion's gesture and promptly dropped through the narrow opening into the rank sewer water some ten feet below.

Standing in the narrow channel of water, which to Blackmore's relief was no more than calf deep, he awaited the imminent arrival of the wolfman, only to be surprised once more on this most extraordinary of days, by the unexpected arrival of James Bass, now fully restored to his human form...

"James; how on earth... what the devil... as God stands witness, how..."

Displaying his characteristic demeanour of total calmness and offering his answer with a customarily economic use of well-chosen words, Bass raised his right hand sharply in a bid to silence the inevitable torrent of questions that he anticipated would almost certainly spill from Blackmore's inquisitive lips, and merely imparted...

"Hush, Tiberius. Now is not the appropriate time for explanation. Suffice to say that mine and Connie's regular sojourns into the isolated solitude of our beloved Hebridean wilderness have been very well rewarded in part by what you have just witnessed here."

With that, and accepting that their prime concern remained to abscond and re-evaluate their options in a safer, more secure environment, Bass and Blackmore proceeded to navigate the narrow, red brick-arched sewer tunnel system for a distance that they both approximated to measure at least one mile on from their point of entry until they came upon an iron ladder that led upwards about fifteen feet to an iron grating above.

CHAPTER 11

Raising the rusty old grating with relative ease, Blackmore was able to survey the surrounding terrain for the 360-degree perimeter all around in order to ascertain if it was safe enough for them both to emerge.

Satisfied that the coast was clear, the two fugitives climbed through the grating and found themselves close to what they perceived to be the outskirts of the city of Pretoria.

Scanning the circumference of their location for himself and realising that cover and concealment was of prime importance, Bass made a suggestion…

"See over there, Tiberius. The dense tree line that begins approximately twenty feet away to the north of the city boundary will provide adequate cover for us to shelter and take stock of our situation."

Once the short distance between their escape hole and the edge of the forest had been successfully traversed as swiftly as their ageing limbs would allow and the dense canopy of deciduous greenery enveloped them, the pair of detectives' senses were simultaneously alerted to the fact that they were not alone…

"Tiberius; half a league to the east!" exclaimed Bass with some urgency…

"Clear evidence of heavy footfall. Standard British military issue footwear; a small cohort of not more than a dozen bodies, plus two others… affirmative; two others not affiliated directly to the main group…

"Jackson and Sura have honoured their pledge and returned to aid our cause, bearing a significant, if somewhat discreet, force of arms."

Blackmore eyed Bass and shook his head, and with the clear sign of a grin forming upon his gnarled, ageing features answered merely with silence, yet barely able to conceal his admiration towards the plethora of enhanced senses that now belonged to his remarkable lycanthrope companion.

***

"This is a prime location. From here, we shall mount our rescue attempt, Marcus," began Lucius Sura…

"Agreed, Lucius. Our reliable intelligence sources inform us that the contingent of British officers is incarcerated within the State Model Prison that is situated but a short half-mile march within the eastern quadrant of the city…

"We should reasonably assume, therefore, that Churchill and our bold comrades, James and Tiberius, are detained behind the very same walls."

Sura offered a wry grin as he began to answer, his response curtailed almost immediately by a most unexpected presence arriving unannounced in their midst…

"Never be so presumptuous as to assume anything, my good friend. One day, perhaps when it is least expected, assumption might conspire towards your premature demise…"

Unsheathing his twin 'gladii' instinctively and setting his stance for combat, Sura turned sharply towards the direction from whence the familiar voice of James Bass emanated. Joined by an equally prepared Jackson, a cocked pistol at the ready in each hand, their initial shared sensation of the ice-cold terror instilled into the heart of every soldier the instant before battle commences instantaneously evaporated to be replaced, at first by relief, and then, especially in the case of Marcus Jackson, euphoric glee at the sight of his two closest friends, safe and sound…

"James… Tiberius… You… You're alive; may the good lord above be praised!" …he exclaimed as the three comrades embraced each other warmly.

Noticing immediately that Churchill was conspicuous by his absence, and with no shortage of concern present in his voice, an agitated Sura spoke...

"And what of Churchill? Choosing to ensure personal liberty in order to save your own lives; to relinquish your sacred oath given towards preserving the sanctity of Churchill's well-being; I would pray that for your sakes sound reasoning exists for such a questionable decision to have been conceived."

At once, Blackmore was aware that the eyes of Bass had turned jet-black and for a terrible, fleeting moment, as his enraged brother rounded and faced directly at Sura as though poised to strike, feared that the wolf spirit would instinctively be unleashed in order to wreak unanswerable, horrible violence upon the unsuspecting Roman, who, after all, was merely exhibiting a human concern for his still incarcerated friend.

Positioning himself between Bass and Sura as a human buffer of sorts, Blackmore proceeded to offer sage words of his customary wisdom in an attempt to quell the rising bloodlust of the beast, and preserve a life that he was now certain remained a valuable asset to the future success of their mission...

"JAMES. RESTRAIN YOUR INNER DEMON, MY FRIEND! SURA'S ANGER IS BORN FROM A GENUINE CONCERN HELD FOR A BROTHER, A BOND FORGED IN BLOOD AND FIRE AS WAS OUR OWN MANY MOONS BEFORE THIS MOMENT WAS EVER CONCEIVED."

Sura, his pair of 'gladii' remaining poised and battle-ready, now prepared himself in anticipation of an imminent assault from the legendary 'Wolfman of Whitechapel'.

"I AM AWARE OF YOUR 'AFFLICTION', JAMES BASS; THE 'CURSE' THAT WRESTS FOR EXCLUSIVE OWNERSHIP OF YOUR SOUL. UNWITTING RECIPIENT OF A WEREWOLF'S BITE, DAMMNED TO ROAM ETERNITY FOREVER AS A LYCANTHROPE. THE HOUND FROM HELL DESTINED TO

SCOUR TIME IN SERVICE PLEDGED TO BOTH THE 'TIME ENFORCEMENT AGENCY', AND TO 'THE LEAGUE OF GHOSTS'.

"WHY THEN, FOR ALL OF YOUR ENHANCED ABILITIES, COULD YOU NOT LIBERATE CHURCHILL?"

Bass stepped around Blackmore displaying the deft agility of a cat and as the demonic blackness of his lycanthrope eyes bored into the deepest soul of the Roman, his manner surprisingly softened and he spoke with reassured calmness of their immediate intentions with regards to their plan for the urgent repatriation of Churchill...

"Have a care, Roman," warned Bass, the fangs of a wolf formed and clearly visible in the jaws where once human incisors had lain...

"Had you not already proved yourself an integral player with vital scenes still yet to act out in this perpetually unfolding drama, I would see fit to end your days here in payment for your impudence just imparted alone...

"Now, I advise you to sheathe your pathetic toothpicks, for they would serve no meaningful purpose against the iron constitution and lightning swiftness of a werewolf, nor, should it please you to be aware, would they either prove any deterrent when raised in anger upon the human form of James Bass...

"Make your choice wisely, Centurion. Yield now and serve further useful purpose or persist with your predictable, pedestrian human assault and prepare to take your final breath on earth...

"In either case, Tiberius and I shall seek to carry out the sacred pledge we made to 'The League of Ghosts' and preserve the life of Churchill."

Bass and Sura faced each other across a small space within the circle that had opened up around them, made up of the British soldiers who had accompanied both Sura and Jackson on their rescue mission. Both men maintained a full stance of readiness in preparation for hand-to-hand, or more to the point with regards to this instance, sword-to-

CHAPTER 11

fang-and-claw combat.

After little more than thirty seconds, which appeared to the anxiously awaiting Blackmore, Jackson and the nervously attentive squad of soldiers, to span the course of a millennia, Sura relaxed his stance and, in a gesture of unexpected compliance that signalled his willingness to Bass that his action would offer recourse, at least momentarily, with regards to their potentially fatal impasse, sheathed his 'gladii' into the leather scabbards strapped onto his back...

"You chose wisely, Centurion," was the simple, uncomplicated answer proffered by Bass in acknowledgement of the Roman's decision to yield.

Curtailing what he perceived to be an inevitable retort from Sura, Blackmore imparted hurriedly...

"Excellent, gentlemen. Now that this latest charade of petty posturing has been, at least for the present, consigned to history may we now proceed with the matter in hand, which would undoubtedly entail the liberation of our still incarcerated companion, Winston...

"Might one suggest that we proceed to utilise the labyrinthine network of sewage tunnels that run beneath the prison through which James and I made good our escape, and set a 'sapper's fire'?"

"A 'sapper's fire'?" enquired a puzzled Sura...

Blackmore proceeded to offer his briefing that outlined in fine detail the proposed strategy that both he and Bass had conceived...

"During our brief time spent navigating the sewer tunnels beneath the prison, James and I noticed that several key load bearing sections of the foundation that support a significant weight of the building above comprise of a heavy wooden joist and sandstone construction...

"If, therefore, a series of fires was to be set at strategic points below the compound, utilising pig fat as the fuel, then the ensuing high temperatures that would be generated by the pig fat inferno would prove more than adequate to bring even the stoutest construction of wood, stone and molten metal down into the pit...

"The squad who accompany Marcus and yourself are Royal Engineers who, as we had previously arranged with Marcus here, count amongst their ranks personnel bearing the necessary 'sapper' skills to accomplish this task to our satisfaction."

"You gambled upon the foundations of which you speak being susceptible to such a procedure?!" exclaimed Sura incredulously...

Blackmore offered a wry grin as he answered...

"Experience affords us the opportunity to anticipate all possibilities and grants that we procure any available resource in order to accomplish the perceived task at hand...

"Not only do engineers possess the effective 'sapper' skills that we require, they too are excellent combat troops; a portion of their skillset that I have no doubt we shall need to call upon at some stage during these proceedings."

"So, the foul stench emanating from the barrels that we hauled with us in those two wagons is..."

"Rendered pig fat, I would surmise, my Roman friend," answered Blackmore in conclusion.

Chapter 12

'A Sapper's Fire.'

As though impatiently awaiting the cessation of Blackmore's detailed briefing, Bass commenced issuing orders to the engineers as he segued flawlessly from the feral beast in waiting, into the commanding guise of an experienced British army Colonel...

"Engineer commander; to us," he barked as a fairly short, solidly built man wearing the characteristically khaki uniform of a Royal Engineer Captain approached Bass and Blackmore, standing to attention and instinctively snapping out a textbook perfect salute...

"Captain Bryce Witherspoon, commander of the first Royal Engineers and elite 'sapper's' squad, sirs."

Whilst respectfully returning the salute, as army protocol demanded, Bass continued to speak without pause whilst gratefully re-acquainting himself with his varied selection of weapons, all of which had been discarded at the moment of their arrest in an attempt to negate any notion on the part of the Boer soldiers that might give suspicion to the fact that either Bass or Blackmore was affiliated to any British military cause, by firstly introducing himself and Blackmore by rank, thus establishing the correct chain of command, and then outlining in detail the strategy they proposed to adopt going forward...

"Stand easy, Captain...

"My name is Colonel James Bass; this gentlemen to my left is Colonel Tiberius Blackmore; Captain Sura and Mr Jackson have already made your acquaintance, I trust. Our immediate task will entail the setting of a 'sapper's fire' directly beneath the foundations belonging to the State Model Prison that is situated a few hundred yards due east of our position here...

"Exact placement of the charges will be entrusted to your capable judgement, Captain. I would respectfully ask that all questions appertaining to our intended strategy be deferred at present until the appropriate moment arises when a detailed briefing will be forthcoming, and that we move with all haste from here towards our point of entry into the sewer system that runs beneath the whole area of the prison complex."

Upon locating the iron grating from which Bass and Blackmore had exited the sewers, the engineers' first task was to hurriedly erect a block-and-tackle in order to lower the dozen heavy barrels filled with the rancid, incendiary pig fat down into the tunnel system and traverse the mile or so distance through the stinking, knee-high water to a point which the two wily old detectives had previously marked as being directly below the central hub of the prison complex.

Set in four groups of three barrels at equidistant points around what the sapper commander perceived to be the four stone pillars that were the key load-bearing stations supporting the entire mass belonging to the central part of the prison compound, Captain Witherspoon then ordered his demolition specialist to prepare four hundred feet lengths of thirty second fuse cord that were attached to each of the four groups of barrels and consequently played out back down the tunnel in the direction from whence they had come, in order for all of the charges to be ignited at a safe distance away from the impact point.

"Beggin' your pardon, sir; with your permission, I've allowed for thirty seconds delay on the fuses. Ample enough time to get gone

CHAPTER 12

an' safe whilst the pig fat burns up to its 'ighest temperature an' does its worst on this brittle wood an' Stinkwater sandstone foundation. Should 'ave this 'fakker' down an' dusted in forty minutes or less, sir," Witherspoon reported assuredly...

"Excellent, Captain. Please proceed at once," replied Blackmore before addressing Bass, Jackson and Sura...

"We must seek without delay to exploit fully to our good advantage the chaos that ensues as the edifice crumbles. Over all the other potential opportunities that might present themselves in the moment, remember that the location and liberation of Churchill remains our shared prime directive."

Whilst hastily back-tracking down the tunnel in the direction from which they came, to a point that Witherspoon approximated to be a safe distance from the devastating effects of the high temperature blaze of the 'sapper's fire', Bass spoke plainly to Blackmore, suggesting at once although he had understood implicitly the reminder tendered by his colleague appertaining to the importance of fulfilling their primary responsibility, in addition they should also be prepared to exploit the random element of chance concerning securing once and for all the final conclusion of a more privately conceived, yet no less important sanction...

"Tiberius, mindful as I remain with regards to my commitment towards the liberation of our man, I would offer a reminder that should clear opportunity present itself to terminate both Severin and 'The Architect' during the chaos that will undoubtedly unfurl during our unconventional assault upon the prison, then either one of us should be prepared to exploit any such fortuitous opportunity to maximum effect."

Blackmore, reluctant though he first appeared to admit that the suggestion made by Bass was born not entirely of sound reason, but rather a personal blood feud that had festered malignantly between

'The Architect' and the two detectives over a protracted period of time, chose to answer firstly with a single silent nod of his head, prior to eventually stating cautiously...

"Have a care, James, that this burgeoning ambition bordering on an obsession with delivering a final, fatal justice in the moment does not appear as the unwarranted catalyst that defines our failure, or indeed, perhaps more of a grave concern, become the incontrovertible harbinger of our doom."

***

Attaining a modicum of comfort once more, attired in their customary pin stripes and tweeds, their signature sidearms and varied assortment of blunt and sharp weaponry returned to them by Marcus Jackson, the pair of ageing warriors respectively proceeded to load a 'yellow boy' Winchester rifle and a sawn off 'Purdy' shotgun whilst Bass continued to speak...

"When the edifice tumbles, there will be no need to seek covert entrance from the lower levels, as was first expected. The unfolding confusion will suffice as ample enough cover for us to gain entrance through the front gates of the compound."

"So, upon entry into the prison, are my engineers to aid exclusively in securing the safe repatriation of Mr Churchill above all other concerns?" was the enquiry made by Witherspoon, eager to clarify the exact expectations of his squad after listening to what he had perceived to be mixed messages emanating from the two detectives...

The withering response offered by Bass from behind his now jet-black eyes caused the stubbly hairs on the back of Witherspoon's profusely perspiring thick neck to prickle uncomfortably and sent an ice-cold shiver down the full length of his spine...

"Affirmative, Captain, and do remember to exterminate anyone who would appear to be not affiliated to our cause or seeks to hamper our progress in any way... Absolutely no exceptions."

Chapter 13

'An Unexpected Turn of Events.'
('From the Jaws of Victory.')

"Beggin' your pardon, sirs, thirty minutes 'as elapsed since the pig-fat caught aflame. Should be about time to proceed with phase two of your plan," Witherspoon reminded the two detectives as he meticulously scanned the dial of his pocket watch for the umpteenth time.

As the squad broke the cover beyond the boundaries of their forest sanctuary to which they had mutually agreed to retreat after igniting their 'sapper's fire' barrels, the rather conspicuous presence of an advancing group, consisting of several uniformed British soldiers accompanied by four other heavily armed non-uniformed individuals, courted little attention as a result of the chaos unfolding around the area of the inferno that was now consuming a large section of the State Model Prison.

Upon gaining unchallenged entry through the unguarded prison gates and, thankfully, encountering little resistance amounting to either any relevance or stubborn fortitude, the almost discreetly invading British engineers made their way along corridors that were now very familiar to both Bass and Blackmore before arriving at the location where both men were certain that the central hub of the complex once stood...

"I see that our 'sapper's fire' has served its purpose very effectively, James. Notice how a large portion of the building's central core has already crumbled down into the abyss," alluded Blackmore as potentially lethal shards of stone, wood, slate and iron proceeded to rain down dangerously and explode randomly onto the flagstone floor all around them...

"TIBERIUS. TAKE HEED OF YOUR LEFT FLANK. THE 'BLACK GUARD' ARE UPON US," warned Bass as he fired off a trio of rounds from his 'yellow boy' Winchester rifle, each deadly projectile finding the unguarded chests at which they were aimed with unerring accuracy.

Blackmore wasted little time in offering his own inimitable contribution to their initial engagement with their enemy by discharging both barrels of his old 'Purdy' shotgun into the chests of a further pair of the advancing 'Black Guard'.

Upon discarding his spent shotgun, Blackmore drew his old LeMat revolver and proceeded to lessen the numbers within the ranks of their assailants substantially by unleashing a volley of projectiles that found each of the targets for which they were meant.

Whilst employing his pair of pistols, and proceeding to unleash his own deadly barrage of ordnance, Bass became instantly aware that the rumours to which he had been privy, regarding Sura's ability to deflect bullets using a deft sweeping motion of his twin 'gladii', were indeed no falsehood.

He even afforded himself a brief moment of admiration in tribute to the impressive show of combat skills being showcased by the Roman centurion as the twin blades arced and twirled mesmerically in the gifted hands of a master swordsman, scything through flesh and bone clinically and without mercy, expertly dissecting any unfortunate foe who crossed his path in battle.

Amidst the rising cacophony of chaos that was erupting all around them, Blackmore was able to isolate Witherspoon for a few precious seconds so as to offer a suggestion as to how the British engineers' involvement in proceedings should progress...

"Witherspoon, have your engineers concentrate their attentions exclusively upon the Boer contingent of the enemy force. Your bold command, myself, Colonel Bass, Captain Sura and Mr Jackson personify the random aberration that threatens to de-stabilise the correct order as to how events should naturally unfold here, as too do Severin, 'The Black Guard' and 'The Architect'.

"We four alone shall endeavour to contain and crush their lofty aspirations here once and for all."

Almost as though some pre-arranged protocol had been systematically engaged in order to in some way subliminally manipulate the opposing factions towards their pre-designated areas of combat, Bass noticed the focus of the 'Black Guard' offensive alter directly towards the four non-engineers...

"Gentlemen, the 'Black Guard' favour us and shift the impetus of their assault exclusively towards we four, just as you'd surmised, Tiberius...

"And see there, beyond the blinding confusion of this killing floor on the parapet above; Severin and 'The Architect' make good their attempt to flee, bearing our man Churchill in their custody."

"Yes, James, I see. Be ever mindful, however, that 'The Architect' seemingly always endeavours to act only when a sound basis for reasonable logic is assured. He clearly has a use for Churchill beyond this skirmish, possibly to serve as a live hostage."

Resorting to unleashing their uncompromisingly brutal, well-drilled martial arts skills as hand-to-hand combat commenced, the four companions proved more than a match for their 'Black Guard' opponents.

CHAPTER 13

Sporting his well-used pair of heavy brass 'knuckle dusters', Blackmore proceeded to showcase the dexterous grace and professional poise of a champion prize fighter as blow after powerful blow was relentlessly and precisely aimed into the unprepared bodies of his hapless assailants.

Meanwhile, Bass favoured a brass-pommelled hunting knife as his chosen weapon, a single razor-sharp talon which he wielded firstly to cripple his luckless assailants with either deft slashes across key leg tendons supporting balance, or multiple swift stabs from close quarters into unprotected torsos before employing a combination of clinically-precise technique and remarkably powerful physical force to tweak weakened, disorientated heads first one way and then the next in order to cleanly snap the neck as if it were no more than the rotten branch of an ageing tree, often all of the components belonging to this particularly macabre 'dance of death' undertaken in one quicksilver blur of motion.

Marcus Jackson, much to the relief of both Bass and Blackmore, proved more than able to offer his own unique contribution to the affray; a somewhat naïve and untutored form of 'street' pugilism combined with an obscure form of gentleman's martial art known as 'Bartitsu' that merely required a common walking cane to wield, albeit with a well-tutored precision and graceful poise.

The trio of companions from the streets of Whitechapel, though only able to steal the occasional briefest of glimpses as they toiled tirelessly, each man focusing intense concentration upon fulfilling his own obligations, could do little but admire the showcase of scintillating and quite exquisite swordsmanship being displayed by their centurion colleague, Sura.

His twin 'gladii' whirled and twisted with the speed of a steam-powered threshing machine, the arc of each razor-sharp blade finding its intended target with each deadly slash. Chests were split wide open, limbs were amputated, whilst pistols continued to spit their aimless bullets still ignited into life by the taught muscle spasm of a severed hand, torsos falling like limp rag dolls minus the heads that had once sat atop proud and confident shoulders...

'This man truly purports to be the Devil himself incarnate'...

...mused Bass, inwardly.

All at once, Blackmore adopted a defensive posture back-to-back with Bass, offering open respect for the centurion's remarkably competent prowess in battle...

"Our Roman compatriot fights like a man possessed of Satan's influence. His skills are mesmeric, his feral brutality tempered and controlled by the experienced hand of a very adept, highly trained killer of men. I believe that we have unearthed a kindred spirit, James."

"So it would appear, Tiberius. If this man sets example with regards to what once constituted but a minute portion of the elite military might of ancient Rome, then the unassailable dominance of that relatively small empire over much of the then chronicled world could never be underestimated, nor upon this remarkable evidence, be doubted in any way," was the eloquent and respectful answer offered by Bass.

As he continued to repel what thankfully now appeared to be the substantially diminishing swathe of the 'Black Guard' assault, Bass drew each of his colleagues' attention towards a troubling chain of events which was proceeding to unfold high above them on the iron gantry that for the present had, in some fortuitous way, survived the ruination wrought by their 'sapper's fire'...

"EYES ABOVE AND TO YOUR LEFT! 'THE ARCHITECT' AND SEVERIN, WITH CHURCHILL STILL ENSCONCED BY THEIR SIDE. IT IS IMPERATIVE THAT WE..."

His sentence was curtailed by the vexatious spectacle of the gantry upon which the focal point of his observation stood, beginning to crumble. Still frustratingly occupied by the insistent remnants of the

CHAPTER 13

'Black Guard' assault, the four companions were only able to watch with disbelieving eyes and remain transfixed in the momentary horror of their helplessness as 'The Architect' and Severin faded from view into the safe and welcoming embrace of the fourth dimensional ether, and the remainder of the iron and stone gantry, upon which Churchill had been abandoned to his fate, crumbled into dust and ten thousand pieces of hopeless despair all around them...

'CHURCHILL; WHERE IS CHURCHILL! OH, MY LORD; THERE, LOOK THERE, HE TUMBLES INTO THE PIT!...

...were the last desperate words, falling from anonymous lips, that Bass was able to clearly distinguish amidst the cacophony of chaos and destruction erupting all about him as his senses became momentarily overcome by a familiar sensation of blissful oblivion and a serene sensual flux...

"NO, NOT NOW... OF ALL TIMES, NOT AT THIS PRECISE MOMENT," Bass cried out loud as his surroundings blurred into a mist and he entered into the now familiar process of a dimensional shift.

**

"TIBERIUS!" exclaimed Bass, as his temporarily displaced consciousness returned to the sight of his semi-conscious companion, in the process of gingerly seating himself from a prone position not five feet away from the place where Bass had raised himself up a moment earlier into an unsteady crouching position...

"A certain familiarity with our immediate surroundings persists and yet my innermost senses subliminally gnaw at my willingness to reason as to exactly how, let alone why, without consciously engaging either of our portkeys, we find ourselves here... wherever here proves to be!"

Blackmore tentatively raised himself to his feet from the patch of damp ground where he had lain unconscious and, his senses now fully restored, proceeded to survey their surroundings in greater detail...

"James, thank the gods you are well, my old friend."

"I am restored in some part, Tiberius, though still I remain somewhat disorientated from the rigours of what I now perceive to have been an unsanctioned dimension shift, forced upon us, no doubt, by a capable third party..."

"I am under no illusion whatsoever that 'The Architect' is wholly responsible for our current predicament. I fear that his ability to access our portkeys and, in some fashion, manipulate them in order to spirit us away from our intended point of reference, provides a problem of unprecedented magnitude that we must, with some urgency, seek to rectify."

Finally able to recognise their surroundings, Bass continued...

"Tiberius, the river that runs beside us is undoubtedly the Thames, and the old towpath upon which we now stand. Are we not merely a few short paces from Traitor's Gate, behind which lies the concealed entrance into Trajan's Vaults and onwards into the inner sanctum of 'The League of Ghosts'?"

"Indeed, James, though the glass towers rising high on either side of the riverbank offer an unfamiliar contour to the city skyline suggesting initially that we now inhabit a time that exists a good number of decades on from our own, possibly even many years beyond the new millennium that was close to its eve before we left."

As he spoke, Blackmore continued to survey their immediate surroundings and noticed something else of note that made such a profound impact upon him that he felt compelled to pause for a few seconds in order to compose himself before he was satisfied his words would convey precisely that his observations were made by engaging both a rational and logical thought process...

CHAPTER 13

"And notice there too, James; see the flags that flutter, somehow incongruously, at the apex of each pinnacle belonging to all four towers of the 'White Keep', coupled with the twin banners that hang from the river-facing façade of the Tower battlements. See the striking statement of a bright red background bearing the white circle, inside which is the offset black, geometrical symbol; distant memory suggests, however, that the symbol is presented here clockwise, as opposed to its anti-clockwise original configuration...

"A bold symbol... an emblem that is in some way known to me, but... displayed here, so conspicuously and in such a prominent place where the flag of St George and the Union flag once proudly flew as a world-renowned emblem of the glorified union of the British Isles... If only I could recollect...

"OF COURSE!" exclaimed Blackmore, now able to recall the significance held by the mysterious, and the ever more increasingly ominous symbol, and even its name...

"The symbol was adopted from ancient origins as a sign of divinity and spirituality by Eurasian cultures in recent centuries, though its true origins could possibly be traced back to well before 500BC...

"...and now I remember its name... The 'SAUASTIKA'."

Chapter 14

'The Legends Are Alive!'

'March 2022'

"This place, Tiberius, it feels... every aspect of the place... an air of incongruity hangs in a stale, subliminally oppressive atmosphere... the whole aura is... WRONG!" Bass imparted brusquely, offering little in the way of a specific appraisal, though Blackmore understood in an instant the direct meaning of his colleague's simple, if rather unspecific, statement...

"Almost as though the militaristic emblem we witness adorning the 'White Keep' should not exist here, let alone be displayed openly on such a grand scale adorning almost completely the river-facing facade of such a prominent London landmark as the Tower of London."

Their conversation was interrupted by the familiar deep, commanding baritone voice that belonged to an old and trusted friend...

"James, Tiberius, by all the grace of the gods and their ancestors, you are alive!"

Compelled by the ever present, instinctive telepathy shared by the pair of old warriors, each man drew and cocked their pistols and prepared themselves for whatever might occur next to accelerate events towards even greater disadvantage on this already most curious of days...

"Please, lower your weapons, my old friends. Your safety here, for a brief moment at least, is assured, "continued the familiar tone of Pontius Aston as he emerged from the concealed entrance that thankfully remained where they remembered it, behind Traitor's Gate, his hands held aloft with empty palms wide open as a gesture of there being no malicious intent on his part...

"Follow me quickly, gentlemen, lest we risk this entrance into our sanctuary below being compromised by 'The Gestapo'."

Holstering his weapon immediately, prior to clasping hands heartily and embracing in a brotherly hug, Blackmore asked but one simple question...

"Gestapo, Pontius?"

Expecting a similarly warm greeting of friendship from Bass, Aston found himself inwardly bemused in the first instance that his colleague's cocked pistol remained drawn and firmly to hand, and in the second, to receive merely a single curt nod of the head and the customarily conspicuous blank visage that gave no indication as to what searching questions, or indeed what random intentions, lay waiting behind those impassive, menacingly pitch-black eyes.

As he proceeded to usher his two still slightly bemused colleagues towards the open portal, Aston continued to speak...

"Please, enter inside quickly, my brothers. I promise you, all will be revealed upon reaching the secure confines of the inner sanctum."

Once beyond the threshold, the heavy iron door shifted silently into place behind them and an array of bright LED lights burst into life, illuminating the now familiar maze of corridors that led towards Trajan's Arch.

Upon passing beneath the imposing monolithic relic of once-great Roman architecture, the two detectives would have been able to navigate the labyrinthine warren of tunnels that they were both aware would eventually lead them to the place that once was the covert headquarters belonging to 'The League of Ghosts'... 'but'... pondered Blackmore to himself as he now became fully aware that Bass had chosen to retain his primed pistol ready to hand and adopt a potential covering position to the rear of their reception group comprising Pontius Aston and six Covert Special Forces operatives...

'What awaits us, I wonder, in the one place where peace and security was once assured... and, by the gods, what could James have sensed at the moment of our reunion with Pontius that could possibly have vexed him so?'

Approaching the point where both men perceived the vast library and ornately carved round table where 'The League of Ghosts' once, perhaps still did, convene, Bass and Blackmore became acutely aware of several aesthetic changes made to their surroundings that altered profusely the once intimate and very private aura once insisted upon by the League to that of a vibrant, busy modern office environment.

Glass panels partitioned off private office spaces, inside each of which both men and women were seated behind desks, furiously tapping the lettered and numbered keys on what appeared to resemble a journalistic typewriting device, whilst the words being engaged at a remarkably brisk pace miraculously appeared on a board before their eyes.

When the pair of detectives strode into view, the men and women halted their labours immediately and, as they left the self-contained privacy of their personal glass-walled enclaves, a mellow buzz of excitement began to permeate throughout the entire maze of Trajan's Vaults...

'IT CAN'T BE... SURELY NOT... BUT, THEY WERE LOST, THOUGHT DEAD LONG AGO... IT'S THEM... IT'S REALLY THEM... IT'S BASS AND BLACKMORE... THE FATHERS HAVE RETURNED TO US... THE LEGENDS ARE ALIVE!'

Chapter 15

'A Harsh Reality.'

Upon passing through the tessellating stable of glass boxes, they entered a much larger, open-plan space that was furnished with a great many more desks, each one bearing 'flat' typewriting machines and 'magic' screens similar to those in each of the glass rooms they passed, and devices which Blackmore perceived to be telephones.

Stepping into this area, both Bass and Blackmore became instantly transfixed by a plethora of wondrous sights that confronted them on the large facing wall.

Several moving pictures depicted instantly recognisable locations from all over the world, the most striking of which were of London, the Houses of Parliament, Tower Bridge, Buckingham Palace and other prominent landmarks throughout the city, each one adorned with similar red banners and flags bearing the identical 'sauastika' emblem which, when viewed in this context, appeared to imply that a more sinister, even perhaps inherently evil, regime had in some way taken control of the sovereign isles.

Shortly after their initial wonderment with regards to their somewhat impromptu introduction to advanced twenty-first century technology had at least in some small part subsided, Bass and Blackmore became aware that the entire area in which they now stood, save for the hum of electrified cyber-chatter and the subtle buzzing of muted cell-phones, had fallen into a deathly, attentive silence.

Aston elected to pause for a few seconds before breaking the unnaturally prompted hush himself...

"Everyone, pay very close attention. It is my very great privilege to introduce you all to the founding fathers of the 'League of Ghosts': Colonel James Bartholomew Bass and Colonel Alan Tiberius Blackmore."

Aston's revelation prompted sharp intakes of breath and murmurs of stunned disbelief among the assembled group...

'GOD SAVE US... 'IT IS THEM... BASS AND BLACKMORE... THE FATHERS HAVE FINALLY RETURNED... THE LEGENDS HAVE COME HOME!'

"Colleagues, I implore you, listen to me. Please... allow our brothers the time they require in order to gather their thoughts and to settle into their new surroundings. Then, I am certain that all of our questions will be answered, all of our curiosity and remaining doubts satisfied. Please, friends, give the founding fathers of our league time to recoup both addled wits and dissipated strength."

Adopting the initiative, Aston proceeded to lead the way through an avenue of outstretched hands, offered by the group in a gesture of welcome and friendship, or perhaps in some cases to convince themselves that the physical reality of this most unlikely of scenarios was in fact a legitimate truth, the two detectives were directed towards the welcomed sanctuary of their old library.

Instinctively taking their customary seats on three of the seventeen high-backed oak chairs that were set equidistantly around the large, round, highly polished wooden table, Aston, Bass and Blackmore proceeded to re-acquaint themselves whilst partaking of the vices that constituted their favourite Italian Del Vecchio brandy, Rajah brand cigars for Bass and several pipes of Hindu Shag tobacco for Blackmore.

CHAPTER 15

Curiously, Bass chose not to holster his weapon, but rather place it onto the table directly in front of him: a blatant, passively aggressive action that did not go unnoticed by a somewhat perturbed Blackmore.

Wishing not to openly dwell on his puzzlement for the present, Blackmore chose to momentarily divert his thought process towards the more agreeable creature comforts that he was now enjoying...

"Ah, how one misses the simple vices afforded to satisfy oneself, if only for one fleeting, precious moment," he sighed as he drained his second large tumbler of brandy in one grateful gulp, helped himself to a third and proceeded to blow perfectly formed rings of white pipe smoke into the air, still unable to erase the sight, and the potential intent, of the Schofield revolver belonging to Bass still placed provocatively on the table.

Satisfied that the necessary pleasantries of cordial re-acquaintance had been duly and satisfactorily realised, Aston took it upon himself to revert the conversation towards more pressing concerns...

"Gentlemen, if we now may address the matter of your de-brief. I am elated that you are both here, and most importantly, rude of both mind and health. The fact that you were lost to us for so long, thought slain during the assault upon the State Model Prison so many years ago..."

"'Slain... So many long years ago, you say?" interjected Bass...

Aston sat forward on the very edge of his seat, his back ramrod straight, as he countered the query posed by Bass with an inquiry of his own...

"What specific details do you recall of your recent past experience, James, prior to your arrival at Traitor's Gate this afternoon?"

Bass pondered for a moment before offering his answer, surmising that the response he would receive would, in all probability, offer not the slightest morsel of discernible comfort, nor would it present an immediately viable explanation as to their sudden appearance in this, thus far, perplexing future that already, in so many ways, had presented to the pair of marginally re-animated detectives a troubling aura of unease and contradiction...

"Tiberius, myself, Marcus Jackson and a Roman centurion named Lucius Sura, accompanied by a small supporting unit of Royal Engineers, were engaged in direct conflict within the central prison complex with both Boer militia and an unexpectedly sizeable cohort of 'Black Guard'...

"Our mandate, as you are no doubt well aware, was to secure the liberty of Churchill from the unwanted attention of 'The Architect' who had, utilising manipulative traits known only to himself, coerced the Boer authorities into relinquishing custody of this greatest and most coveted prize directly into his grateful charge...

"It transpired, during a particularly fierce argument in which I found myself engaged with a burly and somewhat irked 'Black Guard' Captain, an argument which, incidentally and I'm sorry to say for him he lost, that I caught a glimpse directly into the eyes of 'The Architect'."

Bass paused for a few seconds in order to take a long pull on his 'Rajah' cigar, allowing the smoke to intrude deep into his lungs before expertly forming his customarily impressive array of grey rings in the air, as though he were continuing his oration by utilising the silent smoke signal code as used to great effect by the native American Plains Indians.

"They were the eyes of supreme confidence, which afforded one the distinct impression of arrogant self-satisfaction and gave grave indication of one single, disconcerting certainty: that he was about to reap the ultimate reward of his final, fatal victory."

Blackmore, who up to this moment had contributed very little to the conversation, continued the thread allowing barely a pause for breath...

"The moment I was aware that we had begun to 'shift', I swear that some form of subliminal contact between myself and 'The Architect' took place."

CHAPTER 15

"Just as it was for myself, Tiberius; as though he were speaking to me directly," added Bass...

"...and, in that instance, as our helplessness became apparent to him, his message, a shard of damning truth, somehow empathically forced upon the consciousnesses of ones who had knowingly failed at their moment of triumph, not only their man, but quite possibly also the future freedom of the entire human race...

"As our minds joined, I distinctly sensed him impart...

'I cast you now deep into the vortex, my worthy opponents, where time has no meaning, and where torment has no end. A desolate place where your achievements, your families, your friends, your very lives have never existed as you remember them in this your final moment; your futures will be forever ensnared within the cascading maelstrom that is the unbounded temporal nexus of the fourth dimension...

...I now bid a fond farewell to my ever-tenacious adversaries of old and hope never again to lay these eyes upon either of your faces.'

Aston listened with great intent as Bass and Blackmore each took turns to recount the final, fatal few seconds of their cataclysmic confrontation with 'The Architect'...

"Pontius, but a short time ago, you alluded to the suggestion that we were 'lost' to you... for so long. Exactly, how long?"

Once again, Aston paused for what appeared to be an inordinate period of time prior to offering his considered answer, realising that his response would, at first, prove difficult for his two old friends to comprehend...

"Your assault on the State Model Prison took place on December 12th 1899. Today's date is March 15th 2022. You have been lost to us, within the maelstrom of the temporal vortex, for more than 122 years."

Following a further lengthy pause, during which both Bass and Blackmore reflected upon the startling revelation imparted by Aston, Blackmore raised his right index finger sharply in order to silence his equally inquisitive comrade, thus affording himself the opportunity of first response...

"Of course, the perpetrator of this grand deception could only have been 'The Architect'. In some way, he was able to manipulate the natural function of our portkeys and in so doing, cast us into oblivion."

"Precisely, Tiberius," was Aston's immediate reply...

"One of the great privileges afforded the 13th Meister is the ability to wilfully disrupt every temporal 'shift' undertaken by all T.E.A. agents, at any time, under a given premise...

"A great power, either to be used wisely and in context with the ancient laws upheld for centuries by the Council of 13, or alternatively to be manipulated unscrupulously by a malevolent anomaly."

Aware that a further enquiry needed to be made regarding this matter, Blackmore wasted little time...

"Are we then to understand that 'The Architect' holds in his grasp a method whereby not only is he able to preclude the temporal intentions of any one agent, he too has the ability to imprison that agent for an indefinite period within the infinite confines of the vortex?"

"So it would appear, Tiberius. For many years after your disappearances and prior to the true ramifications of what proved to be your exile were fully comprehended, 'The Architect' was able to access and manipulate all portkey activity at will, resulting in the consignment of a good many active T.E.A. agents to a fate equal to that of your own...

"Eventually, after extensive, painstaking labour on the part of our brilliant technicians, we were able to formulate a complex coding system made up of in excess of a billion possible combinations which is regularly rotated in order for our system to remain secure...

"This technological breakthrough of unprecedented importance enabled us to wrest control of our portkeys from 'The Architect' and begin to use them once more with supreme confidence within the usual secure parameters of safety that their original function intended."

CHAPTER 15

At the precise moment when a pair of familiar faces from two lifetimes long past entered the library, Bass posed a most pertinent question, the answer to which became momentarily delayed as firstly fond greetings were exchanged between old friends, and then the conversation was dominated by Aston for a time as he offered an in-depth briefing appertaining to the rise of fascism, firstly as it cut an unchallenged swathe across Europe, and then how it was manipulated by unscrupulous means to eventually conquer and subjugate the free world...

"What became of Churchill?"

Marcus Jackson greeted both of his old comrades with a hearty bear hug apiece as he imparted emphatically...

"James, Tiberius, my dearest friends; I had given up all hope long ago of ever laying eyes upon your dour, menacing features again. My heart is enraptured by your return, and my confidence that we shall now be able to vanquish the Nazi spectre that has blighted our shores, and indeed our world, for so long is in this moment instantly restored."

"Nazi spectre, you say, Marcus?" enquired Bass of his now somewhat emotional colleague as he merely nodded once to acknowledge the presence of a smiling Lucius Sura, who reciprocated the tepid Bass greeting with a single, cordial nod of his own, directed towards both of the detectives, as he took a seat at the great oak round table of King Arthur.

Gesturing for Jackson to cease his intended briefing and for him to be seated beside Sura, Aston addressed both Bass and Blackmore directly...

"Since the time of your disappearance, the world endured the almost cataclysmic repercussions brought about by the onset of two World Wars during which horrific conflict divided and decimated entire countries across all continents of the globe...

"Populations which had previously thought themselves brothers and sisters fought each other over depreciating political and social issues; petty differences that once might have been settled amicably over time in the highest echelons of government office were in some fashion manipulated and managed beyond the remit of capable diplomats into what was ultimately to manifest into an unassailable empire that was built upon the foundations of total, dictatorial rule to be overseen by a dominant, genetically perfect race of super beings...

"A fascist autocracy that used fear as its key component in maintaining a balanced, subservient social order...

"The First World War, between the years late August 1914 to late November 1918, began in principle soon after the assassination of the Austro-Hungarian heir Archduke Franz Ferdinand by a rogue Bosnian Serb Yugoslav nationalist...

"Unable to placate an expectedly incensed Austrian government, the Serbian authorities were left with little choice but to prepare for war with Austria, a war that would inevitably destabilise the network alliances between the European countries and exacerbate their already tenuous political relationships, thus fundamentally dividing Europe into two factions that would stand against each other: the allies of the Triple Entente consisting of France, Russia and Britain, and the Triple Alliance consisting of Germany, Austria and Hungary...

"An escalating chain of catastrophic events, and the continued stalemate of a political impasse throughout Europe, prompted more countries worldwide to take opposing sides and fuel the inferno that had become referred to as the Great War, or the 'War to end all Wars'...

"This horrifically brutal conflict ground on relentlessly for five long years, responsible for the loss of an estimated forty million lives in total...

"As if to compound this catastrophe on a world scale still further, a Spanish flu pandemic proceeded to spread a black cloak of death over an already decimated world population, exacerbating this total and the catastrophic effect of the conflict upon the world's infrastructure substantially...

"With its allies defeated, and its own infrastructure both socially and politically in turmoil, Germany finally signed an armistice on November 11th, 1918 and so, in effect, ended the First World War."

"You alluded to the fact that there were two World Wars fought, Pontius," remarked Blackmore who, along with Bass, had been listening intently to every word of the brief account being presented for their information by Aston of a particularly turbulent period in Earth's history...

"Might one assume, then, that judging by what little we have witnessed of the emblems that adorn major landmarks throughout our capital city, that a new allied coalition formed, perhaps some years after the Great War ended, failed to suppress an even more potent threat?"

"Indeed, Tiberius," continued Aston...

"Following the total collapse of the German government and its entire infrastructure post-war, a new form of totalitarian government arose from the ashes which presented a single policy that dictated all aspects of life be governed exclusively by the state...

"Between the years 1933 and 1945, what the world would come to know as the Nazi Party rose to absolute power in Germany under the leadership of Adolf Hitler. A gifted, influential orator and a decorated veteran of the First World War, his rise to the pinnacle of prominence from out of the eternally festering and dangerously unstable cauldron of post-war European politics was proved nothing short of meteoric...

"By 1933, after staging an attempted coup, which on this occasion was doomed to failure, Hitler was arrested by the ruling government and spent a year in prison...

"Upon his release and undeterred by his incarceration, he continued to build upon his vision of a totalitarian state and even though the

Nazi Party held no clear majority of seats in the German parliament, Hitler had been appointed Chancellor on the recommendation of his influential supporters and was afforded the opportunity he had craved for so long to sow the seeds of his ultimate vision by first implementing a most severe foreign policy...

"On September 1st, 1939, Hitler's re-equipped and fully re-vitalised 'Wehrmacht' invaded Poland, thus forcing allies Britain and France to declare war on Germany...

"As 1941 dawned, the relentless Nazi war machine proceeded first to dominate, then mercilessly crush all allied forces sent against it, and to blacken the landscape of Europe into a barren wasteland by implementing its horrifying 'scorched earth' tactic...

"Satisfied that a vanquished and totally subjugated Europe posed no further threat to his ambitions of global domination, Hitler shifted his focus and the attention of his all-conquering 'Wehrmacht' towards the east, where Russia was soon to fall under the ever expanding, impenetrable shroud of the rapidly burgeoning Nazi empire."

Adopting a somewhat perplexed tone, Bass enquired...

"But should not the Americans' participation at this critical stage of the war have been a formality?"

"One might assume so, James, but at this juncture Europe and the remainder of the free world each experienced the catastrophic effects that a major alteration to the intended timeline would undoubtedly cause...

"In May 1940, what remained of the British Expeditionary Force in Europe had been forced into a desperate retreat until, beaten and exhausted, they were contained by superior German forces on the beaches of the Northern French town of Dunkirk...

"Here, in what had been transformed by the incessant ravages of battle from an idyllic northern French coastline into a living hell on earth, the historical texts regarding the history of this particular timeline inform us that, rather than halting their advance upon the beleaguered and poorly armed British soldiers, as should have been the case, and now separated from their vanquished French and Belgian allies by forces belonging to the German army group B, the bedraggled survivors of the British Expeditionary Force were mercilessly ground deep down into the bloody sands of Dunkirk by the merciless vanguard of the unassailably advancing 'Wehrmacht'...

"As a consequence of their heavy defeat in Europe, the allies, unable to offer reinforcements in support of the African campaign, swiftly capitulated on that continent also."

"As for any potential involvement on the part of the Americans, with what little remained of the allied resistance all but vanquished, Hitler was able to consolidate his now supreme command of the war at sea by strengthening both his 'Kriegsmarine' (navy) and his formidable U-boat fleet..."

"U-boat fleet?" enquired a puzzled Blackmore...

"Please forgive me, Tiberius, underwater boat; a remarkable, heavily armed craft able to travel at great velocities and for long distances deep below the ocean surface, and capable of inflicting catastrophic damage onto the unprotected hulls of both the allied Navy and commercial shipping fleets, the latter upon whose unmolested supply runs were vital to the continued success of the combined European war effort."

"Ah, of course, Tiberius and myself happened upon such a craft during the course of this mission. A truly remarkable vessel, endowed with identical capabilities to the ones which you allude, Pontius; the name given to this mechanical serpent was 'Leviathan'," imparted Bass...

"So, 'Leviathan' is not the stuff of legend concocted in many a rum-addled mariner's mind of many years past to the present day!" exclaimed Aston as he raised himself sharply from his seat, his large palms slapping the table top with considerable force, denoting to all those assembled with whom he was well acquainted a most uncharacteristic demeanour that had shifted alarmingly from that of his usual controlled logic to one of a highly agitated, irrational state which bordered on mild hysteria.

None of the surprised group was more aware of Aston's erratic outburst, however, than the now extremely suspicious Bass, whose sensitive lycanthrope nostrils twitched upon detecting a rogue pheromone emanating from deep within his old friend...

'How can it be that the rancid stench of malevolent evil permeates from every perspiring pore of your skin, Pontius?'

"Of course, of course, how remiss of me," retorted a profusely perspiring, highly agitated Aston...

"Let us then explore a hypothetical theory: a wondrous vessel boasting the formidable combat prowess of 'Leviathan', coupled with an ability to traverse dimensions, gave the ship not only virtual invulnerability from prospective harm inflicted upon it by any existing vessel, but also aided in consolidating its legend throughout the myriad dimensions it freely terrorised, unchallenged in its spectral guise as the ghostly hell spawn from oceans deep."

Remembering that a key part of the history lesson was yet to be divulged, Blackmore intuitively offered his own brief appraisal as to the reason why he believed America had declined to enter the fray...

"So, the German 'Kriegsmarine', supported, no doubt, by 'Leviathan' and more vessels of a similar design and capability, was able to consolidate its superiority throughout all of the world's oceans...

"The introduction of American forces into the conflict at this juncture would, without question, have proved a pivotal moment in turning the hitherto disastrous fortunes of the allies towards eventual victory over the rampaging Nazi war machine."

His composure suitably regained, Aston persevered with delivering the remainder of his briefing...

CHAPTER 15

"As the history of this timeline recounts, soon after Japanese forces attacked and all but obliterated the American fleet as it lay berthed within the supposedly safe waters of Pearl Harbor, located just off the coast of Oahu, one of the Hawaiian islands in the Pacific, the now numerically enhanced fleet of the 'Kriegsmarine', supported by Hitler's U-boats and the superior speed and weaponry of 'Leviathan', were able to seal a resounding victory for the Reich in the Pacific within the matter of a few short weeks...

"On a subsequent note, as a result of the failure by the allies to quell the Nazi threat, with regards to the brilliant engineer, Professor Werner Von Braun, chiefly responsible for the design of a revolutionary rocket propulsion system; instead of defecting and pledging his great knowledge to both the allied war effort and to the future NASA space exploration programme, remained loyal to the Nazi cause, thus enabling Germany to complete its nuclear development experimentation ahead of the Americans by at least two months...

"This unhindered development of Von Braun's propulsion unit culminated with the deployment of the first nuclear weapons on the field of combat...

"A pair of tactical nuclear strikes were subsequently launched from the now Nazi occupied London, the first aimed directly at the heart of American democracy and the capital city of the free world, Washington DC, the second razing New York City and a great portion of the Eastern sea board to a radioactively contaminated wasteland...

"Both of these devastating, unanswerable strikes effectively ended the war and resulted in the unconditional surrender of the combined allied forces to the victorious Nazi Chancellor and soon to be proclaimed first 'Uber Fuhrer' of the world: Adolf Hitler."

An eerie silence befell the group as the truth dawned that the unimaginable fate suffered by all of Mankind was the direct consequence of a single seed that was sown over a hundred years ago.

None present were more aware of their own part in this disastrous turn of events than both Bass and Blackmore...

"Lord preserve us," imparted Blackmore as the full extent of the two detectives' complete failure became wholly apparent...

"Churchill: the catalyst upon whose survival the freedom of the free world was to depend. He did not survive the assault on the State Model Prison?"

"Alas, Tiberius, he did not," replied Aston gravely...

"Should the true course of history have followed its natural path, Winston Spencer Churchill was destined to escape from prison by purely conventional means, utilising a strategy known only to himself, his friend Captain Aylmer Haldane, a trusted subordinate, and a pair of anonymous personages whose identities history did not record...

"His subsequent rise through the ranks of British politics would have proved meteoric by conventional standards, earning him a formidable reputation as a compelling orator, his ability to motivate and instil vitality, confidence and belief in a morally defeated population becoming the stuff of folklore and legend...

"All of these remarkable qualities, coupled with his impressive raft of military experience were attributes that qualified him, when called upon by both a British government bankrupt of a motivational war time leader, and by the rudderless governments of allied Europe and Africa, to forge a clear pathway back from the abyss and onwards, battling against insurmountable odds towards the unlikeliest of victories against the tyrannical overrule of the German Wehrmacht...

"Alas, his intended destiny remained unfulfilled, his great potential to one day accept the mantle of the greatest Briton of all time never realised, all of history as it was destined to unfold altered irrevocably as a direct consequence of his young life ending prematurely on that fateful day in 1899..."

"So, Britain; indeed... the whole world..."

CHAPTER 15

Blackmore's retort was instantly curtailed by the insistent, troubled tone displayed by Aston...

"...the whole of the free world was subjugated in a very short period of time and accepted their lot as conquered nations, Tiberius, subjected to the unconditional rule implemented by the dominant Nazi world order..."

"Overseen by the 'Uber Fuhrer' Adolf Hitler until his death by natural causes in 1965, Adolf Siegfried Rolfus Hitler is the third descendant in a family line to inherit the title, the responsibilities and the privileges afforded to the 'Uber Fuhrer' of the known world."

"One senses an inevitable 'but'," alluded Bass somewhat prophetically as he casually lifted his Schofield revolver from where it lay on the table in front of him and provocatively cocked the hammer backwards and forwards whilst he spoke; 'click'... 'click'... 'click'...

"I would surmise that this 'Uber Fuhrer' is now, as has always been the case, a manipulated marionette, a subservient puppet retained as merely a redundant figurehead in order to appease an unaware public, answerable entirely to the dominant higher authority of 'The Architect'."

'click'... 'click'... 'click'...

Bass noticed that tiny beads of perspiration had begun to form on Aston's temples as he teasingly continued to toy with the hammer of his revolver...

'click'... 'click'... 'click'...

Ever watchful of his companion's curious actions, somewhat perplexed by the blatant obviousness of Bass' seemingly provocative behaviour towards a trusted brother, Blackmore chose, for the moment, to remain silent...

'click'... 'click'... 'click'...

His attention fixed upon the revolver being continuously cocked before his eyes, Aston attempted to maintain his composure...

'click'... 'click'... 'click'...

"Erm, yes, very astute reasoning, James. All of his ambitions realised, every one of his enemies either eradicated or subjugated to a level where their former ability to resist his influence could no longer pose either any effective, or tangible threat towards his now supremely dominant regime, his victory was complete, his diabolical kingdom here on Earth assured forever... PLEASE, JAMES, IS THAT INCESSANT TOYING WITH YOUR REVOLVER ABSOLUTELY NECESSARY?"

Having satisfied himself of an issue that had been troubling him for some time since his and Blackmore's arrival, Bass slammed his heavy old Schofield pistol down hard onto the table...

'THUNK!'

"Please excuse my 'incessant toying', Pontius," Bass imparted, a definite note of sarcasm present in his voice that was meant for all to hear...

"I had no idea my old revolver was causing such consternation with yourself, and amongst the ranks also it would seem. One can never be too prepared for any eventuality, does one agree?"

"Erm, yes, quite...," spluttered Aston, his heightened sense of anxiety with regards to the attitude displayed by Bass towards him, matched equally by the confusion and disbelief that permeated throughout the assembled group...

...All except Blackmore, whose mind as ever it was, remained impartially open, calm and focused upon speedily returning towards some semblance of sanity to what had begun as a routine briefing between reunited friends...

"So then, our failure alone is the sole cause of this... abomination?"

"Your failure was meticulously engineered, Tiberius," countered Aston immediately, nervously avoiding the piercing, cold glare fixed upon him by the now spectacle-free, raven-black eyes of Bass...

"By obtaining in some way exact copies of both yours and James' unique genetic profiles, 'The Architect' was able to use these key components, in conjunction with the immense power afforded to a 'Grand Meister' who once sat as one of the Council of 13, to access and control each of your portkeys in such a way that would result in you both being cast adrift within the infinite complexity of the temporal nexus for the past 122 years."

"Our portkeys were compromised?"

"They were, Tiberius, as were those of a good many T.E.A. agents, resulting in them being dispatched thankfully to moments in time from whence they were eventually able to return of their own volition...

"By the time it became clearly apparent that 'The Architect' was in command of such a formidable weapon, the ability of the 13 'Grand Meisters' to formulate and implement any form of effective contingency measures that would disrupt the abduction of our key agents had been all but diminished...

"The fact that our best, most capable agents were first identified, then systematically erased from existence on this timeline for a good long while provided 'The Architect' with the opportunity and ample time to exert total control over the rising Nazi regime and to cunningly manipulate its rapidly expanding influence into supporting his ultimate ambition to become master of the world."

"Why, then, were we not able to leave the temporal nexus of our own volition, as were the other agents...?"

"Ah, Tiberius, because you two, of all our operatives, weigh heaviest upon the mind of 'The Architect'. Ever since you first frustrated, and then curtailed, his strategy during the case of the Whitechapel Ripper murders all those years ago, the pair of you have always posed the greatest threat to him realising the successful culmination of his plans...

"Your indefatigable tenacity, your superior mental and physical strength plus your overwhelming desire to succeed when faced with a plethora of insurmountable difficulties are traits that he both truly admires, and fears, to the point of investing an inordinately substantial portion of his personal time and energy into devising ever more cunning and irreversible methods designed to not only frustrate your consistently valiant and creative attempts to thwart his plans, but also now it seems, to erase completely all traces of your ever having existed at all."

Turning towards Jackson and Sura, who had chosen to remain silent during this most extraordinary exchange between the three old warriors, Bass imparted bluntly...

"And what of you two fine gentlemen? What events transpired after both myself and Tiberius were taken down that might have hindered your resolve with regards to fulfilling our shared obligations?"

Marcus Jackson was swift to answer...

"Alas, we were able to achieve very little, my old friend. Amidst the unfolding mayhem of battle and destruction that served only to hamper our designated task immeasurably, I was severely wounded..."

"And my own portkey, too, was compromised, Colonel Bass," interjected Sura...

"I swear that as I sensed a 'shift' beginning, and my consciousness was enveloped momentarily in the familiar haze one experiences upon entering the temporal vortex, I witnessed Churchill tumble with the rubble of the collapsing gantry upon which he had stood, down into the raging inferno where once lay the foundations of the prison. He could not have survived such a fall."

"What was the duration of your absence from the fray, Roman?" persisted Bass venomously, the forthright bluntness of his tone showing little sign of abating...

"I, myself, along with most of our colleagues and the key commanders necessary to maintain the T.E.A. as a relevant, potent opponent of 'The Architect', were exiled into the nexus for 50 years; ample time for our cunning nemesis to steer his plan towards fruition, totally unhampered by the attentions of the one external agency that

CHAPTER 15

held at its disposal the means and the exceptional roster of personnel that could undoubtedly have thwarted that plan, and brought to an end, once and for all, his recurring threat towards the normal equilibrium of all things..."

"Regarding the matter to which Captain Aston alluded earlier, so indelibly was the lasting impression cast into his psyche by both yours, and Colonel Blackmore's quite exceptional methods of detection, so great became his unbridled admiration for your stubborn tenacity as you relentlessly implemented your seemingly inexhaustible raft of resourceful attributes towards the merciless quelling of whatever cruel injustice became the focus of your keen interest, even the intrinsically brilliant mind of possibly the most perfect criminal intellect ever conceived became overwhelmingly consumed by the one basic emotion that cripples the ability to engage logical thought processes and freezes the very core of one's soul into a petrified stupor... FEAR!"

"An effective weapon that he has seen fit to unleash on so many occasions in order to achieve his own ends; latterly, of course, to such devastatingly spectacular effect..."

"This simple, raw emotion consumes him to such a degree that he seeks to purge the human catalyst of this from his life forever; to, as you so rightly attest, Captain Aston, erase our two bold friends here, now miraculously returned to us, from existence."

Blackmore once more exhibited the razor-sharp keenness of his acumen with the insightfulness of his retort...

"And so, with our network of agents' portkeys compromised, thus neutralising their ability to resist, the future landscape of history was laid exposed and vulnerable, enabling 'The Architect' to create whatever vision for his twisted, dystopian future he chose..."

"So, the ripples that we began have, in no doubt, brought about this travesty...

"Now falls to James and me the responsibility of, in some way, devising a cunning ruse that will both rectify this great wrong and see an end, once and for all, to the reign of 'The Architect'."

Blackmore sat back in his chair and surveyed each of his companions' focused expressions, awaiting patiently in the protracted silence for the first response to his insightful, if somewhat professionally naïve, appraisal of the psychological profile belonging to their sociopathic nemesis.

Just as Blackmore had expected, Bass was the one to break the silence, with his characteristically forthright retort brief and customarily worded in his uniquely unnerving manner so as to leave no doubt in undecided minds as to the direction in which they must proceed, and of the unorthodox methods they must agree to deploy in order to satisfactorily achieve their goals...

"Fear! Rest assured, he will come to know fear intimately, for the true essence of fear is to both myself and Tiberius an old and familiar bedfellow...

"He will feel the tentacles of its ice-cold, intrusive caress as it infiltrates the guarded portals of his inner sanctum here in this time and proceeds to eradicate all levels of meaningful support affiliated to his twisted cause until, alone, afraid and desperate, the only foreseeable hope for salvation left for him will be to revisit that fateful day in Pretoria 122 years past and attempt to end, rather than merely exile, his accursed harbingers of doom forever..."

"Tiberius and I shall deliver unto 'The Architect' the very essence of fear incarnate. An ever-present, constricting terror that will plague his every waking hour until the moment his tortured, isolated, blackened soul is cast forever into the perpetual wilderness of the temporal nexus, where an eternity of torment and insanity awaits, to welcome its worthiest victim."

CHAPTER 15

***

So deeply were each of the group engrossed in their conversation that none of them was remotely aware of the appearance, towards the rear oval wall of the library, of a tall, cloaked figure whose raised hood shrouded from view a darkened, anonymous face.

Whilst becoming simultaneously aware of the stealthy intrusion in each of their peripheral visions, both Bass and Blackmore instinctively bore their revolvers to hand and levelled them directly towards the mysterious presence who, undeterred by this sudden display of controlled hostility, began to move towards the great oak table.

Raising both hands, fearlessly facing the pair of cocked pistols, the curious intruder proceeded to lower the hood of his long robe to reveal the grey bearded features of a man, whose ageing face bore the horrific scars of many a hostile encounter and, as the two detectives also observed, whose piercing blue eyes and impassive expression betrayed no outward sign of a man who was either tactically disadvantaged or who feared for his own immediate well-being in any way...

"Please, forgive my awkward intrusion, gentlemen. It was not my intention to cause consternation here. Nor was it my wish to announce myself in such a clumsy and informal manner, but my own agenda demands that this is the correct time for us to become acquainted...

"I am known across the ages by many names, but one such title above all others is more commonly used and familiar to some of you here seated I think; I am the 13th Meister, the gatekeeper to the temporal nexus of time."

Chapter 16

'The 13th Meister.'

"Never heard of you," was the dismissive answer proffered by Bass as he aimed his primed Schofield pistol directly at the forehead of the grey intruder...

"James, Tiberius, lower your weapons, if you please," came the earnest request from Aston...

"Rest assured that this man poses no threat to either our security or our personal well-being. On the contrary, his timely and welcomed contribution in aid of our cause might well be the catalyst we seek as we strive towards securing our lasting salvation from the suffocating grip of tyranny."

"Ah yes, of course; this gentleman is one of your council of 13 'Grand Meisters', one assumes, Pontius?" quizzed the ever-insightful Blackmore as both he and Bass reluctantly lowered their weapons as requested, Blackmore content to holster his LeMat out of sight below his heavy grey overcoat, but Bass, displaying yet another blatantly provocative act that did not pass unnoticed for a second time by the assembled group, chose to once more place his pistol strategically on the table directly in front of him, turning it slightly so as to make certain that the barrel pointed ominously towards Pontius Aston.

CHAPTER 16

Having swiftly been re-acquainted with his discomfort, Aston nonetheless attempted to ignore this latest gesture of flagrant provocation by addressing the observation made by Blackmore, whilst simultaneously embracing the grey stranger warmly as he would any returning long-estranged brother...

"That he is, Tiberius. But let us allow our esteemed guest a moment to introduce himself, and then perhaps to speak of the invaluable worth that he offers with regards to aiding us in planning the architecture of our redemption."

"Thank you, Pontius, my fellow Meister. The name with which I began life in the year 1070 AD is Hugues de Payens. Born into French nobility, I was later instrumental in founding the Order of the Temple, more commonly known as The Knights Templar, 20 years after the first crusade, in order to protect the passage of European pilgrims, who set forth on the road to Jerusalem, from brigands and cut-throats..."

"You are, then, a Templar?" enquired Blackmore...

"I am, sir, the first Templar knight of the old order, the first Grand Master of the order of The Knights Templar."

"Then explain, if it pleases you, your obvious close association to Pontius."

De Payens seated himself at the table...

"My tenure as the first Templar Grand Master came to an end when official documentation of my death was submitted in the year 1136, though..."

"Though your death was fabricated so as to enable your seamless recruitment to sit at the table of 13 'Grand Meisters', and so become an integral cog in the machinery of the Time Enforcement Agency..."

"An appointment of truly inspired genius on the part of Pontius Aston, not merely upon the acquisition of your formidable military, historical and political acumen, but more importantly in enabling the 'Grand Meisters' to finally become sole custodians of the many priceless historical artefacts held within the jealously guarded coffers of your former esoteric brotherhood; the Arc of the Covenant, the nails and remaining timber belonging to the True Cross upon which Christ was crucified, the Spear of Destiny, the Turin Shroud, the Golden Fleece of Colchis, Excalibur, the Holy Grail, the lost gospel written by Jesus himself, and the Round Table of King Arthur, around which our league has convened for so many years; all now ensconced here, deep within the catacombs of Trajan's Vaults under the watchful patronage of 'The League of Ghosts'."

"Impressive, Colonel Blackmore. Your keen insightfulness does you much credit," retorted an admiring de Payens instantly...

"All of these wondrous artefacts, their priceless intrinsic value as totemic icons alone, bore such significant importance that each one, regarded as a single talisman, would undoubtedly de-stabilise and call into question the entire doctrine of religious dogma and the validity of ancient theological and historical texts across all known beliefs and cultures throughout the ages, and therefore could no longer be permitted to remain in the care of a single fragile order."

"So, Arthur's legendary quest for the Holy Grail was authentic, as was Jason's search for the Golden Fleece of Colchis?"

Brother de Payens simply nodded his affirmation to Blackmore's enquiry, allowing Aston the opportunity to speak...

"As you are aware, gentlemen, at any one time just 12 of the 13 'Grand Meisters' are summoned to council. The serving 13th Meister, in this instance, Brother de Payens, sits alone in vigil as sole guardian of the physical portal that exists here on Earth which allows access directly into the temporal nexus, the infinite maelstrom of time from which there is no escape, unless..."

"Forgive me, Pontius, unless the guardian grants freedom to the hapless soul cast adrift within the vortex," interceded de Payens whilst first addressing Bass and Blackmore directly...

"It was during a moment of meditation, as I searched the eternal chaos of the abyss through the eyes of the all-seeing 'Skull of the Ageless One', that I became aware of the resourceful attributes belonging to each of you that would prove pivotal in repairing a catastrophic rift that had appeared in the timeline, threatening to unbalance the correct order of all things...

"It was I who found you both, imprisoned in mindless stasis within an impregnable temporal prison without hope of escape, and it was I who returned you to aid our cause once more."

Now addressing the whole group, de Payens concluded...

"Now finally reunited with the fathers of the 'League', together as one entity at last, I feel confident that we are at last readily equipped to conceive a cunning ruse that will repair that which should never have been broken, and ultimately imprison 'The Architect' within the maelstrom of the temporal vortex for all eternity."

"Then mine and Tiberius' primary goal here in this century is made abundantly clear," afforded Bass in earnest...

"We must look to instigate the immediate and unequivocal destabilisation and subsequent dissolution of the entire Nazi regime. We shall endeavour to infiltrate its highest echelons and exterminate with extreme prejudice and without exception every single party member bearing influence, including all of those who offer fealty towards, or support, any government or institution that pledges loyalty unto their cause."

Brother de Payens continued...

"Agreed, Colonel Bass. An extreme, though necessary strategy that culminates in the isolation of 'The Architect' to the point where he perceives there to remain but one place of safety to which he might abscond in order to once more evade our insistent attentions...

"I have no doubt that he will make good his attempt to enter the temporal nexus through its physical portal here on Earth, for only if a

'Grand Meister', who once was tasked to guard the portal himself, enters at will, may that person be in command of their passage throughout the complexities of the nexus."

"A 'GRAND MEISTER' WHO... 'THE ARCHITECT' ONCE HELD THE TITLE AND COMMANDED THE POWER AFFORDED THE 13TH MEISTER!"

"That he did, Colonel Blackmore, and damn his everlasting black soul ten thousand-fold to the hereafter for debasing the hallowed privilege of office to which, in all innocence and with good faith intended, he was gladly exalted by those of us who should have known better," conceded de Payens ruefully, unbeknownst to himself betraying for a brief moment, to experienced observant eyes, an aura almost approximating a contrite admission of guilt...

Following a protracted silence, de Payens sharply raised his right index finger to his lips in an attempt to quell the inevitable deluge of enquiries he anticipated would surely emanate from all quarters...

"In order to match, and then best, this quite extraordinarily brilliant intellect, you must first understand something of the unequivocally remarkable ethos that encapsulates the character belonging to the man himself, and a portion of what warped desire compelled this unashamedly sociopathic, flawed genius relentlessly onwards towards his own perceived appointment with destiny."

Chapter 17

'An Appointment with Destiny' ('The Rise of 'The Architect.')

"Might one assume, then, that 'The Architect' is either a title inherited from the sometimes imaginative, but all too often grindingly tedious proclivities which the media possesses? An annoying habit frequently and unashamedly displayed when referring publicly to a serially offending criminal bearing high profile, or perhaps alternatively an egotistical self-proclamation to what the man himself perceives to be a world in waiting to benefit from his benevolent patronage and receive in return the rapturous rewards and unwavering fealty bestowed upon him in return for their doting obedience."

"Very much the latter, I would probably surmise, Brother de Payens, when considering the self-grandiose, arrogant and outwardly sociopathic tendencies often frequently displayed by the man," interjected Aston, the beads of perspiration returned to his greying temples and the greatly enhanced beating of his heart, both uncharacteristic signs of extreme anxiety that had not gone unnoticed by the extraordinarily keen senses of Bass...

"I would concur, Pontius. The pathologically warped, yet brilliantly refined, supremely balanced intellect that continues to frustratingly elude our minute attentions was conceived sometime in the mid-seventeenth century...

"Born into a wealthy family, bearing a long and illustrious history of service at the highest level of command within the Royal Navy, high expectations abounded that the young Artemis Granville de Courcy would honour the generations-old family tradition and build a successful naval career for himself...

"A youthful de Courcy rose at an astonishingly brisk gallop through the ratings, excelling in all areas of advanced seamanship and tactical seaborne warfare aboard several high-profile war ships commissioned to the fleet, whose supreme commander at that time was the great Admiral Lord Horatio Nelson...

"Captain Artemis Granville de Courcy was to consolidate his legendary reputation as the master tactician who held Nelson's ear and stood by his great friend on many glorious occasions, and was privately vaunted by his many subordinates, supporters and peers alike for his invaluable contributions to both planning, and even executing, many of the acclaimed victories accredited to the great Admiral himself...

"Etched forever into the folklore of the service, several of his revolutionary tactical manoeuvres conceived to assure resounding victory for the many campaigns that he commanded, still remain required areas of study on the roster of renowned naval institutions throughout the world to this day...

"Whilst never officially proved to be anything other than the opportunistic killing shot fired by a French marine stationed high in the rigging of an adjacent man-o-war at the height of the Battle of Trafalgar, it was in fact the treacherous and already dangerously ambitious de Courcy himself who arranged for the Gallic sniper to fire the fatal round into the chest of Nelson at an appointed time, thus exerting his subliminal influence upon weaker minds in prompting the admiralty, oblivious of his heinous crime, to promote its next prime candidate to

CHAPTER 17

the rank of Admiral in charge of the mightiest naval fleet on Earth, albeit for but a short period of time."

"Promoted to Admiral, for but a short period of time you say, de Payens?" queried Blackmore...

"Yes, Colonel. By this time, his quite extraordinary achievements had not gone unnoticed by the ever-watchful eyes of the 'Grand Meisters'....

"Identified not only as a prime candidate for consideration, but potentially as the finest candidate ever to be selected to undergo the rigorous induction process and the intense training programme that would follow in order for the successful candidate to earn the right of acceptance into the agency; a process which promised much personal discomfort, not unfamiliar to yourself, to Colonel Bass or to Captain Sura, I think."

Whilst delivering his assertive speech, de Payens fixed his steely grey gaze upon Bass, Blackmore and Sura, each of whom in turn offered a silent nod of affirmation, recounting privately to himself the physical and mental hardships they had endured whilst experiencing their own personal hell during the rigorous induction process...

"The initial observations made by the 'Grand Meisters' were proved to be correct; those of a brilliant prodigy who spectacularly surpassed expectations in every conceivable fashion. In a relatively short period of time, serving as one of the 12 council members, Admiral de Courcy elevated himself into prime contention to be considered for the coveted title of 13th Meister and Guardian of the Temporal Nexus."

"Might one assume then that de Courcy did indeed accept the mantle of 13th Meister?" enquired a transfixed Blackmore...

"Yes, Colonel. Artemis, already displaying a remarkably robust constitution with regards to absorbing both the complex library of knowledge and developing the strict mental discipline required for a candidate to be even considered for such a unique and powerful position, was, unbeknown to the council of 12, already undergoing a disconcerting metamorphosis from the gifted, world-renowned naval officer who had first courted the interest of the Council so spectacularly, into the sociopathic arch-villain mastermind that we now identify by his self-administered sobriquet of 'The Architect'.

"His voracious appetite for knowledge, bridled with his understanding of the great mental discipline required in order to harness and control the immense power required when overseeing the safe passage of all T.E.A. agents through the unpredictable complexity of the temporal nexus as they went about their business in service to the agency, was matched only by a dark personal desire which was festering deep within his ever more blackening soul...

"As a result of the unanimously favourable vote cast by the council of 12, myself included, Admiral Artemis Granville de Courcy was appointed as 13th Meister and Guardian of the Nexus, inheriting with these auspicious titles the great power and knowledge required in order to access the portkeys of every temporal agent and, if so motivated to do so by whatever dark influence was soon to overwhelmingly consume his rational thought process, to use this incredible gift in order to sow the first virgin seeds that would, in time, lead to the fruition of his own evil plan."

"Never more so than regarding this case was the phrase 'absolute power corrupts, absolutely' more applicable. Not merely, then, a rogue temporal agent, nor even an estranged 'Grand Meister', but, even more disconcertingly, a former '13th Meister'...

"In what possible fashion, then, could one so privileged, one so brilliant and meticulously conditioned to accept the great responsibility of maintaining the equilibrium across all of time, become such a potentially unassailable weapon pledged to serve the forces of darkness that harbours such evil intent towards the Human Race to which he once so honourably and selflessly pledged his allegiance."

CHAPTER 17

The somewhat rhetorical question posed by de Payens remained unanswered. Instead, a lengthy period of silence ensued, following which, the grey Gatekeeper of Time resumed his speech...

"Also, of worthy note, at this time in his spectacularly advancing career, whilst engaging his extraordinary prowess as an engineer, de Courcy began formulating, in secret, his great vision for the planning, construction and inauguration of a fleet of revolutionary submersible vessels...

"Each one capable of travelling great distances at a time whilst submerged deep beneath the ocean surface at a fantastic rate of knots, these 'sub-marines' would carry on board an array of revolutionary armaments, with a view to each of the seven vessels belonging to the fleet designated to roam the seven great seas of the world...

"By the sheer terror of their formidable reputation, consolidated whilst threatening the security of the world's oceans throughout time, and heightened, somewhat fortuitously, to hysterical levels by the seafaring legends and ancient mariners' folklore left in their wake of countless attacks made upon shipping by giant, mythical serpents, these remarkable craft enhanced the already established invincibility of Hitler's 'Kriegsmarine' and reinforced his dominion over the war at sea."

"'Leviathan' is one of those ships?" enquired Blackmore...

"'Leviathan' was the first. Commissioned as the flagship to resemble a giant serpent and capable, as you are now aware, gentlemen, of 'shifting' through time, corroborating beyond all doubt the persistent claims from mariners attesting to the sighting of a monstrous, single-eyed serpent that had terrorised the shipping lanes and trade routes of the world's oceans for hundreds of years, feeding on the souls of any hapless seafarer who was unfortunate enough to cross its path."

The lengthy pause, that followed the revelatory speech given by Brother de Payens, was rudely curtailed by the intrusive buzz of a cell phone...

Chapter 18

'Family.'

"YES! I gave strict instruction that on no account was I to be interrupted unless... Excuse me, gentlemen, a pressing matter of some importance necessitates I honour this call."

A conspicuously agitated Aston rose from his seat and moved a few paces away from the table in order to proceed with his conversation in private, or so he imagined...

As he did so, Bass, Blackmore, Jackson, Sura and de Payens remained in reflective silence, stealing the occasional glance across the table in an attempt to gauge the blank, expressionless eyes belonging to a colleague that might betray the merest hint of a sign that would engage the necessary debate as to how they might proceed.

For the entire duration of Aston's conversation, however, Bass listened intently, his sensitive lycanthrope hearing able to decipher with ease the words that were being imparted...

'Yes, yes, it's true; de Payens, blast him to hell... located them within the nexus and brought them back.' 'No... nothing... Absolutely... I assure you, Master... yes, I am certain. It is too soon for them to be aware of any tangible details.' 'Yes... Yes, Master, rest assured that I will settle the matter personally.'

"Please accept my apologies, gentlemen, I..."

CHAPTER 18

'CRACK'... 'CRACK'... 'CRACK!'

Aston's attempted apology was unceremoniously curtailed by the loud, high-calibre discharge made by the three shots that emanated from the barrel of the Schofield revolver belonging to Bass that had been toyed with so provocatively, and then slammed with such threatening intent upon the table with its barrel pointing towards Aston. Customarily accurate in their selected trajectories, the first round impacting squarely into the centre of Aston's forehead, the second and third rounds grouped tightly together in his chest, all life was extinguished before Aston's body fell backwards onto the floor...

"HAVE YOU COMPLETELY TAKEN LEAVE OF YOUR SENSES!" exclaimed Blackmore aloud as instinct guided him to rapidly draw his LeMat revolver and level its primed barrel directly at the chest of his companion...

Anticipating the brief moment of unease that would surely follow such an act of blatant, seemingly senseless brutality, Bass calmly laid his pistol on the table and raised both his now empty hands above chest height.

Sura, meanwhile, his twin 'gladii' promptly unsheathed and adopting a posture that suggested an act of instant retribution, added incredulously...

"Whatever reasoning that could conceivably justify such an atrocity had better prove sound, Bass, or there must surely be but one consequence offered as just retribution for perpetrating such a heinous crime."

Remaining the epitome of serene composure, Bass proceeded to offer his appraisal of what had just occurred...

"Gentlemen, I will gladly and without offering meaningful retaliation, of which you are all aware I am more than capable of administering on a whim, yield to whatever justice you may deem fit recompense for such a crime, but hear me well as I assure you that whatever lies here dead before us is not the mortal remains of Pontius Aston."

"ARE YOU OUT OF YOUR MIND? How could you even begin to imagine that such a thing might be possible, let alone expect us all to believe that it is fact!" exclaimed an equally apoplectic Marcus Jackson.

Even amidst the tense atmosphere which now permeated the library, that had been enhanced considerably by the arrival of several Covert Special Forces operatives brandishing semi-automatic weapons, Bass lowered his hands and began to speak, offering no indication to any of those assembled that here was a man who had 'lost his mind'...

"Please, everyone, lower your weapons, for all the good they will serve you against a lycanthrope, and I shall endeavour to explain the treachery within our midst that necessitated my extreme response."

Looking instinctively towards Blackmore, possibly more for assurance rather than guidance, the entire group did as Bass requested and reluctantly lowered their weapons upon receiving a single nod of affirmation from the wily old Colonel.

Satisfied that a modicum of calm had been achieved, at least for the present, Bass began to deliver his remarkable supposition...

"Good. Now please, my friends, listen very carefully, for what I am about to suggest will, at first, seem as ludicrous a proposal to present in any logical sense as it may be an improbable peculiarity to even contemplate existing at all...

"The corpse that lies here at our feet is, in fact, an impostor, an almost exact doppelganger of our brother Pontius Aston, who, if my summation proves to be regrettably correct, languishes ensnared and helpless within the very same temporal prison from which both Tiberius and myself were recently liberated."

Blackmore answered, still bearing an agitated tone...

"A DOPPELGANGER! Even the astute deductive prowess of a detective bearing such a widely renowned reputation as your own could not possibly possess the intelligence, nor the acumen, that would justify committing such a spontaneous act of unbridled aggression against one of the Council of 13..."

"No, Tiberius, never could a justifiable decision to pursue what would appear to imply a seemingly impromptu act be sanctioned by the deductive prowess of a mortal man alone, non-cognisant to the opposite physical or forensic evidence, but consider perhaps the validity given to the testimony offered, based upon the richly enhanced senses of a lycanthrope."

All at once, Blackmore's mood turned from one of anxious, incandescent vexation to a lighter sensation of relief, even elation upon the realisation that the remarkable abilities belonging to his lycanthrope brother had once again proved a pertinent factor in revealing the machinations of a covert plot to infiltrate the once thought to be impregnable inner sanctum belonging to 'The League of Ghosts'...

Instinctively aware that Blackmore was sufficiently satisfied that trust placed in the validity of his abilities was a sound investment, Bass continued to explain precisely why he had decided to pursue his chosen strategy in such a doggedly stubborn manner towards its final, fatal conclusion...

"I was able to eavesdrop every word imparted by the Aston impostor as it spoke into its 'cellular telephone device' but a few moments ago. Its constant referral to the owner of a frustratingly familiar voice as 'Master', aligned with my sudden recognition of that voice as belonging to 'The Architect' himself, presented a final damning indictment of guilt."

"Would not the more prudent course of action have involved maintaining the impostor's ignorance regarding your knowledge of his... its existence, thus utilising its continued presence in some way to our advantage?" Blackmore offered, not unreasonably...

"Had the normal parameters of officially sanctioned protocol been adhered to, then yes, my old friend, your suggested recourse would, without question, have been the correct tactical strategy to employ, but alas, the extreme action that I chose to employ, though appearing to resemble nothing short of a wanton and seemingly random act of cold-blooded murder, was born out of necessity...

"When the 'The Architect' had been assured by the impostor that the initial reports he had received from his covert network of agents ensconced within our midst concerning our return were genuine, his order to the doppelganger was a simple one: 'ELIMINATE THEM ALL, NOW!'

"Had I not terminated the 'bogus' Aston in our midst, I fear that without delay the impostor might have alerted more 'sleeper' agents loyal to 'The Architect' who do indeed continue to operate covertly as we speak within these walls, and that it would be we, and not it, who lie upon the floor here deceased."

A further protracted silence was punctuated by Blackmore as he began to outline the genesis of an audacious plan...

"Remarkable, quite remarkable; if all that you purport is true, James, with regards to our inner sanctum being compromised, then we face not only the potential implosion of the infrastructure that supports 'The League of Ghosts', but also the very real possibility that the council of 13 may well be on the cusp of involuntarily relinquishing into the custody once more of 'The Architect', the great power that maintains the equilibrium of time itself...

"I see our immediate course as clear, gentlemen: we must root out and eradicate the infectious disease of treachery that infects our organisation from within...

"I propose that we announce the exposure of the Aston doppelganger to the entire staff and thereafter monitor all avenues of outbound communication...

CHAPTER 18

"If possible, secretly monitor every cell-phone and electrical device capable of relaying word and observe closely all exits in the event of an immediate desire for the guilty to abscond."

"Might one ask what action be taken against those proved to harbour treacherous intent towards our cause, Tiberius?" Jackson enquired pensively...

"Instant termination. No quarter nor reprieve offered, nor given," came the terse reply from Blackmore.

Bass interceded immediately...

"A decisive and necessary proposal, Tiberius, however, might one suggest erring towards caution before engaging our wrath...

"Consider this for a moment: though we must accept that 'The Architect' is now without doubt cognisant of mine and Tiberius' return, should he be made prematurely aware of our intentions his immediate recourse would almost certainly entail him cravenly absconding once more beyond the remit of our attentions into the secure embrace of the temporal nexus where a former 13th 'Grand Meister' could evade even the most meticulous and insistent scrutiny of even the current 13th 'Meister', Brother de Payens."

"A wise observation, James," conceded Blackmore as he turned his attention towards Marcus Jackson, whilst simultaneously retrieving and meticulously scrutinising the cracked glass screen of the cell-phone which the impostor had discarded as he fell...

"These quite extraordinary communication devices, Marcus. Might one assume that they are common property belonging to all persons of this century?"

Jackson nodded his affirmation...

"Could they be utilised in some fashion so as to, somehow, at the precise moment of our choosing, reveal to all persons herein that we possess intelligence appertaining to the existence of a major security breach of internal systems, and that we, too, are aware of those traitorous personnel who pledge loyalty to the Nazi regime?"

Jackson again nodded his affirmation whilst he offered his reply...

"Yes, indeed, Tiberius. A network-wide 'text' message may be sent to every operative's cell, with the identical message arriving simultaneously on all personal workstation screens."

"Have a care, Marcus. It is imperative that these 'text' messages be sent secretively, so as to court and coax the required response from our sleeping enemy within."

Whilst Jackson nodded his agreement to the request made by Blackmore, Bass took the opportunity to speak...

"It is imperative that we seek to learn all that we can from the corpse of this impostor, and I am able to suggest but one person that I would trust implicitly to perform a thorough post-mortem and to garner the relevant information that we require in order for us to fully understand this latest weapon sent to test us by our cunning enemy: my Connie; oh Marcus, please tell me that she is safe and well..."

Jackson first answered Bass, before turning his attention towards Blackmore...

"She is, my friend, as are Pandora and your kin, Tiberius. Each of your closest family remained in service to 'The League of Ghosts' after your disappearances. Pandora, Alanis and 'The Undertaker' became predominantly responsible for overseeing the affairs of 'The League' in the twilight embers of the 19th century and beyond for many years into the dawning of a new millennium."

"And what of my sweet Connie, Marcus?" came the understandably concerned enquiry from Bass...

"Connie fares well, James, and what is more, she is present, here in this century. Inaugurated into the service of the T.E.A., during the tenure of your absence, Connie has developed substantially her already considerable knowledge of surgical medicine and has proven instrumental in furthering the advancement of forensic science techniques. She too has remained an active agent affiliated to 'The League of Ghosts'.

"A coded message has been dispatched to the Whitechapel Hospital where, under the protection of a pseudonym, Professor Hildegard Bronwyn Trenwith, Connie gives regular seminars regarding the subject matter relating to her areas of expertise."

"Now, gentlemen, if I could ask you both to surrender your portkeys to Brother de Payens. He has been able to devise a method by which the unique melding of the symbiotic/mechanical matrix you each share with your portkeys may be adjusted so as to prevent a foreign third party from accessing them, so preventing such consternation from occurring ever again."

De Payens addressed Bass and Blackmore, his languidly impassive demeanour at first quarters diverting their attention from the fact that he was in possession of a supremely tempered intellect...

"It is also within the remit of my powers to bestow upon you both a privilege previously only granted to a member of the council. With just a thought, and a minute tinkering with your portkeys, you will each possess the ability to travel backwards and forwards in time and space to both a precise moment and an exact location of your choosing, from any fixed point in time."

Blackmore remained thoughtful for a moment before offering his response, all the while casting a wary eye towards Bass in the hope that his well-intended proclamation of gratitude on behalf of his friend did not appear to be a presumptuous error on his part...

"Though grateful to become the recipients of such a rare and precious gift, as I'm certain we both are, might one proffer the simple question: why us?"

De Payens wasted no time in delivering his measured answer...

"When our dear, momentarily absent friend, Pontius, brought the potential eligibility for induction into the T.E.A. of both yourself and Colonel Bass to the attention of the 'Grand Meisters', the ensuing vote cast in your favour by the council of 13 was overwhelmingly unanimous...

"As you are now aware, not since the induction, many years past, of one other, the one who we now identify as 'The Architect', had the general consensus of opinion between the 13 been so positively aligned in unanimous agreement as to the unequivocally great service the pair of you were capable of rendering in support of the perpetual fight against the constant threat of an all-encompassing evil arising from deep within our own house...

"Only now that you are restored to us, following all of the hardship and oppression suffered by the ensuing generations of humanity post-war, born out of a great wrong that should never have been, are we now truly on the periphery of reconciling our fractured alliances with the exiled leaders of our truly recognised authority, and at long last stand united and prepared to unleash upon the enemies of mankind the merciless retribution they so richly deserve...

"Let them finally understand the terror that has been unleashed by them so readily as a weapon of subjugation for so long, as the harbingers of our wrath go forth and let loose the quintessential anatomy of fear."

'Chapter 19

'The Anatomy of Fear.'

The arrival of Constance Bass coincided perfectly with the conclusion of Brother de Payens's speech. Upon entering the library, and her tear-misted eyes meeting the soulless black return gaze of her husband, Connie nevertheless suppressed the torrent of emotion she had long held to heart for a millennia over countless sweet reunions as they took each other in a loving embrace that neither of them had a desire to end...

"Oh James. The days and nights have been never-ending as I waited for this day of all days, this day of which I had convinced myself long ago would never dawn. My broken heart is mended once more."

"Connie, my sweet Connie. You remain the one thing in my life of true, untainted beauty; who radiates a guiding light upon my dark and complex existence, and draws me back from the ever-enticing beckoning of the eternal abyss...

"You are, as you have always been, my salvation; my only reason for being. I appeal with all of the humble pleas that may be tolerated by a contrite sinner to whatever god may choose to listen when I offer sincere thanks that you are safe and well...

"Please listen now, my love, as I make some attempt to elucidate the reason for our longest parting, and to what perilous ends both myself and Tiberius must once again endeavour towards in order to right the terrible wrong that compromised and stole the righteous and just course of history so many years ago."

Connie interjected and offered apology to her husband for having curtailed his speech prematurely. Nevertheless, her perceptiveness regarding the reason for his absence, and the unprecedented maelstrom of peril that both he and Blackmore must surely revisit, was a stark reminder to her admiring husband that hers was indeed an intellect of formidable standing...

"Forgive me, my husband. I was aware that 'The Architect' was, in some way, responsible for our parting, as I too accept that you and Tiberius must once more seek to champion the true course of justice, for I have always known, ever since your spirit became intertwined with that of the wolf, that one single, fateful moment in time would draw both you and your soul brother, Tiberius, towards your own epoch-defining appointment with destiny."

Finally parting from their long embrace, each of them satisfied that little more of discernible value was to be gained from pressing their initial conversation further, Bass proceeded to brief his wife of other relevant matters, particularly the manner in which her extensive surgical and forensic science skills might be put to immediate use...

"The moment that we returned, Connie, Pontius was the leader of our reception committee and yet, the thing that purported to be Pontius Aston proved to be an impostor; a doppelganger that in almost every fine detail resembled our dear brother."

"Your suggestion alludes to the fact that it was exact in 'almost every fine detail', James?" enquired Connie of her husband thoughtfully, her keen scientific mind preparing for the enticing possibility of a forensic puzzle forming...

"Yes, my love, almost; but alas for its creator, not the perfect facsimile he had anticipated which would successfully deceive all those with whom it interacted...

"Aside from the initial misgivings I experienced during our re-union, which at that moment I was at a loss to comprehend, my first sliver of good fortune appeared when I was able to overhear a conversation between the Aston impostor and the distinctly recognisable tones of 'The Architect' as he spoke into his cell-phone device..."

"I distinctly overheard the doppelganger as it made a pledge to its 'Master' that it proposed to 'take care of the matter personally', the 'matter' in question referring to the instant extermination of all those here present...

"At that precise moment, satisfied that foul treachery was afoot within our ranks and indeed brazenly standing personified directly before us, I shot the impostor dead."

Connie found herself momentarily incensed, almost incandescent before immediately regaining her composure and continuing along her logical course of enquiry...

"BASED UPON THE EVIDENCE OF AN EAVESDROPPED CONVERSATION YOU OVERHEARD?... WHAT IF PONTIUS HAD BEEN?... JAMES... What if Pontius was in fact engineering a cunning subterfuge designed to infiltrate the Nazi high command, perhaps even to gain access into the sanctified enclave of 'The Architect' himself?"

"The possibility of such subterfuge had occurred, Connie, but please understand. Regarding a detail to which I alluded earlier; at the moment of our reunion with the thing that purported to be Pontius Aston, my senses became alerted immediately to several inconsistencies regarding the behavioural patterns belonging to the impostor, perhaps the most indicative of all its distinctive scent, or, to be more specific, mixture of scents."

Without pausing to offer his wife the opportunity she craved to air her thoughts, Bass continued...

"Please, indulge me a moment longer, Connie. Though the keen instincts and heightened senses of a lycanthrope would, in all probability, be regarded inadmissible as evidence to whatever judicial authority we recognise, perhaps as a plausible alternative to a reliance on the instincts of nature's folly, a thorough post-mortem conducted by one possessing such renowned credentials as your own might suffice?"

Connie took both of her husband's battle-gnarled hands in her own and gazed tenderly into his eyes…

"The credibility of any evidence presented to me as prima-facia by way of your extraordinary lycanthropic instincts would satisfy me, my love…

"However, for us to understand intimately this latest weapon that our wily nemesis has engineered and set against us, I will do as you suggest and set to work at once. The results of my preliminary examination will be forthcoming within the hour."

***

"I shall deliver tidings personally to Pandora in 1898 of your wellbeing and offer detailed report of what your immediate obligations entail, before you seek to return home yourself, Tiberius."

Waiving the onset of Blackmore's inevitable protestations, Marcus Jackson continued…

"Mine is a familiar presence to Pandora, Tiberius. Though your heart beckons you towards a fond reunion, you must remain here and endeavour to focus your undivided attention in this century upon first, the destabilisation of the Nazi regime, and then, setting to the task of forcing 'The Architect' towards playing one final endgame."

Though initially reluctant to acknowledge that the sound reasoning of his friend was wise, Blackmore conceded that Jackson's was a major role to play in the ensuing proceedings, if their audacious strategy was to stand even the remotest likelihood of being nurtured towards a satisfactory conclusion...

"Go now then, Marcus. God speed to you and please convey all of my fondest love to Pandora, Alanis and Don. Speak this simple message directly to their ears only...

'The wolves remain in the fold.'

"...These words alone, spoken in this context, will suffice and assure them of our safety, and that our resolve towards fulfilling our designated orders remains true and on task."

Waiting until Jackson had departed the library, Bass then began in earnest to address the remainder of the group...

"Gentlemen, I propose that Tiberius and I alone attempt to infiltrate the inner sanctum of Nazi high command where we shall proceed, in our own inimitable fashion, to exterminate, with extreme prejudice, all high-ranking personnel...

"An audacious attritional act of this magnitude will not be expected and, before this vile infestation musters the notion to retaliate, our intended mandate to totally eradicate its capability to govern will have been achieved, sending a stark message to 'The Architect' that the accursed harbingers of his doom have returned."

Directing his attention first towards Hugues de Payens, then, following a brief intercedence by the 13th Meister himself, the C.S.F. Commander, whose stocky gait appeared vaguely familiar to him, Bass continued...

"Brother de Payens, your presence will best serve our purpose by returning to your place of vigil at the entrance into the temporal nexus where, should the initial phase of our proposed strategy prove successful, we shall deliver 'The Architect' so as the 13th Meister may administer the sentence of banishment into the temporal abyss for eternity."

Brother de Payens eyed Bass thoughtfully...

"An admirably proposed, exceedingly audacious endgame solution, Colonel Bass, but may one enquire by what miraculous means 'The Architect' would be compelled to even contemplate attending the sacred place of vigil at the appointed moment of your choosing?"

"Only at the precise second when realisation dawns that but a single course of action remains available for him to contemplate, that of erasing from existence the 13th Meister, the one true hope for the salvation of humanity...

"At that precise moment, as he stands before the portal of the temporal nexus and on the cusp of inheriting the power of the 13th Meister once more, only then, upon casting eye once more upon the returned, accursed usurpers of his empire, will he finally comprehend that his deliverance is at hand."

"Commander, Colonel Blackmore and I intend to infiltrate the fortress of our enemy and bring it down, piece by piece, until both the faculty to command and the will to continue is duly compromised and eroded into dust. We shall deliver to them the quintessential essence of terror, the anatomy of fear in its purest, most unyielding incarnation imaginable."

Whilst speaking, Bass noted that the attention of his colleague had rested upon the C.S.F. commander and concluded that he too had observed a certain distinct familiarity with regards to his robust physical appearance...

"Forgive me, Commander. If one might enquire... What name do you go by?"

"Witherspoon, sir, Captain Roderick Bryce Witherspoon, currently of Her Majesty's Covert Special Forces."

Both Bass and Blackmore afforded themselves a knowing grin as they simultaneously recalled a brief, but nonetheless valuable acquaintance made many years ago...

CHAPTER 19

"You had, perchance, a distant relative serve in the army many years past, Captain?" quizzed Blackmore expectantly...

"Great-great-grandfather, sir, Captain Bryce Witherspoon, Royal Engineers. Recipient of the Queen's medal for Distinguished Service during the second Boer War and the Victoria Cross for single-handedly saving the lives of several isolated colleagues pinned down and without hope of reprieve by relentless German advancement during the First World War...

"He always spoke very highly of two British Colonels whose impressive efforts to save the life of Churchill during the State Model Prison assault his squad of Engineers were privileged to support in Pretoria during the second Boer war, round about 1899 if memory serves...

"Both of those Colonels mysteriously disappeared on that day without a trace, by all accounts," imparted Witherspoon as he glanced towards Bass and Blackmore, affording each of them a wary glance and an informal nod of recognition...

With their grins slightly widened upon learning of the distinguished accolades earned by an officer they clearly recalled as possessing the experience, cunning and guile of a very capable 'Sapper' commander, Bass and Blackmore each nodded their affirmation prior to Blackmore revealing a humorous facet to his nature rarely exposed in public...

"Ah yes, of course... Witherspoon, the 'sapper' commander. If he had been but a fraction more solidly built, his ability to expertly secrete himself swiftly and covertly beneath the enclaves of his enemies would have proven an impossible task...

"I remember a courageous soldier of exemplary character and skill who commanded one of the finest 'sapper' squads with which it has been my privilege to serve, if only for a short time. Might one enquire what became of him?"

Captain 'Rod' Witherspoon took a sharp intake of breath and visibly bristled with pride upon gaining the knowledge that his great-great-grandfather had stood proudly shoulder to shoulder in battle with this pair of 'legends', thus finally corroborating once and for all the validity of the facts from the written testimony of an infallible eye witness, and at long last consigning to the vault of historical travesty the conjecture and rumour that had for so many years surrounded the extraordinary events that were always alleged to have occurred during the prison assault.

Observing that a wave of emotional pride had momentarily struck Witherspoon dumb, Blackmore concluded...

"Rest assured, Captain, that your great-great-grandfather's pride, so obviously in evidence whilst pledging his unyielding service to Queen and country on that day, is duly matched by your own on this."

Composing himself, the young captain, his confidence enhanced a hundred-fold, began to offer relevant tactical and logistical suggestions of his own which might aid their cause...

"Our extensive network of covert agents, who, to this day still remain on active deployment throughout the city, have sacrificed much and suffered great hardship and personal discomfort for decades as they toiled tirelessly to procure intel that has proved an invaluable resource as we strove to compile a database that consists of the exact whereabouts of every key Nazi party member at any given time...

"Referring to classified schematic diagrams that were filched from a top-secret government facility, our team of quite exemplary engineers were able to construct a device that enables us to read the hourly-changed passcodes that unlock the electronically sealed doors securing their closely guarded inner-sanctums...

"In addition to this electronic 'skeleton key', we are now also able to access the ingenious identification system that allows unchallenged passage beyond their otherwise quite impenetrable security protocols,

'CHAPTER 19

by means of injecting a microscopic device directly into the bloodstream that allows any authorised DNA to pass freely. Every citizen is 'chipped' in this manner, with access to high security areas permitted by a simple electronic scanning of your sanctioned chip...

"The rather ingenious method developed, which allows us to bypass this elaborate and difficult to replicate technology entails, somewhat ironically, a simple enough code reading device that is built into a common cell-phone."

Witherspoon handed each of the attentive detectives a cell phone. As Bass and Blackmore proceeded to allow their 19th century fingers and thumbs to explore the not unfamiliar devices, Witherspoon expressed his surprise at the obvious familiarity that the detectives confidently displayed for such a relatively modern piece of technology...

"Excellent; I see that both of you are well versed in the use of a cell. In order to utilise the device for the function that suits our purpose, simply engage the app resembling a spiral; a keypad will then open on the cells' glass screen...

"All that then remains to do is position the cell over the lock one requires to open as one would an electronic scanning device and the required pin number configuration will stand out on the cell-phone screen. Simply depress each key in the sequence they light up and access will be duly granted."

Toying clumsily with his cell, Blackmore enquired directly...

"We shall require access to both the extensive database to which you allude being made available to us and a wide-ranging selection of 21st century weaponry."

"Access to all of the relevant intel you require regarding this mission and any other technical or research based subject matter: the names, the whereabouts and the target value of each individual based upon their rank and worth to the Nazi party, is accessible via the network app on the touch screen of your cell. As for weapons, allow me to introduce you both to some very personal acquaintances of mine..."

Witherspoon proceeded to lay on the table before them two pairs of semi-automatic pistols, the matching clips, silencers and ammunition compatible with each, and enough hand grenades, smoke bombs, flash-bangs and semi-automatic small arms to sufficiently equip a compact invasion force...

"The pistols and grenades should suffice, Captain," interceded Bass, before Witherspoon had the opportunity to complete his impromptu presentation.

Taking one of the pistols in his right hand and its seventeen-round clip in his left, Bass studied the weapon briefly before reasoning out its function himself, courting the instant admiration of the intently observing young Captain...

Sliding the fully loaded clip into its correct recess in the grip, Bass then proceeded to screw the silencer into place at the gun barrel's end. Perceiving that the weapon must somehow be primed in order to be readied for discharge, he took the grip in his right hand whilst running his left hand across the top of the pistol, detecting as he did so a slight sliding movement of the breech along the top of the gun.

By sliding the breech as far as possible and back again into its original position, and satisfied that his weapon was now 'primed', Bass noticed a small catch nestled at the top of his weapon's grip that was simply labelled 'SAFETY: ON/OFF'.

Selecting the 'SAFETY: OFF' setting, he panned around the library in order to locate an inanimate object of suitable size to serve as an appropriate test target.

Finally settling upon an ancient, stately, yet somehow forlorn looking suit of armour standing equidistant to others of a similar style around the library's circumference, Bass took aim dead centre of the forehead belonging to the helmet of his chosen target and gently squeezed the hairline actioned trigger of his pistol... 'THUP'... 'CLANK!'

'CHAPTER 19

Upon habitually completing his accustomed trio of 'kill' shots by discharging a further pair of perfectly sighted 'taps' into the steel breastplate of his silent knight, Bass first re-loaded his spent weapon, then prepared a second pistol in an identical manner to his first...

Then, taking a primed weapon in each hand, emptied both of the seventeen-round clips into the armour, erasing all recognisable characteristics above waist level that likened it to the stature of a man.

Choosing initially to observe intently, as though studying a presentation specifically tailored to instruct a layman in the basic use of a semi-automatic firearm, Blackmore selected for himself from the formidable cache of ordnance laid before him on the table a larger weapon which would obviously require two hands to operate it...

"Colonel Blackmore, perhaps I might..."

Blackmore returned the affably meant offer of assistance from Witherspoon with an icy, silently indignant glare whilst taking up a full forty-round clip and inserting it expertly into the empty recess on the underside of the breech... 'CLICK'.

Locating what he assumed to be the loading breech that ran along the side of his weapon, he proceeded to ease it towards the stock as far as possible before screwing a silencer to the barrel and clicking the easily located safety catch to 'OFF' before looking across towards Bass, who had re-loaded both of his pistols and stood awaiting his companion's readiness, an expression of impish satisfaction now clearly apparent across his grinning, stubbled features.

Both men, by means of a long-nurtured silent coded combination of eye contact, that incorporated the slightest nodding of heads and the remarkably effective subliminal communication they appeared to share, selected another pair of armoured suits and proceeded to empty the entire clips of all three of their weapons into them, reducing each one to a pile of pulverized scrap metal...

As a result of this impromptu display of impressively accurate target practice, a brief period of pandemonium ensued. Though each weapon was silenced, the sound generated as the multiple rounds of semi-automatic gunfire ripped into the steel plate of the ancient armour resonated around the cavernous confines of Trajan's Vaults as though each single impact had been inordinately amplified within the confines of a vast echo chamber.

Even outside the relatively private enclaves of the library, the thrum and chatter of silenced small arms fire, plus the clank of high calibre, hollow point ordnance ripping into its steel target alerted the attentions of a second squad of six heavily armed C.S.F. operatives and activated the full lockdown protocol for the entire complex that was engaged in the event of a confirmed perimeter breach.

With the smoke still emanating from the barrels of their spent weapons, the air filled with the acrid stench of sulphur and gunpowder fumes, Bass and Blackmore faced each other and, each brandishing his weapons as though proudly displaying to his best friend a brand-new toy, nodded their silent approval to each other, oblivious at first of the chaos they had wrought.

Witherspoon took immediate command in order to placate, possibly more so hopefully diffuse, a potentially volatile situation from escalating towards a higher level of concern by firstly standing down the containing squad of C.S.F. operatives now training their weapons upon the swiftly reloaded and battle-ready detectives...

"STAND DOWN. DISENGAGE AT ONCE AND STAND DOWN. THAT'S AN ORDER!"

Turning to engage Bass and Blackmore, whose weapons remained poised and primed for discharge, Witherspoon decided that subtle cordiality would prove a more acceptable method of persuasion in attempting to disengage the intense combat focus of the two men, both of whom he now surmised were quite obviously a pair of vastly experienced, battle-hardened soldiers, each one in possession of a superior level of both guile and intelligence...

"Gentlemen, I implore you; lower your weapons. Rest assured: we are all friends here... please."

Deciding collectively that no further threat was immediately apparent, Bass and Blackmore clicked the safety catches on each of their new toys to 'ON' and placed them onto the table, well within their reach should a negative regression of the improved mood occur that should require 'instant correction'.

"A wise decision on both our parts, Captain," alluded Bass dryly as he offered no indication to any of the assembled group that the potentially catastrophic events just this moment averted had affected either his own or Blackmore's unnaturally calm demeanours in any way...

"These toys will suffice," he continued, tapping each of his newly acquired 'toys' whilst casting a furtive glance towards the rifle now ensconced in the jealously-guarded custody of Blackmore...

"I believe that Tiberius has discovered a new soul mate."

Raising his pistols slightly, he continued...

"A second pair of these rather fine implements for Tiberius, if you please, Captain, and lots of compatible ammunition for each piece as well."

"Marvellous. Now, Captain, assuming that our credentials pass muster, and you are completely satisfied that a pair of relics from a time long past are capable of functioning to the highest level of your exacting standards, let us venture forth and unleash 'the anatomy of fear'."

Chapter 20

'Return of the Ghosts'

Bass was interrupted by the combination of a low, steady 'thrum' and a mild vibrating sensation emanating from the left inside pocket of his overcoat. Removing the cell-phone which Witherspoon had handed to him a moment ago, he noticed the name 'Connie' had appeared in large white type on its flat glass screen, underneath which a red icon in the shape of a conventional telephone pulsated insistently in unison with the thrumming of the phone; '...an indication of an incoming message, perhaps...'

...he supposed, not unreasonably, to himself.

Bass prodded the red telephone shaped icon, intended as no more than an instinctive reaction designed initially to quiet the insistent, mildly irritating 'thrum', and immediately upon doing so, convinced himself that he could hear the very distant, but nonetheless unmistakable voice of his wife speaking to him...

"CONNIE... YES... I CAN HEAR YOU, THOUGH YOUR VOICE IS VERY DISTANT."

As Bass continued to speak, the volume of his own voice increasing profusely with every uttered syllable, Witherspoon caught the irascible old detective's attention by sharply lifting his right hand up towards his ear, as though subtly instructing, or perhaps reminding Bass to raise

CHAPTER 20

the cell up to a similar position beside his own ear...

Doing as he had been instructed, the voice of his wife improved substantially...

"Ah, yes, Connie... much better, thank you. What news of our recently deceased doppelganger, my love?"

Connie answered in earnest, her desire for the minute details of her findings to be divulged in person, becoming immediately apparent as she spoke...

"A report containing details of such great importance is best suited to be delivered within the confines of a more private enclave than to be shared over such an impersonal device as this, James...

"I call to ask that you, Tiberius, Marcus, Lucius, Captain Witherspoon and Brother de Payens make haste to our medical facility, which is situated a short distance from your current location, where I shall deliver some quite remarkable news regarding the extraordinary genetic footprint left by our impostor."

Upon entering the area designated as the forensics laboratory, a section of the medical facility equipped with state of the art technology used exclusively in the specific area of genetic and forensic studies, it became immediately apparent to both Bass and Blackmore that not only did Connie Bass command the total respect of her colleagues and subordinates, who continued to work at their stations undistracted by the sudden appearance of a pair of so-called 'legends', but also, as she proceeded to expertly interface with computer consoles whilst simultaneously conversing freely with her colleagues of technical matters relevant to their immediate concerns, that she, too, had mastered completely the complexities of 21st century technology, modern forensic science techniques and medicine; all areas of excellence within her field of expertise that she had been instrumental in both formulating and developing during the process of their late 19th century genesis, to the present day.

Rather than enjoying a much-anticipated reunion with his wife, however, Bass, along with Blackmore and their companions, was escorted onto a long corridor that was separated from a spacious, brightly illuminated room by a large glass wall.

Inside the room were six long, steel tables, set at equidistant intervals. Bass recollected a memory from long ago of the tables resembling those that were arranged in a similar fashion in the old mortuary room at the Whitechapel Hospital, the scene of many a grisly post-mortem briefing for the two detectives.

Clearly visible upon one of the steel tables, lay the partially dissected corpse belonging to the Aston impostor, its chest cavity exposed and the skull opened up so as to facilitate respectively the removal of vital body organs, and the brain.

Upon learning of Bass' and Blackmore's arrival, Connie looked up from her work to acknowledge them both. As her eyes sought out those belonging to her husband, her words, slightly borne on the breath of emotion for a few seconds prior to regaining her composure, focused upon the more serious concern of delivering her detailed report regarding the startling discoveries she had unearthed to the eagerly anticipating group...

"Damn and blast this impersonal glass edifice inside which we must work!" she grumbled into the intercom that relayed the sound of her voice out beyond the thick glass wall that separated them...

"But alas, for the purpose of maintaining the sanitised environment essential for preserving the delicate samples of forensic evidence, I must remain within its sealed parameters until such time as my work here is complete...

"As you can quite plainly observe, gentlemen, several key organs from the chest cavity, the lower abdomen and the brain have been removed from our subject. I have made a detailed analysis of the central nervous system and insisted that both blood and tissue samples be meticulously scrutinised...

"The initial findings of these tests prove that James' initial instinct to shoot was correct; the Aston we see here is proved beyond all logical scientific doubt, an impostor...

"On first impression, the tissue samples I identified, the arrangement of organs within the body, even the bone structure of our doppelganger conform exactly to those recorded in the official medical records of Pontius Aston, but certain minute discrepancies in the complex DNA chain belonging to our subject expose him for what he really is. What lies here before us is an example of a brilliantly engineered 'clone'."

"A 'clone'?"

"Yes, Tiberius, an almost exact copy of a person. Constructed from samples of selective DNA strands, carefully harvested from the subject, the 'clone' is engineered in a laboratory environment to look, to move, to sound, to think, in actual fact to adopt all of the familiar characteristics of that person, thus enabling the 'clone' impostor to walk freely amongst those unsuspecting souls who would ordinarily never assume to perceive otherwise its true intent."

"You allude to the fact of this being 'almost an exact copy' of a person, Connie?" queried Blackmore...

"Almost, Tiberius, but not quite. The complex technology involved in engineering the cloning process has yet to be perfected and refined in order to reach its full potential of producing a genetically perfect copy...

"With reference to a previous point made, a sample of DNA belonging to Pontius was in some way purloined and utilised in the construction of this 'clone'. Its genetic profile, however, could not be finalised as a result of the vital DNA chain, itself the quintessential essence of sentient life, remaining incomplete, necessitating the addition of a further DNA sample to the process, harvested from a second source, in order to complete the sequence...

"Were it not for the alertness of the exceptionally enhanced senses belonging to my lycanthrope husband, the Aston 'clone' would, in all probability, be walking amongst us still..."

"James, might one enquire: what characteristic first alerted you to the presence of this almost perfect anomaly?"

Remaining pensive for a moment, Bass finally answered his wife...

"Firstly, my love, the eyes: each one bore a startlingly contrasting shade, one emerald green, the other, aquamarine blue, whereas those belonging to the true Pontius Aston are of a hazel hue. Secondly, the distinctive scent, or to be more specific, mixture of scents: the unmistakable aroma of Pontius melded with that vile stench of the rogue that seeps from every pore of this abomination, a recurring stench to which I have become very much acquainted these past few months..."

"It would appear that 'The Architect' has seen fit to instil something of himself within his creation by submitting a sample of his own DNA in order to complete the genetic strand."

Maintaining a brief silence, Connie offered her husband a smile of understanding, a subliminal melding of the senses that they had shared together on countless other occasions in the past, prior to imparting...

"Quite remarkable, my love. That you are able to discern by scent alone the unique pheromone excreted by each of us. Might one enquire, was the distinction between true and false entity determined upon the presence of a single pheromone, or perhaps..."

"As I imparted previously, Connie, a distinct pair of scents were clearly discernible: one unquestionably belonged to the true Pontius, while the other was an unmistakably cloying, putrid stench of inherent evil, undoubtedly that routinely excreted by 'The Architect'."

***

"What now, James? Both you and Tiberius were returned to us for good reason, of that I have little doubt, but though my heart sings for your return, my head is filled with troubled thoughts appertaining to naught but dread in anticipation of what perilous strategy is to be implemented in order to correct what has been proved to be the heinously conceived ambition of a truly malevolent individual."

"Ah Connie, my sweet, perceptive Connie," retorted Bass in return for the intuitive aside made by his wife...

"Of course, and somewhat inevitably as your ever astute awareness attests, in order to right this terrible wrong that should never have been conceived, Tiberius and I must become 'ghosts' so that we might once more engage evil at its very core until, vanquished and fleeing in fear, it retreats to the last remaining place it may feel safe and able to effect one final, desperate bid to steal victory from the gaping jaws of defeat...

"'The Architect' will seek to enter the portal that grants access to the temporal nexus that lies in the hidden crypt beneath St Michael's church, located in the grounds of Highgate Cemetery here in London.

"It will be there, in that ancient location where the physical manifestation of this entity exists exclusively in the late 19th century, when a single gilt-edged opportunity will be presented for both Tiberius and I to banish the blackened, bitterly twisted soul of 'The Architect' into the waking nightmare of temporal incarceration forever."

Chapter 21

'Into the Viper's Nest.'

Blackmore remained in silent contemplation whilst Bass continued to speak. The experience of many historical cases and military campaigns shared with his old accomplice, served as a reminder to him that should either man choose to present a strategy that appeared to suggest a logically reasoned course of action, then the bond of brotherly trust shared between them was ample enough of a sign for him to grant his great friend the time he required in order to share his thoughts...

"I propose that both Tiberius and I venture forth into the city and commence with our seek and destroy mandate, wherein the immediate 'retirement from office' of the 'Uber Fuhrer' himself, Adolf Hitler III, becomes our initial priority...

"Wherever he is, I would raise a high ante for certain that several members of his key staff would surely be in attendance, thus affording us a prime opportunity to convey a bloody message directly to 'The Architect', informing him that there is no safe haven in all of time that remains accessible to whence he might run and hide, save perhaps for one..."

"Upon realising our proposed strategy to save the life of Churchill, he will turn tail and regress to the 19th century, firstly to the exact moment during the prison siege where he will once more make attempt

CHAPTER 21

to curtail our intentions, and then, should his altercation prove successful or otherwise, he will proceed to 'shift' across continents directly to the crypt under Highgate Cemetery where he will seek to assassinate Brother de Payens and reclaim the great power of the 13th Meister which once belonged to him," countered the ever-insightful Blackmore...

"Precisely, Tiberius. There must be naught left to chance as we endeavour to repair the fractured timeline; we simply must not conceive of failure a second time."

Addressing Witherspoon directly, whilst simultaneously making certain that each of his weapons was prepared for the ensuing firefight, the question posed by Bass was simple, concise and direct...

"Captain Witherspoon, where precisely might we find the 'Uber Fuhrer'?"

"Reports submitted by our covert agents reliably inform us that he rarely ventures forth from the top two levels of the tallest building in London, the Shard, located at Bankside, SE1...

"The passcode finder app on each of your cell phones will grant access to the less secure lower level magnetic door locks but between you and the prize rise over a thousand feet of fortified glass and steel, 96 levels serviced by 36 elevators, all protected by both a state of the art security system and a constantly rotating cohort of 'Black Guard', personally commissioned by 'The Architect' as his own 'Pretorian Guard' to offer their unyielding loyalty in their protection of both himself and the 'Uber Fuhrer'."

"The Bankside area is well known to us," remarked Bass...

"Ergo, the tallest building situated in 21st century London should prove simple enough to locate."

Gesturing firstly towards himself, and then Blackmore, before once more addressing Witherspoon, Bass continued...

"Our, erm, rather distinctive 19th century attire might prove something of a disadvantage with regards to initially maintaining a discreet anonymity, one might assume."

Witherspoon afforded himself a wry grin as he gave his answer...

"Oh, I shouldn't be too concerned with regards to your attire, Colonel Bass. Even though we reside firmly under the boot heel of a totalitarian military dictatorship, the appearance of a pair of potentially harmless, ageing 'steampunks' on the capital's streets will be viewed as merely one of the 21st century's more traditional European eccentricities that is still moderately tolerated, albeit somewhat grudgingly, by the Nazi authorities."

"STEAM-PUNKS!" mouthed Bass silently in the direction of Blackmore as each man looked at the other and shook their heads with incredulous disbelief, prior to Bass imparting...

"Welcome, indeed, to the 21st century, my ageing 'steampunk' compatriot."

***

Relying upon the natural black shroud of the night for cover as they had done so often in the past, and moving stealthily through the eerily silent, curfew-governed backstreets which they had once known so well, Blackmore's hushed tones betrayed a slight indication of the mild sense of trepidation that each of them was experiencing...

"These streets, James. So much has changed and yet, the familiar façade of a building here, a recognisable bend in the road there, and mercifully the street names remain predominantly unaltered."

"Indeed, Tiberius. These secondary streets serve well to shield our presence from the intrusive electronic voyeurism of the surveillance cameras and drones that are advantageously, or so it would appear leastways, not as prominent on these less than salubrious enclaves that skulk menacingly, casting their dark shadows, still bearing their vivid and now, thankfully, secret memories of a feral, brutal underworld that thrived beneath, betwixt and behind old London... our London."

Whilst picking their way cautiously along a short, secluded alleyway an uncharacteristically perplexed Bass halted their progress abruptly...

"Hold here for a moment, Tiberius," he hissed, his attention piqued by a certain familiarity to their current surroundings...

"I find myself recognising no discernible landmarks with which to verify our current location, but should not this 'snicket' open out into Broadstreet Square, from which was once accessible, via the old railway arches across the way, a concealed entrance that led into the Bankside embankment tunnel system?"

Blackmore remained pensive for a few seconds, until his reply was curtailed abruptly by an unexpected interruption...

"That it should, James. If indeed this open space before us goes by the name 'Broadstreet Square' as once it did, then I see no obvious alternative but for us to risk crossing it in order to best reach our destination from this point."

"What... What are those curious red spots that have just this moment appeared upon your chest that dance and flutter so randomly?"

"I'm at a loss to explain," countered a puzzled Bass. "But you have an identical pair reciprocating their curiously crazed dance dead-centre of your bowler. I..."

"HALT, STAND STILL AND BE RECOGNISED!"

Upon receiving the precise, clear and most officiously-delivered command, indicating at once that their position had been compromised, Bass and Blackmore realised, only too well, that should they relinquish the partial cover which the long shadow cast by the ancient brick archway belonging to their 'snicket' afforded them, where they had expected to retain their anonymity for at least a few more precious seconds in order to consolidate their next action, that the modern surveillance devices they had discussed earlier, indigenous 21st century technology that intrusively eavesdropped upon the largely unsuspecting population below from vantage points located high above virtually every city street corner, would surely reveal their identities to their arch nemesis 'The Architect'.

"Quickly, James, feign intoxication!" hissed Blackmore, his mind immediately engaged by an instant flash of inspired improvisation...

"The appearance of a pair of inebriated, ageing 'steampunks', caught out long after curfew, might just afford us the precious few seconds that we require in order to best assess our immediate options."

Stepping backwards slightly into the partial cover of the arch, Blackmore began his impressively improvised dialogue belonging to a drunken cockney 'soak' as though a vocation as a thespian had remained for many years an undisclosed talent...

"An' she pushed 'er 'wheel Barrer, through the streets broad an' narrer, singin' cockles, an' muscles, halive, halive oh..."

Upon observing the impressive command performance delivered by Blackmore, Bass reciprocated in kind, delivering an admirable supporting role of his own which would have undoubtedly honoured the boards of any reputed West End theatre...

"Awtergevvanah'... halive, halive oh... halive, halive oh... singin' cockles an' muscles halive, halive oh my word, wot the 'fakkin' 'ell is goin' on 'ere then?" slurred Bass convincingly as the familiarly dark-apparelled figures belonging to four 'Black Guard' approached, each of them training their laser sighted, semi-automatic weapons upon the pair of totally convincing faux inebriates...

"Don't you two realise it's an hour past curfew? Why are you out at this time? Papers... Both of you, show me your papers... NOW!"

"Ere, don't you go getting' snotty wi' me, you little 'fakker'," Blackmore belched disdainfully into the face of one whom he had assumed to be the 'Black Guard' Commander...

CHAPTER 21

Irked considerably by both the lack of compliance shown, and what he considered the disrespectful behaviour to which he had been subjected, the young 'Black Guard' commander barked out his demands...

"ON YOUR KNEES, HANDS BEHIND YOUR HEADS... NOW!"

"Nah, nah... no need for all o' this 'fakkin' 'palavah' 'moi' 'san'... 'ere, 'ave a little drinkie 'wiv' us 'hofficer," chipped in Bass, now settling somewhat over-confidently into his portrayal of an ageing lush, prompting the now seething and totally distracted young officer to forcefully swat the hip flask offered by Bass out of his grasp...

"Ere 'moi' 'san', that 'weren't' very friendly like... "thash a fine old 'hitalian brandy you just 'schpilled' there, boy..."

"ON... YOUR... KNEES, OR I SHALL..."

"Nah, nah, shhh... tut, tut, tut... jus' settle 'dhan' young 'un. Sh'all 'bin' a mish... a mish (burp!) ... a mishunder... Sh'all 'bin a mishtake, 'hofficer. Nah' 'jusht' gimmee a 'fakkin' second while I..."

Bass commenced his impressively choreographed charade by clumsily rummaging through an inside pocket of his overcoat, feigning to retrieve the identity papers he knew were not forthcoming, but instead, engaging a single, fluid motion, sending his brass-pommelled hunting knife powerfully arcing through the air with unerring accuracy to embed itself deep into the shoulder of the astonished 'Black Guard' Commander...

"My credentials, all in order, I believe," deadpanned an obviously sober Bass as he bore down upon his prone quarry and stooped to retrieve his blade from the stricken commander's shoulder.

Looking up at Bass, as though searching for some sign of mercy or compassion, the perplexed young officer was merely greeted by the expression of a hardened, experienced soldier whose soulless, jet-black eyes, quite possibly the eyes of the Devil himself, bore down deep into his soul...

"Who... Who in God's name... are you?" he whimpered pathetically...

"Oh, I'm just the hapless, sozzled old 'steampunk' inebriate whose rather fine Italian brandy you just wasted," quipped Bass as he stooped to retrieve first the precious hip flask that had moments earlier been flagrantly batted to the ground, and then his blade that was embedded deeply into the incapacitated commander's shoulder...

"Thank you and please accept my apologies for the absence of both gentlemanly decorum and humane civility regarding my selected method of farewell to you."

Whilst still adopting his crouched position, and facing minimal opposition from his crippled opponent, Bass slid behind the prone Commander's body, placed his head in a tight lock between his own shoulder and forearm and very gently, utilising a remarkable economy of physical effort, moved the commander's head first one way, then the other, snapping his neck as though it were nothing more than a sliver of dry kindling.

Rising to his feet and dismissively stepping over the corpse he had created, Bass had correctly anticipated that accounting for this century's penchant towards all public interaction and confrontation scenarios concerning strict politically correct guidelines and full human rights protocols being observed to the letter at all times, even the habitual behaviour of these 21st century 'Black Guard', blindly facilitating the whims of a fascist regime, most probably held their modern weapons in 'safety' mode unless directly confronted by confirmed hostile intent, thus affording him the further precious few seconds he required in which to adroitly engage his second target.

Bass aimed a deftly-targeted right boot at the left kneecap of his momentarily disoriented second opponent, shattering the entire knee joint instantly and forcing the hapless 'Black Guard' to re-distribute his entire body weight upon his now completely over-compensated and openly vulnerable right side.

CHAPTER 21

Able now to exploit this imbalance that he had purposefully and expertly engineered to the full, Bass proceeded to gracefully execute, in a single, flawless movement, a full 360-degree pirouette whilst simultaneously re-drawing his brass-pommelled hunting knife and burying it into the throat of his already incapacitated perspective antagonist.

Meanwhile, Blackmore had required little enticement to forego his own remarkably adept subterfuge and immediately set to task in dispatching his designated pair of woefully inept intruders by displaying a very similar and decisively swift array of martial arts skills to those so expertly showcased by his clinically proficient companion.

Upon proceeding to characteristically punt his own heavy-handled blade with such powerful ferocity that it became too heavily embedded in the forehead of his first assailant to retrieve with ease during his first fleeting pass, Blackmore adjusted his intended strategy slightly in order to compensate for the minor irritancy of momentarily nullifying the availability for use of his primary weapon.

Acting purely on instinct alone, he raised his left boot with some considerable force, so as to connect directly with the semi-automatic weapon slung tightly across the chest of his second adversary.

This inspirational act of foresight pressed the weapon tightly against any other threatening implements that the 'Black Guard' might have thought to engage, thus rendering them momentarily useless to hand and affording Blackmore several vital, precious seconds of tactical advantage.

Showcasing all of the deftness and poise of a man half his age, Blackmore moved firstly to the side, then to the rear of his perplexed opponent and engaged him in a choke-hold not dissimilar to the one demonstrated by Bass a moment earlier which had produced such a devastatingly final effect except, rather than break the neck of his now incapacitated mark, Blackmore chose to squeeze every last breath of life from the constricted larynx held firmly in his vice-like grasp...

"Will these 'Black Guard' whelps ever be trained to assess every last one of the myriad of possibilities presented by random confrontation, however ludicrous they might first appear?" sighed Blackmore as he discarded the corpse of his second victim, as would a child cast aside an unwanted rag doll, and then proceed to retrieve his blade, not without some considerable difficulty, that had remained embedded almost up to its brass guard within the forehead of his first 'retiree'.

"Something of note of which you should be made aware, Tiberius," afforded Bass as he scrutinised each of the four 'Black Guard' cadavers...

"All four of these recently deceased 'Black Guard' are, without a shadow of a doubt, 'clones'. Even prior to our recent pugilistic engagement with them, the pungent dual pheromone excreted by these things, to which Connie alluded in her meticulously-detailed post-mortem report, presented a distinctly offensive stench that set my sensitive lycanthrope nostrils twitching...

"I am now certain that 'The Architect' has seen fit to use his own DNA as a catalyst for the creation of these abominations."

"So, it transpires that the long, intrusive shadow of a formidable nemesis from our past is cast large over these proceedings, James," retorted a somewhat perturbed Blackmore.

"If, as it would now seem likely, 'The Architect' is indeed a major protagonist in this immoral distortion of history, then it follows that he must surely have access to the advanced scientific, technological, and biological techniques necessary to engineer the raising of such a formidable army."

"CLAVEL AND Von WALDHEIM!" Bass exclaimed perceptively...

"This cloning process reeks of their influence, or perhaps a more plausible theory would be that this latest process is in fact a progression of their original vision."

"The thought had occurred, James," answered Blackmore...

CHAPTER 21

"One might be correct in the assumption that this indeed represents a natural progression from the crude, piecemeal constructions of human body parts, galvanized into life using nature's own formidable electrical energy, towards a more scientifically advanced method that to laymen such as ourselves, so far as the complexities of science and technology are concerned, is aesthetically more human in appearance to the naked eye, but still presents overall a concept devoid of any justifiable moral integrity or suggestion towards even a minute shred of scientific value."

"Agreed, Tiberius, and what is more, the second pheromone excreted by these abominations of twisted scientific folly, as was apparent with the Aston clone, belongs, without doubt, to 'The Architect'... Shhh!" Bass curtailed his speech abruptly... "Our position here is compromised for a second time."

***

"THERE... IN THE SHADOWS DIRECTLY ACROSS THE SQUARE... ONE PERSON... SLIGHT OF BUILD... VERY FLEET OF FOOT... PENSIVELY CAUTIOUS... OBSERVING OUR EVERY MOVE," hissed Bass, his attention piqued by the unexpected arrival of an intruder in their midst...

"DAMNATION!" exclaimed an exasperated Blackmore...

"More than likely observed our every move. I'm going to casually melt into the shadows and ease around the perimeter in an attempt to flank our little eavesdropper. If you could..."

"It would appear that our 'little eavesdropper' has anticipated and reciprocated in kind your perceived strategy with exceptional effect, my friend," remarked Bass as what appeared to resemble the voice of a teenage girl emanated from the shadows directly behind the pair of momentarily-startled detectives...

"Oh my, you have both been very bad. Very good, but very, very bad boys, indeed."

Turning sharply on his heels, his LeMat revolver instinctively drawn and cocked, Blackmore was confronted by the unilluminated blackness of their ancient alleyway sanctuary, into which his human eyes were not momentarily able to focus.

Alternatively, Bass remained the epitome of calmness personified as he bade his clearly agitated colleague to lower his weapon...

"Steady, old man, lower your guard. No immediate threat to either our security, or to our well-being, is present here..."

"Come out, youngling; have no fear and show yourself. We mean you no harm."

Taking Bass at his word, emerging cautiously from the shadows, the slightly-built, yet quite tall, form of a teenage girl, no more than perhaps 15 or 16 years old, stepped tentatively into view. An impressive mane of long, strawberry blonde, tousled curls cascaded in golden ringlets across her perfectly exquisite features, reminding Bass somewhat of the flawless porcelain face belonging to a child's doll.

Bass was also aware that her piercing grey eyes appeared untroubled by the darkness, as were not his own, suggesting to him a logical thought process that he chose for the present not to share with Blackmore...

"Quick... Follow me now, if you want to live," hissed the girl, wary of the fact that each second they remained exposed risked courting further unwarranted attention from the ever-vigilant authorities...

"What! Who...? Who are you?" was the perfectly rational enquiry made by the calm, yet still correctly cautious Bass...

"Please... There is little time to exchange cordial pleasantries... My name is Nettie Glover and you must accompany me this instant, James Bass."

Choosing primarily to err on the best part of caution, but with both men's interest piqued markedly by this random stranger referring to

CHAPTER 21

Bass directly and somewhat informally by name, the pair of ageing detectives attempted to maintain the quickening pace set by the youngster as she proceeded to lead them down deserted alleyways and cuttings that even in the dead of night presented some form of welcomed familiarity to the two companions...

"Current direction suggests that our enthusiastic young guide leads us towards the Bankside tunnels," Blackmore correctly observed as they approached a series of crumbling railway arches that constituted the remnants of the once grand façade of a disused entrance to the Bankside Underground Station terminus...

Upon gaining entrance to the now long since derelict site through a pair of pre-loosened boards that were part of the poorly maintained perimeter fence, adorned with precisely worded warning messages that clearly read...

'...NO ENTRY. UNSAFE GROUND. PROPERTY AQUIRED FOR DEVELOPMENT BY THE STATE...'

Below this formal warning was emblazoned in high case, bright red typeset an altogether more ominous, infinitely more threatening warning...

'TRESPASSERS WILL BE SHOT!'

Bass halted their progress for a moment...

"Nettie Glover. Tarry a short while whilst two old men regain their breath, if you please."

Taking his opportunity to look deeply into her compelling grey eyes as he spoke, as though Bass was searching behind them for some semblance of an entry directly into her soul, his next words to her forced the unintentionally-eavesdropping Blackmore to puff out his cheeks as he openly displayed his astonishment at their remarkable content...

"Ah, sweet Nettie Glover, there you are. Behind such young, tender eyes lies the truth of a thousand ages, the experience of several lifetimes... but of course, not so young as your outward appearance suggests, for you are indeed one of my kind, are you not... a lycanthrope?"

Chapter 22

'Nettie.'

Nettie reciprocated in kind the intrusive, yet somehow reassuringly familiar, glare aimed towards her by Bass, but she was able to sense only the perpetual darkness within him as it blackened each of his eyes, as though barring entry through tightly-shuttered windows into the tempestuous maelstrom of his securely guarded soul...

"I see nothing and I sense a great emptiness within you, James Bass. You remain the eternal enigma of which the legend foretells."

Addressing both Bass and Blackmore together, Nettie continued...

"Here, finally, against all reasonable expectations, stands before me the lycanthrope and the human, who have returned to us as was prophesied by our ancient forefathers, in order to lead the righteous out of bondage towards their salvation..."

Her mood of euphoria quickly evaporated into one bordering on heartfelt sadness within a second...

"...but to see... the nothingness behind your eyes, James... saddens me. For your return I gladly rejoice, but for the blackened, tortured soul you remain compelled by nature's cruel kiss to endure, I offer my pity."

"SAVE YOUR PITY FOR THOSE WHO BEST DESERVE IT, YOUNGLING!" snapped Bass tersely, his anxiety levels rising profusely
...

"Pity yourself, if you must seek to offer such a thing, or perhaps pity the rest of your kind, who cravenly skulk in shameful concealment within the labyrinthine sanctuary of the sprawling Broad Street tunnels before us."

"OUR kind, James Bass? OUR kind? Hunted, persecuted and repressed to the point of extinction, the few meagre packs of survivors that remained alive either fleeing towards their eastern European homelands or forced to seek sanctuary in any safe cesspit available to them in the secret 'underverse' languishing beneath the festering streets of this once great metropolis," retorted Nettie sharply, somewhat perturbed by the dismissive tone adopted by Bass with regards to his damning slight towards both the misplaced pride and the systematically eroded courage of his own race.

Bass nodded contritely, conceding that in sharing publicly his ill-advised outburst of ignorance, he had, in fact, offered an affront to the very race of which he was now revered as a blood brother...

"Of course, Nettie, quite right you are. I stand soundly rebuked for my unnecessary display of indiscretion. Please understand that I meant no disrespect to you, or to the pack that resides within these catacombs..."

"YOU MEAN THERE ARE MORE OF THESE?"

"Yes, Tiberius, there are a good many more of us within," interjected Bass wisely, his own tactfulness rapidly re-instated just in time to curtail the lack of discretion Blackmore was about to show whilst hastily airing his own somewhat misaligned, naive prejudices...

"Yes... well... of course, it's the smell of damp dog, you see... very pungent... distinctive aroma... not altogether abhorrent, though, you understand?"

Conscious of both Bass and Nettie's raised eyebrows, informing Blackmore that the more he rambled on with regards to this subject, then the further into a mire of self-imposed embarrassment he would

CHAPTER 22

sink, he decided that his speech should be brought to its timely conclusion by making what he considered to be a pertinent enquiry...

"Well then, answer me this: how does such a distinctive aroma fare with regards to both of your keen snouts?!"

Bass and Nettie first looked at each other, and then back towards Blackmore, who fidgeted uncomfortably with the tactile curves of his silver pocket watch. Each of them offered him the widest grin as they answered in perfect synchronicity, as if prompted to do so by a subliminally transmitted signal that was transmitted between them...

"THE SAME."

***

Replacing the pair of dislodged boards behind them, so as not to arouse suspicion of any unlawfully clandestine entry, Nettie proceeded to lead Bass and Blackmore into the imposing Gothic-styled arc of a disused railway tunnel which, as they approached the solid stone wall that grew larger in their midst suggesting a dead-end, seemed to offer little clue as to the location of an opening that might allow access into the now long since decommissioned Bankside underground tunnels.

Just as each of their noses was almost touching the damp Derbyshire gritstone of the tunnel wall, Nettie bade the detectives follow her to their immediate left and enter into a narrow service archway that in turn led them into a low, even less spacious tunnel.

Barely high and wide enough for Bass and Blackmore to pass through, the length of time that they were required to uncomfortably shuffle along almost doubled over was mercifully short before the old service conduit into which they had been so unceremoniously shoe-horned opened out, much to their great relief, into the more familiar surroundings of an underground station platform.

Its curved tile walls were grubby and crumbling after decades of neglect, long forgotten faces of once prominent celebrities, and pointless non-celebrities, still stared out enticingly from the remnants of rotting advertising posters that remained adorning much of the decaying ceramic façade in a now forlorn bid to promote either their current piece of indispensable, yet instantly forgettable art, or perhaps the next must-have, extortionately expensive gadget; 'one simply must own'.

The now rusty, long-ago decommissioned train tracks, too, still remained in place, as did the several iconic red, white and blue coloured circular signs that heralded to the three companions that their intended destination was close at hand: 'BANKSIDE'.

There was an eerie stillness prevalent throughout this once vibrant public area, that now stood for little other than perhaps a reminder of what once existed a golden era of peace and prosperity, the silence punctuated occasionally by the rumbling sound of the trains thundering at intermittent intervals along the modern Bankside line that ran on a parallel course to the decommissioned old tracks.

The newly-acquainted trio made their way along the station platform towards a prominently placed metal sign which was riveted to a securely locked and bolted heavy cast iron door, the stark warning upon which was writ large in bold red type so as to accentuate, beyond all doubt, the extreme danger that lay beyond its secure portal...

'KEEP OUT: DANGER OF DEATH.'

Undeterred by this blatantly stark warning from another era, intended, no doubt, to dissuade the curiosity of a public long since passed, Nettie proceeded to unlock two heavy padlocks that fastened the pair of bolts securing the solid iron door using the key that hung from a brass chain around her neck.

The rusted, weighty door was now able to be swung inwards effortlessly, revealing a ladder that dropped vertically into the ominous

CHAPTER 22

pitch blackness of what appeared to be a dusty, bottomless shaft.

Sensing a certain reluctance on the part of Blackmore to venture into what she instantly understood represented to him, from a purely tactical point of view, an advance into unknown territory, Nettie revelled in her unexpected opportunity to offer a slight reciprocation of mild scorn towards Blackmore in return for his own contemptuous, near-affront towards her 'kind' a few moments ago...

"Not afraid of the dark are you, Mr Blackmore? All those 'things' that might lurk in the shadows, those damp 'doggy-smelling 'things'!"

Blackmore's initial rejoinder was in the form of a stern glare towards their young companion that melded instantly into a wry grin and a shaking of his head as he imparted in a somewhat contrite manner...

"Touché, my young friend. Now if you can find it within your heart to forgive the taciturn blathering of an ageing soldier, please lead on, if you would be so kind."

Nettie duly obliged Blackmore's request, offering her exquisitely beguiling smile in return for the grateful offer of his metaphorical 'olive branch', and they began their long descent into the pitch-blackness of a long disused service shaft.

Remaining silent for the duration of their fifteen-or-so minute descent, upon reaching ground level once more, Nettie produced a petrol-fuelled cigarette lighter from one of the pockets of her well-worn leather motorcycle jacket and upon igniting its unnecessarily high, dancing yellow flame, used its petrol-incensed flickering luminescence to locate an ancient switch panel hanging on a facing wall of the tunnel in which they now stood.

Selecting a rusting old isolation switch on the panel, Nettie pulled down on the lever until a heavy 'click' ignited the incandescent bulbs that had been hung intermittently from the tunnel sides by railway men of old; relics from another age, as were in essence both Bass and Blackmore themselves.

Whilst the three companions picked their way gingerly along the barely illuminated tunnel, Bass attempted to glean more information from their extremely confident and street-smart new acquaintance regarding details appertaining towards both that of hers and her packs' current dire circumstances, and perhaps a brief synopsis explaining their origins...

"For how long have you and your pack been forced to reside here, Nettie, in this dark, desolate place?"

"You wish to learn about me, James Bass? About my people? Very well then, you'll be told more soon enough at journey's end, much more, when you are formally introduced to 'The Baron of Bankside'."

Nettie paused for a moment, perceiving wisely that indeed revealing a little of her past may offer the two detectives an insight into the ancient counter-culture that had thrived almost unnoticed under London for many hundreds of years; unnoticed, that is, until one fateful, cold winter's night on the snow-dusted cobbles of the infamous Whitechapel 'abyss' 122 years ago...

"I was born in Nottingham, don't rightly remember the exact date, though I do remember that William the First was King of England and near to death so... late 1087, I s'pose..."

"1087!" spluttered Blackmore... "But that would make you..."

"Nine hundred-and thirty-three-years young, give or take a month or two. Don't look too bad on it, do I," imparted Nettie, whilst flashing a cheeky wink in Blackmore's direction...

"How were you...? Your lycanthropy, Nettie... in what manner did you...? were you...?"

"I was the age I appear to you now, 15 or 16 years old... not certain... so long ago, you see. Difficult to recall...

"I do remember vividly the monster that turned me though. Oh yes indeed, that cold, merciless she-wolf hell spawn whose continued malignant existence upon this earth I hope never to erase from my every day waking thoughts until the moment dawns when I tear out her throat."

Pausing for a few seconds, forcing suppressed emotions and distant memories suppressed long ago to momentarily surface, Nettie regained her composure and continued to recount her tale...

"She was referred to in both the superstitious whisperings of Eastern European folklore and the dusty tomes written by supposedly learned scholars, as the very first of our kind: 'The Queen of the Damned'.

"No one knows for certain how long she has prowled the earth, raising 'packs' of feral lycanthropes bound slavishly to her uncompromisingly brutal regime of command in her wake, across the vast ocean of eternity...

"She remains the strongest one amongst us and, contrary to the ancient sacred code that decrees 'lycanthrope must never kill lycanthrope', she will think nothing of murdering her own kind in order to retain her jealously-guarded crown...

"Known by many names across the centuries, the one sobriquet that you will hear uttered most often, should you prove foolish enough to delve too deeply into her affairs, is 'THE MATRIARCH'."

"Well, unless this 'Matriarch' presents a stern challenge towards the successful completion of mine and James' immediate task, I suggest that we tarry not a moment longer and hasten on our course towards whatever awaits us at your pleasure, Nettie Glover," reasoned Blackmore, not wishing to cloud essential matters of importance in the present by overtaxing their minds unnecessarily with thoughts regarding perspective issues best, for the time being, mothballed for future concern.

"Destiny decrees that one day your paths will cross, of that there is no doubt, but not today, nor for that matter any time soon... Ah, our reception committee is here."

Emerging from a series of tunnels and ducts that opened out onto the platform of another disused underground station that they had ventured onto, several of what Bass and Blackmore instantly identified as fully transformed werewolves crept furtively towards the three companions, flanking them on all sides and sniffing the stale underground air, wary of the fact that one of the three intruders into their lair presented them with the unexpected opportunity to feast upon fresh human meat.

In an instant, both Bass and Nettie instinctively formed a protective perimeter around Blackmore by circling him whilst facing outwards towards his potential predators, their own salivating fangs that had swiftly protruded from each of their jaws barred, and their razor-sharp claws that, too, had sprouted with miraculous speed from their bloodied finger ends readied in anticipation of a potentially bloody skirmish.

As though warning away the circling pack from any notion they might harbour of purloining an easy meal courtesy of Blackmore's invitingly tender human flesh, Bass and Nettie proceeded to mark assertively both their territorial dominance and to present beyond reasonable doubt their alpha dog status by snarling disapprovingly towards each of the stalking lycanthropes.

All at once, the sound of a confident, booming voice that commanded the instant respect and obedience of the circling werewolves and dissuaded them from their hunt, was given human persona in the large frame of a man who appeared out of the darkness of an adjoining tunnel...

"Please excuse the rudeness of my all too often unruly children, gentlemen. Hunger for them is, regrettably, a daily constant and the chance arrival of human meat into their midst provides great temptation for them to satiate their discerning palates...

"Rest assured though, Mr Blackmore, that your personal well-being in this place is guaranteed."

CHAPTER 22

As his features and hands returned to their human form, Bass spat out a venomous warning towards his momentarily startled host as his opening gambit, thus intentionally asserting his own 'alpha-dog' credentials amongst the Bankside wolf pack for all to witness ...

"And you, sir, remember this well: I offer no credence to your so-called and just lately often quoted lycanthrope code that states 'werewolf shall not kill werewolf'. Should any of your 'children' decide that my very good friend Tiberius is a tempting prime cut on the daily meat menu, then all of your fates are sealed. Make no mistake, I shall endeavour to hunt every last one of you to extinction!"

The large man smiled and, showing no sign of being intimidated by the cold ultimatum delivered by Bass, proceeded with a hearty greeting...

"Please, James Bass. No affront was intended on my part. Allow me to introduce myself formally: I am 'The Baron of Bankside'.

Chapter 23

'The Baron of Bankside.'

Though faced with a potentially life-threatening situation, Bass and Blackmore exuded their usual aura of calmness personified, much to the admiration of their host, whose own keen lycanthropic instincts were instantly attuned to both the suppressed rage, and to the latent menace that lurked beneath the surface of each of their otherwise expertly guarded personas...

"Your exemplary reputations precede you, gentlemen. I have long held the ambition to make the acquaintance of the two finest detectives ever to police the dour, unforgiving streets of our not so fair city...

"That I find you here, on the threshold belonging to the inner sanctum of what remains of a once revered and proud society poses something of an intriguing conundrum, however...

"The presence of Mr Bass one can comprehend: a lycanthrope discovering, if only by chance, a 'pack' of his own kind, after a near-fatal encounter with a rogue wolf many years ago, made immortal and so cursed to roam the earth for all eternity unless granted merciful release by means of a knowledgeable personage, or perhaps..."

As though anticipating a priceless sliver of information about to be casually divulged by 'The Baron' might prove somewhat premature with regards to the great benefit of Bass retaining his lycanthropic tendencies

CHAPTER 23

for the present could offer to their survival, Nettie interceded...

"Baron, I observed in wonder from concealment as these two men dispatched four 'Black Guard' with consummate ease...

"The importance of James Bass, if one were to consider the heritage of his blood alone, is of great value to this pack; but neither should the usefulness of the varied and quite formidable skill-set belonging to Tiberius Blackmore be underestimated as something of great worth to us also."

Addressing Nettie by mistakenly adopting the condescending tone of a chastising parent, 'The Baron' began to speak...

"Ah, Nettie. Welcome home, my dear. I'm so glad that you see fit to return when the moment suits..."

"DO NOT THINK TO PATRONISE ME, YOU POMPOUS, SELF-AGGRANDISING, FESTERING PIECE OF WORM FOOD!

"I alone established this 'lair' five hundred years prior to your arrival. I was the one who offered sanctuary to a persecuted and bedraggled Eastern European 'wolf pack', running in terror for their lives across continents from squads of hunter-killer agents loyal to 'The Matriarch'.

"Do not ever forget that for whatever transgressions your 'pack' was responsible for perpetrating toward your European bloodline that so earned the uncompromising wrath of 'The Queen of the Damned', remember that the sanctuary of my home has thus far served you all very well!

"In my house, 'Baron', 'MY HOUSE!' I come and go as I please, and I invite over its threshold guests of my own choosing."

'The Baron appears somewhat perturbed'...

...Bass mused inwardly...

'Due, without doubt, to the suppression of an incandescent rage that burns within him as a result of the humiliating affront this minute received, delivered with such venomous bile and in the presence of strangers to boot, by one whose outward appearance of naïve, innocent

221

youth conceals a razor sharp, superior intellect, and a seasoned, street-honed acumen.'

'The Baron' shifted uncomfortably on his spot whilst seeking in some fashion to regain his bruised composure...

"But of course, Nettie, but of course. Any friend of yours etcetera... etcetera... as it were..."

"Be welcome and please, leave a little of the light that you bring into our world of perpetual darkness."

'The Baron' beckoned towards Bass, Blackmore and Nettie to enter an area of several abandoned offices that had been crudely converted into a makeshift living quarters, the most spacious of which appeared to have been specifically furnished with a large semi-circular, highly polished mahogany table and a random selection of antique furnishings, late of an archaic Victorian aristocracy, and arranged in such a fashion so as to suggest that one had entered the distinctly officious, ominously overbearing atmosphere of a courtroom, prompting a wary response from each of the two detectives' right hands to instinctively, and discreetly, reach towards the stocks of their holstered pistols ...

"Have a care, Baron, lest we perceive that our liberty is to be threatened by your counsel in this place, where I'm certain that the fate of a good many others has been deliberated upon and sentence declared on several occasions in the past."

"Mr Blackmore, I..."

"Colonel Blackmore, and Colonel Bass!" exclaimed Blackmore brusquely, his patience worn ever thinner by the constant whiff of insincerity that permeated the atmosphere surrounding 'The Baron' and the increasing likelihood of a tactical conundrum growing ever nearer...

"You will refer to each of us using our full military titles, 'Baron', if you please. If official platitudes are to be recognised here regarding use of your own 'unofficially sanctioned' title, until we are satisfied that your interest in our affairs offers no discernible hindrance to our plans

CHAPTER 23

and a modicum of trust might be present in our developing relationship, then we insist that such tiresome protocols be adhered to."

"Of course, Colonel Blackmore... and Colonel Bass... Of course. Please understand that neither harm, nor disrespect was intended towards either of you fine gentlemen. Now sit, and let us drink a toast to the potential dawn of a new age, for on this day of all days the age-old prophecy foretelling of the bringers of salvation returning home to lead..."

"BRANDY!" demanded Bass curtly, his own patience eroded to dust by what he considered the infinitely tedious and falsely ingratiating manner of 'The Baron'...

"A vat of fine Italian brandy and an instant cessation to your insipid toadying might improve your standing minutely in our perception, 'Baron of Bankside'..."

"I shall ponder upon respecting you perhaps just enough, Mr Baron, when I am satisfied that the respect of both myself, and that of Colonel Blackmore, has been well earned," snorted Bass indignantly as he drained his first generously-sized, fine cut glass crystal tumbler full of brandy in one gulp and, without waiting upon invitation from his host, helped himself to a second...

"You may choose to liken our coincidental arrival here into the midst of your 'pack' as being foretold, 'Baron', and that remains your sacred right of choice, but I choose to believe that randomly occurring happenstance, such as I assure you that our presence here most surely is, sometimes, above all other things, has a fortuitous habit of proffering the most fruitful solution to even the most taxing of conundrums."

His composure fully restored, rather than adopting a defensive posture against the venomous verbal assault delivered by Bass, 'The Baron' calmly took a sip from his own tumbler and, his expression softened as though becoming instantly reacquainted with the familiar features belonging to a trusted compatriot of long standing, smiled understandingly at the astonished detective...

"Ah yes, of course... there you are, James Bartholomew Bass. There is the cynical old wolf whose acquaintance was one's privilege to make so many long years ago."

Both Bass and Blackmore gawped incredulously for several discomforting seconds at 'The Baron', each attempting to comprehend and assimilate the remarkable statement they had just heard, prior to Bass eventually stammering...

"I... I fear that you have me at a disadvantage, sir. I don't ever recall having met you."

Now fully aware that he had gained the high ground with regards to maintaining a composed demeanour, his smile now a good deal broader as he proceeded to deliver the following salvo of his remarkable revelation, 'The Baron' proceeded to utilise his fully restored confidence in order to interrupt Bass...

"Ah no, James, my old friend... Not for a good while yet."

Both Bass and Blackmore, struck dumb by the fantastic rhetoric delivered by 'The Baron', all at once turned sharply on their heels upon becoming aware of the arrival in their midst of an unnervingly familiar presence.

Seating himself at the head position of the curved table that 'The Baron 'had hastily vacated on the instant of his appearance, as though the mysterious stranger expected such a gesture to be made by a subordinate, even the horrific scar that ran from his forehead, passing through the eyeless left socket and down the left cheek to join myriad battle-related facial wounds could not conceal the certainty of his identity, nor could it detract from the potentially paradoxical connotations that were possible as a result of such an unorthodox meeting...

"Hello again, Tiberius, my oldest and dearest friend. On this day, my heart is gladdened beyond words."

Alternating his attention, firstly to the stranger, and then to Bass several times whilst attempting to rationalise the improbable sight that had manifest itself before their eyes, Blackmore remained silent as words that would even begin to logically explain such a remarkable phenomenon were momentarily not forthcoming.

Alternatively, Bass, who studied intently the now 'not so strange' stranger, whose one good eye scanned him in a very familiar manner, as ever retained his controlled composure and on this occasion proved the antithesis of his dumbstruck companion as he began to speak, all the while curiously sniffing the air as he did so...

"Greetings... James," he began as, turning towards Blackmore he nodded his affirmation that the battle-scarred features belonging to the man who sat before them did indeed belong to James Bartholomew Bass...

Blackmore looked on incredulously, still attempting to give relevance to the sight that was unfolding before his disbelieving eyes...

"Rest easy, Tiberius, for as I... he has just confirmed to you, I am James Bass," came an attempt from the surrogate Bass at placating the perplexed detective.

Referring to both himself, and his past incarnation, 'future' Bass persevered with his intention to offer a simple explanation for this extraordinary phenomenon of two separate versions of the same person inhabiting the exact same space in time ...

"I am, in essence, one and the same person from one of an infinite number of realities that exist parallel to your own, momentarily inhabiting the same space in time by means of random coincidence."

Blackmore, his powers of cognisance now fully restored, began to offer a pertinent cross-examination, the ability of which to deliver in a confident and effective manner had previously eluded him, whilst 'his' Bass chose, for the present, to observe matters as they unfolded in silence...

"So, 'James'; you allude to the space that we, in this moment, inhabit as representing mine and James', 'MY' James, that is of course, possible future... A future that, however, may be altered. A future that need never come into being."

"But of course, Tiberius," countered 'future' Bass without observing the merest hint of a pause for thought...

"Throughout the constantly undulating eddies of time, an infinity of possibilities co-exist, all of which may be affected by either a single random occurrence, a well-conceived decision, or even the most spontaneously realised whim."

Transfixing each of the detectives with the startling content of his revelatory words, 'future' Bass winced as he shifted his battle-weary and broken form uncomfortably in his chair in a futile attempt to gain some form of painless comfort, and continued...

"In actual fact, my friends, this particular reality should never have been allowed the credence to exist at all. The specific reasons for such a catastrophe to have been allowed to occur are now consigned to the annals of history, reasons appertaining to which you have no doubt already drawn your own conclusions, but thankfully and due largely to the tireless labours of Brother de Payens, we are once more able to foresee a time when equilibrium throughout the cascading myriad of infinite timelines will be restored once more."

"Then answer me this, James," countered a somewhat perturbed Blackmore...

"Why in God's name were our alter-egos, indigenous to this dimension, not able to affect the required motivation for an effective reprisal to be mounted, amongst what must surely have existed a willing resistance force? Where was the resolve, where lay the courage, the fortitude and leadership to command arising from the abyss and onwards towards the dawn of a new hope?"

CHAPTER 23

"Because, my old friend, though retaining my lycanthropic tendencies, a near-fatal altercation with positively the fiercest and most physically capable nemesis that you will ever meet very nearly ended my life and did in fact rob me of my..."

His words faltering as a wave of spontaneous emotion overcame him, nullifying his ability to speak, the ensuing silence was compounded by a rising inner turmoil within Blackmore as he became instantly aware of an awful truth...

"One assumes, then, that I perished during this 'altercation' of which you speak?" an air of resigned acceptance now apparent in his manner...

"Alas, yes, my old friend," answered 'future' Bass simply, his raw emotions re-ignited by the vivid memory of a past tragedy that cast a dark, indelible shadow across his obviously grieving heart...

"The Matriarch?" interceded Bass, finally electing to break the silence he had maintained for quite some considerable time, as though wishing to spare his physically and spiritually ravaged 'doppelganger' from completing, for the present, his already emotionally compromised response to Blackmore's enquiry...

Regaining his composure, 'future' Bass answered...

"Yes, James, damn her festering black soul to eternal torment, 'The Matriarch'; an inevitable confrontation that beckons from your future, but as you are now aware, a confrontation that need not bear the same tragic consequences."

"Oh, you may rest assured, Tiberius, that the end result of such a confrontation will culminate in an altogether more favourable outcome for both of us. This is my pledge to you, from brother to brother," interceded Bass assertively, as though assuring Blackmore that both his loyalty and resolute commitment towards preserving their well-being in the face of impending adversity could never be either doubted, or compromised.

Blackmore, meanwhile, unsurprisingly, remained resolutely focused upon the complexities of their immediate concerns...

"Yes... quite... well then; might one suggest that the potential harbinger of my demise, and of course the possible architect of James' quite radical facial re-adjustment, be regarded as a matter best earmarked for future concern?

"I suggest that our immediate mandate retains paramount importance; in that we seek to gain access into 'The Shard', wherein our intent to eradicate once and for all the evil that festers cravenly within the confines of its lofty crystal portals will be realised."

The one 'good' eye of 'future' Bass perused both his reliably taciturn 19th century alter-ego and Blackmore intently, provoking a heartwarmingly familiar single silent nod of affirmation from each of the two detectives.

This simple, instantly recognisable mannerism, that he recalled using himself on so many occasions in the past, invoked within him the merest sliver of hope that after so many lost decades cast hopelessly adrift in an all-consuming maelstrom of self-recrimination and regret, he may now once again be afforded the opportunity to join forces with his brothers at arms in order to effect one final, glorious offensive against the malignant forces of injustice...

"Gentlemen, even though my prime years are long since behind me, I assure you that I may still be of some valuable assistance to your cause, as will Nettie Glover here, 'The Baron', and what remains of the Bankside 'pack'.

"If we agree to collude and to pool our knowledge of the much-altered 21st century topography of London with your stoic, untainted, politically incorrect 19th century cunning and resolve, then I feel certain that our endeavours shall ultimately bear the sweetest fruit."

Bass surveyed the half-blind, crippled shadow of a man who sat before him. Intensively trained to expertly mask his feelings

CHAPTER 23

from inquisitive eyes, it hadn't escaped his attention that his future incarnation now presented a broken, bereft, cruelly distorted mirror-image of the once proud, indefatigably resilient force of nature which should be facing him...

"Indubitably, all of you may yet indeed prove to be of some use," was the witheringly terse response given by Bass in the wake of the generous offer of assistance proffered by his dishevelled alter-ego..."

"Tiberius and I have at our disposal items of modern technology that will enable us to gain access into 'The Shard' where we are reliably informed the unwary recipients of our wrath remain ensconced within."

"Your source of intelligence is sound," answered 'future' Bass...

"The 'Uber Fuhrer' himself, surrounded by the entirety of his festering, sycophantic cabinet of acolytes, oversees the whole of his tyrannical Nazi empire from atop that glass and steel monstrosity...

"From the 72nd level observation lounge, up to the 96th level penthouse apartments that were once the exclusive domiciles of the very wealthiest of the world's leading financiers and aristocracy, it now serves as the chosen location for both the Chancellery Headquarters and the residential area for the entire relevant governing core of the Nazi cabinet...

"Unsubstantiated rumours abound that 'The Architect' himself oversees the machinations of his odious puppet government from atop this once revered symbol of progressive 21st century architectural engineering, but confirmation of such reports have yet to be verified."

His interest piqued, the response given by Blackmore was coloured by an unexpectedly elevated level of exuberance...

"Excellent! All of the rotten eggs gathered together in one basket. How arrogantly foolish of them not to anticipate their glass fortress in the sky being susceptible to compromise. Let it soon become their tomb then."

'Future' Bass retorted immediately...

"Ah but, Tiberius, their arrogant superiority is well established upon a solid foundation of confidence, and a supreme belief that their counterfeit empire here upon these once sceptred isles is the truly ordained kingdom of the Olympian gods, now physically reborn in them and descended to earth once more to rule the children of their creation."

'Of gods and men, lest the two shall ever meet.'

"Oh, how very poetic!" spat Bass dismissively...

"I recall being not so fluent in the ways of classical verse and quasi-relevant proverbs but alas, when one considers that our beloved and rightly revered metaphysical deities of choice offer spiritual comfort freely and without condition to any tormented soul who believes in them, then these counterfeit 'gods' of mere flesh and blood are exposed as the conniving, manipulative charlatans that we know them to be...

"Let us tarry not a second longer in satisfying ourselves that these false idols can be made to bleed."

***

As the newly-conceived alliance navigated the labyrinthine Bankside tunnels towards the rapidly darkening city scape above, Blackmore, occasionally cursing under his breath as he stumbled over a succession of concealed obstacles, attempted with varying degrees of success to focus his eyes as best he could upon his hampered footfall along the inadequately lit passageways...

'DAMN AND BLAST, CLUMSY OAF THAT I AM!'

"Follow my directions, Mr Tiberius. I 'knows' these tunnels an' their man-traps better'n anyone," offered Nettie in a show of genuine sympathy towards the very human frailties of the ageing detective...

"Yes... of course... by all means, lead on, Nettie."

As Nettie took the lead, Blackmore glanced backwards for a second and noticed that Bass and his future incarnation were nowhere to be seen...

"James... Where the deuce are you!"

"Oh, I shouldn't fret any over them two's whereabouts, Tiberius. These tunnels 'is' narrow, dusty 'n' dark. They'll be along soon enough, you mark my words."

Though Nettie's words were offered as merely an innocent and well-intentioned form of comfort, Blackmore's guarded retort expertly concealed his instinctively suspicious assumption that plans were afoot of which it had already been deemed he should not be made cognisant for the present...

"Yes, of course they will, Nettie. Please, lead on."

Chapter 24

'A Fortress of Steel and Glass.'

"SEVERIN. GET UP HERE, AT ONCE!" The call from above had instilled in the usually calm demeanour of Septimus Severin a rare, most uncharacteristic sensation of nervousness.

Being summoned into the presence of 'The Architect', as opposed to receiving a cordial invite, always gave him a feeling of mild trepidation.

His master's well renowned penchant for venting the spontaneous fury of his indefatigably dominant will upon countless legions of his hapless minions, was the stuff of legend, but on this occasion, the lack of even the merest hint of civilized cordiality present in this particularly curt summons gave Severin great cause for concern.

Arriving promptly in the spacious outer-atrium belonging to the collection of inter-connected rooms located at the Shard's very apex, from which 'The Architect' was able to cast an all-seeing gaze over the entirety of his empire, Severin shifted on his chosen spot uneasily and fidgeted with his collar as it seemed to tighten, noose-like, around his throat with every excruciating second that he was forced to await what he perceived would undoubtedly prove to be a most uncomfortable audience.

Wincing as a sharp, familiar pain racked his subconscious mind, momentarily curtailing his ability to engage rational thought, Severin was nevertheless well aware, throughout this albeit brief moment of agony, that 'The Architect' had forced his malignant, prying consciousness upon him. An uninvited violation of his most intimate, private thoughts to which Severin was no stranger...

"Ah, Septimus. Please enter, and join us."

'He used my Christian name; perhaps my initial instinct of trepidation was, on this occasion, unfounded?'

...reasoned Severin to himself as he stepped over the threshold beyond a pair of great iron-hinged oak doors that were in their grand, middle-aged regality, totally out of context architecturally with the surrounding bland sterility of the contemporary glass and steel décor of the 21st century room into which he had entered...

"Septimus, please come in and be at your ease," sounded the unexpectedly cordial greeting offered by 'The Architect'.

Standing a few paces to the left of 'The Architect', Severin recognised the 'Black Guard' Commander who had been responsible for overseeing the previous night's watch.

Nodding his recognition to the Commander, an informal gesture between master and subordinate officers that was duly and respectfully reciprocated, Severin waited in silent, slightly nervous anticipation, for their often-unpredictable master to reveal the reason for their curt summons into his presence.

Following what seemed to both men an inordinately lengthy period of time, during which all semblance of earthly reality appeared to momentarily cease, 'The Architect' finally began to speak whilst pacing the perimeter of the large, sparsely furnished room which offered a spectacular 360-degree panoramic vista of the spectacular London city scape.

Tentatively obeying their master's request to accompany him, the wary pair of colleagues joined 'The Architect' on each flank as he proceeded to pace languidly around the observation walkway that encircled the spacious room...

"Quite breathtakingly beautiful, is it not, gentlemen? Ever more so when the dying embers of a glorious, mid-autumn sun segue sublimely into the brief sepia of the enchanting golden hour of twilight."

Displaying an almost wistful demeanour, the like of which neither of the perplexed soldiers had ever before witnessed, 'The Architect' continued...

"On many such similar evenings, as one stood watch on the bridge of 'The Royal Sovereign', with topsails drawn in, deck and hold locked down, and ordnance prepared in readiness for the ensuing battle, one would look beyond the quarterdeck astern and quietly, contemplatively whilst adopting a self-satisfied, proud manner, remind oneself of... THE HARSH DISCIPLINE REQUIRED IN ORDER TO MAINTAIN SUCH A PRISTINE, PERFECT ORDER AMONG ALL THINGS!"

His manner altering with alarming swiftness, from that of uncharacteristically informal cordiality to his more familiar trait towards spontaneous acts of manic, unfettered brutality within the space of a mere micro-second, 'The Architect' dramatically raised his right hand and aimed its wide opened palm towards the throat of the 'Black Guard' Commander.

Making neither physical nor direct eye contact with the distressed and completely incapacitated commander, 'The Architect' continued with his diatribe whilst revealing a hitherto unrevealed ability to use the power of his mind initially to asphyxiate his hapless victim to the point of unconsciousness.

Then, in a callous display of unnecessary force that was specifically intended to remind Severin of the consequences one might expect as payment for the price of failure, and just to reiterate how little value 'The Architect' placed upon the lives of even the most loyal contingent of his acolytes, finally proceeded to make direct eye contact with the helpless 'Black Guard' Commander as he casually flicked his still-

CHAPTER 24

open palm in a sideways motion, first to the left, and then to the right, snapping the neck of his helpless captive with ease, as one might a rotten piece of kindling...

"As you can plainly see, Septimus, the cost of failure is high. Are you prepared to pay such a price for bearing the ultimate responsibility of that failure?"

As the corpse of the 'Black Guard' Commander slumped limply to the floor, 'The Architect' diverted his attention towards Severin, whose incredulous expression, coupled with his stunned silence at having witnessed such a callous demonstration of his master's great power, was ample enough of a response to satisfy the psychotically-warped thought process of 'The Architect' that a necessary lesson in obedience had been given, and duly noted...

"And there you have it," proclaimed 'The Architect', rubbing his hands together vigorously, as though merely denoting the completion of yet another tiresome item on a never-ending list of mundane, inconsequential everyday tasks...

"Now that this rather vulgar, but nonetheless necessary, presentation of instant discipline has been concluded, I feel obliged that I should enlighten you as to exactly why I considered it an appropriate example to give, extreme though I readily admit it must have appeared even to one bearing the resolutely solid constitution of a seasoned veteran soldier such as your good self, Septimus; one who, regardless of an unyielding loyalty pledged long ago to my cause, still regrettably bears the irritatingly fragile and infinitely flawed traits of human nature."

Gesturing towards the crumpled, broken corpse lying at his feet, 'The Architect' continued...

"Fleeting moments before your arrival, our recently-retired commander of the watch had brought to my attention closed circuit televisual images depicting an altercation which occurred late last evening between a quartet of your highly regarded, so-called 'elite'

'Black Guard', and a pair of, at first mysterious, very pugilistically competent personages."

Whilst delivering his speech, 'The Architect' proceeded to stab impatiently at the keyboard belonging to a desktop computer that lay on the glass table located at the centre of the room, bringing to life a sequence of poorly illuminated images upon a connected monitor screen...

"The fact that such an altercation was allowed to take place at all, troubled me greatly, thus demanding that this extreme example of discipline be meted out to the serving commander of the watch, who bore, at your order, Septimus, the sole responsibility of assuring that my stringent curfew parameters be adhered to."

Severin remained attentively silent, wrestling with his thoughts and realising that to intercede whilst 'The Architect' remained engaged in speech was inadvisable, until his gnawing conscience dictated that he at least respectfully offer a comment, albeit somewhat reluctantly...

"Still, it would seem to have been a harsh reprisal upon a loyal soldier who was merely performing his designated duty... Master."

"I readily welcome your thoughts, Septimus," imparted 'The Architect' somewhat surprisingly, even though Severin sensed that the unexpected invitation offered by his Master to wilfully contribute his own appraisal of the situation without fear of reprisal, was tempered with the suspicion that nothing more than a false gratuity had been proffered, as though perhaps 'The Architect' had in fact withheld vital components appertaining to the importance of his intelligence deliberately, in order to perversely gauge the response of his wary commander-in-chief.

Deciding to err on the side of extreme caution with the thought of preserving his own life very much now a prime concern, Severin employed the cunning politician's ruse of answering a request for guidance by first making a politely presented, but nonetheless searching

CHAPTER 24

introductory enquiry of his own...

"Excuse my candour, Master, but with the greatest respect intended, do these rather substandard quality pictures represent the entirety of all closed-circuit televisual images that were available from every camera located within the vicinity?"

Instantly aware that his fiendishly conceived gambit had been anticipated, 'The Architect' continued, his mock contriteness instantly sensed by a wily Severin...

"Ah yes, of course; just one more frame that one neglected to reveal, an oversight for which I must offer to you my unreserved apologies, Septimus...

"See here; the quartet of 'Black Guard' approach and appear to challenge a pair of inebriated citizens breaking the curfew. Imagine, then, my chagrin, upon observing closely this portion of footage and laying eyes upon these two particular faces."

Whilst he spoke, 'The Architect' stabbed indignantly at the tortured keypad, enhancing clearly upon the screen the unmistakably dour features belonging to James Bass and Tiberius Blackmore.

Glaring menacingly upwards, directly into the camera lens, each man waved nonchalantly, almost as though an epiphany had simultaneously occurred to them both that upon realisation that their identities had been compromised, a gesture of almost puerile intent, aimed at the one-person least expecting ever to lay eyes upon them again, would, in all likelihood, provide a very beneficial destabilising tactic.

As hoped, the desired effect upon the dangerously unstable mind of 'The Architect', as a direct result of this impudent act, was instantaneous. His mood shifting towards incandescent rage, he proceeded to destroy both the already abused keypad and the image-bearing monitor by focusing the full force of his mind to channel a concentrated burst of energy powerful enough to reduce both components into a molten mass of melted plastic and computer circuitry on the glass desktop.

Preparing himself as best he was able for the inevitable tirade that would surely commence, Severin looked on uncomfortably, aware that within seconds he would bear the brunt of his psychotic Master's rising fury...

"BASS AND BLACKMORE! DAMN THEM TO THE PORTALS OF HADES' HALLS; THEY HAVE SOMEHOW MIRACULOUSLY DISCOVERED A PATHWAY BACK TO THE LIGHT!"

All at once, at the precise moment his anger was approaching its unpredictable zenith, a sudden sharp bolt of rational thought struck 'The Architect', ceasing abruptly his mounting tidal wave of rage, which was in turn replaced by a mood of focused, controlled rationality whilst becoming acutely aware of the extreme course of action he must now be forced to consider as an effective riposte to this outrage...

"Of course: de Payens."

Severin pondered as to whether these words, which he noticed had been uttered aloud, were meant for his ears, or merely delivered as a form of self-psychotherapy.

Convincing himself that his continued silence was conducive towards the most effective form of self-preservation, Severin proceeded to allow the curiously frenetic dialogue of 'The Architect' to continue unhindered...

"Only the intrusive, meddlesome intent of the 13th Meister could possibly have facilitated their reprieve from temporal incarceration."

Gazing out wistfully over the sprawling night-time canopy of London, illuminated by thousands of city lights far below that resembled the encampment fires of a vast army, 'The Architect' paused momentarily, as though to gather and process the relentless cascade of thoughts that proceeded to flood his already increasingly overburdened mind...

CHAPTER 24

'Could this curious thing I am witnessing be the last vestige of sanity deserting a once brilliantly ordered mind?'

...mused Severin to himself, just as 'The Architect' spun theatrically on his heels to face him...

"And what news of the Aston clone dispatched to roam amongst our enemies, Septimus? What news indeed."

Given no time to answer, Severin was bound to listen as 'The Architect' proceeded on with his increasingly erratic diatribe...

"No word since its last documented interim report over six hours ago. I'd confidently wager your life, Septimus, that our pair of recently re-patriated, irritatingly resourceful detectives have, I fear, already unearthed our cunning subterfuge and permanently retired our agent from service..."

"That being the case, one too should assume that our entire network of covert operatives ensconced deeply within the infrastructure of the resistance, is compromised, leading one to the conclusion that..."

His rhetoric halted abruptly by the loud, piercing shrillness of a warning siren, 'The Architect' looked towards Severin, who had, in turn, answered a message that had appeared on the screen of his cellphone...

"Priority one proximity alert, Master. Our perimeter has been severely compromised."

Looking blankly towards his security commander, his lack of any facial expression a sure sign that extreme levels of anxiety were present and increasing at great pace within him, 'The Architect' responded to the message delivered by Severin with an emotionless, unnerving simplicity...

"'Personas non grata', Septimus... THEY ARE HERE!"

***

Approaching a heavy, seemingly impregnable iron door, the threshold beyond which led into a network of disused service tunnels that ran adjacent to the older, long since decommissioned Bankside underground railway line, Blackmore removed his cellular phone from an inside pocket of his overcoat whilst addressing his eclectic band of companions...

"Now is the time to test rigorously the effectiveness of these 21st century 'tranklements' and ascertain whether their worth merits the sacrifices that were made in order to attain the confounded technology."

Stabbing impatiently at the spiral-shaped icon on the glass screen of his cell-phone, Blackmore then held the device over the electromagnetically sealed lock that secured the door barring their entry into the tunnels beyond.

Immediately, a rectangular box appeared upon the glass screen, inside which an array of eight digits began to randomly click over for a few seconds until finally settling on what was assumed to be the correct eight figure key code required in order to open the lock.

Blackmore proceeded to punch the code, '24:30:09:17'...into the keypad securing the lock, resulting in the sound of hefty iron bolts sliding open, possibly for the first time in many years, and the door automatically opening inwards to reveal an unilluminated tunnel before them...

"Excellent," he murmured to himself, prior to addressing the group as a whole...

"Captain Witherspoon, James and I, accompanied by four of his men, will proceed from here along this tunnel to its end where I am certain we shall gain access to 'The Shard' and proceed to unleash the fury of Hell that follows in our wake...

"Baron of Bankside and Nettie Glover, deploy your werewolf hordes throughout the city with a view to causing a consternation the like of which has never before been witnessed, a strategy designated primarily

CHAPTER 24

to occupy the attentions of whatever security forces are prevalent...

"Have a care, mind you, that the safety and well-being of the innocent is of paramount importance, but by all means, feel free to unleash your savage proclivities upon those whose actions best merit them."

Both Nettie and 'The Baron' silently nodded their affirmation. Well aware that time was becoming ever more a priceless commodity, Nettie nevertheless decided that in light of the new trust she had instinctively placed in the hands of the two detectives, coupled with the respect she had developed with regards to both their integrity and formidable combat skills, a few stolen minutes would be well spent in order to share some of the details relating to her past life...

Tossing her exquisitely cascading strawberry blonde curls aside to reveal her beguiling, unblemished features, Nettie began...

"Yes, Tiberius Blackmore... and James Bass, my brothers and sisters are indeed sentient and capable of logical, free thought. Long ago, whilst engaged upon my extensive travels I happened upon a feral pack of lycanthropes...

"Still overcome by their untempered, unpredictably savage tendencies and roaming aimlessly throughout their Balkan heartland, lacking either logically reasoned direction or decisive leadership, I joined them and, once having gained their trust, proceeded to offer them the possibility of a purpose beyond the merest bare instinct to survive; to look with clear, open minds towards the future and embrace a bold optimism that promised, in time, to deliver them an improved quality of life the like of which they could scarcely have dreamed imaginable...

"Eventually, in the early part of the sixteenth century, if memory serves, we arrived in London and discovered a concealed honeycomb of Roman-built tunnels that served as our home for many years until, in the late nineteenth century, an altercation with 'The Matriarch' and her fanatical minions ensued that virtually wiped-out my pack and forced the few survivors that were left to re-locate into what we considered the more defensible enclave of Bankside."

As Nettie continued to speak, she glanced towards 'future' Bass, her gaze softening as her eyes met his across the group...

"Here, in this desolate, forgotten place, we came upon 'our' James. He was horribly wounded, crippled and close to death...

"We nursed him back to some semblance of health and, in time, possibly as a gesture of gratitude, he willingly became our mentor, aiding in furthering our understanding of how the feral tendencies within us might be tempered, even mastered, by utilising the discipline that had always laid dormant, buried unchecked for centuries deep within each one of us...

"You see, gentlemen, James is our father. 'The Baron' here, however, bless his huge, benevolent heart, remains the totemic figurehead of our pack. He provides for our everyday needs and he leads, based upon the advice and mentorship proffered by our true patriarch, James Bass."

Sensing that Nettie's rising emotions had conspired to momentarily curtail her curious tale, 'future' Bass placed a steadying, paternal hand upon her shoulder...

"Ah, sweet Nettie; the eldest and wisest of us all. Self-nurtured through the demanding process of enlightenment and completely sentient towards the taxing rigours upon her senses wrought by this terrible curse of lycanthropy long before my arrival, Nettie selflessly retains the true, life-affirming essence of this pack, and quite probably that of the whole lycanthrope race."

Diverting his attention towards Bass, the closing sentences of 'future' Bass were tinged with an unmistakable air of solemnity...

"Assuming that this attempted 'correction' of ours proves successful, and the course of time as it should unfold is restored, then assure me, James, that whatever plane of existence you choose to inhabit, you will seek out Nettie and together strive to preserve both the well-being, and the unhindered future of our race."

Dissuaded from giving a verbal answer by the sharp raising of a silencing finger to lips from his solemn alter-ego, Bass instead signalled his affirmation by offering a single nod of his head, allowing his future self to conclude...

"Ask of me no more concerning this matter, James, for to divulge further what destiny lies before, or indeed behind you, would enhance the possibility of a further potentially catastrophic ripple effect in the ebb tide of time which might well once more de-stabilise the repairing equilibrium."

Taking heed of the request made by his 'future' self, Bass proceeded to re-focus the minds of his companions on the task in hand...

"Captain Witherspoon, with us, if you please; 'Baron of Bankside' and Nettie, go now and take from this rising 'wolf moon' the gift of its unbridled energy to our kind but be wary: though your cleansing task be of vital importance throughout the entirety of our city, choose not this side of the river as the focus of your attentions in one hour's time, lest your children of the moon be eradicated by the fall of our enemy's glass and steel Olympus into the dust."

Nodding her understanding of the ominous warning issued by Bass, Nettie turned towards the Bankside tunnel entrance where the remnants of her werewolf 'pack' patiently awaited her return. As she did so, 'future' Bass imparted towards Bass and Blackmore...

"Due to certain pressing responsibilities that demand the entire focus of my attention at present, I shall endeavour to rendezvous with the pair of you in the year 1898, at the designated time in the crypt situated beneath St Michael's Church where, if all our hopes and plans come to fruition, history will be on the cusp of realising its destiny, one way or the other...

"Now, god speed to all on this night of nights, when from the desperation of our present rises a new hope for both the salvation of our past, and the affirmation of a future free from the shackles of tyranny."

***

Referring first to his pocket watch as the unmistakable sound of howling wolves filtered across the still night air of London, and the flames of chaos began to rise all across the city skyline, Blackmore proceeded to speak in hushed tones directly to Bass whilst simultaneously making certain that each one of his considerable cache of formidable weaponry was fully loaded and prepared for instantaneous use...

"The wolves have commenced their designated mission with a fortitude and zeal one might least have expected from a race that was once so vilified and persecuted to the point of extinction by the very same human race whose freedom from beneath the suffocating shroud of evil they would now seek to secure."

"Witherspoon, we enter here, one would assume," hissed Blackmore close to the ear of the C.S.F. Captain...

"Refresh my memory, if you would be so kind, Captain; during our briefing, was not the fact alluded that the 72nd to the top-most levels were allocated for the exclusive patronage of the entire regime hierarchy?"

"Indeed, sir, the entire government both resides and governs from within those levels, rarely, if ever, venturing beyond its heavily guarded and technologically fortified ramparts."

"Excellent," exuded Blackmore, his adrenaline level rising sharply towards its peak battle readiness...

"The moment our squad reaches the 72nd level as one, James and I shall detach ourselves and press on upwards alone with a view to flushing out the most venomous serpents languishing within this nest

CHAPTER 24

of vipers and retiring them from office permanently."

Witherspoon surveyed Blackmore intently, his eyes clearly betraying the thoughts that spiralled behind them; thoughts of concern and incredulous disbelief at the very notion of what he now felt certain was the act of wanton devastation that was about to be perpetrated...

Engaging a 'saved documents' folder on his cell-phone, Blackmore selected a detailed blueprint of the steel super-structure of 'The Shard', which he brought to the attention of Witherspoon and his men...

"James and I were able to identify what appear to be the key load bearing steel support stanchions of the building from level 72 here, here and here, all the way up to the penthouse summit, here...

"In theory, and I apologise unreservedly in advance for my lack of knowledge in the field of explosive demolition, a single charge of adequate yield at these points here, plus random charges set intermittently so as to weaken these areas where the supporting steel triangulates and bears the entire mass of the higher levels, should suffice to raze this edifice to its foundations, the spectacle of which alone would prove an ample statement to all of humanity that the oppressed had finally risen from their enforced slumber and claimed back, with one mighty blow, the liberty and freedom that was for too long denied them."

Utilising once more his cell-phone code-breaking app, Blackmore proceeded to access the electro-magnetic locking system which secured a second pair of stout iron gates that allowed them access, from the darkness of the tunnels, to a much more spacious, brighter illuminated area.

Witherspoon instantly recognised their current location as being one of the many underground car parking areas that ran throughout the entire basement area of 'The Shard'.

"We're directly below the main concourse level of our destination," Witherspoon hissed before his well-intended attempt to communicate

AN APPOINTMENT WITH DESTINY

quietly was rudely curtailed by the arrival of six armed 'Black Guard', whose sudden appearance surprised the bold companions during their attempt to gain access to a service elevator...

"HALT! YOU THERE! STAND TO AND BE RECOGNISED!"

Neither waiting for the 'Black Guard' commander to complete his tersely delivered request, nor allowing his men the precious few seconds they required in order to raise and prime the breeches of their weapons, Bass and Blackmore each drew their pair of silenced semi-automatic pistols and, displaying the remorseless efficiency of the assassin's creed that they each steadfastly upheld, proceeded to systematically gun down all six of their hapless challengers.

Surveying the latest deceased examples of their clinically undertaken handiwork, whilst momentarily still inhabiting the mindset of cold, emotionally-detached enforcers, the resulting comment made by Bass proved to be as profound as it was characteristically brief...

"And so, it begins."

Performing a second questionable action that appeared unnecessarily barbaric on first impression to Witherspoon, his revulsion towards their initial extreme actions was compounded as Bass and Blackmore stepped cautiously among their latest collection of 'retirements' and coldly fired off a further pair of rounds each into the prone 'Black Guard' corpses.

With the precise efficiency of the experienced military commander he was, Blackmore sounded off as protocol demanded...

"Six marks down," to which Bass duly responded...

"Six marks down. That's an affirmative."

"Purely habitual, you understand, Witherspoon?" alluded Blackmore, his somewhat insincere attempt to justify their seemingly pointless actions prompting the incredulous young captain to privately suppose to himself, as the team prepared to enter the now secured elevator...

CHAPTER 24

'I can't recall happening upon military personnel affiliated to any regiment that I'm aware of who possess even a minute percentage of the focus, the guile, the skill set and the cold, unashamed brutality of this quite extraordinarily barbaric pair of arcane Victorian 'monsters'.'

As though perceiving the troubled thoughts permeating throughout the mind of Witherspoon, the response Bass chose to give the young C.S.F. officer offered neither a calming fatherly comfort, nor any vestige of compassionate, brotherly sympathy...

"Wise up, Captain, and compose yourself. QUICKLY! Forget all of the things you perceive to be 'just so' and focus your mind only on survival, at any cost. Survival is the key; the single most important thing of value that affords one the opportunity to seek the ultimate victory...

"Quite probably the simplest, most visceral tactical decision that you will ever be compelled to make, Witherspoon. A decision of such monumental importance that it will impact upon the continuance of your very existence; whether to survive, or whether to die."

Without waiting for a response, Bass entered the elevator compartment. Witherspoon followed closely behind, still processing the stark, sobering lesson just received from the ageing, taciturn warrior...

"Up to the lobby first, gentlemen, where one might suggest that we continue on with our 'purge'."

With no sign of resistance forthcoming from any of the group towards the proposal made by Bass, Witherspoon, his mind now suitably cleared so as to form patterns of logical thought once more, proceeded to offer a suggestion of his own...

"The moment our presence is detected, all of the building's 36 elevators will be automatically locked-down as part of the site-wide security protocol...

"If I am able to access the main computer terminal that is located on the ground floor, somewhere in the south quadrant, I will endeavour to override the system and upload my own program that will allow us both unhindered use of all the building's elevators and wilful access through all of the on-site security protocols."

***

Upon entering the spacious entrance concourse belonging to 'The Shard', the band of companions was afforded little opportunity to tactically assess their surroundings before a sizeable squad of 'Black Guard', who had obviously been alerted to their unauthorised presence, and too, judging by the fact that they chose to open fire immediately upon the band of nefarious intruders without offering the obligatory challenge, were also plainly aware of the wanton violence that had been so mercilessly meted out to their hapless colleagues in the basement just a few moments earlier.

Drawing from his vast well of combat experience, Bass barked out his uncomplicated commands in his own brusque, quite unorthodox 19th century fashion, with a view to the entire squad of C.S.F. operatives, Blackmore and Witherspoon included, taking note and obeying without question...

"TAKE COVER; LEFT AND RIGHT FLANKS; UNLEASH HELLFIRE AND FURY AT WILL!"

Joining Blackmore as he sought concealment behind the fortuitously large marble sculpture of a lion, Bass raised his voice so as to be heard over the increasingly deafening sound of semi-automatic small-arms' fire as it lethally bit into the opulent marble and glass décor of their surroundings...

"I fear that the element of surprise we so coveted no longer rests in our favour, Tiberius. No matter, assuming that Witherspoon is able to make good on his proposed strategy, then the successful completion of our designated mandate should remain a formality."

CHAPTER 24

As he attempted to be heard over the rising cacophony of potentially lacerating glass and stone shards that were randomly exploding in all directions around them, Bass drew Blackmore's attention towards the red flashing light on an active security camera which spied on them from a location high above their heads, more than likely alerting 'The Architect' himself as to their presence within his inner sanctum...

"Look aloft, my old friend. Our calling card is duly delivered to our host, and, it would seem, our attendance has been well documented and duly received in kind."

Choosing to offer a physical reaction in response to the remark made by his observant companion, Blackmore raised his LeMat revolver and expertly discharged a single round towards the invasive surveillance device, that proved sufficient to blind its intrusive electronic eye permanently...

"How rude," he quipped dryly, raising an uncharacteristically cheeky smirk and a satisfied huff of approval from Bass...

"Witherspoon, you and your men discharge a suppressing cross-fire from secure positions on each flank. Taper your rounds with exacting precision so as to reduce the risk of incurring friendly-fire casualties," ordered Blackmore as he waved his left hand accordingly so as to visually corroborate his commands.

A protracted period of relentless weapons' fire appeared to exhibit little indication of abating due to the seemingly constant re-enforcing of the 'Black Guard' ranks, a curiously repetitive occurrence that had not gone unnoticed by the ever-observant Blackmore...

"Has it ever given you cause to notice that, regardless of the ever-increasing numbers of these 'Black Guard' that are retired, a dozen more appear in order to reinforce their depleted ranks?

"In light of the recent forensic evidence brought to light, courtesy of the minutely detailed report submitted by your good Connie, James, I would be inclined to offer the theory that these 'beings' each possess a similar genetic inheritance to the one discovered ensconced within the Aston clone."

"Yes, Tiberius. The unmistakable stench of 'The Architect' is prevalent, buried deep within the DNA of each one of them. Even with regards to his own army, arrogance compels him to infuse each and every one of them with strands of his own irremediable DNA."

'And God created man in his own image...'

"Could one deluded, incalculably flawed individual, giddied by the intoxicating fumes of his own great power, harbour such a grand delusion as to perceive his own existence as being omnipotent? An invincible, unimpeachable deity overseeing his minions from atop his glass Olympus, perhaps?"

Bass nodded his silent affirmation to the sage suppositions proffered by Blackmore, prior to addressing Witherspoon directly...

"Set your remote fuses for a twenty-minute delay, Captain. Then, without hesitation, lead your men away to a secure vantage point on the far river bank, safe in the knowledge that your mission here is completed to the satisfaction of your commanding officers."

"Sir, with respect, we could..."

Witherspoon's well-intentioned attempt to offer aid was instantly curtailed and rebuffed by Bass, who fixed the perplexed young officer with his piercing, jet-black glare...

"Tiberius and I press on upwards from level 72 harbouring naught but sound mind and reason, Captain. Rest assured; we do not proceed towards what might be perceived by either our peers or subordinates alike as being little more than a forlorn hope without the assurance of an infallible exit strategy being factored into our plans...

"Now, you have your orders, Captain. Please be so kind as to cover our rear guard as you vacate the 'kill-zone'. God's speed and good fortune to you all."

Chapter 25

'The Fall of Olympus.'

Bass and Blackmore gratefully reached the secure confines of a vacant elevator car, the insistent chatter of semi-automatic small-arms fire becoming less apparent as the doors slid shut behind them, and they proceeded to ascend towards the upper levels of 'The Shard'.

Discarding their spent semi-automatic weapons, each man drew from concealment beneath his heavy overcoat his trusted, now antique revolvers: Blackmore his battle-grey LeMat, Bass his pair of Smith and Wesson Schofield specials.

Taking the limited, infinitely precious time afforded them during their brief elevator journey, whilst being serenaded somewhat bizarrely by the inanest, soporifically bland elevator music imaginable, the chambers, hammers, triggers and breeches of each revolver were meticulously checked for maximum efficiency, as were the four spare separate interchangeable chambers of ammunition that each man carried in two of his several overcoat pockets. Both Bass and Blackmore then confirmed their readiness to each other with a single nod, and prepared themselves for the imminent inevitability of deadly confrontation.

Almost as though he considered it a necessity to air his thoughts, Blackmore nonetheless waited for a further few seconds before speaking, a lull made all the more surreal by the increasingly nauseating strains of 'Popular Organ Classics of Our Time' which were being piped incessantly through the elevator speaker system...

"To state the blindingly obvious, James: the moment that these doors slide open, the ensuing barrage we face will, in modern terms no doubt, equal in the percentage of deadly ordnance alone the intensity of the one we encountered during the forlorn charge upon Sevastopol."

Concluding that the observation made by Blackmore was perfectly valid, Bass frantically scanned the cramped confines belonging to the interior of their rapidly elevating potential 'coffin' in the hope of locating some form of concealment from the approaching firefight...

"There, Tiberius. Directly above our heads. What appears to be an accessible aperture of some description."

Noticing a service hatch located in the ceiling of their elevator compartment that was barely wide enough for a man to squeeze through, Bass began feverishly formulating the semblance of a plan...

"Quickly, old friend, time is short. Lend me that ageing back of yours so that I might make attempt to gain access onto the roof of this rapidly rising 'steel tomb 'we find ourselves in."

Reluctantly doing as he had been bid, Blackmore bent over, thus allowing Bass his human step, as requested.

Almost buckling under the combined mass of both Bass and his weighty array of assorted weaponry, Blackmore grumbled aloud...

"Uhm... Should not a lycanthrope possess the ability to leap such a short distance with relative ease? Oh, upon my life... James, please... I fear that I may never recover from..."

Just as the last few strained words left Blackmore's lips, Bass used his considerable upper-body strength to lever himself upwards and through the now forced open trap door cover.

Anchoring his feet between a pair of iron stanchions located on the elevator roof, Bass reappeared at the opening and offered his outstretched arms to Blackmore...

"Now, I think, would prove to be the optimal moment to cease your griping and join me up here, do you not agree, Tiberius?"

Requiring no second bidding, Blackmore gratefully reached up and tightly gripped each of Bass' forearms. Anticipating a tricky ascent, he was surprised, then, to experience the entirety of his own body weight, weapons and all, being raised effortlessly through the narrow aperture as though he bore the weight of no more than a young child...

"A truly remarkable turn of physical strength for a ruined old war dog such as yourself, James," quipped Blackmore dryly, his stab of spontaneous mock sarcasm masking his true feelings of absolute astonishment at being witness first-hand to the remarkable feat of physical strength displayed by his ageing companion...

"A consequence of eating well, taking regular exercise and copious amounts of rest," quipped Bass congenially, as Blackmore joined him on the roof of their still rapidly ascending elevator car.

***

"DEPLOY MORE UNITS TO QUELL THE FRAY!" 'The Architect' spat frantically towards Severin, who had by this time ascertained that the self-proclaimed 'Master of All Things' was no more capable of rational thought than any mortal being plagued by the sensually-crippling effects wrought by the one human condition that radiates the power to numb and confound the senses, and send them careering hopelessly towards the brink of unbridled, emotional collapse... FEAR!

'So, not only does 'The Architect' appear concerned for the potential havoc the assault led by Bass and Blackmore will wreak throughout his empire, he, too, is quite obviously now afeared of the men themselves.'

From the moment of his epiphany forth, Severin finally accepted that no longer would he perceive 'The Architect' as the infallible, immortal, all-powerful entity he once had...

'And so, in his moment to be severely tested is the 'god' exposed as being merely a man, made vulnerable by all of the frailties, all of the indecision, indeed, all of the human flaws which, when combined, make humankind the sentient, compassionate, benevolent, extraordinarily unique beings that they are.'

Deciding, too, that self-preservation must now be regarded as being the better part of judgement, Severin took great care to temper his next words meant for 'The Architect' with extreme caution...

"Master; they retain complete control of any elevator they wish to utilise. All of the security codes that govern the lockdown protocols for the entire site have somehow been compromised. Might one suggest, Master, that we first contain this situation directly, and then..."

"YES, YES. CONTAIN, SEVERIN... CONTAIN THE SITUATION DIRECTLY AT ALL COSTS... AT ALL COSTS, DAMN YOU... DO YOU HEAR!"

Convinced that his empire now spiralled uncontrollably in a calamitous freefall towards its doom, 'The Architect' considered his psychotically deranged perspective now refocused entirely upon self-preservation and the immediate invocation of what he perceived to be his cunningly conceived alternative contingency plan, a plan which was so outrageous in content that if it were to prove successful would ensure the power of the 13th Meister remaining his to command forever...

Whilst concentrating his thought process almost entirely upon securing his unchallenged exit strategy, 'The Architect' continued to issue what appeared now as little more than token, hollow commands towards Severin, who was now completely aware of the distinct possibility, fast approaching, that the lives of both himself and his men were about to be sacrificed in order to cover the retreat of nothing more than a craven coward...

CHAPTER 25

"Call out the entire garrison if you must, Severin. This time, it is imperative that my initial error of deciding to banish them into the vortex for eternity is not repeated. Now get out there and supervise the demise of Bass and Blackmore personally."

"And what, if one might be so bold as to enquire, might one expect as your next course of action?" enquired Severin, his tone purposefully altered to blatant informality, as he was now devoid of any thoughts appertaining towards the fear he might once have harboured in lieu of the expected abusive response he might receive for his openly unashamed display of flippancy...

"THAT IS NONE OF YOUR CONCERN AT PRESENT; YOU SHOULD ONLY ASSUME THAT MY AFFAIRS, WHATEVER DIRECTION I NOW INTEND FOR THEM TO PURSUE, ARE OF MY OWN VOLITION, AND THAT SHOULD YOUR PARTICIPATION IN THE SUCCESSFUL CULMINATION OF THOSE AFFAIRS EVER BE REQUIRED, THEN REST ASSURED YOU WILL BE SUMMONED IN DUE COURSE. NOW GO AND DO AS YOU WERE TOLD!"

Presenting a torrent of vitriolic abuse exactly as anticipated, Severin looked on incredulously as, without looking backwards, 'The Architect' bolted towards the large brick sphere that was situated against one of the sizeable window panels behind his glass desk...

'How on earth could I not have noticed this incongruous obelisk here?'

...puzzled Severin to himself as the bricks parted on either side, affording the fleeing 'Architect' an entrance into the black interior of the sphere, closing tightly behind him as he disappeared within, suggesting no indication that the mortar binding each brick together ever having been disturbed.

Remaining silent for a few moments, the sphere then began to emit first a low-pitched humming sound that after a few seconds developed into a louder pulsating thrum, which in turn manifested into a painful, high-pitched whine as the sphere began to rotate on the spot at great speed, a shock-wave emanating from its core shattering all of the windows in the room as it dissolved amidst an arc of spectacular lightning bolts and blinding white light into thin air before the still disbelieving eyes of Severin...

'So, in the defining moments of his reign, the so-called 'Master of All Things' reveals himself as the fearful, spineless absconder that he is. GOOD RIDDANCE, SAY I!'

'As for oneself, perhaps an honourable death served by the hands of two former friends who bear the highest repute amongst their peers is the least one might hope for in return for one's many transgressions against his own kind'...

...mused Severin inwardly, as he afforded himself a rueful grin whilst preparing his sidearm for the inevitable confrontation.

Chapter 26

'A Most Rhadamanthine Pair.'

"Pray tell, what manner of curiously pyrotechnic delights were deposited into the sack that was entrusted to your care by the good Captain Witherspoon, Tiberius?" enquired Bass of the contents packed within the hessian sack that had remained tightly strapped to Blackmore's back throughout the entire melee thus far.

Loosening the drawstring that secured the top flaps of the sack, that resembled an old-style, hessian military kit bag, Blackmore commenced revealing its lethally explosive inventory…

"Even as we speak, Witherspoon and his men traverse downwards towards the concourse located at ground level, their own cache of neutronic charges being placed at precise locations on several levels below the 72nd, where the giant crossed steel stanchions bear the full mass of the building…

"Within this sack is an assortment of our own neutronic explosive charges, each of which we shall deploy along our route of ascent so as to wreak maximum destruction upon detonation…

"In addition to these devilish baubles of destruction, we have, at our disposal, these delectable little 'hors de oeuvres'," Blackmore quipped as he produced from inside the sack an object that resembled a matt-green, label-less baked bean tin, on top of which a metal ring secured a 'dead-man's' trigger by means of what appeared to be the steel pin to which it was attached.

Bass remained transfixed, his interest piqued by this intriguing device of simple design and construction which bore obvious incendiary promise, whilst Blackmore continued his impromptu munitions presentation...

"A rather devilish little trinket, appropriately named a 'stun grenade'. Simply remove this pin and toss it towards the advancing hordes, the ensuing voluminous bang and blinding flash of phosphoric light momentarily befuddling the senses, thus affording one the opportunity to secure an unchallenged, if somewhat cruelly one-sided, victory over one's momentarily sensually incapacitated enemy."

Glancing upwards as Blackmore addressed him, Bass became acutely aware that their elevator car was still ascending rapidly towards the ceiling...

"All things to which we aspire will count for naught should we be crushed betwixt the swiftly approaching elevator shaft ceiling and the roof of this car!"

With less than six feet to spare, the elevator car halted abruptly. Taking a 'stun grenade' in his left hand, his right index finger poised to remove the pin, Bass bade his attentive companion to mirror his action...

"Patience, my friend. Hold fast until their initial volley is spent."

Sure enough, even before the elevator car doors were completely open, a deafening barrage of semi-automatic small-arms fire began mercilessly strafing the inside of the exposed, empty compartment below them.

Just as Bass had predicted, a brief, almost ethereal, lull occurred post-volley during which was plainly audible both the ejection of spent cartridge magazines to be replaced with fully loaded clips, and the sliding breeches that denoted the re-loading and priming of semi-

CHAPTER 26

automatic weapons.

Identifying this scant few seconds of inactivity as their optimum opportunity to strike, Bass and Blackmore each removed the pins from a pair of 'stun grenades' and punted them as best they were able through the narrow opening in the elevator car ceiling so they bounced out of the bullet-riddled compartment, thus enabling each of the 'live' devices to roll effortlessly towards the now tentatively advancing group of 'Black Guard'.

The remarkably effective results of the 'stun grenades' presenting no discernible discomfort to the battle-hardened constitutions of the still-concealed Bass and Blackmore, a deep-rooted instinct alone provided them with their next obvious course of action.

Exploiting to full advantage the pyrotechnic combination of a deafeningly loud bang and a blinding, phosphorescent flash, the pair of old warriors dropped effortlessly through the narrow aperture and, with revolvers cocked and raised, began their merciless cull of the incapacitated 'Black Guard'.

Scrutinising the familiar tableau of carnage laid out before them, six now lifeless souls, fresh bullet wounds still smouldering amidst the acrid stench of gunpowder and the haze of gunfire residue, Blackmore's voice became noticeably tinged with raw emotion and perhaps a suggestion of underlying anger...

"To kill with impunity at the behest of one's government; to take lives without question in the name of the perceived righteous cause, has quite possibly rarely appeared less relevant than in this moment, James...

"Have we truly as a species evolved so little from wearing animal skins and sheltering in caves that the prime concern of our finest technical minds this past century has involved the development of more devastatingly effective weaponry with which firstly to dumbfound, and then to exterminate ourselves...

"Wherein lies the soldier's sacred code of honour?"

"A question of unequivocally great import that demands due and careful consideration at a more appropriate juncture, my brother," reasoned Bass in reply to the extraordinarily philosophical query raised by Blackmore.

***

Severin attempted to prepare, as best he was able, both himself, and what meagre numbers of his 'Black Guard' cohort remained cognisant of his ability to still issue decisive commands...

"Steal yourselves, my brave, loyal soldiers, for the true, quintessential essence of wrath incarnate is almost upon us. Offer no quarter yourselves, as surely none will be given, and be mindful that to hesitate, even for a micro-second, is to accept readily and without question what little time remains of your existence here on this mortal plane."

With the ominous sound of multiple explosions, raking small-arms fire and the pitiful death throes of his forward placed bridgehead, tormenting his tortured ears drawing ever closer, Severin persevered with his attempted motivational monologue as best he could, accepting of the fact that in all likelihood he was in the process of issuing his final raft of commands to his beleaguered troops...

"Easy now, boys, have courage... steady yourselves. Raise those weapons and take a solid stance for death is coming to call on this day and rest assured, its greeting is rarely cordial and its touch is as cold as ice."

The blinding white phosphorescent flash and deafeningly loud discharge of a stun grenade heralded the anticipated arrival of Bass and Blackmore. In their momentarily disoriented state, the meagre remnants of Severin's much-depleted rear guard offered little tangible resistance to the formidable vanguard offered by the pair of determined

CHAPTER 26

old warriors advancing on a relentless course directly towards them.

Dispatching all that remained of the now completely demoralized 'Black Guard' squad with considerable ease, Bass and Blackmore wasted little time in locating and confronting Septimus Severin, who somewhat surprisingly offered no resistance after having come to terms with the stark reality that he was, in all probability, and with just cause, about to reap the ultimate reward in return for his hitherto unyielding fealty towards the house of 'The Architect'.

Finally finding themselves eye to eye with their once highly respected mentor, both Bass and Blackmore simultaneously, and without hesitation, discharged a pair of rounds each into the chest of Severin.

As was ever the case, the customarily unerring trajectory of their lethal lead projectiles found their target with consummate ease, the spectacle of which prompted a sense of surprise within each of the two detectives, as though in attempting no malicious action towards them Severin had accepted that this moment was fated in order for his time on earth to draw finally to its ignominious and inglorious end.

Kneeling respectfully beside the prone form of Severin, from whom the final few embers of life were fading from his once proud, vibrant and strong warrior's frame, a mixed combination of feelings encompassing both regret and remorse, coupled with the joy of many fond reminiscences of the more brotherly and cordial association that they had shared whilst serving in the military together, darted through the minds of both Bass and Blackmore, who remained respectfully silent as Severin uttered his final words...

"Ah, James... Tiberius... The two most stoic, least corruptible, keenest upholders of true justice that in all probability the world has ever known, and quite probably shall ever know; Indeed, a most Rhadamanthine pair.

"I celebrate, with fondest regards, our once highly-prized friendship and the small part that I was able to contribute in both unearthing and nurturing the unique potential that both of you possessed for future greatness, just as I am in this moment contented that it is you two who now justly end the mortal journey of this hopelessly corrupted old sinner...

"May one now, as the final few breaths exhale from these tired, spent lungs for one last time be permitted to regard you, James Bass, and you, Tiberius Blackmore, as my revered brothers in arms?"

With genuine tears of sorrow finding the copious deep lines of age that etched each of their weathered faces, Bass and Blackmore each took a hand of their fallen comrade in theirs and proceeded to offer him the comfort that befitted the strong bond of friendship they had once held for each other...

Blackmore's voice faltered momentarily as the strain of intense emotion took its toll...

"Was it ever thus, my brother? Never should you have harboured any doubt that our unifying bond of brotherhood, anointed in the blood of our enemies spilled on countless fields of battle long ago, remained true, despite your idiosyncratic tendencies of late...

"Rest assured, my old friend, that the spiritual unity shared by we three old soldiers will prevail until time has run its course."

Bass reciprocated the comforting, compassionate words offered in all sincerity by Blackmore at first with only a single, silent nod of his head: a characteristically cold gesture of mute affirmation to which Severin was well accustomed...

"Ah, James, ever the silent, brooding assassin in our midst. The dark Rhadamanthine character towards which a thousand choice epithets could offer meaningfully relevant testament...The champion of... true justice."

CHAPTER 26

Words faltering as the final few breaths emanated from Severin's frail lips, Bass seized upon his opportunity to speak...

"Know this, Septimus: whysoever, and indeed howsoever, your vicarious fragility of will was exposed and manipulated to the extent that it was, is of little import now...

"Take to your grave, my old friend, that your heinous crime of high treason against your Queen, your country and your colleagues merited only one end: the journey towards which the waiting ferryman now beckons.

"Be at peace in the knowledge that 'The Architect' of your corruption will surely be invited to join you very soon after you embark upon your final voyage across the dark waters of the Styx to reside for eternity upon the Isle of the Dead."

Barely able to impart the merest smile of affirmation, and all at once now seemingly with the weight of a thousand past transgressions lifted from his troubled spirit by the comfort of a renewed brotherhood thought forever lost to him, the purged soul of Septimus Severin breathed no more...

"His torment is ended. May his soul find redemption and eternal peace."

Blackmore's brief eulogy was curtailed abruptly by the necessity to proceed with some urgency with regards to the suggestion offered by Bass...

"Tiberius, engage your portkey at once and form a clear image in your mind of the opposite riverbank, as though looking back across the Thames towards this soon to be smouldering pile of neo-capitalist symbolism...

"Now is the time to put a portion of the gift, recently bestowed upon us by Brother de Payens, to a stern test."

In what appeared to be seconds after their simultaneously-shared thought of the suggested location, Bass and Blackmore found themselves facing 'The Shard' from their safe vantage point located on the opposite bank of the river…

"A most impressive ability to command at will," alluded Blackmore aloud, his comment eliciting the now customary single nod of the head, accompanied by the hint of a raised eyebrow from Bass, who in turn reached for an inside pocket of his overcoat and retrieved a small metallic box, at the centre of which was situated a single red button…

Glancing first towards Blackmore, then turning to focus his attention upon the towering stature of 'The Shard', Bass raised the box purposefully to the level of his right eye and forcefully depressed the red button with his right thumb.

Almost as though that one simple 'click' of an insignificant little button had engaged the entire chain of events that duly proceeded to unfold not only before their eyes, but throughout the entire city, Bass and Blackmore nonetheless retained their characteristically impassive demeanours and proceeded to observe whilst pandemonium erupted all around them.

Regarding the point they perceived to be the 72nd level, all of the windows around the entire circumference of the building were blasted outwards by the huge explosion which emanated from within.

Initially, and somewhat eerily, for a scant few seconds no sound was audible at the precise moment the spectacular blast occurred, so that when aural evidence of the monumental pyrotechnic display finally reached civilian ears, the wave of shock and terror combined that ran through the witnessing population, similar to that of a pre-engaged electrical charge, proved all the more prevalent…

'OH MY GOD!'… 'LORD HELP US!'… 'WHAT THE HELL IS HAPPENING? 'THE SHARD; 'LOOK AT THE SHARD!'… 'WE'RE UNDER ATTACK!'… 'GOD HELP US ALL!'

Regarding the cacophony of dismay that resulted from the activation of one innocuous little device, the entire gamut of human

CHAPTER 26

emotions was clearly filtering throughout the perpetually swelling ranks of the observing throng; from confusion and panic, to stunned disbelief, as the unfolding onset of potential Armageddon continued to substantially re-arrange the once spectacularly impressive skyline of the far riverbank.

Bass looked on impassively as an ensuing chain reaction of explosions proceeded to obliterate several of the lower levels of the building in an identical manner to the first, all the way down to concourse level, providing something of a compelling spectacle of precise and expert demolition work.

All at once, an eerie silence befell the now very large crowd that had herded together, bonded by both a shared terror and a supressed apprehension as each one wondered what more atrocities were to follow, separated by the wide, moat-like security of the Thames from the raging inferno that now consumed the Shard almost entirely below its 72nd floor.

"A confounded disappointment and something of an annoying inconvenience that the structure didn't…"

Blackmore's vociferous frustration was instantly alleviated by all of the levels above the 72ndat first buckling, then collapsing in an almost perfectly-engineered vertical trajectory downwards as the now super-heated molten iron and steel supporting girders throughout the entire structure gave way to the monumental mass teetering precariously above them which they could carry no longer.

Rather than the wave of mass hysteria that might have been expected to permeate throughout the witnessing throng in the wake of such a monumental cataclysm, a subtle, gently undulating sub-current of largely unintelligible murmurs suggested a mood of disbelief, and even of a remarkably belligerent disquiet of sorts becoming apparent as the sound of the buckling iron and glass superstructure belonging to The Shard cascaded towards its foundations, with the resulting acrid residue of demolition enveloping the once spectacularly pleasing panoramic vista of the cosmopolitan eastern river bank in a thick haze of suffocating dust.

Immediately snapping to attention, as though having received a direct order to do so, Bass and Blackmore each gave a formal salute in respect to the memory of a once highly regarded soldier.

Blackmore eulogised aloud, standing stock-still whilst orating his personal tribute to a fallen brother...

"Finally, Septimus, may you now find the peace in death that always eluded you in life."

The retort offered by Bass, though less of a testimonial in word, nevertheless suggested a poignant, heart-felt pledge of vengeance in the name of their once revered mentor towards their now shared nemesis, 'The Architect'...

"Go rightly to Hell now, brother, where an eternity of harsh retribution awaits you in payment for your folly, and rest assured that 'The Architect' will be dining beside you at Lucifer's table on this very night."

Standing at ease, Bass caressed the tactile metal casing of the remote detonation device, with which he had moments earlier induced Armageddon on the eastern city skyline, within his right hand for a few seconds before casually tossing it into the brown, soulless murk of the Thames, where, no doubt, already lay several thousand other dark secrets submerged in the cloying riverbed slurry of mud and filth, never to be revealed.

As he did so, he became instantly aware, in his exceptionally acute peripheral vision, of a young child gazing directly towards him from no more than six feet to his right.

Assuming correctly that this pair of innocent eyes and ears had not only overheard the words spoken by both himself and Blackmore, but also observed the remote detonation device being cast into the depths of Old Mother Thames, Bass nonetheless casually proceeded to remove his portkey from an inside pocket of his overcoat…

"Well, Tiberius, our task in this century is now concluded, I think. Witherspoon obviously laid his portion of the neutronic charges as directed, and assuming that he and his men, supported by the Baron of Bankside and Nettie Glover with her pack of lycanthropes, were able to evacuate that area of the city most at peril from the substantial chaos that ensued as a result of this most effective and impressive example of controlled mass demolition in a confined area, then this phase of our mission must ultimately be deemed a resounding success…

"Should the outcome to the impending critical phase of our task prove as favourable, then my understanding is that this entire timeline we currently inhabit will never occur, and all that is now will, in fact, cease to have existed at all, therefore allowing all that should have been to unfold without further irritating hindrance from the corrupt element of random chance."

Blackmore glanced to his right, initially to offer silent courteous acknowledgement towards both the succinct summation of their mission thus far, concisely and logically delivered by Bass, and in support of the suggested course on which their shared destinies should steer, but his attention was seized by the fixed, attentive gaze of the young child, still standing a few feet to the right flank of Bass…

"Ah yes, my friend, as you are now plainly aware, our position here is compromised, and by all things, the innocent eyes of youth," alluded Bass upon realisation of his comrade's awareness that their presence was being scrutinised intently from very close quarters…

"Quickly, Tiberius, engage your portkey and clear your mind of all thoughts other than the assault upon the State Model Prison, Pretoria, in the year 1899…

"Focus your mind, and prepare yourself as we regress and make good our attempt to complete successfully phase two of our task."

Turning his head towards the child, Bass removed his dark lensed spectacles to reveal his pitch-black eyes.

As he smiled at the transfixed youngster, who reciprocated in kind the friendly gesture offered by one of these strangely-attired men, who were themselves now beginning to attract more unwarranted attention from other less innocent and more inquisitive quarters, Bass offered a nonchalant wink and, as he and Blackmore dissolved into the early evening ambience of a rising west bank mist, offered the parting words..."It's quite alright to believe in ghosts, child, for as you can plainly see... they do exist."

Chapter 27

'A Strange Sensation of Déjà Vu.'

'Pretoria: 1899.'

Somewhat fortuitously, Bass and Blackmore materialised inside the open doorway arch of a vacant prison cell, thus enabling them to maintain a modicum of anonymity whilst still somewhat surreally able to both observe and overhear events and conversations respectfully that were already well-remembered past history to them for a second time.

Upon clearly hearing the familiar words that he recalled orating, Bass proceeded to propose a spontaneously conceived, perilous strategy which he hoped might alter this misaligned course of history back towards its intended course...

'EYES ABOVE AND TO YOUR LEFT! 'THE ARCHITECT', ACCOMPANIED BY SEVERIN... AND THERE... CHURCHILL... STILL ENSCONCED BY THEIR SIDE... IT IS IMPERATIVE THAT WE...'

"Tiberius, I suggest that your participation in proceedings here be limited to that of a covert supporting role. I ask you respectfully to please remain here in an observing capacity until called into action and avoid contact with any members of our group who may become aware of our dual presence, particularly regarding unwarranted attention from both yours, and my own, alter-egos...

"Now stand aside for your own well-being, my brother, for I intend to unleash the wolf."

Beckoning upwards, towards the gantry each of them had surveyed earlier, Bass continued without pause...

"At the precise moment the wolf achieves footfall upon that gantry above us, and you are certain that Churchill is safely in its charge, make all haste in transporting yourself to St Michaels's Church at Highgate Cemetery at this parallel moment in time...

"I'm certain this is both the time and the location 'The Architect' will traverse to next upon accepting that his plan is in tatters, in order to murder Brother de Payens and claim the great power belonging to the 13th Meister for himself once more."

Prior to Blackmore even contemplating acknowledgement of the audaciously bold proposal offered by Bass, let alone presenting a tactically adequate counter-strategy of his own, the fantastic metamorphosis from man to lycanthrope had already commenced.

At exactly the same time that Bass, now completely altered into his lycanthropic form, began his seemingly effortless ascent towards the landing above, Blackmore became aware that the conspicuously alien form of the brick sphere portkey he surmised belonged to the future incarnation of 'The Architect' had materialised into a secluded apse just a few feet away from his own position of concealment, adjacent to the main corridor where the intense skirmish commenced in earnest and without respite, Witherspoon's cohort of bold engineers stoically maintaining a worthy advancing force against the infinitely swarming hordes of 'Black Guard'.

Instinctively, and without the merest thought of hesitation to ponder the request made but a few moments earlier by Bass, Blackmore proceeded to relinquish the cover of his stone prison cell in order to facilitate the impending reunion between two arch-enemies.

CHAPTER 27

Opting to gamble on the premise that facing 'The Architect' directly would unsettle the customarily indefatigable resolve of his nemesis sufficiently upon learning that both Bass and Blackmore had been granted the great power of the 'Meisters', enabling them to not only 'shift' through time, but also to traverse the great distances separating entire continents at will in a few seconds, and so raising them up to the elevated level of his equal, Blackmore picked his way between the battling factions as best he could, taking care not to engage in any unnecessarily protracted bouts of single combat that would surely attract undue attention to his presence.

The actual purveyance of such a well-intentioned tactic in hindsight, however, provided a more favourable result in theory, rather than in actual deed.

Inevitably, within seconds of him breaking cover, Blackmore encountered a marauding pack of three 'Black Guard' troopers, whose intense focus upon the raging conflict was cast into total disarray by the sudden confusing appearance before them of the very same tenacious force of nature from whom they had, just seconds previously, barely survived a most challenging encounter in a corridor they had exited just a few yards to their rear!

Afforded little choice to adopt an alternative strategy, Blackmore seized full advantage of the obvious disorientation present within the thought processes of his perplexed opponents and proceeded to dispatch each of them with relative ease, utilising devastatingly effective examples of his coldly efficient, lethally effective martial arts skills.

Very much as both Bass and Blackmore had feared, the theatrical altercation with the hapless trio of 'Black Guard', unavoidably undertaken by Blackmore, had not passed unnoticed.

From their vantage point on the crumbling iron gantry above, both 'The Architect' and Severin witnessed every nuance of the impressive display of single combat etiquette unfolding directly below, each of them simultaneously drawing to the conclusion that...

'If indeed there are now a pair of Tiberius Blackmores sharing the same dimensional space, then an astute, informed logical thought decrees that...'

Their attentions were focused immediately forward as the wolfman effortlessly propelled himself upwards, emerging from the ensuing chaos below, and over the iron railings to land gracefully a mere 12 or so feet away from their startled faces...

"JUDAS PRIEST, IT'S TRUE!" exclaimed Churchill, who found himself in some part relieved to be re-united with half of his sworn protectorate, convinced though he was that this remarkable folly of nature's cruel humour that stood before him was, without question, Colonel James Bass, nonetheless realising within himself an uncharacteristic dual sense of uncertainty and terror in the wake of the sudden appearance in their midst of this feral and potentially unpredictable, snarling monster.

"BASS! (JAMES!") spat both 'The Architect' and Severin respectively in unison as the wolf snarled menacingly and barred its grotesquely salivating yellow fangs ferociously towards its sworn nemesis and now potential prey...

"Of course, the lycanthrope Bass from... our future, one would surmise?" sneered 'The Architect', his characteristic arrogance immediately returning, his composure now fully restored.

Momentarily glancing downwards and to his left, 'The Architect' was clearly able to discern the rather rueful visage belonging to the future incarnation of Tiberius Blackmore gazing back directly towards him.

The right hand of Blackmore was raised and waving as though, having been recognised, he offered some sort of spontaneously conceived, sarcastically-inclined greeting to his arch foe as he supposed to himself...

CHAPTER 27

'The very least you can do, Tiberius old chap, is to retain a modicum of civility, even towards that psychotically misaligned, deranged pile of festering privy dung aloft.'

From his rapidly decaying, now precariously unstable vantage point above the chaotic melee that continued to rage below, 'The Architect' was also able to observe his future self-materialise and concluded that a confrontation with the future incarnation of Tiberius Blackmore was inevitable.

Harbouring an ingrained, bitter frustration, agitated considerably by the realisation that each of his reviled adversaries now possessed, and were able to command at will the 'dimensional shifting' power of the 'Meisters', 'The Architect' proceeded to spit venomously a final desperate order at Severin prior to retreating towards the welcomed sanctuary of his brick portkey, that lay open and awaiting his back-scuttling, craven retreat at the far end of the now precariously teetering remnants of the doomed iron landing.

"LAY THIS SORRY DEBACLE TO REST, SEVERIN… ONCE AND FOR ALL… END THIS NOW!"

Flashing an incredulous glance, between the hastily retreating back of his once revered master 'The Architect' and then the glowering, snarling, ferociously contorted features of the wolfman, now strategically positioned between himself and Churchill, Severin hastily concluded that to remove himself from this hopeless scenario, with the likelihood of victory in favour of his forces a rapidly diminishing possibility with the passing of every second, was to guarantee another opportunity in the future where scores might finally be settled…

'This is not my time to die. I will see you again, James Bass, and you, Tiberius Blackmore, when we shall each of us settle old scores once and for all'…

…Severin reasoned to himself as he first eyed the advancing form of the salivating wolfman, then the unmistakable figure of the future incarnation of Blackmore, as he fought his way towards a confrontation with his future Master below.

Turning on his heels, Severin sprinted towards the still ajar entrance that led into the inner blackness of the brick portkey belonging to 'The Architect' and without glancing back over his shoulder, terrified that the hot, rancid breath of the wolf would be upon him in a heartbeat for sure should his pace falter for a second, he was overcome with relief when in crossing the welcomed threshold of the portkey unmolested, the bricks that had parted on either side to facilitate an entrance closed silently behind him.

Turning his back dismissively on the portkey as it dematerialised into a theatrical arc of lightning bolts and steaming, acrid vapour, the wolfman proceeded to take a firm grip on Churchill's shirt collar from behind with his strong left hand, and, hooking the long, claw-like fingers of his right hand into the waist band of the remarkably compliant second lieutenant-cum-war correspondent's breeches, proceeded to leap from the collapsing gantry onto the relative safety of a lower mezzanine-type platform situated about 30 feet below them and well to the right of the crumbling debris, just a few feet above where Blackmore was advancing at pace to confront the meddlesome future incarnation of 'The Architect'...

"On how many more occasions must we conceive a cunning ruse in order to facilitate your ultimate failure?" Blackmore gloated as 'The Architect' surveyed the spectacular unfolding of his grand scheme before his eyes...

"BLACKMORE!... OF COURSE. So, both you and that rancid, feral dog Bass are now fully cognisant with the glorious, unimpeachable power of 'The Meisters'.

"Do you feel its electricity coursing through your veins? Have you yet experienced the full rapture of its invigorating energy upon your soul? All of the power of the ages is now yours to command...

CHAPTER 27

"Your wildest dreams, your loftiest ambitions now laid at your feet to be realised as you traverse your pathetic, subservient world to be worshipped as gods among mortals."

"BE SILENT, FOOL!" hissed Blackmore, his stinging reply meant as a disdainful, mocking rebuke towards the abhorrent misuse of the great gift bestowed upon them by the 'Grand Meisters', leaving no doubt in the mind of 'The Architect' that his rather clumsy attempt at a crude form of brinkmanship, in order to ascertain even the slightest possibility of a weakness in the stoic resolve belonging to the two detectives, had failed...

"Harken to the hollow, baseless words of a proven megalomaniac that will soon be buried forever deep beneath the dust and debris of this decaying edifice that crumbles around us...

"The power of the 'Grand Meisters' is bequeathed into the safe hands of true justice, where it rightfully belongs. As the chosen custodians of that priceless gift, James and I pledge that is where it shall remain, for the good of mankind."

During his speech, Blackmore, though retaining his minute attention towards 'The Architect', had become aware that the unmistakable form of the wolfman had conspicuously arrived on his left flank, still bearing before him, as one might tote a large sack of potatoes, a clearly perturbed Churchill.

Altered back once more into his human form, Bass caught his Schofield pistol as it arced through the air, tossed towards him by his companion, who remained focussed upon their sworn enemy as he did so, and together proceeded to level their cocked pistols directly towards the black heart of 'The Architect'.

As though compelled to do so by a shared subliminal instinct, Bass and Blackmore simultaneously demanded the identical damning instruction of their old enemy prior to emptying the respective chambers of their weapons towards their target...

"GO TO HELL!"

Though their aim was true, the lethal barrage of searing lead joined with the surreal ambience of the moment, as time appeared to cease.

All senses numbed into a waking stupor that nullified the desire to intervene on the part of Bass and Blackmore, the pair of stricken detectives were able only to stand by as helpless observers.

'The Architect', who had, in some fashion, frozen this moment in time, affecting all of the protagonists within the immediate vicinity except for himself, and retreated to the sanctuary of his awaiting portkey that lay just a few steps away.

Once safely ensconced behind its secure brick façade, real time immediately resumed and the volley of bullets, that were only seconds earlier discharged with such unerring accuracy at point-blank range from the weapons of Bass and Blackmore, ricocheted harmlessly off the solid crust of the portkey as it first began to emit a low, insistent hum before beginning to spin on its axis at a great many thousand revolutions per second, finally de-materialising amidst a spectacular arc of brilliant white forked lightning bolts…

"Now that, gentlemen, is how to facilitate one's exit from an impossible, tactically untenable position," Churchill alluded humorously, his composure now restored, as the final fizzes of electrical charge settled upon the charred, smoking concave indent which had been scorched into the solid concrete floor.

***

Turning his attention towards Churchill, Blackmore began…

"Winston, it is imperative that you now follow my instructions strictly and succinctly to the letter, with no thought of deviation on any count, do you understand?"

CHAPTER 27

"Well, I...," Churchill spluttered prior to his attempted protestation being vehemently curtailed by a venomous riposte from Blackmore...

"DO YOU UNDERSTAND, ACTING SECOND LIEUTENANT CHURCHILL? Even after all the fantastically unprecedented events that have transpired thus far throughout our association to which you have borne witness, do you still fail to understand that the future freedom of the entire human race depends upon the choices you make from this moment forth?"

"Y... Yes, Tiberius... Colonel Blackmore, sir; I... Please... rest assured that the herculean efforts made by our loyal supporters, those of yourself and Colonel Bass, and the selfless sacrifices offered by many good souls in order to preserve the liberty and well-being of this, as yet undeserving, minion will not be in vain, and shall never be forgotten," was the brief and yet impressively statesman-like and poignant reply offered by a contrite Churchill...

His taciturn, authoritarian tone continuing unabated, Blackmore interceded...

"Do not speak! Retire yourself from this melee immediately, for there are no cheap laurels of war to be earned here, nor is there reputation-enhancing glory to be had by you. Seek out Captain Haldane, James and I, and then abscond from this desperate place utilising the strategy that was previously conceived by both yourself and Haldane."

Substituting his contrition for confusion, Churchill assumed that surely further rebuke would not be forthcoming should he make just a single, harmless observation...

"Forgive me, Tiberius, but I... I must concede to being somewhat bemused as to how current events are unfolding at an extraordinarily swift pace, and in a most unorthodox manner. You both quite plainly stand here before me now, and yet you send me off to find...yourselves!"

His own patience eroded, Bass interceded; the rising frustration within him provoked a brief, curt response...

"Know only that Tiberius and I have affairs of the utmost importance still to address here that demand our unhindered attention. Now, make no more enquiries of us and go with all possible haste as directed to prepare the foundations upon which you shall lay the cornerstones of your formidable legacy."

Though the duration of their association thus far had been brief, Churchill had developed a deep respect for both Bass and Blackmore, so much so that when a direction was given by either man, or even a suggestion made that might present an advantage in favour of their cause, his better judgement dictated that their strategy was, in all probability, both tactically and logically sound, and acceptance of their word was mandatory.

Nodding his head in uncharacteristically silent approval, Churchill observed, for the few seconds that were necessary, Bass and Blackmore disappear from view into a dense mist of spent gunpowder residue down the facing corridor and beyond the still-smouldering concave crater blasted into the concrete floor, where only moments earlier the brick sphere belonging to 'The Architect' had vanished into thin air.

Turning back to face in the opposite direction, Churchill was dumbfounded, therefore, to be confronted by the rapidly approaching, unmistakable forms of Bass and Blackmore...

"HOW THE DEUCE ARE YOU ABLE TO BE HERE WHEN... YOU WERE BOTH JUST THIS SECOND... THERE?"

Regarding with puzzlement the wild gesticulations made by Churchill in opposite directions as he attempted to offer some form of credible visual support to his curious enquiry, the pair of flummoxed detectives were initially devoid of suggesting any meaningful response between them, finally deciding that silence and a raised eyebrow each would in this instance, prove the kindest, and most tactful response...

"Winston, thank the stars you are safe and unharmed," began a relieved Blackmore, electing to re-focus their attentions onto more immediate concerns...

"We three must locate Haldane and utilise this somewhat fortuitous skirmish to our best advantage as we seek to secure our liberty beyond these crumbling walls."

"As was just this moment quite rudely conveyed, Tiberius, by your somewhat taciturn lycanthrope colleague," imparted Churchill brusquely whilst scowling towards Bass with all the ferocity he could muster before concluding that his unnecessarily immature display of pique would, in all probability, be wasted and have little effect upon the impervious, granite-like constitution exuded by the brooding old warrior in his midst.

Bass, not unexpectedly, reciprocated with the merest shrug of his broad shoulders and almost as though to offer a silent, chastising rebuke, aimed a characteristically withering stare of disdain from his soulless black eyes at the now regretful Churchill.

Chapter 28

'Completely Human.'

Bass and Blackmore materialised outside the decaying grey gritstone façade of St Michael's Church that was situated within the western grounds of Highgate Cemetery in London.

A cloying, dense fog had descended upon the city, creating an eerie ambience that befitted the mood of their current situation to perfection: that of a late 19th century gothic melodrama rapidly approaching its epoch-defining endgame.

Before the impressive iron-gated entrance to an extensive network of catacombs, whose labyrinthine maze of tunnels stretched beneath the entirety of the western acreage belonging to the vast cemetery, a rusty padlocked chain which secured the gates was easily 'jemmied' by an enthusiastic Blackmore utilising a heavy iron bar that he had located conveniently lying nearby. The detectives then paused awhile in order to discuss how best to proceed…

"Alas, I have no recollection of ever having set foot inside this place before; neither the church, nor the catacombs. This rather familiar dour gothic façade is the one single clear image that I was able to recall from memory with a view to achieving even a close proximity to our intended final destination of the crypt that lies somewhere within."

CHAPTER 28

The consternation openly displayed by Blackmore upon realisation that their intended journey's end had yet to be reached, was reciprocated in the response given by Bass...

"It would appear that my own recollection of this place matches that of your own, Tiberius. I believe that should either of us have pictured the crypt in our minds, then the linked subliminal patterns of our conjoined thought processes would undoubtedly have transported us to the same, pinpointedly accurate location."

Wasting no more time, Bass led Blackmore through the now open gates and into the half-light of the upper catacombs, the barely-adequate illumination facilitated by a welcomed placement of gas-fuelled lamps that were conveniently hung intermittently along their way and ignited as they made their way ever deeper into the claustrophobically narrowing vaults that covered the entire acreage in all directions beneath the cemetery.

"Here, Tiberius, down these stone steps, and remain vigilant for any sign of an entrance that might grant us access into the crypt that we seek," alluded Bass earnestly as the pair of detectives darted between one apse and the next belonging to the small chapel inside which they now found themselves, in a frantic bid to locate a point of access into the lower catacombs that lay cold, dark and forgotten beneath the ancient foundations of St Michael's church...

"TIBERIUS, OVER HERE... BEHIND THE ALTAR!" ...Bass exclaimed, his attention instantly drawn towards brilliant white flashes of lightning emanating from behind the altar and the unmistakably familiar combination of the almost deafening whirring and electrostatic cracking sounds generated by the conspicuous arrival somewhere in their immediate vicinity of the spherical brick portkey belonging to 'The Architect'.

Selecting the closer flight of two sets of steep, well-worn stone steps, located on each side of the altar, Bass and Blackmore descended onto a fairly narrow flag-stoned platform that boasted as its impressive backdrop the great stained-glass window of St Michael's church, through which the entire area before them was now illuminated by the crystal-clear natural light emanating from a late September full moon: a wolf moon.

Reaching the centre of the narrow platform, Bass and Blackmore could plainly see, at the foot of a second flight of wider steps, underneath an ancient array of stone arches that spanned the considerable width of an open cloistered area, a grey cloaked figure seated upon a stone plinth, its face made anonymous by a heavy hood, with its back to the pair of detectives, as they cautiously descended the time-worn, uneven steps.

Even as the raging form of 'The Architect' emerged from the opening made by the receding bricks of his portkey brandishing menacingly a pair of high calibre revolvers and proceeded to advance at pace across what appeared to resemble the face of a giant clock hewn into the stone floor of the cloisters that rose up on all four sides around them, the mysterious shrouded figure raised to its feet, placed the human skull upon which had been the sole focus of its concentration gently upon the stone plinth seat and threw back its hood to reveal the gnarled, white-bearded features of Brother Hugues de Payens, who simply acknowledged the arrival of Bass and Blackmore with a nod of his head towards each man in turn…

"Welcome, my friends, to your appointment with destiny."

Noticing their own revolvers already drawn and cocked for immediate discharge, de Payens raised each of his hands sharply, as though to firmly dissuade the notion either of his companions harboured towards facilitating the immediate demise of 'The Architect', and continued…

"Stay your hands, my bold brothers, and allow the nexus its opportunity to claim this blackened soul before us forevermore."

CHAPTER 28

Dramatically raising his now fully outstretched arms higher, the whole of the ancient edifice around them reverberated violently with a sound not dissimilar to that emanated by the portkey belonging to 'The Architect', yet ten-fold more pronounced in both its volume and intensity.

Bolts of brilliant white forked lightning were summoned by de Payens and proceeded to strafe the quadrangle, seemingly on first impression at random intervals, until it became apparent that each one of the 12 Roman numerals upon the face of the giant clock hewn into the stone flags of the quadrangle floor before them was being specifically targeted.

Halted at the centre of the clock face, initially by the sheer spectacle of the events as they unfolded around him, 'The Architect' remained dumbstruck as the solid stone flags of the quadrangle floor gave way beneath him and crumbled into a bottomless maelstrom of swirling mist and a raging, orange hue of ten thousand dancing fire wraiths, rising up from the pits of hell in eagerness to claim their promised bounty.

His body now completely incapacitated and suspended over the abyss by the all-powerful, superior force of will exerted mercilessly upon him by de Payens, 'The Architect' now resembled the sorry, terrified husk of a condemned man helplessly awaiting his inevitable fate.

Holding the ensnared, prone form of 'The Architect', whose arms were forcibly outstretched as though the victim of some form of bizarre mock crucifixion, de Payens delivered his sentence to the pitiful excuse for humanity that hung helplessly before him…

"Only in this moment do you finally accept this great power, that has a uniquely synonymous association to the 'Grand Meisters', once relinquished, can never again be manipulated to support the perpetration of evil that you have on countless occasions both wilfully and purposefully advocated…

"Therefore, as a just and merciful punishment for your multiple crimes against humanity, taking into careful consideration the once-revered commander and world-renowned military tactician and gifted polymath you once were, I now cast you down into the eternal labyrinth of the temporal nexus, where, I'm certain, several millennia spent alone in forced exile contemplating a life of wasted opportunities will, in some way..."

"NO!" interrupted Blackmore curtly, aghast at the remarkable decision made by de Payens to mercifully incarcerate for life rather than to execute summarily the times many-proven mortal enemy of humanity.

Taking barely a pause for breath, a tone of agitated incredulity that bordered on blind rage rising within him by the second, he continued...

"Merely to be held captive within a vortex of temporal incarceration, yet still existing, still drawing breath, whilst at any moment the distinct possibility of liberation remains a very real possibility, especially for one in possession of such manipulative guile and devious cunning...

"Brother, the sentiment you propose here is commendable, but to suggest that the malevolent, inherent evil coursing throughout the scorched and barren consciousness of this man might, even over an inordinately lengthy period of time, be neutralised...

"...or perhaps by utilising some spiritually cleansing meditation techniques of which we have yet to be made cognisant, be suitably enough rehabilitated to be considered at some juncture for both pardon and release... well... both myself and James say to you, with the greatest respect given to your largely unimpeachable wisdom, and with all humility intended... NEVER!"

Weapons already drawn and cocked, in the fleeting moments that followed the normal passage of time appeared to cease. The volley of 12 or more potentially lethal projectiles, that had exited the trio of smoking gun barrels aimed towards 'The Architect', physically slowed

CHAPTER 28

in their trajectory until each searing shard of lead hung stationary in mid-air, still yards away from finding their mark.

Helpless to conceive of any response that might alter this unprecedented chain of events, Blackmore was unintentionally reduced to the role of observer as Bass proceeded to fling his arms wide, as though experiencing a bout of major convulsive distress...

'Please almighty God, not now James... Not the wolf' ...he mused, not unreasonably, to himself.

Rather than the anticipated metamorphosis from man to wolf, however, an apparition embodying the familiar form of a great white werewolf appeared to emanate from within the now violently convulsing body of Bass, prior to adopting its full physical form a few yards in front of them.

Falling to his knees, both pistols discarded to either side as he did so and his capacity for logical thought and sound reason momentarily failing him, Bass remained physically incapacitated for a few seconds, leaving both Blackmore and de Payens to confront the snarling beast before them that had manifest itself in the racing mind of Blackmore as the physical embodiment of the malevolent lycanthrope spirit that had for so long wrested for total domination of his brother's tortured soul, with the exception, it would appear, of one plainly obvious characteristic...

...that of a horrific network of scar tissue, running from its forehead all the way down to below its right jaw-line whilst bisecting the vacant right eye socket...

"YOU... FROM THE FUTURE... JAMES?" stammered Blackmore, comprehending almost instantly, his enquiry answered without prompt, that this was indeed the physical manifestation of the future embodiment of the werewolf spirit belonging to Bass.

Replying to the familiar tone of Blackmore by imparting a full-throated, feral roar of recognition, the intensity of which was not impaired one iota by the rows of yellow, salivating fangs through which it emanated, the wolf turned 180 degrees to face the now visibly petrified visage belonging to 'The Architect', whose pathetic, prone body was still being held in suspension over the raging chaos of the temporal nexus by the vice-like will of de Payens.

Aware that one more step forward would result in him being lost into the embrace of the temporal wilderness prematurely, and realising that its preordained final obligation towards restoring equilibrium to both timelines was approaching completion, the great white wolf steeled itself on the edge of the precipice for a moment before taking an almighty leap towards the pulsating energy stream that continued to lock 'The Architect' securely in stasis.

Grasping tightly its intended prey, the wolf was able, after some considerable effort, to rotate itself within the restrictive force of the stasis beam and face the three companions.

There they hung: the majestically regal form of the crusading, battle-weary white wolf, now his every bodily fibre becoming inextricably conjoined with the lamentably pathetic remnant of once-impervious, inherent evil to which he clung; two dominant alpha male entities; each one fated to chart his own course towards a perceived righteous future, yet each bearing completely opposite values of morality.

Remaining fused tightly together in perfect disharmony for what appeared an eternity until, exhausted to the point of surrendering his grasp, the wolfman emitted what appeared to resemble a plea-like whine directed specifically towards de Payens, as though imploring the '13th Meister' to show mercy and neutralise the paralysing stasis beam inside which both he and 'The Architect' remained helplessly imprisoned: an action that would enable them to tumble into the maelstrom of an eternally recurring nightmare together.

De Payens, sympathetic to the heartfelt appeal made by the wolf, duly obliged his request and immediately neutralised the stasis beam,

CHAPTER 28

thus enabling the pair of reluctant companions to be consumed by the swirling vortex of the temporal nexus.

As the final distant roars of the wolf, coupled with the pitiful screams of 'The Architect' faded from earshot, the gaping chasm before them instantly returned to the familiar stone flags of the quadrangle upon which the clock face reappeared, as though it had remained undisturbed for centuries.

Diverting his focus towards the abandoned brick portkey belonging to 'The Architect', lying where it had been vacated by its Master a short while ago on the far side of the quadrangle, de Payens once again dramatically raised his arms.

On this occasion, however, he immediately brought them together in front of himself and began a circling motion with both hands, one way, and then the other, as though he were first sighting, and then cradling the sphere between his rotating palms.

This curious gesticulation began an identical cycle to the one that transpired as the portkey revolved at great pace on its axis and disappeared into a crackling crescendo of blinding white lightning bolts and acrid fog.

Attempting in some way to make sense of the fantastic chain of events that had just transpired, Blackmore's words were instantly silenced by the '13th Meister' sharply raising his right hand…

"Brother de Payens… I…"

Without uttering a word, the ageless first Templar covered his grey, grim features with the heavy hessian hood of his cloak. He then proceeded to retrieve the ancient human skull which had been the sole focus of his attention prior to all that had just occurred and calmly re-seated himself upon the stone plinth that was situated in front of the stone clock face floor.

His concentration once more focused upon the mysterious skull he had gently placed in his lap, the parting words uttered by the 13th

Meister left Bass and Blackmore with the distinct impression that they were final and required no response on their part...

"All that was, is as it was so written... All that will be, is returned to its designated course... It is done."

***

Shifting his attention to his still mildly disorientated companion, Blackmore reasoned that the inevitable de-brief regarding the complexities appertaining to this most remarkable of capers would best be cogitated over in the altogether more salubrious surroundings of 'The Brown Bear' public house whilst imbibing a decanter of their preferred brandy...

"JAMES... ON YOUR FEET, SOLDIER... COLONEL BASS... WE ARE LEAVING!"

Raising Bass up onto his unsteady feet, Blackmore decided to tip the entire heft of his still incapable colleague onto his shoulders, fire-fighter-style, and beat as hasty a retreat as he was able, backtracking up the wider stone steps directly behind them.

Then, after pausing briefly to witness the motionless figure of Hugues de Payens still hunched in total concentration over the mysterious ancient skull gradually beginning to fade from sight, Blackmore, his groggy and incoherently grumbling companion still slung over his shoulders as would be an awkwardly balanced, substantially weighty sack of potatoes, navigated the much narrower flight of steps that led upwards and out from behind the altar into the small chapel belonging to St Michael's Church.

Unceremoniously dumping Bass onto the nearest pew facing the altar, Blackmore hastily returned to the altar with the intention to descend once more into the crypt and quiz Brother de Payens further, only to be confronted, inexplicably, by a solid mass of old stone floor slabs that appeared to have lain undisturbed for centuries, covering the location where the pair of narrow stone stairways had descended onto the platform overlooking the hidden quadrangle a few moments earlier.

Feeling mildly perplexed and momentarily devoid of any logical explanation for such a bizarre occurrence, Blackmore returned to the chapel and seated himself beside his now mildly coherent old compatriot...

"How fare you, James? Had I not witnessed with my own eyes the extraordinary manner in which your future incarnation entered the fray, I would never have believed such a thing possible."

Bass paused briefly prior to offering Blackmore his response, gratefully utilising the precious few moments to unravel his myriad befuddled thoughts into some semblance of coherent logic, aided no doubt by several hearty and most appreciated gulps from the hip flask filled with Del Vecchio brandy, proffered by Blackmore.

Taking multiple long pulls from the stogie that too had been ignited on his behalf by Blackmore, through an impressive array of grey cigar smoke rings and patting himself down, as though to reiterate to himself the startling revelation that he was about to divulge, Bass delivered his short, extraordinary answer...

"Remarkably... I feel... Cleansed; completely human, in fact."

Chapter 29

'A Curious Tale Recounted.'

" And so, James; there remains no conceivable doubt. The malevolent spirit of the werewolf has indeed relinquished its tenacious quest to wrestle for command of your soul. It would appear that you are restored back to complete humanity once more."

Bass reclined as easily as he was able in the uncomfortable hard oak embrace of his ornately carved chair, one of 17 identical seats placed equidistantly around the great round table of King Arthur, each one occupied by a member of 'The League of Ghosts'.

Puffing out his cheeks, in part to offer for the benefit of his assembled colleagues a public exclamation of disbelief, but quite probably more of a private expression to himself, and to both his understanding wife, Connie, and to his wily old companion Tiberius Blackmore, of much welcomed relief…

"Human you say, Pontius…

"Little had I dared to imagine that one day my inner torment would cease, for as much as God may be my judge on this earth, every waking and sleeping moment had become an unprecedented trial, each agonising metamorphosis from man to wolf, and then from wolf to man, eroded away a little more of the man's humanity, erasing a fraction more of his soul that allowed the lycanthrope to flourish and

CHAPTER 29

to dominate my increasingly weakening resolve...

"I truly believe that this raging conflict between the warring spirits embedded deep within me has presented, without question, the single most challenging ordeal that I have ever encountered...

"Indeed, I had even become compelled to enquire of myself on numerous occasions of late when the wolf spirit had risen...

'Could the next battle of wills force what vestige of humanity remains, to concede finally and be vanquished forever?'

A protracted hush permeated throughout the great library hall, each of the astonished assemblage remaining unwaveringly transfixed, as Bass continued to recount the details of his remarkable tale, turning his attention first towards Blackmore as though to offer his old friend an explanation of his mysteriously covert actions as they traversed the Bankside tunnels...

"It was whilst Tiberius and I navigated the long-derelict Bankside underground tunnels sometime in the early part of the 21st century, 122 years into one possible dystopian future that is now, by the grace of God and good fortune, thankfully consigned to the deepest recesses of both mine and Tiberius' memories, that we became first acquainted with the bombastic façade and the pseudo-autocratic pretence permeated by the 'Baron of Bankside' over his pack of lycanthropes and the pitiable remnants of the mentally exhausted, battle weary and, as it would soon become apparent, deeply in-mourning husk belonging to a possible future incarnation of myself...

"Merely existing from one day to the next, a recluse by choice for many lonely years and resembling little more than a dishevelled, aimlessly-wandering vagrant, all of his loved ones, friends and colleagues long since passed and consigned to the labyrinthine maze of his distant memories, this once-formidable man who was held in such high esteem amongst his peers, and even throughout the criminal underworld which he had once so vigilantly policed, was first encountered mired deep within a quagmire of remorse and self-loathing.

"A bereft, grieving soul in mourning for the loss of his great love Connie, and harangued constantly within the tormented confines of his tortured mind for failing to avert the demise of his beloved brother, Tiberius Blackmore, whilst engaged in mortal combat with possibly the most powerful entity that we had, or rather shall, ever encounter; the Queen of all lycanthropes known as 'The Matriarch'."

Indicating with a sharply raised finger to his lips a desire for each of his enthralled colleagues, particularly an ashen-faced Blackmore, to allow him the courtesy of concluding his curious tale, Bass persevered...

"Close to death himself and horribly wounded during the frenzied onslaught each of the overwhelmed companions had endured, my future incarnation was able only to observe helplessly whilst 'The Matriarch' took the life of his now isolated and woefully overmatched comrade."

A short pause ensued, the silence during which clearly indicated that the assembled 'League of Ghosts' would respectfully stay their eager tongues until they were certain that Bass had concluded his remarkable account...

"And so, my friends, in a desperately barren place, far into a possible future blighted by the spectre of misery and oppression, a chance encounter between two disparate souls ensued; each one's consciousness, subliminally conjoined in perfect synchronicity across the intertwining, infinite multiverses of time, was physically introduced; each one so similar in a multitude of characteristics, and yet different in both physical appearance and social circumstance due to the opposing courses throughout time that each entity was fated to travel...

"...One soul so overwhelmingly blighted by the torment of his perceived monumental errors in judgement that, cast helplessly adrift upon the oceans of unquantifiable guilt that saturated his clarity of thought and reason, cost the life of his brother, and was compounded

CHAPTER 29

a hundred-fold by the black shroud of mourning for a beloved wife long passed, and a future free from the constricting shackles of tyranny, alas never to be realised as a direct consequence of his abject and complete failure...

"... and the other; incessantly harangued by an unfeasibly persistent inner strife, only at this precise moment to comprehend finally that his own ebbing humanity would soon be completely erased forever by the increasingly dominant influence exerted upon him by the werewolf spirit which incessantly conspired to consume him from within."

"So then, James, might one suppose that your 'future self' offered an audaciously ambitious suggestion as to how his own selfless sacrifice might afford himself the inner peace and redemption he so desperately craved, and assure salvation for your own rapidly diminishing humanity?"

Preparing his mind to conclude his recounting of a quite extraordinary encounter, Bass afforded himself a wry grin in recognition of the perceptiveness displayed by Aston, to whom he first addressed, awarding his old friend a simple, well-deserved accolade...

"My compliments, Pontius. Your logic, as always, is impeccable."

Bass paused once more, clutching tenderly the outstretched hand of his wife, whose loving support he gratefully accepted.

Reluctantly turning away from the piercing blue-eyed gaze with which Connie Bass was able to melt the most impervious resolve, Bass proceeded to address Blackmore, Aston and the remainder of his colleagues...

"And so, following the direction of our unwarranted escort 'The Baron of Bankside' and his lycanthrope hordes, we happened upon my future self: bereft, tortured by insurmountable ravages of both guilt and grief, hopelessly adrift in self-imposed exile and no longer recognising a justifiable cause or reason to continue drawing breath until a chance encounter, leading to a private conversation shared between a pair of disparate entities, might fashion an opportunity whereby their shared inner demons may be exorcised indefinitely."

"Ah, so the moment that 'The Baron' and I noticed you had fallen back into the shadows to our rear as we navigated our exit from the Bankside maze..."

"...Was the moment, my old friend, I was enlightened of the fact that should a lycanthrope be conceived as a 'pure blood', then that spirit is cursed to prowl the earth for eternity unless granted a merciful release by means of which we are now all quite familiar...

"If, however, the werewolf has randomly become the unwilling victim of nature's cruel folly, then there remains a possibility that the malevolent spirit ensconced within might be completely cleansed, returning full humanity to the wrongly afflicted soul."

"So, it would appear that this unlikeliest of wonders has indeed come to pass, and thank all the gods for it; my brother is restored to humanity," alluded Blackmore, signs of raw emotion clearly evident as his usually measured demeanour faltered for the briefest moment...

"Yes, Tiberius, I stand here before you all, human once more. During the conversation that transpired between myself and my alter-ego it became evident that each of our personal agendas would benefit substantially from a particularly hazardous strategy which was agreed to be implemented only by unanimously sanctioned mutual consent...

"Having decided upon ending his solitary existence, and becoming cognisant of our intentions to rid this world once and for all of the influence and misery exerted by 'The Architect' and his oppressive regime, my future self proposed a fantastic strategy whereby he would gauge with pinpoint accuracy through my own eyes across the constantly rippling eddies of the temporal wake, precisely the time, the place and the exact date when both Tiberius and I would next confront 'The Architect': at the opening of the temporal vortex by Brother Hugues de Payens in the lower crypt beneath St Michael's church...

CHAPTER 29

"He would then ascertain to the precise second when my body could be utilised as a conduit in order to facilitate his transition between dimensions and, instinctively aware that this metamorphosis from man to wolf would be his last, thus extinguishing the final flickering ember of humanity within him forever, proceed to secure 'The Architect' in his powerful grasp and plunge them both into the waking hell of a temporal nightmare together for eternity."

Barely allowing seconds to pass, Aston remarked...

"So, James, the werewolf spirit, passing through the fibres of your physical being, in some way cleansed your soul entirely of the lycanthrope curse?"

"That it did, my old friend. Exactly how this miracle was achieved, I remain at a loss to fathom, though one might assume that in some supernaturally unorthodox fashion my werewolf alter-ego from the future, now transposed from man into beast for the final time, was able to absorb the lycanthrope spirit within me into his own being."

"A truly remarkable story, James, that thankfully for all here assembled culminates with the restoration of your humanity. But what of 'The Architect'?" enquired Aston as the extraordinary tale recounted by Bass drew to its conclusion...

"You might well ask, Pontius. In the end, nought but a mortal man, bound for eternity to grapple with a raging, unrelenting, unintelligible beast whilst incarcerated within a temporal nightmare... What indeed of 'The Architect'... God only knows what waking horror he now endures...

"However, were it not for the meddlesome intercedence of 'The 13th Meister', his demise would have been assured and swift at the hands of both myself and Tiberius, but..."

"But might one offer an alternative suggestion in return, James? Was it not a more fitting judgement that 'The Architect' spend all of time imprisoned in his own purgatory... conscious and aware of every passing second within the inescapable portals of his personal hell?"

Appearing to offer unerring support for the justice meted out by the '13th Meister', as opposed to the spontaneous, yet surprisingly humane alternative of the attempted execution by Bass and Blackmore, Aston's coldly observed endorsement prompted a lengthy silence to fall upon the echoing stone chamber of the vast library.

***

After a considerable amount of time had passed, Aston broke the silence and proceeded to address Bass and Blackmore directly...

"Gentlemen, consider these final excursions as drawing to a conclusion once and for all this, your most extraordinary of all missions...

"It may please you to consider this...Should you so wish, it now falls within the remit of your considerable powers to visit a significant moment in our near future, during which a gentleman of your acquaintance will inspire a nation teetering on the brink of capitulation and defeat, to rise up contrary to all expectations and lead selflessly towards the eventual salvation and rejuvenation of a lasting world peace."

Chapter 30

'A Phoenix Rises.'

'18th June, 1940'

An expectant hum permeated throughout the opulently grand, neo-gothic corridors and colonnades belonging to the old Palace of Westminster.

Winston Spencer Churchill, first Lord of the Admiralty and recently invited by his Majesty King George VI to form a coalition government to facilitate the immediate commencement of unhindered governance during wartime, was preparing himself to deliver the maiden address in a series of key motivational speeches.

The first would be to the unusually subdued rows of his right honourable colleagues from both sides of the house, assembled expectantly in this austere chamber. The second would be via a worldwide radio broadcast into the homes, workplaces, public houses and the lasting consciousness of a nervously anticipating British, and world public.

Whilst the unmistakably familiar, authoritative tones of Churchill reverberated throughout the densely populated, yet eerily silent chambers, the materialisation of two unfashionably attired gentlemen into the shadows of a deserted service gallery which fortuitously overlooked the entire area of the house floor went completely unnoticed...

'Upon this battle depends the survival of Christian civilisation. Upon it depends our own way of British life and the long continuity of our institutions, and our Empire...'

Listening intently as Churchill delivered his inspirational clarion call to a world in rapt anticipation, both Bass and Blackmore readily agreed that these impressive, soon to be regarded as iconic words were exactly those that might have been expected to emanate from this ageing potential world leader who stood alone in stoic defiance on the cusp of achieving finally the laurels, and perhaps even the immortality, which he had so desperately craved throughout his eventful life.

What occurred to Bass more readily, however, was not just the genuine passion with which this emboldened, motivational rhetoric was being delivered, but possibly even more of a privilege and a revelation to behold were the massed supportive cheers and the near-hysterical fervour emanating from the now unified assemblage that punctuated this remarkable speech upon the completion of virtually every sentence towards its enthusiastically-received conclusion.

Here was a man who had, through the frequently fraught endeavours during his many tempestuously challenging formative years, finally recognised and embraced both the charting and the meaning of his own destiny and here, in his defining moment of truth, he stood in readiness to convince a nation, and all of the oppressed peoples of the Earth, that if they chose to rise up and stand together as one formidable, allied force, then both the Nazi and Imperial Japanese threats posed to world peace would be vanquished forever...

'Let us, therefore, brace ourselves to our duty, and so bear ourselves that if the British Empire and commonwealth lasts for a thousand years, men will still say... This was their finest hour.'

CHAPTER 30

"Impressive," alluded Bass respectfully as the final sentence of Churchill's speech was greeted by the rapturous ovation of his peers and a newly motivated nation...

"So... It transpires that this was indeed a man worth saving after all, Tiberius."

"Aye, judging by the evidence of our own eyes, it would appear so, James. An appointment with destiny duly kept, I think, and here begins the genesis of a legacy that will no doubt guarantee him the accolade he so craved, of becoming the greatest Briton of all time... and rightly so," replied Blackmore sagely.

Bass reciprocated with his customary single silent nod of acknowledgement and allowed Blackmore the courtesy of suggesting the location for their next port of call...

"Well then, one last call to make that will draw this most extraordinary caper to its timely conclusion, I think, James."

Even as Blackmore's final words were uttered, the physical embodiment of the two detectives had dissolved into the veil of secretive darkness from whence they had come...

Chapter 31

'The Unlikeliest Farewell.'

'January 4th, 1965'

The entrance hall to number 28, Hyde Park Gate was somewhat busier than usual. Servants, colleagues, family members and personages of both national and international import circulated and exchanged cordial conversation amongst themselves, creating an aura of nervous anticipation throughout the gathering whilst awaiting the news that would shock the world.

Regardless of this unprecedented level of anxiety hanging over a place widely noted for its reputation throughout London society as a domicile of family joy and serenity, an eerily hushed atmosphere permeated throughout the assemblage, as though each one remained respectfully wary of unnecessarily disturbing the final few days of privacy and peace in what precious few moments remained of the life belonging to one of the greatest, most remarkable men who had ever lived.

The rapidly failing health of Sir Winston Spencer Churchill had become a matter of national concern for some considerable time, ever since he had celebrated his 90th birthday on 30th November, 1964 in his own inimitable fashion by flashing his iconic 'V' for victory sign to

CHAPTER 31

the rapturously responsive multitude gathered expectantly outside his Hyde Park home.

Bass and Blackmore, though still attired in their blatantly unfashionable 19th century tweed suitage, were nevertheless able to mingle discreetly amongst the nervously undulating people around them without arousing unwarranted attention, until a familiar voice echoed forth from their distant past...

"Well, bless my soul... Colonel Bass... Colonel James Bass... and, of course, Colonel Tiberius Blackmore. Well, heaven preserve us... It truly is undoubtedly you, but... your appearance... you both remain exactly as you were the moment we became acquainted... well, it must have been... 67 years ago... give or take... But... no... no, it can't be you; for this fantastically improbable anomaly there exists no feasibly rational explanation... unless..."

"Unless the tall tales with which you were regaled 67 years ago by a questionable pair of so-called commuting precious stone merchants, whilst still a naïve whelp of a first mate serving aboard a second class cargo cutter who was tentatively finding his way in the world, were all in point of fact quite true," interceded Bass dryly in riposte to the observation made by the white-whiskered octogenarian standing before him, splendidly regaled in a full ceremonial Admiral's uniform that sported an impressive array of campaign medals and insignia of high rank upon the left breast of the gold braided, highly polished brass-buttoned tunic.

"What grave travesty of naval protocol could possibly explain this outrageously formal choice of attire, Jennings Pike?" enquired Blackmore, making a well-intentioned attempt to divert attention for a brief moment from the scenario of growing anxiety and despair that was prevalent all around them, by infusing a sliver of well-intentioned humour...

"I could never have dared to imagine that those, erm, 'tall-tales', as you refer to them, Colonel Bass, could possibly be true and would contribute immeasurably towards the salvation of mankind...

"That you each were able to achieve even a fraction of the wonders which you claimed to be capable... well..."

Allowing for a moment to compose himself as best he was able, Admiral Pike continued...

"If you will forgive an old man his retrospective asides for just a moment...A grateful nation, nay, an indebted world, should have bestowed upon you both all of the laurels and accolades deserving of your great service, which each of you selflessly provided towards the sacrifices made by the many in order to secure world peace..."

Both Bass and Blackmore fixed their battle-worn, stern expressions upon the well-intentioned old man as though fully intending to offer a silent rebuke, Bass finally delivering his candid, yet totally appropriate response...

"Medals, accolades, laurels are not for ghosts. Anonymity is our trusted companion and ensconced deep within the shadows that ordinary people fear, are the places we call home."

A further brief pause ensued, during which the ageing Lord Admiral of the Fleet, Jennings Pike, proceeded to gather his composure, and to arrange his wildly-vacillating thoughts into some kind of logically coherent perspective...

"But gentlemen, contrary to all the discernible laws of physics and far beyond the acceptable parameters of logical possibility, here you both undoubtedly are, remarkably unaltered by the unforgiving passage of time, time whose unrelenting gallop bears us ever onward towards the one guaranteed appointment in life that awaits us all...

"It is truly an honour to see you both once more. Might one assume then, that your unexpected appearance here denotes a desire on your behalf to pay your final respects to a much-respected companion of old standing who rapidly approaches the twilight moments of his extraordinary life?"

"Lord Admiral Pike, the honour is ours, sir. Your own great career achievements are plainly obvious, thanks to both your impressive cache of honours and your impeccable choice of tailor, as, it would appear, is the brotherly bond you share with Churchill."

"Ah yes, Colonel Blackmore; it is a lasting brotherly bond the value of which I would surmise you greatly appreciate, as, I suspect, do you too, Colonel Bass," retorted Pike informally whilst shooting a crafty wink towards Bass, who reciprocated with his inevitable single nod that was supported, on this occasion somewhat uncharacteristically, with a wry grin...

Shaking his head once more in disbelief, his heart warmed by the realisation that a long overdue union between trusted companions of long standing had taken place before his own demise, thus completing an extraordinary chain of events, the first tenuous links of which were forged many years previously below the creaking, salty decks of an old tea clipper named 'Rocinante', Pike continued...

"Gentlemen, though I would appreciate greatly the indulgence afforded by a more informally cordial reunion between compatriots of old, I fear that time on this earth grows short for my dear friend Winston. If you will accompany me, I will show you to him where I must insist that you be both gentle of manner, and brief."

Without further delay, the detectives were led through a modest dining area adjoining a spacious orangery that offered through its ornately forged, iron framed windows a picturesque view of what, in the summer months, would be an impressively landscaped garden.

Approaching the ailing figure of their old comrade, Churchill, a picture of serenity and dozing whilst seated comfortably in a woven cane bath chair and facing out towards his beloved garden that had been tidied and lovingly prepared for its inevitable re-growth during the early post-winter months, Bass and Blackmore knelt before the great man and tenderly took each of his frail hands in theirs...

"Sir Winston... Sir Winston..." uttered Blackmore in little more than a whisper, hoping it would be sufficient to provoke a response from their peacefully slumbering friend...

Churchill woke with a start and began to speak with surprising clarity, as ever faithfully in keeping with his legendarily pugnacious temperament...

"WHAT! HOW DARE YOU INTERRUPT ME WHILST I PRIVATELY CONSIDERED VITAL MATTERS OF STATE... I..."

His failing vision gradually adjusting to the unexpected instant glare of a crisp, white winter afternoon, Churchill's still active and extremely sharp mind engaged as he recognised the unmistakable features belonging to the two detectives...

"Well, bless my soul... Colonel Blackmore, and of course, Colonel Bass...

"Still managing to keep that wolf at bay, eh, Bass?" enquired Churchill of Bass playfully...

"Totally at bay these days, Sir Winston," retorted Bass briefly, the chagrin he had harboured in the past towards this once dangerously arrogant, recklessly ambitious man, still presented a rippling undercurrent deep within his consciousness.

Erring in favour of recognising the soldiers' unwritten code of decency and adhering to the demands of acceptable official protocol, Bass elected instead to offer both the respect and compassion towards a dying man that was an acceptable requirement of gentlemanly conduct, a man most of whose earlier, more questionable character traits Bass had quite openly, and often vociferously, never cared for...

Blackmore, realising that any form of dialogue offered by Bass may be somewhat less cordial than would probably be expected in the circumstances, chose to intercede on his taciturn companion's behalf...

CHAPTER 31

"How fare you, old man? Pray tell, what of your life's path post our successful escape from the State Model Prison in Pretoria all those years ago?"

Appearing to be revitalised by the attendance of possibly the two greatest living enigmas to have touched, even perhaps influenced in part, his remarkable journey, Sir Winston chomped fervently on one of the ten Julieta number 2 cigars he still insisted on devouring every day and proceeded to recount a brief summary appertaining to his extraordinary life...

"Very few personages of note are privileged to have places, ships, buildings or streets named after them, or even statues erected in celebration of their great achievements; I have invested in my name a cigar named 'The Churchill'; a creature comfort to which I am honoured to lend my title and for which I remain more grateful than any other accolade or award that I have been fortunate enough to receive during my life."

Inhaling deeply, Churchill took a copious amount of the acrid cigar vapour into his lungs.

A rapidly ailing constitution giving no indication of his declining capability to both inhale and exhale exorbitant clouds of grey stogie smoke, polluting the chilled, previously clean air with the not unpleasant aroma emanating from his slow-burning 'Romeo Y Julieta Clemenceau' brand cigar, Churchill continued...

"Ah yes, gentlemen... Was there ever a finer thing conceived, and so appropriately named, for a man to be remembered by...

"Colonel Blackmore... Tiberius... and indeed... James. Please, if you will see fit to indulge the humble request of a tired old man and grant him the privilege of informality, even though his gratitude for such a precious gift, added to a multitude of debt already owed to you for both services and friendship selflessly rendered on countless occasions, will, in all probability, now remain permanently unsettled, save for the heartfelt gratitude now sincerely expressed by a severely tested, much wiser man than the brash, inexperienced whelp of a lifetime ago.

"From the moment of my absconding from the potential purgatory of Pretoria, I vowed to myself that I would strive beyond the parameters of human capability, following an example recently set by two extraordinary colleagues, to assure that my life would be one dedicated to the service of the many; a life fit for purpose. I proposed there and then to create a lasting legacy of which one might, in time, reminisce fondly upon and be immensely proud...

"I would strive towards nurturing a worthwhile career, firstly in the domestic, and then in the world arena of politics, where both strong influence and forthright leadership are regarded as key requirements.

"Even during my earlier formative years when my rather arrogant self-aggrandisement was regretfully evident for all to witness and endure, I was convinced that these priceless leadership attributes, hard earned by a deserving few after many years' investment of selfless toil and personal sacrifice, were even then already firmly ensconced within the boundaries of my naïvely perceived worldliness, as would be a high rank of privilege or hereditary title be inherited by means of an archaic ancestral heritage...

"Initially, upon reaching Durban, it was my intention to re-enter the fray immediately by taking up with a local regiment by the name of the South African Light Horse. However, a fortuitous opportunity beckoned whereby I was offered a commission, by General Sir Redvers Buller, with whom I had sought an audience and a personage of both high military rank and social standing whom I admired greatly, to command regular soldiers in the ongoing war against Boer forces on the condition that I too was permitted to continue to honour an obligation promised to serve as a war correspondent for the London Evening Post."

Pausing momentarily in order to lay aside his half-smoked cigar, with possibly the intention of affording himself a moment to recount distant memories to which he had not given a thought for over 60 years,

CHAPTER 31

Churchill resumed...

"My career, indeed, my entire life, lived out in the often damningly critical and unforgiving eyes of minute public scrutiny, has, over the many long years of its passage risen to the absolute pinnacle of euphoric success and, conversely, plunged headlong into the gaping abyss of abject failure.

"But never at any juncture did my resolve falter, nor was I ever given constructively argued, tangible reason by my illustrious peers, nor my many detractors, to doubt that the course which I had so readily charted would one day afford me the opportunity of achieving great things for the good of my country, and ultimately for the greater good of humankind."

A further pause ensued, during which both Bass and Blackmore, totally enraptured by the keen, almost auto-biographical memory recall displayed by this extraordinary man, continued to listen intently in respectful silence...

"You see, gentlemen, even when confronted by insurmountably harsh odds, one must inevitably strive beyond all conceivable hardship in order to discover one's own truth..."

Faltering for a third time, Churchill's life light now reduced to barely more than a fading ember, neither Bass nor Blackmore dared to even contemplate speech whilst this latest pause prevailed, waiting in rapt anticipation for the next words to fall from the great statesman's lips...

Looking towards each of the attentive detectives in turn as he spoke, Churchill posed each man a simple question...

"Did we succeed in achieving our ultimate goals, Tiberius Blackmore? Did we, James Bass? Were each of us able to keep our respective appointments with destiny, to fulfil the lofty expectations that our early promise suggested? Were we adequate to the task?"

An uncharacteristic well of tears formed an opaque film that stung Blackmore's ageing eyes as he responded to the faltering words, now barely discernible, uttered by the great man seated before him.

Now so vulnerable and close to exhaling his final breath, Churchill afforded himself a satisfied half-smile as Blackmore answered, his voice tempered with a raw emotion seldom witnessed...

"Aye, that we did, Sir Winston. Might one take this opportunity to impart, on behalf of both myself and James, that the privilege to be acquainted with, and to serve in some small fashion, the greatest Briton of all, has been ours."

Prior to allowing their ailing comrade the honour of concluding their unlikeliest of farewells, Bass seized upon his opportunity to speak, his characteristically taciturn honesty tempered with the deep respect that he was well aware his old comrade ultimately deserved...

"I shall mourn not for the arrogant, unproven, glory-seeking, self-aggrandised young whelp of a lifetime ago, day-dreaming of lofty personal ambition to be achieved at all costs, but rather for the invincible titan who rose up phoenix-like from the smouldering ashes of abject failure...

"Having learned both the priceless qualities of forthright, structured leadership and the arguably more valuable trait of humility from a catalogue of catastrophic errors he made whilst he navigated his perilous course, the man I choose to remember proceeded to galvanise the crushed spirit of a demoralised world order into one irresistible, gloriously unified force that ultimately triumphed over the malignant spectre of evil...

"Good bye, old friend. Go soon and take your rightful place amongst the gods in the gilded halls of Valhalla."

Fervently gripping each of the detectives' hands with all the strength he could muster, Churchill spoke in a voice that was now little more than a whisper...

"The privilege, my very dear and truly loyal friends, and the honour...was mine."

Chapter 32

'Sonata For a Pair of Tired, Ordinary Men.'

'Whitechapel. November, 1898.'

The Brown Bear public house, situated at a crossroads on Leman Street where Prescot Street branched off towards Trinity Square in the west, and Hooper Street likewise in the opposite direction towards Bethnal Green in the east, was humming with the usual late Saturday night thrum of intelligible conversation, clanking glasses and the inevitable brawl that ensued, usually as a result of nothing more than an incongruous word uttered in innocence, or perhaps not, that always spilled out into the street, where it would eventually reach an uncompromisingly violent conclusion.

Another familiar sound permeating this indigenous late evening ambience was that of an ageing upright piano upon which the usually barely competent digits of any number of semi-capable patrons were willing to hammer out on its woefully out of tune keys, in return for a complimentary dram or two of the cheapest gut-rotter gin, what passed as an adequate accompaniment for the often bawdy lyrics that belonged to the latest popular music hall tunes.

On this particular evening, however, rather than retreating to the welcomed sanctuary of their private room of choice located to the rear of the establishment that was always kept vacant for their exclusive patronage, Blackmore, himself a gifted pianist, had chosen to sit at the decrepit old piano and attempt to coax from its tired keys a melody of melancholy beauty which complemented perfectly the tone of the conversation in which he was engaged with Bass, but had in fact only succeeded in prematurely subduing the usually, by this late hour, roistering Saturday atmosphere of cheap liquor and latent brutality considerably...

Affording himself the opportunity of imbibing a generous tumbler full of brandy during a less demanding few bars of his recital which required the use of just one hand, Blackmore proceeded to converse with Bass, whilst impressively retaining his remarkably proficient ability to perform...

"So, James; even though the wolf spirit is purged from within you, why then pray tell, do the dark spectacles remain?"

Reciprocating Blackmore in part by draining his own tumbler, Bass reached towards the black metal frames of his dark-lensed spectacles as though intending to remove them. However, just as he was about to do so his action, and his proposed response, were rudely interrupted...

"Fer 'faks' sake, it's not a 'fakkin' funeral, grandad... It's Saturday 'fakkin' night... Play somethin' we can 'alls' 'shingalong' to or... or, 'FAK OFF!'

Choosing to regard this drunken interruption with the silent contempt it deserved, whilst electing also to leave his spectacles firmly in place for the present, Bass continued to address Blackmore, who proceeded to perform his exquisite recital seemingly oblivious to the ignorant insult aimed in his direction...

"I find that my eyes remain susceptible to a certain level of ambient light. I simply retain the darkened lenses for no other reason than that they offer relief to my sensitive eyes... and perhaps that I, too, have grown accustomed to the 'look' of them, so to speak... and also..."

CHAPTER 32

"'AWTERGEVA' 'NHA'... DAYSEE, DAYSEE, A' GIMMEE YOUR H'ANSHWER DOOO... AH... I'M 'ARF 'CE.. ROISY' H'ALL FOR THE 'LARVE' 'HOV' YOOO... AH..."

Appearing undeterred by the spontaneous 'a-cappella' rendition of this drunken, hopelessly off-key counter-melody offered by his vacuous interrupter, Blackmore persevered with his charming recital, maintaining his composure whilst both continuing his conversation with Bass and becoming instinctively aware that his competition had made the decision to escalate matters further.

Even when the tonally inept inebriate unceremoniously lurched uninvited beyond the threshold of the sacred personal space that surrounded the now sensually aware detective, Blackmore continued to play...

"Wha' the 'fakkin' 'ell do you call that tuneless tripe you is playin'... eh, you old 'fakker'... 'H, it 'h'ain't 'Daisy 'fakkin' Daisy' is it... Ah'm bettin' you can't even play 'Daishy, Daish... y' even, y' old 'fakker.' 'LOOK AT ME WHEN 'AH'M' TALKIN' TO YOU... 'FAKKER!'"

Blackmore proceeded to address his soused inquisitor without first engaging him in eye contact, realising that the deeply ingrained soldier's instinct for immediate close combat readiness, synonymous with both himself and Bass, would already be piqued within his companion and prepared to meet any hostile intent that might be forthcoming from any possible area within the crowded room...

"Ah yes, of course, 'Daisy Bell', or to coin its more colloquially referenced title 'A Bicycle Made for Two'; a quaint little music hall refrain composed, if the weary, brandy-soaked memory of this ivory-bothering 'old fucker' serves, by Mr Harry Dacre," alluded Blackmore playfully as he segued seamlessly from his classical recital into the popular music hall staple in question for a few bars, expertly returning to his original piece utilising the fluent abilities of a very competent musician, abilities with which even Bass was mildly impressed...

"Please, if you will forgive my rather lacklustre rendition of what is obviously a composition that you favour... Perhaps if you were to request an alternative piece, I might..."

All at once, the drunken songbird's mood soured considerably. Somewhat irked that the well-intentioned attempt made by Blackmore to quell a potentially volatile confrontation had, in fact, merely served to make him the unyielding focus amongst his equally inebriated peers to receive merciless jibes of derision and profane personal insults...

"YOU MIGHT JUST... 'FAK OFF' YOU 'LAH-DE-DHA', SUITED-'AN-BOOTED, WEST END 'PONCE!' WHAT 'SHORT' OF 'FAKKIN' SHITE, POSH TRIPE YOU'RE PLAYIN' 'ISH' THAT ANY WAY?"

Turning towards his now baying cronies for support in stoking the fires of his rising bravado, the still formally unintroduced inebriate profanely slurred on...

"'ARRY 'FAKKIN' DACRE... IV'E SEEN 'IM 'DHAN THE OLD 'IPPODROME AT GOLDERS GREEN... 'EE WAS..."

"My dear fellow, as I stated earlier, Mr Harry Dacre was the composer of the piece, not the performer."

Following several perpetually rude interruptions and a slew of personal insults fired in his direction, Blackmore's mood had understandably soured and as he offered his response, prepared himself for what he now perceived must follow the inevitable 'correction' of this profane inebriate's atrocious manners...

"This rather exquisite piece is the first sonata for 'fucking' piano, in the key of C 'fucking' major part two, played 'Andante.'"

"AN... ANDA... ANDANT... WHA'... 'FAK OFF', PONCY OLD FAKKER!'"

"Yes, 'Andante'; moderately slowly. Oh, do try to keep up, 'music lover'. Part three of this rather exquisite sonata, which will follow shortly, should one be allowed to continue, of course, will be played at a brisk allegro, which might offer you the opportunity to at least

CHAPTER 32

dance around a little, accompanied perhaps by your Neolithic brood of inebriated primates here gathered...

"This piece is one of several sonatas written exclusively for piano by Wolfgang Amadeus 'fucking' Mozart and I would expect a little more 'fucking' respect to be shown for the work of a true 'fucking' compositional genius from the soused ignoramus in the 'fucking' troll's gallery!"

"TIBERIUS; BOTTLE AT 3:15!"

Reacting instinctively to the timely warning barked by Bass, Blackmore spun 15 degrees clockwise on the conveniently-threaded piano stool upon which he had been seated, and was able to bat away, with a solid swat of his right hand, the sharp teeth of a broken bottle with which the emboldened, reinvigorated inebriate had armed himself, and was brandishing menacingly with the expressed intent of causing the rudely interrupted detective serious harm.

Continuing on his clockwise rotation, Blackmore raised his left hand and jabbed the extended half-fisted knuckles into the oncoming larynx of his now unsteadily-overbalanced advancing assailant.

Ably assisted by Bass, whom it would appear had himself become a candidate to receive a dose of reciprocal violence from the now-incapacitated inebriate's incensed comrades courtesy of his obvious association with their fallen comrade's nemesis, Blackmore remained seated upon his piano stool whilst proceeding to dispatch a rampaging group of four would-be vigilantes with consummate ease.

Assessing the remnants of their handiwork, a scene of drunken carnage synonymous with the ubiquitous bar room brawls that had ensued in a hundred or more of the less salubrious London hostelries on this very night and satisfied that he was secure from further affray, Blackmore turned around 180 degrees on the stool upon which he had remained seated throughout the entire altercation, calmly opened the lid of the old piano that had been viciously clapped shut onto the hands of an enthusiastic attacker, and proceeded to play the third and final part of his enchanting Mozart sonata.

Upon completion of his eventful recital, Blackmore turned on his piano stool, reached down and grabbed the lapels on the jacket belonging to his bloodied first assailant with both hands, lifted his entire body weight from the sawdust-sprinkled floorboards so that their faces were virtually making contact, and spoke to him curtly before dropping the whining piece of dung like a discarded bundle of dirty old rags to the floor, prior to addressing Bass directly...

"For your own personal information, you rude, inbred piece of festering privy filth; I was raised hard on these very East End streets, as, one would assume, were you...

"I fear, however, accounting for your pathetic showing of single combat etiquette here, I do appear to have assimilated a good deal more of the cunning martial skills required in order for one to survive on these unforgiving streets. Have a care, my filthy friend, and in future do not always assume that either the chosen attire, or the musical proclivities of a man, offer false indication as to his extensive capabilities in, ahem, other less formal and infinitely more hazardous areas of expertise...

"Ahh... Mozart," sighed Blackmore, his attention now returned to the beaming visage of Bass...

"Even when rendered whilst under some considerable duress on this decrepit old artefact of a piano, the opening two parts in particular have always provided one with an invigoratingly cathartic experience."

Idly depressing what appeared to the layman a seemingly random white key, an action which produced a dull sounding, unmusical thud, a wistful grin appeared across the stubbled, time-worn features of Blackmore...

"D'ye know, James, that old middle C string has been missing for years. It's rumoured that it was filched one night during the time of the

CHAPTER 32

Trinity Square garrotting murders... an intriguing case long before our tenure with Scotland Yard began, I think... that still remains unsolved, by all accounts..."

"That crew is always 'spoilin' for a ruck a' lately on a Saturday night," interceded the voice of the previously anonymous young girl collecting glasses whose self-assured, street-smart manner immediately appeared a very familiar characteristic to both Bass and Blackmore.

Surveying each of the six sorry-looking, roundly thrashed, groaning excuses for humanity in turn, that lay dumped like refuse sacks, prone and bleeding, around the area where the two detectives remained seated, their presence completely ignored by the calmly conversing companions, the girl tossed her impressively lustrous, almost waist length mane of golden ringleted curls away from her angelic, porcelain-like features and fixed both Bass and Blackmore with a confident, steely gaze from her compelling blue eyes...

"Looks like they met their match tonight tho'... painfully. The way you put so many of 'em down. 'Is' you two gents 'police, military types'?"

"Sometimes a little of both, but mostly... just a pair of ordinary men, youngling, just a pair of tired, ordinary men... If you'll pardon me, what are you called?" Blackmore first eluded wistfully, then enquired somewhat officiously, as he drained another tumbler of brandy in one gulp...

"Not that it's any of your concern, Mr Policeman, but seein' as 'ow you 'plays' that old 'joanna' so nice an' all, my name is Nettie Glover, an I'm sure that we will meet again sometime down the road a piece. Nah', if you don't mind takin' 'aht' the rubbish when you 'leaves' please," quipped Nettie as she flashed her impudent, yet irresistibly beguiling smile towards the pair of astounded detectives.

Rendering both Bass and Blackmore momentarily lost for any meaningful response, Nettie took her leave whilst delivering a final poignant aside as she continued to honour her laborious in-house obligations to the landlord of The Brown Bear prior to disappearing into the undulating, noisy throng of the Saturday night clientele…

"Piano Sonata Number One by Mozart, you say Mr Police?

"'E was nice, that young Mr Wolfgang, bless 'im, though a bit naïve, I thought… much too young to realise an' appreciate the great gift 'e 'ad been blessed with, I s'pose; 'wot 'e was an' 'wot 'e was capable of achieving, before 'is tragic demise…

"Poor little Wolfy…"

"Whenever I think of that tune from now on, I'll remember it as the 'Sonata for a Pair of Tired, Ordinary Men'.

"Happy trails for now, tired ordinary men. Rest assured that we shall meet again."

"NETTIE GLOVER, OF COURSE!" exclaimed Blackmore as Nettie finally disappeared from sight…

"Quite remarkable. The colourful and intricately woven tapestry of time, in the complex pattern of which we are all but a minute stitch, continues to be woven…

"As both Pontius and Brother de Payens have readily attested on several occasions, for every single person on this earth there exists a doppelganger, who in turn inhabit each one of the infinite dimensions that co-exist throughout time…

"An exact match, right down to the finest-minute details of consciousness, spirituality and thought, sharing an identical anatomy with its dimensionally separated twin… and here, in the public bar of The Brown Bear public house on an unremarkable, typical Whitechapel Saturday evening we meet, completely by chance on the 28th November, 1898, the Nettie Glover uniquely affiliated to our dimension."

Pausing to re-fill his empty tumbler with yet another copious helping of Del Vecchio brandy, and re-ignite the 'Hindu Shag' tobacco flakes packed tightly into the bowl of his old clay pipe, that had somehow miraculously remained gripped tightly between his teeth during the entire altercation, Blackmore took a heavy pull into his lungs of the sweet-scented, Indian- grown weed before exhaling multiple expertly formed rings of smoke whilst resuming his speech...

"I wonder, James, is the spirit of our Nettie Glover plagued by the curse of lycanthropy, as is that of her dimensional twin?"

Bass retorted instantly, as though he had been well prepared to deliver the startling revelation that was to follow for some considerable time...

"It is, my perceptive, wise old friend. I felt certain that I could sense a uniquely familiar presence within the confines of these premises the moment we arrived. My initial thoughts and idle musings were corroborated, however, when I caught the distinct scent of a lycanthrope."

Blackmore spat out a mouthful of brandy upon hearing the extraordinary declaration made by Bass...

"Y... You sensed a..? caught scent of...? What are you implying, James? Are you not, after all, free from the accursed blight of the werewolf?"

Bass remained thoughtful for a few seconds prior to giving a visibly aghast Blackmore his answer...

"Yes, and no, Tiberius. Never again shall I adopt the physical manifestation of a rampaging monster; by the grace of God and good fortune that nightmare is well and truly over; however...

"I appear to have retained a selection of the, ahem, less-feral and thankfully less dangerous characteristics of the beast...

"The ability to sense certain situations of a delicate nature before they occur, remains."

"A useful tool, I suppose," deadpanned Blackmore, who had now resorted to taking huge swigs directly from the brandy bottle...

"My highly sensitive sense of smell, too remains a prevalent, unexpectedly welcomed attribute..."

Another hearty glug of brandy ensued, after which Blackmore gestured mutely towards the dark-rimmed spectacles that Bass was about to remove prior to the moment when their altercation with the less than amiable locals had commenced...

"Ah yes, of course... and these."

Bass duly removed the tortoiseshell framed spectacles to reveal his eyes; the whites, pupils and irises of which had been absorbed into a soulless jet-black abyss... black as pitch.

Chapter 33

'The Land Beyond the Forest.'

'Winter, 1898.'

The exquisitely picturesque hues of a late Romanian autumn melded together into an eclectic palette of summer-bleached browns and layered pastel greens, a landscape dusted by an early light snowfall that thickened considerably atop the distant peaks of the Apuseni Mountains, the 'Mountains of the Sunset', that rose majestically out of the Western Carpathian range to cut a formidable stone swathe directly through the Transylvanian heartland.

For the first time in as long as he was able to recall, aided by the insistent, metronomic chatter of the train carriage wheels upon the iron rails of the trans-Carpathian railway line, coupled with the mesmeric effect upon his senses of the sublime, blurred landscape as it flashed by his carriage window, the leaden eyelids of James Bass had been gratefully lulled to the verge of a restful slumber...or so it had appeared, much to the chagrin of the grumbling, rudely awoken detective...

"JAMES... ROUSE YOURSELF, YOU LAZY OLD HOUND... WE HAVE ARRIVED AT OUR DESTINATION... TRANSYLVANIA... 'THE LAND BEYOND THE FOREST'."

***

As the final few golden shards of a late autumn sunset vanished below the tree line of a dense Carpathian forest, the spartan open-topped carriage which bore Bass and Blackmore along what appeared to resemble little more than a rough cart track towards their intended destination of the central Romanian city of Brason appeared as though at any moment it would be shaken apart as a result of its ancient iron-rimmed wheels failing to avoid a single one of the deep potholes that peppered the entire length of the track.

"Notice, James, ever since the last flecks of sunlight set our coachman has picked up the pace considerably," observed Blackmore...

"Yes, Tiberius, and one senses that his anxiety level has risen substantially to match the pace of his poor, overdriven team," alluded Bass, exhibiting obvious concern for the already overworked and exhausted team of four coach horses...

"COACHMAN... HEY THERE... COACHMAN; EASE UP ON THAT TEAM OR I'LL TAKE THAT SWITCH YOU WIELD ON THEIR DEFENCELESS BACKS AND TAN YOUR WORTHLESS HIDE WITH IT!" exclaimed Bass, his mood of mild agitation rising fervently towards one of undiluted anger that was channelled towards the now quite obviously terrified coachman...

"APERA -TI... APERA -TI... DUENSA DA ROVEND NA DE DOSSE..."

"ENGLISH, MAN... DO YOU SPEAK... DO... YOU... SPEAK... ENG-LISH!"

Slightly embarrassed by his own ignorance, regarding his inability to decipher the obscure local dialect with which the frantic coachman was attempting to communicate, Bass was then quite surprised to receive their raving driver's reply...

"YES, I SPEAK... LITTLE ENGLISH... 'WERY' LITTLE."

CHAPTER 33

"WHAT IRKS YOU, MAN... WHY FORCE YOUR TEAM TO THE VERY BRINK OF EXHAUSTION?"

"NIGHT TIME HERE... NOT GOOD... NO GOOD, ENGLISHMEN.

"IS 'WERY' BAD... 'THIETZE'... THI... THINGS HERE... 'WERY' BAD THINGS HERE... OH, OUVERANTZE DE DI... SOUK...SOUK! MADVE DE VROUANZE ONVURANTOS... SOUK... SOUK!... 'BRANDT CASTALE!"

Beckoning towards the ancient, dour, grey-gritstone façade of a great gothic fortress that dominated the small town which lay beneath the imposing plateau upon which it rested, the coachman's English miraculously improved sufficiently for the meaning of his words to send a familiar chill of wary anticipation down each of the detective's spines...

"THERE, ENGLISHMEN, SEE OVER THERE... 'GHOST DANCER'... 'WAMPYRSCHKE... 'VAMPYRE'... 'NOSFERATU...'

Acknowledgements

Alison Dickson & *Tim Brown*: Dear friends, without whose invaluable assistance this course would have proved harder to navigate.

Heather Burns: For her creativity, mentorship and love.

'The League of Ghosts' & *detective friends* everywhere: For your inspiration, your belief & your friendship. My fondest love to you all.

Ruth Lunn, Jay Thompson and all at UK Book Publishing for their exemplary work, their patience and their commitment.

'The journey continues…'

About the Author

Born in the year 1840, James Bartholomew Bass spent the first twelve years of his life as an orphaned only child in the Derbyshire workhouse where his mother lived and worked for a short time after her husband's tragic death in a mining accident, until her passing during the birth of her only child, James.

Soon after his 12th birthday James absconded from his dour, oppressive workhouse existence and made directly for London where, in the East End district of Whitechapel, he proceeded to live for the next two years of his young life relying on his natural guile and wits alone in order to survive. During this time Bass formed what was to become a lifelong friendship with fellow street urchin Alan Tiberius Blackmore and whilst becoming adept at employing certain questionable methods for the purposes of securing their next meal and keeping a dry roof over their heads, the pair began to develop not only a keen instinct for survival but also, coupled with an encyclopaedic knowledge of both London and Whitechapel, a problem-solving acumen that honed to perfection their rapidly developing intellects, and was in turn supported by the pair's fearsome reputation for employing often uncompromisingly stern discipline in order to achieve their goals.

Facing the unenviable choice of immediate transportation to an antipodean penal colony for life, or joining the Army after being arrested and found guilty of perpetrating various misdemeanours in and around the city, the hapless pair opted for the latter and were pressed into service with the Prince Consort's Own 95th Rifle Brigade. Following a distinguished career of 15 years with the Rifle Brigade, after which five years were spent with Prince Albert's own Royal Hussars Regiment, followed by a further seven years as special agents sequestered to Her Majesty Queen Victoria's special black operations unit CSF (Covert Special Forces), both men eventually retired bearing full military honours in the year 1885, after distinguished service in the second Anglo-Afghan war.

Having been highly decorated for services above and beyond the call of duty rendered to Queen and country and rising to the rank of Major, James Bass and his companion, Commander Tiberius Blackmore, were recommended by their military superiors for recruitment into the London Metropolitan Police force where they were each immediately raised to the rank of Detective Inspector under the command and mentorship of their old army associate and great friend Detective Chief Superintendent Francis (Frank) William Abilene, and were subsequently based at the Leman Street station house, situated deep

ABOUT THE AUTHOR

within the heart of Whitechapel.

Both detectives became founder members of the organisation named 'The League of Ghosts' and a series of novels chronicling the pair's many and varied exploits were adapted from the original journals kept by Detective Chief Inspector James Bartholomew Bass.

The Victorian Detectives, The League of Ghosts, book quotations, character names and images ©jbbass.co.uk

Printed in Great Britain
by Amazon